C000280245

A Good Deliverance

A Good Deliverance

TOBY CLEMENTS

faber

First published in 2024
by Faber & Faber Ltd
The Bindery, 51 Hatton Garden
London ECIN 8HN

Typeset by Faber & Faber Limited
Printed in the UK by CPI Group (UK) Ltd, Croydon CR0 4YY

A CIP record for this book
is available from the British Library

ISBN 978–0–571–34830–5

Printed and bound in the UK on FSC® certified paper in line with our continuing
commitment to ethical business practices, sustainability and the environment.
For further information see faber.co.uk/environmental-policy

2 4 6 8 10 9 7 5 3 1

And for to pass the time this book shall be pleasant to read in, but for to give faith and belief that all is true that is contained herein, ye be at your liberty . . .

William Caxton
from the preface to the 1485 edition
of *Le Morte d'Arthur*

BOOK I

To catch an hardynesse

CHAPTER I

**How Sir Thomas is brought once more unto
Newgate Gaol and how he remains therein constrained
by order of his dread sovereign King Edward,
and of certain other matters**

They come for him in the week before Pentecost, only eight men
when once they'd sent sixty, knowing they would find him in his
garden drowsing under an early summer's sun. They surprise him, of
course, but he them too, for he still keeps about him the dagger his
father gave him all those years ago, and he draws it now, and he gives
one of them a deep nick to the heel of his grasping hand.

'You'll pay for that, you old coot!' the wounded man bellows, and
with his other hand he clouts Sir Thomas hard, driving him to his
knees, and were they sent to kill him, then now is when they would
do it, but they are not, so they don't.

'Harm him not, for the love of God!' one reminds the others. 'Especially not his hands!'

So they thrust him grovelling into the grass, and the stabbed man
is permitted to sit on Sir Thomas's back while another ties those
suddenly precious hands tight and a third is sent to fetch a mule
from Sir Thomas's own stables.

'Damn you!' Sir Thomas manages to croak. 'Get off me' and 'Who
are you?' and 'What do you want?'

But it is only once they have lifted him up – more parcel than person – and set him upon his mule's saddle, with his ankles tied tight
below, that the one who had warned the others not to harm him takes
the time to explain. He is John Smethwick, he says, 'sent by the king to
bring you safe unto London'.

'Safe unto London?' Sir Thomas barks. 'Why, His Majesty need only have sent word and I should be before him within the week!'

'Ah, but he doesn't want you before him, does he, you old fool?' the wounded man bellows over Smethwick's shoulder. 'He wants you back where you belong, back in Newgate.'

Newgate! At its mention, Sir Thomas shies and the mule staggers, but the knots hold firm.

'Go easy, Sir Thomas, please!' Smethwick begs.

And now Sir Thomas's wife **Elizabeth** comes running from the hall, grandson on hip, the boy's nurse in tow, and when she learns that her husband is once more to be taken up she can only cross herself and cry: 'Not again!' and 'What for this time?' and 'By whose order?'

But Master Smethwick has no answers, or none he'll give, and so at length there is nothing left to be said save farewell, and:

'Send word to Master Hartshorne. Tell him I am once more arraigned!'

And so once again, nearly twenty years after that first time, Sir Thomas Malory is led from his hall at Newbold Revel, in the county of Warwick, and taken through the village where his divers servants and tenants look up from their tasks to see him go, and most look away again, knowing this is not a sight meant for them, save **Master Appleby**'s wife — a hard-eyed strumpet with butter-thief's arms — who crosses a sheepfold to rest those chubby arms on a stone wall and watch him pass.

'What is it this time, Sir Thomas?' she caws. 'Up to your old tricks again, is it?'

And once again Sir Thomas shies, and once again the mule staggers, but once again the knots hold.

'Easy, Sir Thomas,' Smethwick cautions, and they ride on all afternoon. As darkness rises, they stop in an inn that Sir Thomas has used before, where he sleeps — badly, as might be expected — between Smethwick and another man, and where he is bitten by fleas, but on the next day he is at least given a horse of his own, a swaybacked mare with a pin mouth, and permitted to ride on licence, with his hands untied, and on the morning of the third day he is given his choice of the next inn's stables, where he takes a palfrey, which is a more suitable horse for a knight to ride into London.

But it cheers him not, because he knows that with every passing league, the road shortens, and his world narrows, and late in the afternoon of that third day he sees the familiar smear of smoke that hangs above the city, and soon he smells it: coal, rotting offal, night soil. At last, as evening rises, they pass through the shadow of the newly re-edified St Sepulchre's, and ahead stands the gaol at Newgate.

'Here we are,' Smethwick need not tell him, and they pass under the middle archway, mutely studied by the men of the watch, and then Sir Thomas is led off the road and into that all-too-familiar courtyard, where he is helped down, stiff as a gibbet after so long a day in the saddle, to face a crowd of warders and turnkeys who emerge from their rookeries, some of whom recognise him from when he was here last.

'Still alive, Sir Thomas?' they call, and 'Couldn't keep away, eh, Sir Thomas?' and 'the usual room is it, Sir Thomas?' and if just one should dare suggest that he has perhaps been up to his old tricks again, then Sir Thomas will . . . Well, what will he do? There is nothing he can do. There is nothing to be done.

'Where is the keeper?' he demands. 'I wish to see the keeper.'

'Oh, **Master Arnold**'ll not wish to see you, Sir Thomas. Not after all that trouble you gave him last time.'

'Surprised he's taken you back, Sir T!'

Sir Thomas stands mute, as it only strikes him now that he has no money.

He has nothing with which to pay the keeper's fees, and without paying them, he will not even be permitted his old cell. He will be taken down to the dungeons below, to lie all apuddle with the common criminals, chained to wet stone walls, begging for scraps and dregs.

Jesu! He will be dead before the week is out.

But then, a surprise: no. His fees are paid already! In advance.

He could almost cheer.

'Already? By whom?'

The porter – a new man – shrugs, and if Smethwick knows he is not saying, but whoever has done so has also afforded Sir Thomas a rush-dip lamp, a loaf of today's good bread and even a pitcher of wine.

'And a top drop it is, too,' the porter assures him, having sampled more than half.

And so Sir Thomas is led up those steps he knows so well – two porters ahead, each with a rush lamp, Smethwick behind – encumbered with yet another uncertainty: what does it mean, that someone would pay his fees?

It cannot be the king, surely? Generations of moths are known to thrive undisturbed in his purse. Then who?

They trudge on, all further questions ignored, weary soles on weary treads, between steadily narrowing walls, winding two, three, four storeys up into the highest reaches of the gatehouse to the south tower, the men's tower, where the gaol scent thins somewhat, and they pass along the short, narrow passage towards the door of his old cell. As they go by the other doors, Sir Thomas senses the other prisoners behind, leaning in to press their ears to the wood, each praying these footsteps signal the worst is come not for them, but for some other poor soul.

And then there it is, through the opened door, second last along the passage: his old cell, the inside of which he has so oftentimes thanked God he will never, ever have to see again.

He stands in the doorway, unable to proceed until Smethwick propels him forward, four fingers and a thumb between his shoulder blades, and in he must step over the threshold into the cell's claggy embrace. He believes he will swoon if he does not sit, so he staggers to sink to the reeking sackcloth palliasse as if felled, and he hangs his head between his knees, and for a long moment he can do nothing except stare at the filthy rushes between his heels and wonder how it has come to this.

The first porter sets one of the lamps upon the stone by his right boot, while the second places the loaf and the wine by Sir Thomas's left. From the doorway Smethwick expresses the fraudulent hope that this has all been a mistake, and that the king will soon send for Sir Thomas, and that all will be quickly resolved. For a moment all three men linger in the expectation of a coin for their troubles, but Sir Thomas can scarcely move, and his purse is empty anyway, and so they turn and go, thumping the door shut and dropping the locking bar behind them with the sound of a falling axe.

Sir Thomas sits in the silent gloom for a long while until he is able to lift his head at last and look about in tremulous dismay.

'Jesu defend me,' he whispers. 'Jesu defend me.'

In the umber half-light of the rush dip, the cell is almost unchanged since last he was locked within its much-abused walls: five paces one way, five the other, under a low, smoke-smutted ceiling, and underfoot a thick, filthy layer of age-old rushes. Come dawn he knows a small square window will let in the east light, and below that sits what must be the same malodorous old bucket that served his privy needs in times gone by. It is only now that he notices the yellow-eyed cat staring at him from the shadows of the fourth corner.

He drinks some wine, which is, as the porter said, good quality, though there is little of it left now, and some bread – likewise of good quality – but while he is chewing it strikes him hard: bread and wine. The Last Supper. *His* Last Supper? Is that what this is intended to mean? He is suddenly certain of it, and he sets aside the meal, jumps quickly to his feet and sets about pacing the room, just as he used to so often before: endlessly, around and across, across and around. He knows what will happen now. He knows that at some time in the short hours the bell in St Sepulchre's will sound – ding ding, ding ding – to announce an execution in the morning, and a priest will come stealing across the way where he'll be greeted by the night porters, who'll give him something hot and strong to drink, to give him the courage to climb the stairs to hear a last confession.

And it will be Sir Thomas's.

But what if Sir Thomas refuses to give it to him? What if he refuses to kneel and when it is done, to cross himself and then to leave with him – what then?

The king's men will come stamping up the steps at dawn and they'll drag him down by his arms if they like him, by his heels if they do not, and he'll cry out to Jesu, just as he has heard so many others cry out to Jesu, and they'll strap him to a hurdle and tie that to a cart they will have wheeled into the courtyard, and after taking ale, they'll roll him out to the crowds that will have gathered on Giltspur Street to follow the cart all the way to Smithfield, where the scaffold is permanent and where they kill men in the worst ways they know how.

But why? Why? Why does the king want him dead? Sir Thomas hardly knows the king, and has done almost nothing to harm him, ever, or not for some while, and so why? Why this? Why now?

It can only be someone else, some new malefactor.

But who?

He believes such mortal enemies as he ever had – and Lord knows he had them – to be dead: the first, his greatest, in battle at Northampton, in the last year of the old king's reign; and the second, his lesser Satan, of plague, near Runcorn, almost ten years ago to this very day.

So who now is there left alive to persecute Sir Thomas in this way?

Around and around such questions turn; endless and intractable, until he can stand it no longer, and he yields to the prisoner's ever-present temptation to believe that doing something will change anything, and he leaves off his pacing to pound upon the cell's stout oak door.

'For the love of God!' he bellows. 'Let me out!' and 'I demand to see the keeper!' and 'Who is it that keeps me herein constrained?', but he is answered only by a scream, far off, then by scathing laughter nearby, and then by nothing. No footsteps. No flicker of lamplight. Not even the rattle of a chain. He hammers again and again, until his hands burn, and still there is nothing save an oddity: someone is playing the harp; soft, melodious trills. The sound makes Sir Thomas pause a moment, before he renews his assault on the door, hammering once more and again.

But finally he tires himself, and he sinks to his knees, aching with misery, and rests his forehead upon the planks, whereupon he almost permits himself a sob, and in the silence the harp continues, and after a moment Sir Thomas's pain fades. He stands and starts pacing again, his feet moving once more of their own accord, and after a dozen or so turns around that compressed space, he notices his steps follow the exact same path they took when he was last here, and that with each pass they go around the void where once his coffer sat, there at the foot of his palliasse, and despite every grim thing, this minor curiosity almost makes him smile.

How long had he spent over that coffer, he wonders now, his pen pressed to the papers, writing out all those tales? Days, certainly, weeks too, if not months and perhaps even years, for he had passed so many in this cell or that cell, drawing out all those marvellous deeds of chivalry as performed by King Arthur and his noble Knights of the Round Table, and thinking of them now – all those knights, all those deeds – he is startled to find himself suddenly overwhelmed by a new rage. Look at him now! Here he is, Sir Thomas Malory, who only ever followed after the good, who

9

only ever left off the evil, back in gaol again, and this time awaiting dawn to face his death.

'What nonsense!' he growls. 'What false, traitorous nonsense!'

He swings his foot through the coffer's space, imagining sending it and its contents flying, and he turns, and sets to pacing again, this time setting his feet to walk through the coffer's space.

Why had he spent so much of his life burnishing the renown of long-dead men whose worship was already assured? Why had he not thought to spend just a moment – a single week, a month or even a year – ensuring his own? Why had he never turned then to the matter of Sir Thomas? He who acquitted himself a knight by performing many a wonderful deed of arms that day outside at Verneuil, and who by worshipful means did preserve the chastity of a damosel whom some now call a saint: Sir Thomas who journeyed far, and saw much, and who kissed the pope's ring? To Sir Thomas who was meek and gentle among ladies, yet the sternest knight to ever couch a lance against a mortal foe? To Sir Thomas who, despite all this, was, through no misdeed of his own, still brought low by the schemes of sly, base-born traitor churls!

Now *that*, he thinks, *that* would have been a tale worth the candle!

But it is too late, and so once more he must cry out: 'Jesu defend me!', for it is no tale any man shall ever hear, for look! The rush dip's bead of flame is already sunk low, and soon, like him, it shall die.

But still he cannot put this idea from his mind. If only he had someone to talk to! A witness! Someone to hear his tale, to marvel at his deeds and to hold his truths.

Had he that man – or lady – before him now, then he would launch into the tale of the deeds of Sir Thomas just as he had so oftentimes in the past launched into the deeds of King Arthur, or those of Sir Lancelot, or Sir Gawain's, even, or any number of those noble Knights of the Table Round, oftentimes for the edification of kings (yes: two of them, though the second was only

King of the Isle of Wight) as well as dukes and bishops and earls, and lords, and a great number of noble knights, as well as many a fine lady too.

That is what he would now do. But there is not a soul here except the cat, still staring at him from the darkest corner, and cats are not stirred by the tales of worshipful men undone by the shenful machinations of base-born churls, however many marvellous feats of arms are described along the way, are they? Cats are interested only in what interests them, and nothing further besides.

At last Sir Thomas comes to a stop. He sits back upon the palliasse, just where he used to, and then he lies back, just where he used to, and as he does so, the rush dip falters, and dies, and Sir Thomas is left in darkness.

The day is done. His race is run.

'Jesu preserve me,' he whispers one last time, before, at last, he closes his eyes and, in spite of everything, he sleeps.

He is almost at once tortured by dreams in which he has chosen to be pressed to death — *peine forte et dure*, as the French have it — rather than be hanged, or beheaded, and so he feels the headsman heaving great weights of iron upon a plank that is laid across his chest, and he feels the life being pressed out of him, and his wind dying, only to wake with a great shout and a flailing of limbs to find that it is the cat who sits upon his chest, and it is the cat whom he now sends screeching across the room in a terror that only redoubles Sir Thomas's own.

'Jesu defend me,' Sir Thomas wails. 'Jesu defend me.'

And then he starts, for he realises that suddenly he is able to see the cat.

It means dawn is come.

And sure enough, through the waxy linen-covered window: cock-crow, and the massed tolling of the city's bells, and the eruption of a hundred thousand furious pigeons from their roosts, for the hour of Prime is come, the last of Sir Thomas's life, and the realisation that he has wasted his final night on earth asleep, dreaming of being tortured, almost makes him laugh, but he steadies himself and rises from his palliasse, only to sink to his creaking knees and clasp his hands together outstretched before him, and close his seeping eyes, to pray as does a child, in the cold grey light of dawn, for the Lord's mercy.

But before he can even finish the Paternoster, there are footsteps in the passageway beyond his door, soft but implacable, and so he must suppress a sudden sob, and though his stomach turns, and he fears his bowels will drain, he is reminded of that baking hot day in that onion field outside Verneuil, when he stood with his brothers-in-arms, readying to receive the second charge of those six hundred magically attired horsemen of Lombardy, and he hears again the Duke of Bedford's exhortation: we are dead men, and all that remains to us is our honour, so let us this day acquit ourselves as gentlemen. For God, Harry and St George!

And so he stands, straightens his pourpoint and turns to face the door, making himself ready to greet Death with a smile, with a nod, with a God-give-you-good-grace, sir, for whatever else men may say of Sir Thomas Malory — and he fears they will say a great deal — let none of them say that in his end, he did not acquit himself a gentleman.

He hears the locking bar lift.

He watches the door open, and he takes a painful, gasping breath that is expelled when he says, 'Oh.'

For there in the doorway stands no priest, no prison guard, only a barefoot boy, of about twelve winters perhaps, in thrice-patched russet and a cap set upon on his head that looks like a greasy, sunken pie. He holds out a leather mug of ale, possibly, as well as an apple with dun-coloured skin near as wizened as Sir Thomas's own, and tucked under his arm is another good loaf. He regards

12

Sir Thomas with sombre grey eyes, each cupped by a ring of darkest lavender.

'God give you good day, sir,' he says in the scraping voice of a young crow. 'I brung you your breakfast.'

Sir Thomas is lost for words, knows not what to do with the hands – his own! – that now seem to dangle on long, useless limbs by his sides. The boy brings vittles that are intended to fuel Sir Thomas's day: it means he is supposed to live, at least to the evening. A warm flush of joy leeches through his aching body, and he confesses to the boy that he had half expected the priest.

'Oh, he is not come by today,' the boy says, his voice settling into a softer note. 'Tomorrow, though.'

And the warmth chills, and Sir Thomas takes the bread and ale, and the apple, with diluted thanks.

'And who are you?' he asks.

'I am John Brunt,' the boy tells him.

Sir Thomas is taken aback.

'No you aren't,' he can't help saying.

The boy scoffs.

'Think I'd know best,' he says.

'But John Brunt is——'

'——is likewise my old man, yes sir. I am named after him.'

Of course you are, Sir Thomas thinks.

'And where is he?' he asks. 'Your father?'

If he is honest – and Sir Thomas is ever that, as he would swear upon the cross of his sword – he hopes John Brunt the father is gone out of this world.

'Abed this last sennight,' the boy disappoints, 'with a boil turned bad upon his backside.'

'Well, that is something,' Sir Thomas supposes, confusing the boy for a moment. 'But he thrives otherwise?'

Sir Thomas very much hopes not.

'Aye sir, he does. And is now become keeper of this whole upper floor.'

The boy proudly gestures around to encompass the expanse of his father's demesne and Sir Thomas silently groans. The boy stoops to stroke the cat as it pauses to rub itself against his shin on the way out.

'How comes you know of my old man?' the boy asks when the cat is gone.

'I knew him when he was but a humble kitchen porter,' Sir Thomas admits. 'A while back now.'

And the boy looks at him beadily, for he is clearly no fool.

'So you've been in before, sir? In here? Is that it?'

Sir Thomas returns the boy's close study. Can it be, he wonders, that this child *doesn't* know who he is?

'You genuinely don't know?' he asks.

'Know what?'

'Know who I am?'

'No sir. I only know you is kept here at the king's say-so, and are to be given——'

He nods at the bread and the ale.

Sir Thomas thinks: Jesu preserve me, this is it. This is my chance. I have been granted a stay of execution – a day, at least – to tell my tale, to recount my deeds, just as I wished this night past, and now here is this boy, unpolluted by prejudice, to be my audience. He is far from the most august of audiences for a man who has recounted tales to kings and so on, but anyway, it is he – this boy – who will hear the true tale of the deeds of arms and gentle acts of valour of Sir Thomas Malory.

'Sit,' he tells him, more certain of being obeyed than he has any right to be, and the boy starts.

'Heh?' he demands, as if sitting is unchristian.

'Sit,' Sir Thomas repeats. 'It is nothing bad. I only wish to tell you a story.'

At which the boy laughs, now more crow than dove.

'Oho!' he says. 'It is not one about how innocent you are, is it?'

Which unsettles Sir Thomas, because, of course, it is – in its way.

'But it is so much more besides!' he assures the boy. 'So much more! It is the story of how a man might rise from nothing to perform many an astonishing feat of arms, including the setting-aside of a thousand magically attired men-at-arms on horseback, and—'

'Boil or no boil,' the boy interrupts, 'my old man will box my ears if he learns I am stood about listening to such tales.'

'This is no tall tale,' Sir Thomas tells him. 'As I swear upon the cross of my sword! No word of a lie shall pass my lips.'

'But a *thousand* magically attired horse riders?'

The boy makes them sound impossible even to Sir Thomas's ears.

'Six hundred then.'

But still. And Sir Thomas was there. He knows what he saw: English arrows bouncing from those breastplates with their bodkin heads bent like lantern crooks and the horsemen coming on, unchecked.

'We shall come to them, by and by,' he tells the boy, 'and I shall tell you how we drove them from the field that day, and not just them either, but two other armies besides – three if you count that of Scotland – and much more too, but like all the best stories, this one must begin at its beginning.'

There follows the faintest breath from the boy, and a creak as he leans against the door jamb and crosses his limbs, just as his father used to, all those years ago.

'Go on then,' he says, 'but quick, mind.'

If the boy supposes this tale will last but a Paternoster's time, he is in for a surprise, for Sir Thomas takes a deep draught of the ale – flat and lifeless compared to the ale from home – wipes his lips, and commences his tale as it should be told:

•

t so befell that on a certain day in the first year of the reign of **King Henry**, the fourth of that name to rule all England, John Malory, a gentleman of the county of Warwick, was blessed with a son whom he named Thomas.

'And that is you, is it?' the boy interrupts almost instantly.

'That is me.'

The boy tuts, as if already disappointed, but really, what else can he have expected?

Now, following the custom of the country in those times, on hearing the news from my childbed, my father took up his bow and a single arrow and went out into the courtyard of his modest hall where, to symbolise my release from womb to world, he loosed the arrow into the sky. He was a skilled bowman, my father, fully able to pin a wren to an oak leaf from a hundred paces, and so any arrow he shot should have flown straight and true. But perhaps he was weak from the month he was confined to the Tower or—

'Confined to the Tower?' the boy intervenes once again. 'Your old man was confined to the Tower?'

Sir Thomas is briefly thrown.

'Yes,' he has to admit. 'Yes, he was, but only for a few weeks.'

'Ha! And what did he do? Must've been something proper bad to land himself in there.'

'We shall come to that,' Sir Thomas promises.

'Oh, and he was innocent too, was he?'

Sir Thomas ignores him, and proceeds with his tale, hoping for fewer interruptions.

Or perhaps it was some other ailment that caused my father to mispluck his bowstring? Whatever its cause, it so happened that the arrow — *my* arrow — drifted on the turn and came back to land not harmlessly in the waters of one of the stock ponds beyond the gatehouse as was intended, but down upon the heads of those gathered in the courtyard to witness the event. No one was hurt, praise Jesus, but every man there would have crossed themselves, and taken a step back, lest my father's ill-luck prove contagious—'

'Which it done,' the boy sniggers. Again, Sir Thomas ignores him.

After that: my baptism, at the parish church of the village of Monks Kirby, scarce a league's ride from my father's house at Fenny Newbold, where — once the priest had stopped us at the porch to anoint my ears and nose with his spit, and to chant the exorcism to drive away such evil spirits as might have entered my soul in the two days since my birth — my father would have carried me into the nave to be welcomed by his friends and family, and by the men and women of his somewhat modest demesne.

The boy blinks drowsily, unintrigued, but silent at least.

But here the mood would have been gloomier than might befit the baptism of a healthy boy, wayward arrow or no wayward arrow, for dark clouds hung over the realm of England, and over Fenny Newbold in particular, for there had recently been made an attempt to kill the new king.

Well, this is more like it, Sir Thomas sees the boy thinking.

For it so happened that my father's good-lord, **Sir Thomas Holland, the Earl of Kent**, had been one of those plotting the king's murder. He claimed King Henry had usurped the throne of **King Richard** — against every law of God and the land — and so they planned to murder him at a tourney held in Windsor to mark the Feast of the Epiphany that year. The plot was foiled and the king's life preserved — thanks be to God (and an informant) — and shortly thereafter, along with all the other known plotters, the earl was put to death (headsman's axe, Cirencester, two days after the Epiphany), and shortly after that, King Henry's inquisitors began running their thumbs down the list of the earl's indentured men and came, by and by, to my father, and they, being conscientious, called him in, and he, having no choice, went.

They kept him under lock and key for fully five weeks before finding him insufficiently guilty to join his good-lord upon the scaffold in the traitor's death, and they released him to make his own way home on foot, but the experience turned his hair and his beard — once handsome fox-red — fog-grey overnight, and much later, when he was on his deathbed, he confessed that just being on the same floor as the brake had made him pass water that was, he said, nine parts vinegar.

At this the boy nods sagely, as if to say he has oftentimes heard such things.

Anyway, on the day of his release, my father was pressed with issues more urgent than the colour of his hair, of course, for though he had been found innocent, it would have been widely known that he had now fallen beyond the king's favour and, worse still, that with Sir Thomas Holland's death, he lacked the protection of a good-lord. This left him and his estates as vulnerable as a duck on a pond for any land-greedy baron, of which — the times then being as wild and scrambled as any yet known — there was no shortage.

A decision needed to be made, and fast, and it is not unlikely that it was made that very afternoon, at my christening feast, in consult-ation with my grandparents and my godsibs, for within the month

18

my father withdrew his allegiance from the disgraced Holland family, and took it to the Beauchamp family, better known now as being the Earls of Warwick.

The boy pulls a face to suggest he has heard of them, which he will have, Sir Thomas supposes, for Warwick Inn is but a stone's throw from where they sit, and the current earl, the sixteenth, is much acclaimed by gentles and commons alike, although he is of course not a Beauchamp but a Neville, though for now that is neither here nor there.

It is strange to think that an event that can most powerfully influence a man's life — the very thing that sets him on this course, say, rather than that course — can happen while he is not present, or looking, or even, in this instance, out of his tail-clouts, but that is what happened to me, for when my father took his allegiance to **Sir Richard Beauchamp** that year, so was forged a connection between our two families that would one day come to govern my life more surely than the planets steer the affairs of mortal men.

All that was yet to come, of course, and unknown to any man then alive, but what was known was that in return for such powerful protection my father must offer something of near or equal value, and since my father had few servants of his own, or none to spare to send in his stead, he himself set out one morning in spring to join Sir Richard's retinue riding for Wales, where the earl was under orders from the king to bring to heel that Welsh miscreant, **Owen Glendower**.

At which the boy gasps, and his eyes grow round with fear.

'Owen Glendower!' he whispers, repeating a name that has long been used by English parents to strike terror into their children.

'The same,' Sir Thomas confirms. 'A Welshman, of the very worst sort.'

And for those first few years of the century, which coincided with mine, of course, my father rode out with Sir Richard every season, setting a household rhythm that soon became familiar: in spring, around Lady Day, he rode out, accompanied by just one servant, leaving my mother to manage the estates – passingly modest, still, as I say – only to return, if God spared him, as He actually did, just as the last chestnut leaves fell, and conkers littered the ground, around Martinmas, when he would come through the gate with his boots worn through and his body hard as *cuir bouilli*. Sometimes he carried a limp, say, or his arm in a sling, and once he came home smelling so powerfully of an unguent that some local leech had applied for a wound hidden under his shirt that it made our eyes stream, and he would unstrap his sword, and throw off his tattered cloak with the Warwick badge of the bear and crooked billet, and he would greet my mother with a kiss on her lips and make her stand while he admired her belly, for she would always by then be about ready to birth another child, and then he would turn to us children one by one, and greet us as was appropriate, by throwing us up into the air and catching us to kiss us, and these were very joyful times.

Physically, he was short and wiry, and only really made sense when he was in the saddle. Mentally and spiritually, he seemed conventionally gruff, but there were odd little things about him which ought to have made me stop and think: such as this throwing us up in the air and kissing us. Often he brought us back some little gift, a present, which was an uncommon thing to do, and which should have alerted me to his more thoughtful side: a ring of Welsh gold for my mother, say, or a belt of finely worked leather, or one of those patterned blankets. I cannot recall what he brought my sisters, but among the things he brought me was a dagger made for a boy's hand (soon lost); a practice bow made of laburnum wood (that I would still to this day struggle to draw); and, once, the skull of what he claimed was a Jacob's sheep, born with three horns and two heads (later thrown out by Master Orme – of whom more later – who believed I was taking it as a false god, which I was not).

Seeing the boy turn restless at such detail, Sir Thomas decides to spare him further description of his father's household, including such things as:

- How Sir Thomas's siblings were birthed; and of how his father's aim with their symbolic arrows improved.

- How once his father needed two horses as well as Thomas's help to bring in the Yule log at Christmas.

- How oftentimes his father played the pipes while Sir Thomas's mother – named Phillipa – worked her wheel, and of how those long winter months passed just as slowly as might be imagined.

- How when the catkins grew long enough to flutter in the spring gales, and Lent loomed large, it would be time for his father to ride out again, clothes patched, body knit-up and with Sir Thomas's mother already green as the next child rooted itself in her womb.

- How Sir Thomas believed his parents loved one another, for though his father lacked the ambition that some men call overweening, he was handsome and hardy, and never unkind to his wife the way most men are, while his mother, who came of better family – her father was **Sir William Chetwynd**, of the manor of Ingestre, in Staffordshire, and was once esquire to the great **John of Gaunt** – cheerfully bore her husband six children besides Sir Thomas himself – though two died before they were weaned, and later a brother named John was drowned in that self-same stock pond at

which young Thomas's arrow was aimed, which saddened
Thomas greatly, though it was not his fault.

'They ever catch him, then, did they?' the boy asks.

It takes a moment for Sir Thomas to realise he means Owen
Glendower.

Sir Thomas shakes his head.

'Very nearly,' he says. 'But just as they almost had him, penned in
one of those valleys of theirs, the king sent word from Westminster
that he needed every loyal man to ride north, to face his great rebel,
Harry Hotspur.'

Someone the boy has never heard of, which does not surprise Sir
Thomas, for whenever does history celebrate failed rebels?

'In truth, he hardly matters,' he tells the boy. 'All that matters is
that at this moment, Prince Hal enters my story.'

At which name, the boy leans forward, agog, for every child in
England wishes to know more of the man who would go on to become **King Henry the fifth**, may God assoil his soul.

'You mean the king what won at Agincourt?'

'The same.'

'And you was there, was you? At Agincourt?'

Sir Thomas takes a breath before telling the boy that they will
come on to that, 'by and by'.

'For a story must have its beginning and its end, and not jump
about as does the frog. And besides: there are battles aplenty to
come before and after Agincourt.'

The boy settles back, wary still, and Sir Thomas has been warned:
keep this interesting, or I'm off.

The first battle comes now: when my father stood alongside Prince
Hal, as he was then, on that calamitous day outside Shrewsbury, in
the third year of this century, where, to our great disworship, we

Englishmen loosed our arrows at other Englishmen, and though my father did not often talk about it, he was there on hand to witness the moment that the young prince — visor up, the better to urge his men forward — caught an arrow shaft full in the face.

It knocked him off his feet, of course, and threw him on his back, as if pinned to the ground, and when his men saw this, they gave him up for dead, for who could survive such a thing? It would kill nine hundred and ninety-nine men in every thousand.

But not the prince!

Thanks be to God, after a little moment, the boy rose to his feet, with the arrow still sticking from his cheek, just below his right eye, here, and then he had his esquire snap the shaft of the arrow half a hand's span from the wound so that he might lower his visor, and after that he led his men in the charge up the slope that routed the rebels, and brought about the death of that great traitor knight, Sir Harry de Hotspur.

What would have happened had the arrow been a finger's width in any other direction? Or if that clever surgeon had not devised his ingenious contraption to pluck the arrowhead from deep within the prince's skull? Only God can know, of course, but man can suppose, and had Prince Hal died then my life — all our lives — needs must have followed a very different path.

That idiot **William Peyto** — of whom more later — once claimed that King Henry was forever conscious of the scar, and that he tried to hide it, as if ashamed because it made him ugly, but that wasn't true: in my experience of the man, by the time he was made king, he was proud of it, for it showed he had been given special consideration by God.

Look, it proclaimed, this man has survived what would have killed any other man, so surely therefore God has a special purpose in mind for him? Surely therefore he may do what he will and only God alone may judge? It is interesting — to me — to wonder why the

Almighty gave him tenure enough to achieve all that he managed – for both good and ill – but did not then choose to let him live long enough to fulfil his purpose, which was to edify the walls of Jerusalem.

Such philosophical questions are not to the boy's taste, Sir Thomas observes, for his gaze drifts to the window, where the light suggests they are getting on towards mid-morning, and it is surely time for him to be gone away about his business, so before he can ask about Agincourt again, Sir Thomas presses on.

My father served further seasons in Wales under the earl, but it so happened that one season he did not ride out with the other men, and he cleaved instead to his estates, such as they were, determined, as he put it, to become a Man of the County. At the time I thought none the worse of him for this, and was glad to have him among us, but I soon came to resent his decision, for it ushered into my life its first great change: for that year I was moved from under the rule of skirts to the rule of men, or more specifically the rule of one man in particular, for in that very first week after Lady Day – perhaps my sixth? – my father sent word for a man to come from nearby Lutterworth, who was to act as my tutor. This was Master Orme.

I do not exactly recall my first day with small, pudgy, ruddy-cheeked Master Orme, but I can be certain it must have gone something like this: we would have met just after dawn, in the west hall, under my uncle's windows – of which more later, perhaps (perhaps not) – first for prayers, then for lessons. We would have sat side by side on a bench before the lectern, and I would have wrinkled my nose at Master Orme's curious hedgerow smell, after which we would have commenced on the alphabet, of which I already knew a little from my nurse, who had been a French woman about whom I can recall not one thing save that she was kind, which only made my early lessons with Master Orme all the more startling.

My first slip – forgetting the letter E, perhaps – would have caused dusty, black-coated Master Orme to purse his wet little lips, and sigh, and to rummage in his bag (a horrible, much-creased leather gourd, not unalike unto a donkey's scrotum) to remove and place upon the bench next to him, within easy reach, a tied brush of hawthorn twigs such as a maidservant uses to clean a bake oven. My next mistake – the letter M, say – would have seen him place my hand, palm down, on the board and then flick my upturned knuckles with those twigs. The pain would have been as nothing to the outrage, of course, for no one had yet deliberately and pointlessly caused me pain before, as why would they?

That first morning I would probably have shouted, I suppose, and looked upon him as if upon an adder that had nipped me in the bracken, and he would have looked calmly back at me, his eyes pale blue and watery as fresh-shucked oysters, and he would have told me that sparing the rod spoiled the child. This phrase grew so wearyingly familiar over the years to come that he became known – not only to me, but to my whole family too, until his shaming end – as Spare-the-Rod.

To begin with, Spare-the-Rod beat me only with the hawthorn brush, replacing it when it wore out, and together we must have worked our way through four or five iterations before I had learned by heart my alphabet and numbers. Then, sometime after my eighth winter, we graduated from English to Latin, from the hazel brush to a thin, whippy hazel switch, and from my knuckles to my buttocks. The switch soon lost its spring, and after my ninth winter, along with the French tongue came a stouter rod, to be replaced every month or so as we wore through it, and each time growing steadily fatter as I grew taller, so that by my tenth winter, it was in girth equal to Spare-the-Rod's little finger, and would, after a few stripes, leave my linen gummy with drawn blood.

'Back of his hand is what my old man gives me,' the boy interrupts with a barely stifled yawn. 'Which is what I'll get if I tarry here a moment longer.' He rises to go.

'Wait,' Sir Thomas tells him. 'I am getting to it.'

'It?'

'The point of my story.'

A lie, of course, but a white one, and still within the spirit of his earlier promise, and the boy relents, reluctantly, so Sir Thomas decides against over-testing his patience with the following details:

➻ How his relationship with Spare-the-Rod changed in the summer after his tenth winter, which was when his father brought down from his counting house the only book he then owned: a hand's span thickness of rough-edged paper, clumsily stitched between two faded leather covers, on which – in tiny letters and pitiless detail – were described the dreary lives and deaths of all the many hundreds of Christian martyrs.

➻ The title of the book – *The Golden Legend* – which he fears the boy will mistake for an inn.

➻ How Spare-the-Rod flinched when he saw it, and how he never once touched it, save to prod it with the end of his rod, and that when he instructed Thomas to learn a passage by heart, and to be ready to recite it to him the following morning, he would let Thomas choose which saint's life he wished to learn.

➻ And how in those early days Thomas chose obscurities (Gentian, say, or Fulcian or even Victorice, each of whom – some of whom? One of whom? Even the author seems to have tired of such details – had molten iron poured into his, or possibly her, ears), believing Spare-the-Rod would be less likely to notice any mistake or omission, but it soon became clear that Spare-the-Rod cared nothing for the lives of the saints or the martyrs, and he was never so happy as when Thomas came to their grisly deaths. He even cheered and happily clapped his damp little palms when Thomas recounted the life and death of St Cassian, the teacher, who died at the hands of his pupils, who tied him up and stabbed him to death with their styluses.

No, Sir Thomas does not tell the boy all this because even now, so very many years later, merely thinking about Spare-the-Rod makes him feel dolorous, and besides, he knows the boy is not likely to spare a thought – just as he himself never did – as to *why* Spare-the-Rod had no time for the Christian saints and martyrs.

Instead he tells him about the second great thing that changed his life.

'Which was?'

It is a risk to tell him, he knows:

'A poem.'

At which the boy rises swiftly to his feet.

'Wait!' Sir Thomas cries. 'It is not just any poem: it is a poem with an enchanted bed that will kill you if you lie on it, and a bridge over a canyon that is made from a single sword as long as two lances, and another bridge that is underwater, and there are a great many fights.'

'Fights? In a poem?'

'Yes,' Sir Thomas blurts, 'as I swear upon the cross of my sword!'

My father brought it to us in the first week after my eleventh Epiphany perhaps, while snow was still thick on the ground, as a gift sent from my grandfather – that good old knight Sir William Chetwynd – while Spare-the-Rod and I were labouring through the last of the martyrs of *The Golden Legend* (St Albine, I think, who lived in Angers and removed an evil spirit from a woman's eye that had taken the form of a whelk, and who had, perhaps, been taken from his crib by a wolf, but who was kept alive by two maids who prayed that they – oh well, that need not trouble us now).

'The boy's grandfather sends word to say he will enjoy this more than that,' my father said, laying upon our shared lectern with somewhat hesitant solemnity a small, ill-treated book between wine-coloured covers. Spare-the-Rod, ever keen never to hear another word from *The Golden Legend*, flapped open the new book's covers.

'*Le Chevalier du Chariot*,' he read, also suddenly hesitant, stepping back as if fearing what he had wished for.

'Oh,' he said. 'A poem. In the French, written by a man naming himself as **Chrétien**, of the city **of Troyes**, Thomas, which is in France, where they are said to enjoy such things.'

By which he meant poetry, I think.

'I am yet to read it myself,' my father admitted, 'but Sir William writes to say that by reading from it, Thomas will learn of the noble acts of chivalry by which knights once achieved honour.'

'Will he now,' was Spare-the-Rod's doubtful reply, the tone of which I only distantly registered, for by then I had taken the book and turned its first pages, where I found two fat columns of text: the one on the left hand in tight, neat French, mostly unadorned save for various names for which the scrivener had used red ink, and the one on the right-hand page, all in black, but arranged within a flower-bordered box around a small, colourful picture of a number of men and women wearing short blue and red mantles, in a garden, talking perhaps of whatever it was that such men and women spoke of in such gardens. To me this was delightful enough for it not being mere text, of course, but of little or no other interest, and so I turned the page.

And it was here — now — that the next great change in my life occurred, for there on the facing page was another illustration, but this was of a knight in harness, outfitted for battle on the back of a caparisoned charger, shield on arm, sword aloft, and before him, another knight, likewise in armour, and likewise arrayed for war, likewise on a caparisoned horse, only this knight's head was sundered clean from his body by a handspan of air to mark the thwacking passage of the first knight's sword!

Jesu preserve me!

I turned the page to find more, and suddenly, there before me, it was: the picture that captured my attention more surely than anything I had yet seen or read or knew of, for here was another knight, in beautiful silver-blue harness, crawling barefoot across a plummeting ravine, upon a bridge made from just one single, lethally sharp, impossibly long, sword.

'How does he do it?' I might have breathed. 'And *why*?'

The answers to these questions, and many more besides, were held within the modest covers of that book, and were revealed over the next few weeks, during which my thirst for knowledge of such things was so great that not one single detail slipped my mind. So voracious was I that the days became too short, and rush dips had to be brought to the western hall, where Spare-the-Rod would shut his eyes and let me read it out, only very occasionally intervening to correct my pronunciation or to help me translate a word here or there. Just occasionally he would bark at me to stop reading.

'Skip to the next page,' he would instruct, and I would, but I would keep my finger in the skipped page, and go back to it later. This is how I learned that Sir Lancelot cut his hand wrenching the bars from Queen Guinevere's window and that they went on to show one another every possible satisfaction, as well as kissing and fondling one another, though I was puzzled that Chrétien de Troyes — having described all this at length — then told the reader (me) that it was not for him (Chrétien) to reveal any further details of the great joy that Sir Lancelot and Queen Guinevere had in one another, for, as he says, such matters have no place in a story.

Which is right, in fact, because I wanted to read only battles, sieges, tourneys and jousts. I wanted shields shivered to pieces, lances smashed to splinters. I wanted to see and smell the burning sparks that filled the air when sword met helm. I wanted to read of smiting on the left and smiting on the right. I wanted to read of men being set aside, of having their brainpans split to their teeth, of their horses trailing their guts below so that their hooves became entangled.

'What next?' I cried, when we finished the book.

'Go out and play,' Spare-the-Rod instructed.

So I did. I set about reclaiming my old stick-horse from my sisters, and got one of the reeves to whittle me a sword from willow, and then a lance from some coppiced hazel too, and for the next howsoever many months my every waking hour was dedicated to the sorts of marvellous feats of arms by which I would soon achieve renown. When I was not treating Spare-the-Rod to my haughty expression, as befits a knight, I was in the courtyard, noisily re-enacting Lancelot's quest to rescue Queen Guinevere from the land of Gore, with my sister forced into the role of damsel-witness, and Rufus, one of the more biddable stable lads, drafted in as traitor knight, and required to offer just enough resistance to my constant lashings to make it feel like a struggle, but never enough to hurt me in any meaningful way.

It was a harmless enough pastime, you would think, of the sort most boys pursue until such time as something else comes along, with no harm done, but for some reason even then I understood that it displeased my father. Coming across me in the courtyard one day, cutting and slashing at my imaginary Sir Meleagant, he stood and watched, his mouth a thin, cud-chewing line, until after a moment he turned his back and walked away without a word, and I was left to come to a puzzled standstill, winnowed by his disapproval, not knowing what at all to do with my hands.

Despite this, as winter passed and spring came in, my obsession with Sir Lancelot's world only became more fervid, until we reached the Pentecost, which brought upon me the third great change of my young life.

Or rather, it was meant to, but did not, as you shall see, for on that morning – Pentecost, as I have said – after hurried prayers and a hunk of bread, my father took me on the saddle horn of his palfrey and we set out through the gatehouse of Fenny Newbold and turned westwards, along the path that follows Smite Brook.

Ah, Smite Brook. How I should love to be sat beside her now, soothed by her constant soft gurgle as she meanders through those mild furlongs and gentle woods, with my dogs and my wife as companions, surrounded on all sides by sweet birdsong, and the smell of mushrooms. I have known that stream so long her name no longer strikes me as odd – though it is oddly appropriate, if you think about it – and nor can I count the number of times I have since followed in the hoof marks that my father's horse that day did imprint on her marshy bank: a thousand? Two thousand? Sometimes at leisure, as then; sometimes in sorrow, as later; and still other times in violent alarum – of which you shall hear more, by and by – and it occurs to me now that that unexceptional little stream – rising beyond Monk's Kirby in the east and easing her way westwards past Newbold Revel and on towards the city of Coventry and beyond – has ever served as a muddy thread running through the great tapestry of my life, for in those few short leagues are crammed many of the divers events that have come to shape it, and me, for good or ill.

'Oh, come to it!' the boy implores. 'This can't just be about streams and poems! Something must happen!'

'It does! I promise. It is just about to!'

Sir Thomas *is* just coming to it, but first he must pause, for surely the boy ought to learn something of what was seen and said on that Pentecost morn ride? There are details that will wax significant as the tale proceeds, he is certain, including:

→ How Sir Thomas's father – in finest doublet and hose, boots polished conker-brown – sighed, just as he always would, at the state of the unmanaged thicket through which the path led, describing it – again, just as he always would – as being 'good only for a bushment'.

→ How because of this, Sir Thomas would likewise forevermore think the same thing, and every time he passed the spot, he would think that it was just the sort place where the traitor knight Sir Meleagant might set his archers in wait for Sir Lancelot so to shoot him down as he rode to rescue Queen Guinevere.

→ How once through those drear woods the path led out into the rich, well-tended fields and pastures belonging to the **Abbot of Coombe**, who was in those days a godly man, unlike his successor, who was a wretch, and a churl, and devoted to every kind of sinful debauchery.

→ How beyond the abbey estate came Caluden Park, wherein once the **Duke of Norfolk** found good sport, but since his execution (four years earlier, York, headsman's axe) it had fallen into decline, and already by then its hedges were overstood with field maples and suchlike, awaiting the lease of that foul, sin-glutted, goose-greased canker, **Sir Humphrey Stafford, Duke of Buckingham**, of whom very much more later.

But no. Perhaps it is best to spare the boy such details, or save them until later, and move on to that which did happen when he and his father reached the village of Gosford Green, a league or two further westwards, where Thomas was seized by an exhilarating terror? Yes, that is more suitable.

For there on the common land before us was gathered a great multitude of people, many, many times more than I could ever believe lived in the whole of England, let alone the county, and so for that moment I believed everyone in Christendom must be assembled here before us.

'Easy, Tom,' my father murmured in my ear. 'Easy.'

And he held me fast until my desire to flee had waned.

'But why are there so many?' I breathed.

'Why,' my father laughed, 'they are come for the tourney, of course.'

I might have bounced from the saddle then had he not still been holding me.

'The tourney?' I squeaked. 'The tourney? They have come for the tourney? Are we — are we likewise come for the — for the tourney?' I could scarcely breathe.

'We are,' my father laughed, but in such a way as to admit the imminence of an ordeal to be endured rather than to confirm a wonderful surprise to an excited son. I ignored him, for there was nothing then that could be said or done to dent my excitement, and still now, thinking about it even after all these years, the hair at the back of my neck rises, and the skin of my arms becomes as that of a plucked fowl, for I can still recall every moment of it: leaving my father's horse with the stable lads in the lines; making our ways through the market stalls, where everything one could ever imagine was for sale, from pomegranates, to caltrops, to jars of foxes' lungs, and where stallholders bellowed the virtue of their wares while disparaging their competitors as wicked pirates, forestallers and counterfeiters. I remember that through the aisles and between the carts poured a crush of all sorts of the most riotously strange and awful people I had ever seen: sickly, wheedling, ill-nourished children dragged along by bun-faced men and women who carried before them bellies alike unto upturned soup cauldrons, and each so garishly dressed, in poorly dyed woolstuffs and moulting cloth, and aperch each turnip-head was a cap the size, shape and colour of a cowpat.

And dear God, the noise! Jesu preserve me, the noise!

I clung to my father's hand until we came to the part of the common where the better folk were gathered, and the noise abated somewhat and we moved more freely among the sorts of folk whom I almost recognised as from home, until we came to a wall of backs turned to us. My father tapped a shoulder and spoke to the man, who spat a reply over his shoulder that made my father angry, and harsh words were exchanged, but I was not listening, for a gap had opened up, and into it I shot, for there, laid out before me – Jesu defend me! – was the tiltyard.

It was a long depression with hoof-pocked sand, a gentle bow-shot from one end to the other, which in those days we did not divide with a fence as we do now. It was roped off from the spectators and in part banked up at its edges with gathered earth and straw stooks. On the far side was a raised platform, which I learned was called a lodge, twenty paces broad under a spreading canopy of red cloth. Its corners were held up on poles to which were pinned blazons of red and yellow, and badges I recognised from when my father used to go away to Wales with Sir Richard Beauchamp: a bear upon its hind legs, clutching a knotted tree stump – the badge of the Earls of Warwick.

Under the canopy were spaced five broad-bottomed chairs behind and around which were set more benches and stools, as yet unfilled, and so my gaze drifted first to one end of the tiltyard, to one cluster of bright-painted tents and pavilions, and then to the other end, where there was another cluster of similar tents. Above them flew banners, held at the fly from long poles thrust in the ground, and it was only after a moment that I divined that these poles were in fact actual, honest-to-God lances. Lances of the sort that a knight might couch, of the sort which Sir Lancelot might have carried, of the sort used in tourneys, and merely glimpsing this magical weapon for the first time in my life was enough to make me gasp. But then I saw, at last, emerging from one of the tents with a bad-tempered flap, one of the magical beings themselves: a knight, encased in what I now know to call full harness, arrayed as if for jousting.

'Jesu preserve me!' I might have breathed, again.

For when first you see a man in harness, the effect is unsettling: it is as if he comes at you from another place, or is another manner of being, inhuman, and for some reason it is impossible not to stare, struck dumb, utterly stilled in awe even as the knight goes about his all-too-human business: in this case shouting for something from someone, and another man in blue came running, carrying I-don't-know-what: a thing, which was passed across, and the knight re-treated into the tent. That, for the moment, was that, for as I was to learn later in life, it is always the case that where men and bits of dedicated equipment are gathered together with a specific purpose there will always be a goodly long delay before anything can be ex-pected to happen.

That day the wait was perhaps as long as it takes to hear Mass said before anything significant next happened, but in all that time I kept my gaze fixed on the tent to my right hand, and whenever there was a glimpse of polished steel, I felt my blood quicken and my breath grow short. As the moments crawled by, everyone in the ever-tightening crowd joined me in craning their necks to spot a knight, and whenever one was glimpsed, all cheered, as if to spur him on, but still they delayed, and the mood in the crowd curdled. The cheers became jeers, and everyone booed when some dark-skinned jugglers were sent out into the tiltyard to entertain us with a performance of acrobatics and so on that at any other time might have been enchanting, but was today surplus to need, and the boo-ing continued until the jugglers threw – and dropped – their dwarf, who was knocked senseless, at which the crowd at last expressed delight.

When he was carried off, another first for me: a small, brown and reluctant bear was brought on, something I'd never seen before, and I confess I was astonished and terrified all at once, just as I had been at the first glimpse of the knight, though I was alone in this, for those by my side, who were more experienced in such things, held it to be a pitiful specimen, with its rubbed-raw flanks and very dolorous mien.

But then – at last – the bear was gone, and there was a trumpet blast, and pipes were blown and drums beaten, and two men and three women appeared under the awning on the lodge on the other side of the tiltyard, each dressed alike, but in such a manner as I'd never seen before: the men in jackets both cinched and short, em-phasising their waists, their cods, their necks, while the women wore tight bodies over vast skirts, and hats shaped like bodkin heads, only as long as your arm, pointing heavenwards, and in such colours too: reds dyed as vivid as any poppy, yellows to shame a yolk and blues bluer than the Holy Mary's cloak. On seeing them, the crowd began cheering and shouting 'À Warwick! À Warwick!'

Hats were waved in the air and a great surge of people came pushing from behind, pressing us against the ropes, and there was much cursing and many threats of violence, but before knives were drawn and any blood was shed, all were distracted by two horses being led stamping forward, one caparisoned in blue, the other in

36

red, each matching their knight's banner, and then at long, long last the knights themselves emerged from their pavilions, to be greeted by great raucous cheers, and they stood for a moment acknowledging the cheers with raised hands.

Then there was more and more delay until, finally, oh dear Jesu, they were mounted, and they faced one another down the length of the tiltyard: two men each hidden by steel and cloth utterly detached and alone in the middle of the arena. It was just man against man, horse against horse, edge against edge, point against point, steel-clad knee against steel-clad knee.

The crowd fell silent. Everyone held their breath. Then a fat man in a scarlet hat emerged from behind the lodge and began shouting something that could hardly be understood, and then at the longest of long last, the two knights gathered themselves and kicked their horses first into a walk and then into a trot. I felt my father's fingers tighten on my shoulder. I could feel the horses' hooves boom through the soles of my shoes, and my teeth chattered, and the crowd seemed to begin a rising roar as the two men careered towards one another. The sand flew beneath the horses, which seemed so big and slow, but the rhythm of their hooves mimicked my heart as they sped at one another, until it became a single thread of pulsing, throbbing noise under the crowd's tensing groan, which reached a peak just as the riders lowered their lances.

And missed one another.

The crowd gasped as one. The knights rode on to the opposite ends of the yard and slowed and turned their mounts. The fat man in the hat stepped forward to shout again, and once more the knights set off towards one another.

Again, the noise rose in pitch and the hoofbeats in intensity, and the two met in the middle, but once again they missed one another.

The crowd, more experienced than me, were becoming impatient.

'He's shy!' someone called. 'Sir Gryffyd is shy!'

'It's Sir John's horse's fault, you dolt!'

There was another lengthy pause and the two knights turned and feutered their lances once more and came at one another with increased speed and ferocity, and this time their lances did touch, but each skittered harmlessly off the other's shield and it was just as bad as if they had missed.

They did it again and again, and each time they hurtled past one another, missing, and their movements became clumsy and jerky as they over-strived to bring the thing to a conclusion – which at length they achieved, but in a manner that neither might have wished, for at perhaps the sixth time of asking, their horses, blindfolded and with ears stuffed with oakum, and ridden by men who were perhaps rendered equally senseless by their helms, collided head-on.

Whose fault it was was impossible to tell, but there was a great sharp crack, loud as hammer on anvil, sharper than thunder, and both horses skittered off one another and went down in a tangle of shattered limbs. The red rider was thrown, but the blue was caught in his saddle, and was crushed by the weight of his thrashing horse. Blood seethed at the joints of his visor and streaked his helmet and stained the sand all about, while the red knight lay totally still, as if he had fallen from a great height, upon his shoulders, with his backside in the air, his neck bent like an elbow. Both horses screamed and the crowd was aghast, most turned away, covering their eyes, covering their children's eyes, as stewards came running and one of them – beefy as a blacksmith – brought a butcher's cleaver and set to muting the horse's screams with wild and dreadful blows. I shied away, and went to block my ears, but now my father gripped me hard.

'No,' he said. 'Look at it. Look at it and remember it well.

Sir Thomas and the boy are so engrossed in the tale that neither hears Brunt the father as he lumbers up the steps in that way Sir

Thomas remembers from times past, and nor do they see him until the door's hinges squeak, until there he is, filling the doorway, slumped in that age-old familiar position, arms and ankles crossed, just as his son had done, looking at Sir Thomas through piggy eyes, pickled with false contempt, and Sir Thomas is very glad to recall he suffers a boil upon his backside.

'Well, well, well,' Brunt rasps. 'Look who it is.'

And the boy springs to his feet like a branded cat, and backs into a corner, while Sir Thomas, caught mid-flow, somewhat confused, stands and sees that Brunt has billowed and sagged with age and bad habits since last he saw him, but he still wears that same greasy old leather jerkin that is the colour of cold dregs, and still wears his horribly stained hose bunched up about his cods.

'Master Brunt,' Sir Thomas greets him, adding no blessing. 'There has been a mistake and I should like you to send word for the keeper.'

'Keeper's busy,' Brunt says, holding Sir Thomas's gaze and then, from the corner of his mouth, he addresses the boy.

'What you doin', boy?'

'Nothing.'

'Been a long time doing nothing.'

'What do you want, Master Brunt?' Sir Thomas interrupts.

Brunt keeps his eyes affixed on Sir Thomas's but ignores his words.

'Telling you his tales is he, boy?' he asks. 'Chuntering on about his Knights of the Round Table, is he? About troth and feats of arms, and honour and whatnot? Well, you're not to listen to a word he says, boy, d'you hear? Because what would he know about it, eh?'

Sir Thomas breaks the staring contest to glance at the boy, who is flushed, and glassy eyed, and Sir Thomas too feels a great weight of sorrow and shame.

But Brunt is not done yet.

'Broken every oath he ever took, this one,' he goes on. 'And many more besides, I'll wager. Come on, son, and if you want to hear a

39

really good story, a true story, mind, then I've got one for you: about how and why a certain Sir Thomas did languish many a day and oft under lock and key in Castle Newgate!'

He laughs, delighted with his impression, and he gestures for the boy to come, fingers to palm, fingers to palm, and the boy crosses to him, just as Sir Thomas supposes he must, but remains wary, and dips past his father's outstretched arm as if expecting a clout, and he disappears down the steps into the darkness, leaving Sir Thomas and Brunt alone, face to face again after so many years. They say nothing, but stare at one another, until at length Brunt concludes he has nothing more to say, and laughs contemptuously, and turns to drag himself after the boy, closing the door and ramming home the locking bar with familiar finality.

'Churl,' Sir Thomas mutters, but it is he who is left in a cell, alone with his fears once more.

CHAPTER 2

How Sir Thomas lives to see Pentecost, and how a certain man of law comes, but wots not well why Sir Thomas should yet languish within-forth so constrained, and of divers other matters

When the bells for Prime ring out Sir Thomas wakes with a strangled cry of conflicted fury. In his dreams he has been back home in dear old Newbold Revel, back in his own bed, with his own wife, under meadowsweet-scented sheets of linen and finest-spun woollen blankets, but on waking here he is still – *again* – after four nights now – locked in Newgate gaol, in a cell he had oftentimes prayed never to see again, alone and upon a palliasse that stinks of other men's worst fears.

But at least he has survived another night. At least he is not dead. There is that.

Though, dear Jesu, death now, this instant, would come as a relief, for he knows the day ahead will be filled once again with the same roiling terror, just waiting for the night to come; for the tolling of St Sepulchre's night bell; and for the soft knock upon his door to let him know the priest is come to hear his last confession.

And yet what has he *done*? What has he to *confess*? Nothing. He clenches his teeth and kicks his feet. Jesu defend him!

If only that boy would come back; that would divert him. But he has not been for two days – is he alive? Is he beaten to death? Or is this some spiteful trick of Brunt's? – and in his place is sent a small, boss-eyed girl who smells very strongly of goat and saltpetre, and who will say nothing save to indicate that she is mute, perhaps, and possibly deaf. She comes again this morning, just as Sir Thomas is gouging another scratch – his fourth – into the daub under his

41

window to mark the passage of his days, and she brings more bread, more ale and another of those mealy apples, which Sir Thomas takes with genuine gratitude, for he is pleased to learn that someone somewhere intends him to live beyond the hour. After she has gone, he says his prayers, and eats and drinks, and then commits himself to pacing his cell, thinking the same thoughts he thought yesterday, and the day before, and the day before that, though this morning there are two new things to think about. The first is that the flies are already gathering in his cell. Not the noisy lugubrious bruisers that hang about his night soil bucket, each the size of an acorn, but the infuriating small ones that cut apparently pre-planned squares through the middle of the room. As the summer wears on, they become unbearable, he remembers. The second is that the man next door is playing, Sir Thomas thinks, the harp, and he wonders why *he* doesn't have a harp. Why did he not think to bring a harp? It is true he has not played the harp since he was a boy. But now he promises himself he will take it up again as soon as he is home.

Nothing else has changed, save that the cat is warming to him, and this morning she allows Sir Thomas to tickle her stomach without latching onto his wrist with every claw, which gives him some sense of achievement, and it is while he is doing this, sat at the foot of his palliasse, that he hears stuttering footsteps beyond his door, and knows with no shadow of doubt that here comes — at last — his private attorney, Master William Hartshorne, bearing tidings.

He detaches himself from the cat and stands with his heart jarring in his ribs, and despite every little thing that he learned from before times, he cannot stop himself embracing the hope that Hartshorne will duck into his cell with a great yellow-toothed smile on his horsey old face, and he'll spread his long arms wide and tell Sir Thomas to gather his things — though he has none — 'for the king acknowledges his error and wishes this day to set you free with some very handsome recompense'. But it is not to be.

42

As soon as the door is opened, Sir Thomas sees Master Hartshorne's face is longer than ever, deathly pale and utterly defeated,
and he knows with a great sinking swoop of his vitals that his lawyer
brings nothing but bad news. Nevertheless, Sir Thomas is still —
for now at least — Sir Thomas Malory, knight, veteran of Verneuil
and of countless other encounters, one-time Captain of Gisors, and
once a Member of Parliament, and so he greets his lawyer with brave
cheer, complimenting him on his very fine emerald-green doublet —
obviously new — made of some sort of water-dappled silk and cut
for a much younger man.

Master Hartshorne ignores the compliment.

'Oh, Sir Tho-omas,' he bleats, for when he is agitated he stretches
out his words to sound not unlike a distant la-amb. 'Oh Sir Tho-
omas.'

And despite himself Sir Thomas cannot keep a similar quaver
from his own voice when he asks: 'Wha-at? The king means to see
me *dead*?'

And as that last word trickles out, Sir Thomas glimpses once
again that fork in the path ahead, where the world and everyone
within it must go one way, while he — Sir Thomas Malory — must
go the other, all alone, into the deep, dark woods of eternal night.

'Well,' he says, turning from Hartshorne to hide his tears. 'So be it.'

To him, this is the bravest thing he has ever done.

'But wha-at have you done, Sir Thoma-as?' Hartshorne bleats regardless. 'What have you done this ti-ime?'

At which Sir Thomas spins back.

'Jesu defend me!' he snaps. 'What do you mean: "this time"? Wit
you well, Master Hartshorne, that I did nothing last time, and that
if I have done *anything* this time — which I have not — then I too am
yet to learn of its nature!'

Hartshorne lets out a mew and steps back, raising his palms in
defence.

'But then why are you herein co-onstrained?' he warbles. 'Why are you back here in Newga-ate?'

'*You* are supposed to know! *You* are supposed to tell *me!*'

At which Hartshorne deflates, and sighs long and loud, and he looks about in vain for something strong to drink, and somewhere clean to sit. He finds neither.

'I have a-asked for an audience with everyone I can think of,' he admits, 'but the king and his Council are so taken up with nego-tia-ations for **Princess Margaret**'s marriage into Burgundy that no man can say whether he is coming or going.'

Having been locked alone with his thoughts for nigh on a week, Sir Thomas finds such tidings from the outside world – a marriage! Into Burgundy! – otherworldly and pointless.

'What of the **Earl of Warwick**?' he barks. 'What of my good-lord?'

He means that sarcastically: the Earl of Warwick is good-lord unto himself alone.

'I have sent messages,' Hartshorne tells him, 'but am told he is again about his business in the Northern Parts, or across the Nar-row Sea in Calais perhaps, or maybe even in Wales again – oh, Sir Thomas, I don't know.'

And the two men are left looking at one another for a length of time – reluctant, unhappy collaborators once more – and both are dretched out of all measure, for this is all so sickeningly familiar, and after another long sigh, and a beating of his cap against his spindly thigh, Master Hartshorne must start again, asking – tenta-tively, haltingly – if there is anything Sir Thomas believes he may have done – 'even by mischance' – to harm the interests of the king?

'I have scarce left my garden these past five years,' Sir Thomas reminds him.

At which Hartshorne makes another of those curious mewing sounds.

'It cannot be the old trou-uble back again, can it, Sir Thomas?' he ventures. 'You know that the earl will not lift a ha-and to help you if he belie-eves it so?'

At which their alliance fractures again, and Sir Thomas rounds once more on Hartshorne and asks him to leave, to return only when he has learned why the king is holding him, what he intends to do with him and how to stop it happening.

'And have my wife send money, fresh linen and a venison pie,' he adds, though he wonders whether there will be any time for that.

Hartshorne is miserable and cowed, and promises to do so, and takes his sorry, angular leave, apologising — just as he should — for all his divers failings, and so once more Sir Thomas is left alone with the cat, who this time scratches his wrist, after which he lies on the palliasse and then, after a further while, he turns to face the wall, and cannot stop himself weeping.

The day passes slowly, warm under the summer sun. Sir Thomas grows more despairing; more fearful, but — praise Jesu! — at None it is the boy who brings him his evening bread and ale, and Sir Thomas is startled to find how pleased he is to see him, alive and unharmed. But his joy is short-lived, for the boy will not hold his gaze, and so Sir Thomas must surmise that Brunt has told him all he believes he knows about Sir Thomas, and so Sir Thomas's pleasure withers on the vine.

He takes the bread and ale with thanks, though, and though he is sure he does the boy too much credit in believing he knows anything of the priest's intentions, he is desperate, and asks after the priest from St Sepulchre's.

'Not been seen for a day or two,' the boy tells him. His manner is gruff, his tone short, and in other circumstances, and in ordinary times, Sir Thomas would take offence and perhaps box the boy's ear, but today he restrains himself and asks after the mute, strong-smelling girl, who turns out to be the boy's sister, Susan.

'Born wrong-headed, but baptised a Christian.'

'And your father's boil?' Sir Thomas wonders.

'Still leaking like an eye, it is, but he's on his feet today, and well enough to lead old Master Bewscel to the moneylender on Cheapside.'

A warden will sometimes accept a payment — two pennies is the going rate — to accompany a prisoner into the city, usually to find credit, taking a cut from both sides, but sometimes to satisfy baser urges, especially so in May.

'And who is he,' Sir Thomas asks, 'this Master Bewscel?'

The boy indicates the wall through which must be Master Bewscel's cell, whence Sir Thomas believes he may have heard someone playing the harp, though he cannot hear it now.

'Nice old boy,' the boy says. 'Plays the harp.'

'What is he held for?'

The boy laughs, visibly unbending now.

'Committing a lewd act on Popkirtle Lane,' he says. 'Though all agree his only crime is getting caught.'

Sir Thomas chews his bread in silence and wonders if there is a guild of children such as this? Coarse-tongued, needle-eyed boys, already steeped deep in hard-bitten cynicism, queuing up to become their fathers? He bets there is. He also wonders what sort of lewd act this Master Bewscel was caught committing? It is beneath his dignity to ask, of course, and he does not particularly wish to distract the boy, who lingers on the threshold and might go, or might stay. Sir Thomas knows not to say anything, but just to sit, and, sure enough, the boy is drawn back in, and if there were anything in the room worth picking up and looking at the bottom thereof — a ewer, say — then that's what the boy would do, but there is not, so the boy must either leave, or ask his question.

He asks his question, praise Jesu:

'So how d'you know all about chivalry and knights and them

things, when you are — when you are what my father says you are?'

Sir Thomas might cheer, but instead he swallows his bread.

'Because,' he says, 'I am not as your father says I am.'

'Ha,' the boy scoffs, moving to the door. 'If I'd a shilling every time I'd heard that.'

'But it is true,' Sir Thomas tells him. 'I was innocent. I am innocent. I swear upon my sword.'

'Upon your sword? You were locked up for nigh on ten years,' the boy levels. 'That don't happen if you're innocent.'

'It does,' Sir Thomas corrects. 'Or it did. And it was nearer five, anyway.'

Which is a slight twist of the truth, rather than an outright lie, for it was seven, though there were weeks, months even, during that time in which he was not — for one reason or another — in gaol. When he was on bail, say, or at large. But perhaps they will come to that.

'Well,' the boy says with a stab at finality, 'my old man says I am not to listen to any of your nonsense, anyway.'

Nonsense! If Brunt were here now, he would— He calms himself. He will not get what he wishes by clouting the man's son, will he?

'Which is a pity,' Sir Thomas manages to croak. 'I was just getting to the good bit, the part that will be of great interest, which is how I came to serve King Henry: he who triumphed at Agincourt.'

Again, and as always, just the mention of Agincourt and the boy is hooked. He sits on the rushes with his gaze fixed on Sir Thomas, his father's words lying forgotten by the wayside.

'But how did you end up a soldier,' he wonders, 'when your old man tried to put you off when he took you to the jousting and all that?'

And Sir Thomas cannot help but smile.

'Oh no,' he tells him. 'My father did not want to put me off being a soldier—'

Or if he did, he could not have been more misguided, as he must have recognised in the week after the tourney, while watching me re-enact both those two gruesome deaths for perhaps the hundredth time. He — who had experienced war cruel and sharp in Wales and at Shrewsbury — had wanted me to see that my make-believe was just that: make-believe; but seeing he had failed, he changed his line of attack, and confiscated *Le Chevalier du Chariot*, and a week later he returned from Coventry with another new book he brought to us in the west parlour just as we were finishing some terrible piece of reckoning that I had got wrong again, and Spare-the-Rod was in a damp sweat, having beaten me nine times on my eleven-year-old buttocks.

'*Epitoma Rei Militaris*,' Spare-the-Rod read short-windedly, 'by Vegetius. Concerning Military Matters? I believed you to be unhappy with the boy's love of fighting, Master Malory?'

'I'm not unhappy with that,' my father told him. 'I'm unhappy that he thinks it is one thing, when it is another.'

Spare-the-Rod read a page of the book with a puckered frown.

'Do you wish the boy to learn Latin from this, or practise its lessons outside?'

'Both,' my father said.

The book — a manual, really — had been written sometime in the fourth century to address the perceived shortcomings of the Roman manhood, which Vegetius believed had declined from its zenith under Julius Caesar, and which was then very popular throughout all of Christendom, where it was believed its lessons were eternal if not universal, and so the very next day I was sent to run to such and such a tree and back, and off I set: once, twice, thrice. The day after that a different, more distant tree was chosen. The next day to an even further tree, with a sack on my back such as fruit-pickers carry, and a stave. On the fourth day the pack was filled with a few shovelfuls of earth. On the fifth a length of flax rope was tied to a lower branch of an even more distant tree for me to run to and climb. Once. Twice. Three times. By the end of the week a leather pack was found that smelled very strongly of the mews wherein were kept my father's falcons and into which a stone was added every day over the next week as the trees got more distant and the rope longer to reach the highest branches.

This was arduous, but a welcome change from *The Golden Legend*.

And nor was it all running and climbing: in the courtyard behind the stables my father had Rufus, the Reeve's son, plant a tree trunk on its end, which, under Spare-the-Rod's nose-in-book tuition, I was set to hack at very fiercely with a blunt sword — the very first I'd ever been allowed to pick up — made of curiously weighty metal that rang more like an iron bar than a blade and sent great pains down my wrists to my shoulders. To begin with, I could keep swatting away for as long as it might take you to say the Ave, perhaps, though by the time Amen was reached, my blows were as weak as a kitten's.

'Is he not too young for this?' my mother asked, watching me dripping with exhausted ten-year-old's sweat, scarce able to pat the sides of the post with the sword held in both hands.

'By about five years, mistress,' Spare-the-Rod admitted.

But still we went on.

The next week a shield woven of rushes — a great oblong thing of my own weight and height — was introduced into my drills with the tree trunk. Spare-the-Rod would sometimes stand behind the post as I attacked it, and he would try to jab me with his rod to encourage me to keep behind my shield. I was instructed to vary my attacks too, so that sometimes I banged the post's shins, other times its crown, which I could only just reach. I learned to stab, rather than cut. I leapt in. I leapt out. Sometimes I was given a spear with which to stab it, and other times I was to throw the spear at it.

In the first week of warm weather I was led down to the stock pond – wherein my arrow was supposed to have landed – to learn to swim. This would pose a problem – though Vegetius was insistent on its practice, he was vague on its method – and with no one else with a clue as to how it was done, my only model was Rufus the Reeve's son's dog, a yellow retriever with a narrow nose and a good nature that he called Meg, who could be persuaded to fetch anything you threw into the water.

Watched by my father, mother, brother and sister, as well as Spare-the-Rod and Rufus, I stripped off my boots, pourpoint and hose, and waded shivering down through the reeds and into the mud-clouded waters where carp sucked at the surface like falling raindrops. Roused by the crowd, I threw myself into the waters and began a constant churn in imitation of Meg's stroke, and in this way I moved slowly across the pond, from one corner to the other and back again. I had not even got my hair wet. When I emerged, the dog woofed at me approvingly.

It might have been about then that my vulnerability to miasmas first revealed itself, for in the week that followed my skin became covered in small cankers and I was laid up in bed with an ague. I was only just strong enough to totter to the window of my room in the eaves to look down to see a harp being delivered, which was the next thing we were to tackle.

The thing about Spare-the-Rod, or *a* thing about Spare-the-Rod, was that although he was well enough versed in clergy, and taught me so well that by the age of eleven I had perfect handwriting, and could read and speak Latin and French as well as any man save the king and the Archbishop of Canterbury, he knew of little else. My father – who had been in battle – guided his instruction of me in fighting skills, such as how to jab at me from behind the post, and in how to look after horses, hounds and hawks – and how to hunt with each of them – but as with swimming, when it came to dancing, or learning to carve at dinner, or playing the harp, all was guesswork.

'You are murdering it,' he said when I first plucked the out-of-tune strings.

'You dance like Death,' he told me as I followed his steps exactly.

Nevertheless, we persevered, feeling our way out of the darkness just as the ancients must have done, refining if not perfecting, and by the time I was twelve — by which time I could swim a hundred paces fully dressed and had got through two harps (never long-lasting things, in my experience) — it was obvious to all that I had exhausted such reserves of knowledge and strength as Spare-the-Rod possessed and that if I were to learn the urbanity and culture of England, as my father put it, I should need a new tutor, or, as many — some — other boys did, be sent from home to be schooled elsewhere.

Which is when, and how, the Earl of Warwick entered my own story, for it was his household that I was to join. My father rode with me to his castle, all the way along Smite Brook once again — no doubt stopping to study the woods in which the perfect bushment could be laid, noting the decline in Coombe Abbey under its new abbot and shaking our heads at the continued decline in the state of the hedges that encircled Caluden Park — and when we reached the town and saw its castle, I was struck with awe, just as I had been at that tourney, for coming to the castle then, for the first time, and from dear old Fenny Newbold, I had never seen anything half its size, half its grandeur, and as we approached the East Gate — where we were to enquire after a certain Master Grimes — I was, for that time, lost for words. I sat in my saddle, slack with awe, and it was then, just at this precise, unfortunate moment when my guard was not so much down as yet to arrive, when my mouth hung open as if on broken hinges, that I first encountered William Peyto, sent there to meet me and take me to Master Grimes.

'Flycatcher!' Peyto called me. 'Catching your dinner are you, Flycatcher, eh? Caught anything nice have you, Flycatcher?'

Peyto — a natural bully — singled me out as his victim from two hundred paces, and having grown up alone, more or less, I was not aware of the ways of boys in groups. Before I had even unpacked my bag, he was laughing at my much-mended hose, and ridiculing me before the other boy with whom I was to share our chamber, **Thomas West**, who would go on to become more important to me than I would ever have believed, and I to him, too, of course, but we will get to that.

I did not then know the code, you see. I thought that perhaps it might be perfectly normal to go through someone's possessions as Peyto was then doing to mine, strewing them about the room, and to find them wanting, as Peyto was finding mine. But as he dug deeper he was as shocked as me when he came upon that copy of *Le Chevalier du Chariot* that Spare-the-Rod must have hidden for me in a folded spare shirt.

'A book!' Peyto shouted with delighted disgust. He snatched it up and danced with it, holding it above his head as if it were some sort of trophy. 'And not in English! Are you a heathen, Flycatcher? Some sort of paynim?

'What is a paynim?' the boy interrupts.

'Oh!' Sir Thomas starts, for he has almost forgotten for a moment that he is here. 'A heathen.'

'A heathen? Cheeky little sod! I'd show him the back of my hand, I would.' He sounds horribly like his father.

But Peyto was by then already an ugly brute: tall and skinny, three or four years older than me, with powdery skin and crusted red pustules, and he had his hair cut under a bowl that came down to just above his ears, as if he were going to war. I must admit he later grew into his looks, but he was a sight then. Thomas West told Peyto that he was unmannerly, and that he should return the book, and while Peyto considered his response, I snatched it back and tore a page, and I was cursing Peyto for the fool he was when Master John Grimes came in.

'Now, now, ladies, stop your love games,' he said.

'Flycatcher snatched that book out of my hands,' Peyto bleated. 'You saw him, didn't you, West?'

West merely raised an eyebrow in disgust and Grimes ordered us both out into the keep, where we were sent to run around the castle walls. I had no idea that this was impossible without a long detour over the bridge, while Peyto — who had done this sort of thing many times before, of course — knew a short cut through the village beyond the second bridge. Therefore, despite my Vegetius-inspired regime, I came in well behind him and was sent out across the drawbridge again. As I ran — laughed at and jeered at by the townspeople, who were used to seeing this — I wondered if this were really what my father had intended when he sent me away. I had said but two words to my new tutor, and those were both 'yes'.

Master Grimes turned out to be an unforgiving satirist, with a powerful faith in mockery and humiliation as the best teachers, but his barbs were aimed indiscriminately and though my harp-playing and my dancing style marked me out for his special attention, the thing that saved me was my ability to fight. Or rather not to fight, since by then I had still not fought a living being other than a cockerel, but I could swing a sword — much lighter than I was used to — and stab at a post for hours on end while leaping forwards and backwards to avoid imagined blows.

'Pshaw!' Peyto laughed when first he saw it. 'Look how Flycatcher jabs with his sword! He's no true Christian: he's a Turk!' Peyto's special skill, I was to discover, was the cheap blow — early or late — whenever someone was not yet ready or no longer ready, and in this way his presence was useful, for he taught the rest of us to be on our guard at all times, though some remembered this lesson better than others.

Master Grimes was to be our henchmaster, chief among the handful of tutors to whom we had to attend, and so in those early weeks, before the Beauchamp family returned to the castle from wherever they were, our days unfolded much the same every day. We rose at dawn, said our prayers, washed, dressed – in green, very finely spun wool – and hurried to Mass, where we were taught not to fidget, but to thump our breast to signify penitence. After Mass we ran to the great hall to wait upon officers of the castle – filling their cups, carving their meat and so on – and when they were done, we sat to be served ourselves, by servants, and we learned from the officers all the good manners and urbanity that we'd need, which included looking one another in the eye while speaking modestly and frankly, talking humbly to superiors, cheerfully to equals and commandingly to inferiors, never interrupting anyone, and above all avoiding all temptation to prolixity.

After that, until dinner at noon, Master Symmington taught us clergy. He had a pair of eyeglasses – very rare then – that made his eyeballs appear huge and terrifying, but he himself was a small and delicate little creature, like a vole, and he had to have a man-at-arms in the room along with him whom he could order to pull the short hairs at our sideburns if we ever yawned or showed signs of nodding off during his lessons. This, it turned out, was why Peyto had opted for his warlike haircut.

After that it was music and dancing, about which the less said the better, but it did bring us into contact with a real-life woman – Mistress Gule – who also taught us manners and respect for women, and to whom I later discovered Thomas West wrote rhyming verse, even though to my eyes – young as they then were – she was alto-gether too solid and ground-bound a figure to be worshipped this way. Despite her size and shape – she had no discernible wrists, but breasts that I could not help noticing were each the size of a man's head – she moved with great poise, and she could do so very quickly, too, when called upon, which she was when first I took her harp — her much-loved instrument — between my knees and began playing.

'Jesu preserve me!' she cried, and she flitted across the room and pulled me away from it, careless that I was sent sprawling, while she soothed it as if I had ruffled its feathers.

'I think I would prefer to see you dance, Master Malory,' she said on that first afternoon. 'Seeing you murder a quadrille would break my heart, but not my harp.'

She found this very funny, and threw her head back, showing us the wonderful whiteness of her throat, the sight of which reddened Thomas West's cheeks.

After dinner, where we once again served our masters before we sat down ourselves, we were to meet Master Yarrow in the tourney yard or at the butts, where he would be waiting to instruct us in various feats of arms. Master Yarrow was a wiry little man — in build not unlike my father — who called us 'gentles', which was short for gentlemen, and started more or less every sentence with 'as I say'. He also stood very close to you, clasping his hands and rubbing them together to make his arm muscles bulge.

'Right, gentles,' he would say, rubbing those hands. 'As I say, today we are going to take another look at the longbow. To wit: one bow, long — not to be confused with the crossbow, which though also a bow, is altogether a different beast, being across, rather than long — and three arrows, less long, ash-shafted, bodkin-headed; intended for the use of: you.'

There would always be groans if we were to shoot arrows, for it was hard work and there was no chance that we would ever win worship using such a thing, because, quite simply, we would never be the best at it. The sons of costermongers, cordwainers and so on, they'd been practising with their bows since they were seven, and while they could hardly read English let alone Latin or French, already by our age they could send an arrow to smash a pilgrim's shell two hundred paces distant. And they could do it ten times to our once.

We all much preferred the riding lessons, during which we were given palfreys from the earl's stables and were taught to keep our seats neatly and cleanly, but it was frustrating that we were not yet permitted to ride with lances at the quintain, or take our horses and go out hunting in the earl's parklands. That would come, of course, but until then what we most relished were the lessons in wearing — and fighting in — harness, which is not so simple as it sounds.

To begin with, we were each presented with a great mound of rusted plate, thick wads of linen and tow, straps of punctured leather and a few square feet of filthy mail. Our task was to make sense of it and harness ourselves 'as if the French were coming'. West pointed out that we'd have a squire for this sort of thing, which earned him a cuff.

'What if he's dead, eh? And the French are still coming?'

'I'd need no armour to beat a mere Frenchman,' the fourth hench-man — **Thomas Verney** — said, and he began again a story we'd all heard a hundred times of his grandfather being given a sword by **Edward of Woodstock** at Poitiers until Yarrow told him he would like to go into battle with him, because the French would kill him first, and perhaps allow Yarrow longer in bed. Verney's brow grew heavy with confusion at this apparently treacherous thought.

We set to work, each pulling out the largest pieces first. It was play armour, if you can imagine it, scaled down to fit a boy such as I was then, and little or no care had gone into its forging, for it was lumpen and heavy, but even so it was complicated to put on, especially if you got the order wrong, and we struggled with straps that we could not reach for they were behind our backs, and so on, until West — it can only have been him — realised that we were not being tested on how much we knew about putting on plate — which in my case was virtually nothing — but on how well we would help one another. Once this revelation occurred he and I strapped one another's cuirass straps and we were ready first to face the French, complete with gauntlets but with mail coifs instead of helmets.

Peyto and Verney finished last and were sent to run around the bailey. Peyto fell, and by the time they were back each was puce and ready to vomit.

Though heavy, the armour made us feel invincible and within moments we were trying to wrestle one another to the ground. As the smallest, I was knocked over first. I got up, my mail coif and arming cap over my eyes, and was knocked down again. I got up more carefully this time, and kept low. I knocked over Peyto by coming at his legs. Peyto kicked me as best he could but bruised the sole of his foot. Yarrow laughed. He watched us for a few minutes with his hands clenched until we were all on our hands and knees, sweaty, and a large red weal had closed Verney's right eye.

We were to keep our armour with us for the next few months, and we were to polish it to make it shine – though it never would, for it had come from the smiths in a rough, dull powdery finish that all our scrubbing with sand and vinegar only seemed to make rougher, duller and more powdery yet. We soon became proficient at helping one another put it on and take it off, and though for those first few weeks wearing it used to make us all short of breath, we gradually became used to it, and soon we were rolling around and fighting one another like noisy iron bear cubs, of which, coinciden-tally, there were a couple in the castle grounds – real rather than iron – and whose scent made the dogs howl at odd times of night. The sight of them took me back to the one I'd seen that day on Gosford Green when I'd stood with my father, and in those days I found I very much missed his hand upon my shoulder.

For all the thrill of those early days at Warwick, the moments that I looked forward to most were the early evenings, when Mas-ter Symmington would reappear, or we would be made to reappear before him, in one of the solars with windows that faced west onto the bailey. There we sat at a table while he read to us from one of the books taken from the earl's library, which was not then so big as it later became, but included a copy of another book by Chrétien de Troyes, entitled *Erec and Enide*—

The boy laughs.

'Eric and Enid!' he says. 'I know them. He's a hog gelder what lives on Midden Lane, and she takes in linens. Haha!'

Sir Thomas cannot tell if he is serious.

'Sir Erec was a knight of France,' he continues, 'who became so soft with love for Enide his wife that he neglected knighthood's sterner duties.'

'And?'

'And? After he overheard Enide weeping for his lost worship, he ordered her to prepare for a journey and that on this journey she was no account to speak to him. They set off to find King Arthur's court and along the way Erec performed a great many marvellous deeds of arms, including the rescue of Cadof of Cabruel from two giants, and, with the help of Guivret the Short, the defeat of Count Oringle of Limors. But on two occasions Enide defied his order to be silent – both times to warn him that he was in mortal peril – and in the end he forgave her, for with his deeds he had reclaimed his worship.'

Again the boy laughs, very uncertainly.

'Really?'

Sir Thomas shrugs.

'So it is written.'

'And such names! How do you know them after so many a year?'

'I have oftentimes recounted the deeds of Erec over the years, and to many a noble ear, including those of kings, even, as well as dukes and earls and any number of lords.'

'Why?'

'Why? So that they may learn how a knight achieves good fame and renown.'

'By telling his wife not to speak to him?'

'By doing after the good, and leaving off the evil.'

The boy remains doubtful.

'Anyway,' he says, 'go on.'

At which point Sir Thomas hesitates to tell him how they were read other books too, including, most especially:

⇥ The *History of Merlin*, as written by a Frenchman named Robert de Boron, which suited Master Symmington's voice and character, which was not at all stern, for though the book described some astonishing feats of arms, such as the defeat in battle of the eleven kings, it also touched upon matters that were less easily understood, such as Arthur's begetting of Mordred, and of what the king did next, which was to set all boys born on a certain specific day into an open boat and push them out to sea, which is an act that can in no wise be seen as worshipful. Despite this, or because of it, the history of King Arthur in Merlin's time lodged itself in Sir Thomas's mind, though when Master Grimes learned of what they were reading, he instructed Master Symmington to turn instead to the *History of Sir Tristram*, which was more in keeping, he said, so long as there was no mention of Isolde.

Since Sir Thomas knows this sort of thing interests the boy less than it ought, he sticks to the story of young Thomas Malory, and of his new life at Warwick Castle.

After a few months settling into it, though, there came an upset, for in the very last years of old King Henry's reign, when I had perhaps twelve winters, it was learned that Sir Richard Beauchamp, and Prince Hal himself, had been expelled from the king's court – because, we were told, disease had turned the king's brain to pickle – and that the earl was coming home for good. This sent a wave of excitement through the corridors of the castle, in which guards now stood straight, plate was polished and we henchmen were given new doublets and hose, even though those we had were scarcely worn.

Sir Richard was then about thirty, his vigour already tempered by wisdom, and he had not only been in command of my father at Shrewsbury when Prince Hal was so nearly killed, but had since then been on a pilgrimage to the Holy Land, about which many fabulous stories were being told, and so on the day of his home-coming, along with his entire household, we henchmen thronged the bailey to watch as he was cheered over the drawbridge by men shouting 'À Warwick! À Warwick!', just as I had heard the crowds bellow all those months ago at the Gosford Green tourney.

The earl was a tall man, broad-shouldered, solid in build, with arms as thick as legs and a dense scrub of brown hair that seemed to wish to throw off the red, pearl-stitched velvet cap he wore. His face was square, his eyes clear and blue, but later I would note that already his teeth were showing signs of the love he bore for dried fruit. He worked his way around the bailey, greeting us all, man, boy, woman, girl and dog. Some he kissed, some he shook hands, some he would not touch for fear of catching something, but to all he was scrupulously polite. He shook my hand.

'Malory,' he said. 'I know your father. Good man in a pinch. Glad to have you here with me. God bless.'

And that, for the moment, was that. He passed on to Peyto, and if Sir Richard knew his father, he made no mention of it, but gave his hand a shake and asked him if he played the harp. For once Peyto, perhaps overawed, did not lie, and instead stammered that he did, but not at all well, which disappointed Sir Richard, and he moved on to Verney, and then to West, both of whom he knew already and West he obviously liked.

'We shall play tables, sir, you and I, only this time I shall have the beating of you.'

But none of that mattered to me then – it came to me muffled, as if through oakum-stuffed ears – for it was at that moment that I first laid eyes upon **Lady Elizabeth Beauchamp**, who trailed behind her husband, taking her turn to greet favoured members of his castle staff. That day she wore a simple jewelled coif with a chin strap and a travelling cloak of darkest red that seemed to give her eyes – well, I cannot say what it was, or how the effect was come by, but when men say they have drowned in a maid's eyes, I know whereof they speak, for when I looked into Lady Elizabeth's deep brown eyes, I was in that moment utterly lost, unsure of what was flat and what was upright, as if I were sinking through warm honey, and so struck dumb was I that I could not even respond to her simplest greeting. Later, even West said something about me being stuck with Cupid's honeyed dart, though Peyto suggested I was struck by something that no man may ever mention, which began a fight (which I lost).

The next day things returned almost to normal, but with the earl's banner up its pole, everyone put in more effort, and after Mass we four henchmen hurried to the great hall in our best doublets and hose, with our fingernails and noses stripped clean, and we prepared to engage Sir Richard in our finest, prolix-free conversation. But, of course, we were frustrated. People were already queuing up for the honour of serving them and we were lucky even to be allowed access to the hall to catch a glimpse of the top table, where they sat with a snow-white cloth laid by many diligent, clean-fingered stewards, their equally white bread cut by past masters of the lateral slice.

When I was finally allowed to serve them, about a week later, my hands trembled so violently the soup – red, cinnamon – very nearly spilled on that snowy tablecloth, which would have caused a great fuss and seen me sent packing in disgrace, but in fact Lady Elizabeth Beauchamp was not at all intimidating. For one thing, she was young — only eighteen at the time, I think — and quite small, with dark hair and those large, soft, brown eyes, and later I discovered that in tender moments Sir Richard was wont to describe her in terms of woodland creatures.

Having said that, she was the cleverest woman I ever met. She ran her household with great care, saving money where she could but never scrimping, so that the candles were always beeswax, even in Lent, and she also read English, French and Latin as well as any man and, as I likewise later learned, she read diligently not just psalters and the lives of the saints, but also of history, philology and even surgery.

And it was she who, having learned that I had damaged a copy of *Le Chevalier du Chariot*, later that summer, when I was somewhat more composed, suggested I accompany her to nearby Bordesley Abbey, where, under lock and key, the abbot kept a great many books and unbound manuscripts, including a much fairer copy of *Le Chevalier* than mine, but also others by the same Chrétien de Troyes; a book about the seeking and achieving of the Grail, and even one concerning the facts of the death of King Arthur, that I had never thought to wonder at. There was also a *History of Merlin* that looked very interesting, and another, of *The Deeds of Sir Lancelot*, that covered the man's life when he was not disguised as Le Chevalier du Chariot, and even one of Sir Tristram which did not seem to over-labour the effects of the love potion.

Until then, though, as the weeks wore by and turned into months, each day similar to the one before, we saw little of the Beauchamp family themselves, for Sir Richard was often away during those months, at Kenilworth Castle with Prince Hal, where the prince was having a lake dug so that he could have mock sea battles as part of a tourney. It was perhaps with this in mind that one day in late spring, nine months after I had first set eyes on Warwick Castle, Master Yarrow and Master Grimes together met us in the bailey. Master Grimes carried a large bag of oiled linen in which was kept some bulky though almost weightless thing, and on seeing it, Peyto groaned.

'Right, gentles,' Yarrow said, rubbing those hands. 'I am assuming you are all broadly familiar with water? The wet stuff? Probably not been bathed in it since you were baptised, but today, as I say, you will be renewing your acquaintance with said liquid, because today is the day you are going to be learning how to propel yourselves across, through or under water, by which I mean, swim.'

Our swimming lessons were to take place in the weir pond of the river that ran on the southern side of the castle, the Avon, into which I believe dear old Smite Brook still runs. As we made our way there, I noticed Peyto was already fretting, swinging his head around like a horse sawing at his bridle, looking for someone to kick. I soon saw why when we were stripped to our shirts and braies and were made to stand in the still-frigid waters, our mottled skin the colour of cured cheese rind: Peyto could not swim at all, and might even have been frightened of water.

'Very well, Master Peyto,' Yarrow said, 'let's see how you get on this time, shall we?'

Peyto turned to face the broadish stretch of puckered broth before us. Beyond were sheep, staring at us with that slightly pitying look, while Peyto swung his arms back and forth again and again, as if he might dive in at any moment. But he couldn't do it, or he wouldn't do it.

'Come on, Master Peyto! Don't keep the ladies waiting.'

We had also attracted a crowd of townsmen watching from the bridge upstream, and the soldiers in the castle turrets were leaning over their walls, too. There was whistling and hooting and sarcastic words of encouragement, but still Peyto couldn't do it. He could not launch himself. Yarrow, standing among clumps of spring flowers on the bank, was taut with compressed laughter. At last he brought it to an end.

'Thank you, Master Peyto,' he called. 'I think you've entertained us enough. Come on out if you will and stand on this here bank next to me.'

Peyto had to wade back and climb the bank. His face was thunderous. His long legs were still skinny and his knees knobbly, and he knew he looked absurd in his sodden linens and muddy ankles as he stood shivering on the grass next to Yarrow.

'Master Verney,' Yarrow called. 'Your turn.'

While Verney performed the same routine as Peyto — knees bent, swinging his arms backwards and forwards, eyeing the water with deep mistrust — Master Yarrow untied the oiled linen bag and hauled out a large ring fashioned of what I would later come to know as the bark of a cork tree, as grown in Portugal. Peyto must have known this was going to happen, possibly from the year before, and he was made to step into it, and pull it up, and stand there, dripping, with it worn around his waist while we watched Verney follow Peyto from the river to take up another of the rings.

Thomas West could swim, after a fashion. He was strong and lithe and muscular and he refused to fail. Bellowing at the top of his voice, he launched himself across the depths and beat at the surface of the water to keep himself above it. Little by little he began to lose touch with the mud of the castle side bank, and to propel himself towards the far bank. We started cheering him on, but then were reduced to silence as the river's current caught him and began to take him away downstream, Yarrow frowning slightly as his charge thrashed his way out of sight around the broad, meandering bend.

'Where will this take him, Master Grimes?' Yarrow asked.

'Gloucester, I believe, Master Yarrow.'

'Well, well,' Yarrow said. 'Your turn, please, Master Malory, if you will.'

As I plunged into the Avon's quick-flowing waters and set off with a powerful, churning stroke, I felt on me not just the startled gaze of Yarrow, or Peyto, or Verney, or even the crowd now lining the banks and battlements, I also felt on me the proud gaze of Vegetius himself, and of my father, who'd made me read his manual, and of Spare-the-Rod, who'd somehow put it into action – and, of course, of Meg the golden retriever, my swimming mistress.

I struck out, nudged by the current, to the far side, which I touched, and then I churned my way back and clambered up onto the bank where Peyto stood glaring at me from under dripping brows, clutching that cork ring about his waist, his kneecaps shuddering with the cold. Ordinarily I would have expected some remark or a cuff or kick perhaps, but Peyto and the others were unnaturally stilled, and I became aware that I was being enthusiastically applauded by a very great number of hands from a little way off. It was only then that I saw the party of men and women who had emerged from the castle and stopped to watch. And among them were not only Sir Richard Beauchamp and Lady Elizabeth, but also the man whom I would soon come to know as Prince Hal.

It was the first time I'd seen the prince, who was perhaps thirty paces distant, so I did not know who he was until my gaze was recalled to the unmistakable puckered whorl of skin under his right eye. He wore dark clothes, very sober compared to the rest of the party, and was not – as I think is obvious from the portraits of him that remain to us – conventionally handsome, but it was he who drew your eye, like a fire on a winter's eve, for he had a powerful presence that came from something more than just being a prince.

'Malory!' Sir Richard called. 'Malory there!'

I bowed my head.

'Go to him,' muttered Master Grimes from the corner of his mouth. 'Go to him.'

Did I know then that the moment that would change my life was approaching? Did I feel the air thicken about me, as if at the start of a storm, when it seems to gain weight, and the sky takes on the colour of the sea? I don't know, but at that moment Opportunity came to me, and I took it.

But it felt strange at the time. I was hobbled with self-conscious-ness as I approached them, all in their velvets and ermines and silks, while I was in my sodden braies and a filthy shirt that clung to my skinny little body, and I am certain some ladies laughed and turned away, for I must have looked more like a shaved greyhound than a man, but my gaze was fixed on Prince Hal, who watched me come with a concerned expression.

'Sir,' I said, bowing my head.

'Where for the love of God above did you learn to swim like that?' Sir Richard asked.

'At Fenny Newbold, sir,' I told him, still childishly certain that all the world knew of Fenny Newbold. He did not. Nor did anyone else.

'Well, never mind all that,' he said. 'Do you play the harp as well as you swim?'

I recalled Peyto's honesty when Sir Richard first came back from the King's Council, and I recalled Sir Richard's disappointment. And I made the decision there and then not to do the same.

'Yes, sir,' I said. 'I do.'

A delighted Sir Richard turned to Prince Hal.

'You see?' he said. 'We shall have musical accompaniment after all.'

There were false delighted murmurs from the men and women gathered behind the two.

'Bring your harp to the great hall for supper tonight, Malory,' Sir

Richard said, 'and we shall hear how a perfect gentle knight plays for his perfect gentle prince.'

I bowed deeply to indicate I was conscious of this great honour, but also to hide my face, which must have been a mask of agonised terror, for I was conscious of Mistress Gule's parting words to me at our last – she hoped – music lesson: that I could no more play the harp than I could fly like a bird.

I returned to Master Grimes and told him about Sir Richard's invitation.

'God's stones, boy,' he murmured, very out of character. 'Why-ever did you tell him that?'

'He asked,' I said.

'Hmmm,' Grimes said, giving me a very piercing study. 'Right. Off to Mistress Gule, now.'

I left my fellows there on the bank of the Avon to continue their swimming lessons, and I spent the afternoon alone with Mistress Gule in her chamber. I broke four strings before the first hour was out, and by the second my fingers were skinned and bloody, but the harp (her third best) survived its ordeal and, crucially, for each string I broke, and for each scream I provoked in her plump little throat, I learned a little more of a tune so that when I played all that I knew, each tune and phrase, the one after the other, I believed I had a full rosary's time of silvery, shimmering sound that I'd be able to send sliding around the hall. That was the plan.

To say I was nervous as the evening approached is to undersell my inner state. I was sick with fright. But for some reason I believed I might just manage to prevail. Thomas West had returned no worse for wear from his adventures downstream, and he acted as my sa-viour, keeping Peyto and Verney at bay while I washed and changed into fresh linen and another new doublet with brocade on it and silken sleeves, and it was he who accompanied me to the castle's great hall where I saw, with a terrible, nauseating consternation, that a harp was already placed in the centre of the horseshoe of tables around which perhaps two hundred people might sit, and – more disconcerting still – that the harp itself was twice, perhaps three times, the size of that which I was used to playing.

That evening will be remembered by everyone who was there: not necessarily for the sight – and sound – of the young harpist who was unused to playing such a large instrument, and who could not reach more than half the strings, and who broke at least three of those he could, but who still would not give up; nor necessarily for how this same aforesaid harpist persisted even as the ill-mannered laughter rose up about him, not even as the blood began to flow from his fingertips to stain the remaining strings.

What they will remember it for was that, at last, Prince Hal himself rose to his feet and walked around the tables and came up onto the dais and stood next to that young harpist, whose fingers were bloody and whose scarlet face was rimed with salty tears – I had but thirteen winters, don't forget – and he placed a royal hand upon my narrow shoulder, and glared at anyone still tittering, or wretched enough to still be holding their hands over their ears while the plinking and the plonking continued, and they will remember that when the harpist finally finished playing, the young prince spoke of his pity for certain gentlemen – 'most like abed' – who would never be able to say they had been here this night to witness such a thing, and that he felt narrow bonds of kinship with those few who had, for they were to him like brothers.

This was a lesson in how a king should conduct himself.

After which he bade me rise to my feet, and he led the applause, with every man and woman standing and clapping for what seemed like many moments. And when I raised my tear-gummed eyes I could see Lady Elizabeth's neck craned to whisper something in Sir Richard's ear, and Sir Richard, with his gaze still on me, nodding agreement to her suggestion, and I knew – God knows how – that she had suggested he take me as his personal page of honour. And I knew — again, God knows how — that others knew this too, for in the shadows I could see Peyto, aghast, staring at those there assembled as if they were struck with St Vitus's disease, and I believe, right then, that we both knew I was set for greater things—

Suddenly the boy is on his feet. He stands poised like a lurcher with the scent of game in his nostrils; his eyeballs twitching as he makes a thousand and one calculations, each based on signals that Sir Thomas cannot sense.

Then he does: footsteps in the passage outside. Two pairs, one heavy-footed, with the stamp and drag of a man limping to favour a buttock on which a boil still weeps like an eye, and the other pair softer, like those of a tired old man fresh from borrowing money at a ruinous rate in the city.

'Your father?' Sir Thomas whispers, and the boy need say nothing for it is so obvious, but he waits, narrow-eyed, and waits, and waits, as the footsteps approach.

Sir Thomas holds his breath.

And then the footsteps pass, up the passage to Bewscel's cell, the last door in the passage, but still the boy waits for some other sign only he recognises, and when it comes he moves, swift as a hawk, stooping to snatch up his cap and darting to open the door just a crack, through which he vanishes, the locking bar making only a faint tap.

Sir Thomas rises to his feet and presses his ear to the door.

He can hear the murmur of male conversation, and then a door being closed and a locking bar dropped, and then, after a further brief moment — the time it takes to say the first three lines of the Paternoster perhaps — Brunt's footsteps return. Sir Thomas holds his breath as they stop just beyond his door, and there follows a moment's stillness, as if Brunt has his ear pressed to the other side of the same door, and Sir Thomas is disgusted to think his and the warder's ears are parted by just an inch (albeit one filled with seasoned oak), but despite the sickening intimacy, he keeps his own pressed to the wood, and listens to the stillness, to Brunt's breath perhaps. It is not a good silence, he thinks. Not a good stillness. It is a pent-up stillness; a breath-held stillness; the stillness that comes before an outrage; and so he steps back and stands frozen in readiness.

But after a long moment nothing happens, and he hears Brunt step away from the door, his feet clumsily descending the steps, and he releases his breath. Then it is just him and the cat, and they remain as they are for a long moment, and she looks at him, and he looks at her, and neither utters a sound.

And in all that time, while he talked to the boy, Sir Thomas gave no thought to the night ahead, with its midnight bell and its priest stealing up the stairs to hear his confession; nor to the king's men who will come for him in the dawn; nor to the agonies that will follow, but now he does. He cannot stop himself, and he throws himself to the palliasse and yields to his fear's full force, and thus does his torment resume.

CHAPTER 3

How Sir Thomas survives a further two nights in gaol, and how he is then visited by a fair lady, and of how a boy falls from the roof unto his death on the cobbles below

It is the ninth day since Sir Thomas was taken from his garden, and he has still heard nothing from the king, nor the keeper, nor anything further from his attorney Master Hartshorne, but this morning, once he has said his prayers, washed his hands, scratched a sixth line in the stone below his window and taken his breakfast, his wife Elizabeth comes unexpectedly and unannounced sometime before noon. When Sir Thomas sees her, he rises and takes her in his arms and presses his nose against the linen of her coif, inhaling her smell, which, even after the rigours of her journey, is the smell he most loves in all the world, for it is the smell of home, the smell of dear old Newbold Revel.

'Have they said why they are holding you?' she asks.

Sir Thomas shakes his head minutely, his nose never losing contact with her crown, and he clenches his eyes to prevent a tear leaking to stain her cap. Despite her best efforts, no doubt, her voice is sharper than it might be, and she has not melted into his embrace as he might have hoped. Her spine, stiff and unyielding, tells him she cannot yet let herself believe him innocent of whatever it is they accuse him of this time, and who, in all honesty, can blame her?

'I've done nothing,' he tells her.

The miasma of suspicion, of his apparent guilt, lingers still, tainting every word they speak, corrupting every gesture they make.

'We heard rumours on the road,' she tells him, 'of a plot against the king?'

Sir Thomas steps back. He knows nothing of this, he promises her, though he is not at all surprised: the old queen, **Margaret**, late of Anjou, and her son **Edward of Westminster** have never given up hope of regaining the throne.

'And there have been more arrests,' she goes on.

'Who? Do you know?'

She does not.

Again, Sir Thomas proclaims his ignorance, his innocence.

'Then what *have* you done?' she presses.

'Nothing! As I would swear upon the cross of my sword!'

'Then why?' she demands, stepping back, holding him at arm's length and looking into his eyes. 'Why are you back here again?'

'I cannot say,' he tells her again. 'I have heard *nothing*, been charged with *nothing*.'

She manages a dry, despairing laugh, and he knows what she means. It is just as it was when Hartshorne came, all so wearyingly familiar: she being back here in this prison cell to hear him swear upon the cross of his sword that he is innocent of anything, and he still cannot be sure she believes a word he said then, or says now.

'And what does the keeper say?'

'They will not let me see him. Or he is away. Or he will not see me.'

'I will write to him,' she says, as if that will fix it, and he feels so unmanned that for a moment he believes that it will, and he is pathetically grateful.

'Anyway,' she says. 'I have brought your coffer as requested.'

She hands him the key, and he thanks her and asks inconsequential questions about home: the dogs, the grandchildren, the fields, the tenants (excluding Appleby's wife, with her fat arms and raucous laugh, whom he will never forgive), and he does not stop to wonder if he did – indeed – ask Elizabeth to send his coffer, and she is too distracted by having to visit her husband once more in Newgate that she cannot talk of anything for any length of time, even of their new grandson.

'I am glad you are back up here at least,' she says, toeing the frowsty palliasse. 'I feared you would be kept in fetters among the commons below.'

'I suppose the king wishes me not too uncomfortable?'

She casts her eye around the smoke-stained and much-abused ceiling and walls, the filthy rushes on the floor, the disgusting old bucket under the window, in which still floats Sir Thomas's morning turd.

'Is it a coincidence,' she wonders aloud, 'that you have been returned to this exact same cell, or a calculated twist of the blade?'

He admits he has not thought to wonder.

'I will ask Brunt,' he tells her, 'though I'll get nothing from him. His boy though. He might know. Yes. I shall ask him.'

Elizabeth doesn't want to hear of the boy, so she absently nods and peers out of the window, through the grimy linen, down Newgate Street, towards the Shambles. On the left is the tower of Christ Church, and on the right, the smaller, square tower of St Ewen's. Behind is Warwick Inn. Seeing it, Elizabeth asks if Sir Thomas has had any word from the earl? Sir Thomas shakes his head, she tuts and they are silent for a while. They have grown old together, Sir Thomas and his wife – though he is considerably further ahead in that race – and he recognises every little crease, fold and pouch in her skin. He knows where each came from, when each arrived and the cause of each, which he must admit is mostly him.

'Did you see him?' he now finds himself asking. 'Down below? A boy. About this height, of the sort you'd expect to see with two clipped ears?'

She frowns.

'London is full of such sorts. Why?'

Sir Thomas knows Elizabeth will not be pleased to learn he is telling the boy the tale of his life, for she will think he ought to get on and finish his book of King Arthur, but he cannot resist seeking her approval, and it turns out he is right: she does not share his enthusiasm.

'You are telling your story to some prison lackey? I wish instead you would finish your story of King Arthur.'

'Well,' he murmurs, 'as you know, I—'

'You lost some book or other,' she cuts him off. 'Yes, yes. I know.'

He wonders, how many times has he told her that? Not often, he is sure. Hmph. But before he can express any sour feelings, he hears heavy feet on the steps beyond his door and a moment later it is barged open, and in stagger two sweating porters, whom Sir Thomas only half recognises, carrying between them his coffer.

'God's Truth,' one of them gasps, for it is quite a weight, and they drop it in the rushes with a boom that sends clouds of dust rolling about their knees. Brunt follows in behind, limping still – good – and on seeing Elizabeth he removes his horrible old cap and bows obsequiously, for he is unnerved by beautiful, well-born women.

'Have you the key, my lady?' he asks in his best voice. 'I needs must go through this here box to see if there is not nothing in there what should not be. In there.'

He means the wherewithal for Sir Thomas to make good an escape – a dagger and a rope, say – which Sir Thomas can scarcely refuse, but of course he really wants to see what there is of value. Sir Thomas fishes the key back out of his purse, fits it into the coffer's stout iron lock, turns it and sets the lid back on its hinges, letting the smell of meadowsweet and rosemary rise up to fill the room and take him back to when he was last herein incarcerated.

The top tray remains untouched, just as he left it all those years ago: some now-wizened goose feathers, his old ink horn, wraps of gum and copperas, a pouch of galls, a small brass hammer and his second-best pricking wheel. Below are just two sheets of rough old

74

paper — all that she could find, Elizabeth says, though she'll have some more sent if she remembers (she won't) — and the very same *zibaldone* — the very one! — in which Sir Thomas was describing the tourney that involved two hundred knights and a diamond, just before **Lord Fauconberg** came to set him free, the year their son, poor young Thomas, died, may God assoil his soul.

In the tray below, interspersed with sprigs of the dried herbs, Elizabeth has packed for him two laundered shirts, three pairs of newly woven braies, three pairs of woollen socks and a pair of fine-spun, part-coloured hose (plum and ochre this time, rather than madder and goldenrod, which those she'd sent the first time had been, and which he'd wanted to save for the day he walked free, but which had soon been pressed into action for weddings, funerals and, of course, court appearances). Under these is another pair of grey woollen hose, a pourpoint in plain linen (new) and another one (old), as well as some spare points, a sponge (dry) and a block of that black soap so beloved of the Castilians. No towel this time.

And below all that, in the base of the coffer, giving it its weight and anchoring it to the floor, just as once it anchored Sir Thomas is a dense pile of all Sir Thomas's divers manuscripts of his book on the deeds of King Arthur and the noble Knights of the Round Table, which, when he sees them, give him a strange start, almost like a thrill, but also a feeling of something like dread.

They are of no interest to Brunt, of course, who rummages through them with rough thumbs and gives a derisive tut that only Sir Thomas can hear, but he is conscious that were Elizabeth not here to witness this search, Brunt would have helped himself to anything he fancied, tossed aside anything he did not and afterwards turned the coffer over, just for the pleasure of it.

'Well, that seems to be in order,' Brunt announces, rising awkwardly to once more remove his cap and bid Elizabeth a formal farewell.

'I am sad to say I have an appointment in town, my lady,' he tells her, still in his best voice, and as if this might be a matter of some regret to her, 'and so my boy will see you out.'

Brunt's performance sickens Sir Thomas, and when he's gone, he takes the time to remind Elizabeth that the man is an odious churl and a bully, and beneath her contempt, which she certainly knows from last time. Later, when she gathers herself to go, she sighs, and says, 'I wish you were coming home with me' as if she really means it, and he believes that to be the single kindest thing anyone has ever said to him, and when the boy comes to escort her down to the courtyard, Sir Thomas goes with them, and when he helps her up into the cart and watches it roll away through the gates, it comes as a withdrawing of the light, and he feels desolation grip him like an ague.

He remembers that he was going to ask her to find him a harp. Too late now.

But the boy is at his elbow.

'The old man's gone badgers,' he says.

By which he means badger-baiting across the river in Southwark, but he says it in such a way as to carry that other meaning.

'And?' Sir Thomas asks.

'And he wanted me to go with him.'

'Oh. Really? To be his crutch?'

'Suppose so,' the boy admits. 'But.'

'But? But what?'

'But there'll always be badgers, won't there?'

Sir Thomas supposes that might be true.

'And,' the boy goes on, 'there won't always be—'

The boy trails off, and waits for Sir Thomas to divine his meaning, which he does, after a moment.

'Ah! You mean there won't always be me?'

The boy nods.

'No offence intended,' he says, and at any other time Sir Thomas might have laughed, for he has long since accepted he is old, and that more years lie behind than ahead, but this is Newgate, and he is lanced by a rising panic, and he grabs the boy's elbow.

'What have you heard?' he demands. 'Is there news come of – of what is to happen?'

'No, no,' the boy hurries to assure him, wrenching his arm free. 'There's nothing. Honest.'

'Jesu defend me,' Sir Thomas whispers, clutching his chest. 'Don't do that to me. I thought my time had come.'

'I shouldn't have said nothing,' the boy says. 'I only wanted to hear about Agincourt.'

Sir Thomas finds he is glaring at the boy.

'*Agincourt*? Ahh. Agincourt! Well. Yes. Of course.'

They start up the steps again, Sir Thomas leading the way, trudging up into the darkness, and he is suddenly suffused with pleasure, for what higher praise can there be than that someone is prepared to give up an evening watching badgers and dogs rip one another to pieces in order to listen to his tale? But as he climbs higher, he becomes aware of a great responsibility: the boy has given up an evening watching badgers and dogs rip one another to pieces in order to listen to his tale!

And so he had better ensure he does not come to regret it.

Out, then, go the following things, which he was going to tell the boy, for they are of great import, but he now believes they might not just bore him but actively drive him mad with irritation:

- How great an honour it was to be appointed page to the Earl of Warwick, and how that oaf Peyto gnashed his teeth with envious rage when young Thomas was lifted up above him.

- How he – Thomas – oftentimes did sit at the end of the top table, and was permitted to serve the family in everyday

77

duties, and if there were any activities or entertainments planned, then he was usually included, and in this way did he come to know — and love — the Beauchamp family, and, he believes, they him.

➻ How it was at about this time that Prince Hal began to slough off his youthful ease and seemed to twist within and harden without, becoming steely, proud and humourless, like a goshawk on its stand, and with a gaze just as cowing.

➻ How Sir Richard's household changed, too, not least Thomas, who during this time learned to hunt every kind of creature with every kind of bird or hound, and learned to fight with every kind of weapon against every kind of opponent. He could ride any kind of horse, even a great destrier if permitted, cleanly and surely, and with a lance he could crack the boss of the smallest quintain nine times in every ten.

➻ How by the end of that year Thomas would wager he was as good as any boy his age — thirteen winters! — in the whole of Christendom at the following things: at reading and conversing in French, Latin and English, at swimming, at tennis, at boxing, at climbing a rope.

➻ How he became well-practised at dancing, at backgammon, at carving bread and any other foodstuff, be it fish or fowl, and he could converse easily with any man or woman, including those of higher station — to whom he was never servile, but always respectful — and those of equal station — with whom he was carefree and jocular — and those of a lower station, over whom he was commanding.

➻ How, though he never mastered the game of chess, even though Prince Hal and Sir Richard both enjoyed playing it and so, as a consequence, did everyone else in their households, and how this might have counted against Thomas had he not, precisely thanks to this inadequacy, discovered his greatest adequacy of all, which was a gift for recounting episodes from history in compelling, vivid detail. For instead of playing the strategist, he sought, and found, renown as the teller of tales, as the recounter of the great deeds of arms of King Arthur – who was the young prince's forefather – and also, and most especially perhaps, of the great deeds of arms of Sir Lancelot du Lac, as recorded in *Le Chevalier du Chariot*, about which few men – or ladies – seemed to know as much as they ought.

➻→ How it was that oftentimes during that year he found himself addressing a room of much older men, many of whom had performed their own deeds of arms against the Welsh and Scots, and the Armagnacs too, and as he spoke of the setting-aside of the King of Here, and the dishing of the brainpan of the Count of There, a hush would descend, and those stern knights would lean in to the firelight and listen intently as Thomas told of – for example – the night Sir Lancelot survived the bed that was designed to first stab him and then set him alight, and how he then removed his gauntlets and sabatons and crossed over the ravine into the land of Gore by clambering along that bridge made from that one long, lethally sharp sword to rescue She-Upon-Whom-He-Would-Most-Wish-to-Lay-Eyes, and how he then fought Sir Meleagant while still weak from loss of blood – from wounds incurred while crossing that sword – and how for the love of She-Upon-Whom-He-Would-Most-Wish-to-Lay-Eyes, Sir Lancelot then spared Sir Meleagant, only for that false traitor knight to entrap him

79

by base means and hold him prisoner while — well. On it went. So many astonishing deeds of arms. So much worship. And by the end of each telling, it mattered not one whit that Thomas could play neither chess nor harp, for he was young Thomas Malory, who could tell stories in such a way as to stir the blood in the heart of every noble Englishman.

But does the boy wish to hear of old tales being told, or does he want drama? He wants drama, and specifically he wants Agincourt, but for that — sad to say — he will have to wait just a little while longer.

For it so befell that in the second week of Lent that year, the thirteenth of this century, King Henry — the fourth, still — died. It was much anticipated, for he suffered the worst kind of leprosy, with his body covered in teat-like pustules, and his mind turned to mush. Some said it was a punishment sent by God for what he had done to old King Richard — whom we were told had pined to death from 'melancholy' but even a child could see that if you take a man's clothes from him and drop him in the deepest, darkest, foulest dungeon you can find, and then deprive him of nourishment for a week or two, he will tend to pine to death from something, or want of it at any rate — while others said it was because the king had ordered the death of **Archbishop Scrope** (in the sixth year of his reign, five blows of the headsman's axe, outside York) for the man's part in a rebellion against him.

Either way, his death cleared the way for Prince Hal to become the fifth Henry to take England's throne. He would have been about twenty-five then: lean as a greyhound, pious as a psalter, honed by hunting and endless endeavour in the saddle, and the joy that his elevation brought us at Warwick can hardly be imagined, for Prince Hal and Sir Richard had passed the last few years banished from court, out in the cold in a strange internal exile, but now — the king is dead! Long live the king! — our place was within, on high and beside the hearth.

We set off from Warwick for the coronation in Westminster in joyous high spirits, the whole household it seemed, many hundreds of us travelling in a league-long train of horses and wagons, all wearing Sir Richard's red, with his badge of the bear and ragged staff emblazoned everywhere, but after four days on the road our festive mood wilted, for as we reached St Albans, still a day from London, we found ourselves marching into a terrible blizzard which continued sharp and spiteful all the way to London. And so it was that I never stopped to look at the city the first time I saw it, never stopped to look at the great cathedral of St Paul, its spire lost in the swirling cloud above, and indeed never stopped to look up at Newgate.

'Nor me,' says the boy, which catches Sir Thomas by surprise, for of course he has given no thought to the boy's experience. But then again, this is, after all, his story.

But I do remember my first spell in the Tower. I was standing sodden before the fire in the hall of the Beauchamp Tower, and hearing Sir Richard laugh and tell us that his father was once imprisoned there, and that if we only looked, we might find his name carved in the stone somewhere, and various other men said the same thing, and so did I, though no one paid me any mind, for we were all burning up with chilblains, and at such times men think only of themselves.

The storm lasted the rest of that week, even unto the morning of the day of the coronation itself, and as our procession left the shelter of the Tower's walls on our way to Westminster, hail came at us from the river like handfuls of flung teeth, and the wind tore down our banners and brought down the hangings that streamed from the windows of the houses along the way. Instead of playing for us, as they were supposed to, all the actors and mummers we passed stood huddled in their sets, out of the icy blasts, watching us, rather than we them, and very soon we were soaked, shivering and bedraggled. No man there can have resisted wondering what this unseasonable blizzard augured.

'This is nothing,' Sir Richard called out, snow on his eyebrows. 'In Russia they would call this summer.'

We pages and henchmen wore silk, which is as protective against the cold as gossamer, and we clung to the warmth of our ponies as we processed behind Sir Richard, who in turn followed the new king, who rode upon a white palfrey and wore cloth of gold – hardly any warmer – but also a velvet cloak dyed the most sumptuous purple and studded with what we were told were rubies and emeralds, but in the weather that day, they might have been pebbles or lumps of coal.

Along the way we were joined by many more knights and their retinues in their now indistinguishable surcoats and cloaks, and then, I believe, came the guildsmen, and behind them the Members of the House of Commons, whom Sir Richard described as 'rascally knights of the hedgerows'. At the back, following on in a vast, unruly crowd, came the great mass of the commons proper – the townsmen and women of London and Kent and Essex – drawn there for the spectacle and the chance of free wine and ale, whatever the weather.

The snow got worse still when we left London through the Ludgate – which, as with Newgate, meant nothing to me then – and made our way along the river to Westminster, where we pressed into St Peter's Church and where some of us – the tallest, or, really, Peyto, standing on the tips of his toes – were able to see King Henry anointed with the miraculous coronation oil that the Virgin Mary had once given to **Archbishop Becket**, and to see him presented with the Sword of Justice and then be crowned King Henry of all England, and France too, of course. There were great crescendos of trumpet-noise, and then the Te Deum was sung, and then all the other anthems, and then we followed him – or I followed Sir Richard and he followed the king – out and across to the great hall for the coronation feast itself.

It started in wondrous solemnity, but the taps of the great water trough in the yard ran with both red and white wine, and soon the silence gave way to whispers and then murmurs and then to ever-louder conversation until by the time the king's champion rode in upon his horse to challenge anyone who dared to speak out against King Henry's right to reign, everyone was bellowing with delight and banging on the boards, in contravention of every lesson in courtly behaviour.

Peyto, of course, was the drunkest of us all, or perhaps the drunkest of all there, and he became so with startling speed. He was garrulous before we sat down, flush-cheeked and glassy eyed before the first course, subsided to the rushes during the second – which was a pike as long as a fully grown man is tall – and by the time the last subtleties arrived – sugar and pastry swans, each escorting a small fleet of cygnets – asleep under the table, his vomit-crusted face being licked by a lurcher.

Not that I was immune. I too felt the unfamiliar swirl and grip of the wine, but instead of befouling my doublet – worth more than me – I took myself out into the freezing air of the courtyard, where the snow had changed character, to become light and feathery, and almost magical, and I walked down through the mire of slush towards the black line of the river, where some soldiers were cheerfully keeping at bay an armada of waterborne beggars. I found a barrel under an eave on which to sit and there I did so for a long moment, warmed internally by the wine, frozen externally by the weather, and I watched the comings and goings with a fuzzy in-comprehension, and a series of soft, rippling burps I hoped would produce something more by way of relief than they did.

The soldiers had put something on a brazier that filled the air with large flecks of black ash that mixed with the snow and blew towards me through the darkness, and above me the abbey bells rang out, and for some reason I felt, for a moment, powerfully mel-ancholic.

And it was then, of all times, that I saw my father again. The first time since the year before, when he had left me in the care of Master Grimes.

'Tom?'

His cloak was thick, his cap was warm and practical and his boots were square-toed, cuffs turned down – perfect for riding along Smite Brook, perhaps, but hardly the thing for Westminster, hardly the thing for the king's coronation – and even now I am sorry to have to admit that I felt a brief flicker of shame of him, for he looked every inch Sir Richard's rascally knight of the hedgerow. Still though, he was my father.

'Sir,' I said, and I slipped off my barrel and stumbled towards him, intensely aware of my dignity and my need to keep it, with what I suppose might have been an awkward hug in mind, because first, I did not know what else to do, and second, I was very, very pleased to see him. In the event, he had to catch me under the elbows and hold me up to steady me.

'Tom,' he said again. 'Sit down.'

He showed me back to my barrel and I sat again and strangely, despite my drunkenness, I recall our conversation even after these years. Not word for word perhaps, but the gist.

'I did not expect you,' I might have said, intending a statement, not a question.

'I wrote to you,' he would have told me. 'A few weeks ago. To let

84

you know that I had become a Member of Parliament?'

'A Member of Parliament!'

I recalled no such letter, of course.

'Or I thought you might have heard,' he went on.

I shook my head. Of course I had not heard.

'I am a page of honour to Sir Richard Beauchamp,' I told him, by way of explanation.

'I know,' he said. 'I heard, and I wrote to say how proud I am of you, my boy.'

'And I served King Henry in Kenilworth,' I went on. 'And he will be a very great king.'

I presumed my father would be impressed, of course, but such hopes are ever to be dashed, and he merely smiled one of his downward-pointing smiles.

'I served with him in Wales too,' he said. 'On and off.'

On and off? He gave the phrase a curious and unpleasing emphasis.

'What do you mean by that?' I asked.

'Nothing,' he said. 'But I am sure you are right. I have heard he has changed a great deal since then, and I am sure he will make a very great king. But tell me, is there much talk of war with France?'

It was such an adult question, not one that I had ever imagined my father asking me, that I was startled and said nothing.

'You have heard no mention of it?' my father went on. 'At Kenilworth? Or Warwick?'

I shook my head. He remained looking worried at the thought, though, and yet, surely, the prospect of war with France was the only thing that made sense of all those hours, days, weeks and months I had spent following Vegetius's regimen? Only war with France made sense of my learning to swim and put on harness in the dark and run half a dozen miles without food or water.

Somewhere in my mind was the thought – though how it had

85

got there is another matter — that when I was old enough, I would always fight the French. We would all always fight the French, wouldn't we? It was as inevitable as the seasons turning, the will of God. Everybody knew that.

Or perhaps I am imagining that was the case, now, after all these years? Perhaps back then, before it all happened, war was not thought inevitable, and the idea of once more taking up cudgels against a country with sixteen times as many men as us might have seemed foolish? All such cavils have been conveniently misplaced in the mists of time, of course, but there must have been some among us — my father perhaps? — who thought that we had ridden our luck just about as far as she would go at Crécy and at Poitiers, and that surely by now the French would have learned their lessons and would not charge pell-mell at their very first glimpse of us?

In the event, of course, it proved we had hardly begun to test our luck.

Still, no man could have known that at the time, so it was not unreasonable for my father, who had fought the Welsh as well as the English, and perhaps even the Scots, and who knew about war, to stand there that night thinking about me departing to fight the French with a worried frown worming across his brow. I think I may have shrugged and lost concentration a bit, for by now he was looking at me, shivering in my drenched finery, and he was smiling a terrible sad smile, and he might have said something that would have made it all better — or worse, who knows? — but at that moment there was a ripple of trumpets and something was underway in the hall.

'Come on, Tom,' my father said. 'Come in and get something to eat.'

And so I did, with his help: a bowl of something and some bread, and that is as much of the evening as I can recall after so long a time. Perhaps it is because of what happened the next day, which was that I was once again – and predictably – struck down with an ague and forced to remain abed in one of the top rooms of Warwick Inn, shivering, sweating and utterly dolorous for what felt like weeks on end while the rest of Sir Richard's household packed up and began their journey back to Warwick.

They did, though, leave me in the care of the household's very worst servant: a man named John Jiggins, who throughout my illness oftentimes sat at the foot of my bed eating strong-smelling pies and spouting confusing nonsense about all manner of things, so that I was never certain if I was awake or dreaming, dead or alive, this way or that, and every morning and evening a thickset nurse – of the sort to populate those tough northern priories where they box rams for sport on St John's Day – would bring me a bowl of greasy pottage and a pint of tepid ale that tasted of rainwater caught in a tree bole, and Jiggins would tell me not to complain or I'd get double.

Once I had recovered – it must have been more than a month before the physician would let me out of bed – we set off back to Warwick, and loitering in an inn just beyond Buckingham, we encountered another of the earl's servants – his second worst, it turned out, named Watkyn Bundsay – who told us that the new king – may God assoil his soul – had appointed Sir Richard Beauchamp to be Captain of Calais, an honour that required his presence across the Narrow Sea no later than the day after Candlemas next, and that Thomas West, Thomas Verney and William Peyto were indentured to serve as lances in Sir Richard's retinue, but that Peyto had taken his pay – twenty pounds a year, paid quarterly in advance – and had passed from St Alphege's to St Dunstan's Day in the bed of the town's plumpest harlot.

'But that is more than three weeks!' I said, unable to imagine such a thing.

Jiggins was delighted and as he set back off the next morning he began a maundering tale about once having to roll a very fat girl in flour before they joined in what he called their 'divers pleasures', without which, he told Bundsay, he could not find the right bit of her into which he was supposed to 'insert' what he called his 'todger'.

I could hardly bring myself to hear all this, of course, for Bundsay's tidings had reminded me that my time as Sir Richard Beauchamp's page of honour must necessarily come to its end, and that I should soon be cast from the pool of light into the cold, dark wilderness, where I would have to make my own way, merely one of many, where once I had been exalted. What would become of me now? The melancholic fugue that had visited me on the night of the coronation had left its bruise, and I thought again of that arrow. I fretted that being page of honour was to mark the high point of my life, and all that lay in store for me now was the downward trajectory, the fall from grace, final failure. I would become one of those witless, shattered men who haunt roadside taverns to tell anyone foolish enough to buy them ale that they were once something to someone. I would become like Jiggins, I thought.

'Naked as a needle, she was,' he was chuntering on beside me, like a mill wheel in the dark, 'though you'd hardly know it, what with all that flour. Anyway—'

When we reached Warwick — two long days later — Master Grimes was on hand to confirm my fears: my name was among those listed to sail with the earl, no longer as page of honour, but as an indentured lance.

'So as I say, Master Malory,' Master Yarrow said, again, 'you'd best be astir. You'll need to arm yourself as best you're able, as well as find yourself two competent archers prepared to cross with you, and a page of your own, likewise competent, though in what it is not clear, and a couple of mounts, serviceable, for the use of lances and archers, mounted.' With that, he clapped those muscular little hands together and clenched his very good teeth and stood very close.

'Shouldn't be too difficult,' he added.

88

But it was. Neither Adam nor Eve can have been more dejected when they were evicted from the Garden of Eden than I was then, for not only was I also cast out of paradise, I had now to recruit my own retinue and buy some horses, and all with just five pounds (actually as well as two and a half marks — again, paid quarterly — which was intended to provide food for the first archer, but not the second). The money was only the first concern: I had not thought ahead as had West and Verney, and even Peyto to a certain extent, and I had been too proud of my position to build up any informal relations among those whom I might ordinarily ask to serve as archers or as a page.

I realised I did not know how this sort of thing worked. My father had never told me, because his father had never told him, and so on; after packing up I rode home, for the first time in what felt like years, to discuss matters, very dretched and disconsolate. I rode through Coventry and then Gosford Green, where the deserted tiltyard seemed haunted by the cheering of ghostly crowds, and then back along Smite Brook — swollen with the recent rain — past the high stockade of the deer park and the abbey, and then on through the estate woods, which was becoming ever more perfect for a bushment.

When I reached Fenny Newbold I rode into the courtyard expecting a great welcome, only to find my father was away, still down in Westminster of all places, on some duty connected to being a Member of Parliament, which my mother told me he had written to tell me so in a letter, and did I not get it? She did her best to cheer me, but she was still bilious with her seventh child and was unable to over-concern herself with my apparent reversal, so she left me to my brother and sisters, who clustered around me shouting their questions. Hearing the commotion, Spare-the-Rod came limping out, much diminished now and startlingly worry-worn, with plum-coloured rings under his eyes.

89

'Master Thomas,' he said, his voice whispery as a handful of barley husks. 'God give you good grace, my boy.'

His hand was like his voice, hot and dry, and lacking the power of old.

'Have they been giving you a hard time, Master Orme?' I asked, indicating my siblings, who were by any standards quite a handful.

He managed a weak smile, and a shrug, but was obviously not going to complain, and meanwhile my brother and sisters were clamouring and dragging at my hands, desperate to tell me some things and show me others, so I did not press him for further details, which to this day I regret.

My mother was pleased with the scarlet I had bought her with the advance on my wages, and I had various little things for my sisters, including a couple of dolls, as well as a slim bow of holly I'd persuaded one of the bowyers at Warwick Castle to knock up for my brother John – who had by now six or seven winters – whom I encouraged in the various drills such as those I'd learned at the fighting post that still stood in the yard. Seeing us at it out there in the rain under pewter skies, my mother shook her head, but my brother was just as keen as I had been when I was his age.

'You'll chop it down!' I laughed.

I told him about Vegetius, whom he was yet to read, and my brother shot an arrow at a heron stood studying the fish in the stock pond, but missed, and we lost the arrow because Meg the retriever – grey-muzzled now, and stiff with rheumatism – refused to go and get it.

'We'll soon be needing every one of them,' I said, because that was the sort of thing a man said.

I wish now that I had stayed longer, if only to teach John to swim, but I was young, with my mind taken up with my own affairs, and later, when I heard that he had drowned, I was very sore with grief and guilt.

But all that was to come later, of course, and in the meantime, I needed to be about my business, only in my father's absence my mother did not believe she could spare any servant who might be considered an archer, let alone two. So I left word for my father to send instruction, and anyone he might suggest in the future, and after a couple of days I bade farewell to my family and to Spare-the-Rod and I returned to Warwick Castle unaccompanied and empty-handed, still with no idea of where to find my archers.

In the end, the answer was simple.

'Look,' John Jiggins said, 'let's not get too concerned about whether I can shoot an arrow or not. Let's just think about the numbers, shall we?'

And he did seem to have them on his side, because he was also offering to bring with him Watkyn Bundsay, that second-worst servant, whom we'd met in that inn outside Buckingham, and with whom it emerged Jiggins intended to go into the cat-farming business, when they retired from service. While Jiggins was long and lanky, but with a drooping belly and numerous chins, Bundsay was proportioned just as is the stoat when it is stood up on its hind legs, with red hair cut in a patchy bristle, and a furtive air, as if he were always waiting for you to absent yourself so that he might continue his own illicit business.

'But can he shoot a bow?' I asked.

'Well, he has shot a bow, I am more or less certain of it,' Jiggins assured me, 'but that doesn't matter, really, does it? Because his wife's father has two horses and a donkey and a mule, and his boy knows horses inside and out, and he can act as your page, and Watkyn's wife can also cook and mend and wash and so on, so that's not really a problem, is it?'

'And who are all these people to me?' I wondered.

'We will be your retinue, Master Thomas,' he said. 'We four.'

I knew he was up to something, and he knew I knew, and so on, but it would probably be harmless enough, wouldn't it? In the grand scheme of things? And besides, what choice did I have?

'Very well,' I sighed.

'That's the spirit.'

Watkyn's son, Folo — whom I was to think of as my page — came as a pleasant surprise, however, as did his mother, for both were solid of limb and pale of skin, with a reliable mien, though Folo had the nervous habit of tugging a fleshy earlobe when you first asked him a question, and had a propensity, as I would much later discover, to wax philosophical. He was, as Jiggins had said, very good with horses and, indeed, with any animal (having looked after Lady Elizabeth's trained bear cub until it became too fierce), and though one of his horses was lame — and the donkey was not for sale (being dead) — he brought with him a mule and a pony that was smaller than I would have liked, late in losing its shaggy winter coat and prone to nip.

'Does the pony have a name?'

Folo tugged his ear.

'John,' he said.

'John? A horse called John? You can't have a horse called John.' This was Jiggins, who barged past me to take control of the haggling. 'There's never been a horse called John. Can you imagine Alexander the Great owning a horse called John? "Come, John, let us ride to slay the Persians!"? Julius Caesar with a horse called John? "Come, John, let's cross the Rubicon!"? No, no. You can't have a horse called John. I'm sorry. It's just stupid.'

But oddly, I liked it.

'And what about the mule?' I asked.

Another little tug on the earlobe.

'Likewise John.'

That was his name: not John as well, but Likewise John. Again, I liked it.

We set off about a week later, gathering first in the great castle bailey, all of us arrayed in Sir Richard Beauchamp's ragged-staff livery and accoutred with new-bought bows and boots, and Jiggins and Bundsay had on their shiny kettle helmets — paid for by me — though neither fit either, the one being too small for Jiggins, so it perched on his head like an acorn cup, and the other being too large for Bundsay, which he peered out from under like a toad from beneath a stone.

'Why don't they just swap them?' Thomas West asked. He, of course, looked every inch the part, and was riding with one of Sir Richard's most experienced captains, **Sir Baldwin Strange**.

I did not know.

'Well, it is your choice to make, Master Malory,' Yarrow told me as we waited to say goodbye, 'but, as I say, them two do not look fit for purpose.'

I knew he was right, but I had no choice.

We rolled out of Warwick Castle barbican and through the town in summer sunshine, onwards heading south, and I was briefly almost moved to tears, for we looked like an army, and I felt part of some mighty adventure — and I was leaving my youth in Warwick, wasn't I? Riding out a man, like one of King Arthur's noble knights, marching for Italy perhaps, to bloody the Emperor of Rome's nose. I rode with a swagger, new boots on my feet, new yellow leather gloves with the palms turning brown from reins, and ahead of me lay feats of arms and great deeds of worship.

The feeling faded all too soon thereafter, for even above all the noise of the hooves and the wheels and the rattle and clink of the other men, I could hear John Jiggins trailing along behind, telling anyone who'd listen that he wasn't much good with a bow, and that Bundsay here didn't know one end of the thing from another, but it didn't much matter, did it, really, because he was riding with 'a fellow named Malory', and 'no, he'd never heard of him either'. As we rode down towards the old Roman road that would take us to London and then to the coast beyond, I started to think of him as a canker in my rosebud, spoiling any sense of martial glory, and by the time we reached Sandwich, ten days later, I almost wished him dead.

We embarked at first light that next day, which was greeted as something of a minor miracle, and were all of us on the same ship – that I learned to call a carrack – with Thomas West and his men; our horses in slings, and our equipment in the hold, while we gathered at the gunwales to catch our first glimpse of the sea, which none of us had ever seen before, and which we came to only after many hours drifting on the river's turbid green waters through dense banks of reeds where all manner of birds shrieked and boomed, until the smell in my nostrils thinned, and became clean, and there, at last, through a gap in the reeds, it was: a broad reach of choppy, mud-coloured sea that stretched as far as the eye could see.

The master was a ratty little Genoese with bandy legs who could hardly keep his eyes – and then hands – from Goodwife Bundsay's rump or breasts. He did not speak any English or French but only a smattering of Latin. He could not tell me how he came to be here on the Narrow Sea, but he did not like it, he said, and he wished to be sailing on clear blue waters under sunlit skies, which sounded fanciful to me.

About a league from the shore the sail filled as a stiff wind came from the right to propel the ship through steadily steepening waves. Jiggins and Bundsay were almost instantly sick ('tainted ale, Master Malory'), but they were not alone, and most men took to praying and gripping fast to the ropes, save Thomas West, who sat in the bow and read a very small book that might have been a book of hours, save that he seemed to be reading as if it were new to him.

'Verse,' he told me. '**Sir John Shirley** lent it to me.'

94

Verse? I felt excluded, second-rate. Why did Sir John Shirley – one of Sir Richard's ablest captains – not lend me verse? I had time enough to ponder this question, though I came to no enduring conclusion, for we did not see the low slump of France on the horizon for what must have been many hours, and it was many more before the ship's captain finally gave the order to reduce the sail and we crept under the great cluster of castle walls and towers that was the city of Calais.

'Don't let Peyto see you like that,' Thomas West laughed, and I closed my mouth with a clack, but I'd never yet seen so many men, women, children, horses, boats, guns, gulls, so many of anything, in fact, gathered in one place. It was dirty, smoky, smelly, incredibly loud like a beehive, thrumming with life as everyone hurried impatiently about their business. I was awestruck and terrified at once, and for a moment I longed to be back in dear old Fenny Newbold, with my mother and father, brother and sisters, and Spare-the-Rod, by the stock ponds, say, or trying to bring down a pigeon in the woods. Such qualms are usual enough, I daresay, and anyway, I soon became conscious that this, here, now, was a solemn moment, for so it was that I first set foot on French soil.

Or rather, set foot in France, because Calais and its Pale were completely and properly English, though by God you could see how hard the place had to work to stay that way: it was ringed with mighty defensive walls and towers, with guns in each, and an enormously tall watchtower from which it was said you could see all the fortified bridges and sluices that could be opened to allow the seawater to flood the land should the need arise. The threat of invasion – not just from the Armagnacs but also from the Burgundians – loomed ever-present. Perhaps this was what drove the pace at which life in the town was lived?

For the men and women of Calais seemed to work all day, which was one thing, but I soon discovered they then caroused all night, ignoring the curfew and disturbing any kind of peace with terrifying, sudden guffaws, crashes, screams and drunken singing. On the day we landed, before we even reached the Church of Our Lady to join in the Te Deum in celebration of our safe crossing, a woman in a doorway on the Market Place showed herself to me — her entire self — causing me to trip and my face to flare scarlet. I hurried on, hearing, I am sure, her cackle ringing in my ears while I mumbled a protective Ave Maria. She was the first Frenchwoman I ever saw, though later Peyto told me not to be so daft, and that she was from Newcastle.

Needless to say, in such a place, Jiggins and Bundsay soon became as elusive as eels in fenland ooze, and trying to get them to appear at the butts for training with Sir Richard's other bowmen was never easy. When I did manage it, it was utterly shameful, for they were wholly, and very obviously, useless. It turned out that they had very quickly sold the bows I had bought them — yew, beautiful and with butter-yellow bellies, and at vast expense — and swapped them for what might have been the sort of thing which a farrier's wife would use to shoot at a fox in her garden, but even then, they could scarce nock them, let alone draw them.

At the butts, John Jiggins would drop his bow and let his arrow skitter across the mud, and then he'd throw himself on the ground, weeping and shouting that it was no good, that I'd forced him to join Sir Richard's retinue against his will — he was a harpist, a lover and not a fighter. If anyone touched him, to help him up, say, he'd scream as if he were being murdered. Meanwhile, Bundsay would appear without his boots, muttering about omens and portents — an owl seen upside down at noon, a child born with the beak of a duck — and stinking of drink. He got into a nasty fight in that first week, and was punched so hard that both eyes were swollen closed. Folo said it was Goodwife Bundsay who'd done it, but it turned out she'd only done one, in anger at the first.

We were billeted in the castle, on the west side of the town, in among the 'ordinaries' of the Calais garrison, who were full-time, paid (occasionally) soldiers under the king's orders, rather than any knight's household men. They felt themselves apart, and kept themselves that way, with their crosses of St George on their buff tunics. Sometimes — when we were on watch on the walkway of the southern wall — we would see them practising at the butts, and John Jiggins — this was before he was caught asleep on watch for the third time — would lean his elbows on the battlements and wonder aloud if they were really all that good.

'I mean, the thing is, yes, they look very pretty going about their business, but how will they be when they're really put to the test, eh?'

But they really were very good. Twenty of them could loose two hundred arrows in the time it took to say the Paternoster, each shaft landing two hundred paces away in a ridge no wider than a hog's back. Watching them roving around the Pale, shooting for the mark and hitting it, was an education.

'Well, I could do that,' Jiggins would say. 'If I had enough practice and wasn't expected to stand up here all day.'

I had long since run out of patience with Jiggins, as had everybody else, and in my still quavering voice I had given him a hundred warnings that he must improve this and work harder on that, but he ignored me, just as he ignored everybody, until at last he was found sleeping on guard duty on that third and final time, and the Sergeant of the Watch — an ordinary named Morrocks — insisted on the traditional punishment for the crime, which was to put him in a dyer's basket and lower him over the battlements on a length of rope to dangle twenty foot above the most disgusting part of the moat, the stretch around the back that was only refreshed by seawater during the spring tides, which was filled with ordure, rotting offal, tannery waste and the carcasses of dogs and so on. He was given a cabbage for sustenance and a knife with which to cut the rope when he could stand it no longer and he was left there to get on with it. A brave man would eat the cabbage, cut the rope and be done with it, but not Jiggins.

At first he wailed and begged to be hauled up, but people just jeered and threw their rubbish at him. Then he crouched down in the basket, hiding, as if he thought that so long as he waited, someone – an adult – would come and rescue him and we would all be scolded. Two days later, after much weeping and cursing, he would still not cut the rope and so Morrocks did it for him.

The basket fell and John Jiggins – long and lanky – spilled from it, cracked his head on the footings of the castle wall and vanished into the thick stew below with a muted splash and a riotous froth of bubbles.

There was a ragged cheer. Everyone had been fed up with him.

Then we waited for him to reappear, perhaps to throw more things at him, but there was nothing save one or two bubbles that after a while stopped. We waited longer still. Still nothing. The crowd – sizeable and rare in a town that never stopped to stare – started murmuring and then laughing.

'He's only gone and drowned himself!'

Eventually they drifted off, partly satisfied, partly dissatisfied, leaving Folo Bundsay and me to wait alone – Watkyn Bundsay had never appeared – and watch a few final bubbles rise and pop glutinously on the filthy ooze's glossy surface, and that was that: we never saw John Jiggins again.

'Shame,' the boy says. 'I liked him.'

Sir Thomas cannot help but shoot a disapproving look at the boy. This is the tale of noble Sir Thomas, who acquitted himself a knight by performing many wonderful deeds of arms et cetera, not of base-born churls such as Jiggins.

Still, though, Folo Bundsay had been of the same opinion.

'Poor old sod,' Folo said, tugging his earlobe, and 'Not what you imagine, is it? When you think of your own life, and God's purpose for it and that.'

He was right, of course. Imagine being brought up to die like that. Is that what Jiggins's mother thought when she first looked into his eyes? I suppose she might have, thinking about it now.

I remained in Calais all that summer, occasionally looking over the wall in case Jiggins resurfaced, but mostly doing what needed to be done in any garrison town. My voice roughened and dropped, I grew tall and my body further hardened with the almost endless exercise at the butts and in the tiltyard. I learned that Vegetius had got it almost exactly right when he laid down what it is to be a soldier: forever running to be somewhere to wait.

And when I was not on duty, there seemed little else for me to do — for I would not debase my honour by joining Peyto in his divers debauches — and the Pale beyond the town's walls and moat had over the years been so over-hunted that it offered little sport beyond that of throwing stones at tethered cats. With my first wages I bought a merlin from a man in the market with one eye, and set her at some gulls that had settled on one of the brackish meres that pitted the marshland behind the town, which men called the Scunnage, but she was lost very soon thereafter, and I believed she flew back to her original owner, who offered her back to me for sale the very next day, though I could prove nothing.

As the days grew longer, so the air around us grew thick and sultry, seeming to shimmer above the marshy ground, and many men fell ill, including Watkyn Bundsay, whom Goodwife Bundsay nursed back to health, but many others were not so lucky and the church bells tolled morning, noon and night all summer long. With my history of the ague, I lived in mortal fear of breathing in miasmas and I kept myself shuttered within my room in the castle wherever possible, from the narrow windows of which I oftentimes glimpsed Sir

Richard coming and going, sometimes taking Thomas West with him. Once I even saw Peyto riding out, and I ached with envy at the sight of them. How I wanted to be riding north with Sir Richard in a small, well-accoutred party, to see the Duke of Burgundy, perhaps, or east to Paris, even, to meet the French king to discuss extending the truce.

I began to believe that I had fallen out of favour with Sir Richard, and that perhaps it had been something to do with Jiggins and Bundsay, and I thought this was hardly fair, since I had recruited them from his own retinue.

'Poor judgement,' Verney said.

I nearly punched him.

But then I heard from my father later in the year, in a letter I was very careful to read properly this time, that he was back home from Westminster, and that he would soon send me two men who had fought with him against Owen Glendower, and on whom I could rely in all matters. I was delighted, of course, though I felt a mild stab of guilt that I would soon need to send the Bundsays home.

My father also sent news of my mother, who was well, as were my brother and sisters, but old Spare-the-Rod had been 'taken'. At the time I thought this must have meant he was dead, and recalling how ill he had looked the last time I had seen him, I was not surprised, though I was more deeply saddened than I would have supposed, and I vowed to pay a priest to say a Mass for his soul (I never did). But there was a puzzling further reference to him being 'never in such right mind as after having fallen afoul of the new abbot in Coombe', which I remember lodging in my mind as something to enquire about further, but like the Mass, I did not do so, of course, until it was too late.

My father's two promised men arrived just after St Michael's Day, in autumn, when the thin rain that usually falls in that part of the world had set in for what would be months to come. They were brothers, William and Robert Boyce, absolutely identical, and apparently immune to the cold and the rain, which seemed to bounce off them as if off bog oak. They were tall, dark-haired, sinewy and very frightening. Each carried at least two sorts of blade, and they were obviously the sort to carry a third secreted elsewhere about their persons.

They surveyed me, and then Folo Bundsay, and both Folo and I took a step back.

One of them – Robert? – said something in an accent I couldn't make out.

'What?'

'Are. You. Tom. Malory?'

I nodded.

'Hmmph,' the other said. A glance between them and an eyebrow raised. Nothing more. William – I think – put his bags down, and Robert – I must suppose – gave me a parcel of something heavy wrapped in waxed linen.

A book! From my father. I would save it for later, because now that Robert and William had arrived, it was time to dispense with the services – such as they were – of Watkyn Bundsay, if I could find him, and, very sadly, of Goodwife Bundsay, who had looked after me very well, and of Folo Bundsay too, who had become, oddly, a sort of companion.

In the event, all three Bundsays remained in Calais, even after I managed to track down Watkyn Bundsay and break the bad news, for it turned out he had been working as a potboy in a tavern from almost the very moment we'd landed in Calais. He wished to stay here, rather than return to Warwick, and Folo and Goodwife Bundsay were of the same mind, so it fell nicely for us all, save poor old John Jiggins, of course.

The book my father had sent with William and Robert Boyce – who, as it turned out, were Welsh – was a version of the deeds of Sir

Tristram de Lyonesse that he had found on his travels in London, he wrote, and thought I might enjoy. It was written in French, of course, but it was not in verse, and, as I discovered later, it lacked the usual poetic flourishes. Instead it seemed almost lifelike, as if Tristram himself were alive that day, and never once did he break into song, as he had in the version of his deeds that I'd read in Bordesley Abbey, and I sensed that perhaps the man who'd written it — or who had had it written for him — knew whereof he spoke, and how such a knight might really have lived, and how such a death might be encountered. It was puzzling at first, and strangely disappointing, as if it were missing something. But then it became oddly thrilling, and I returned to it again and again over the next few months, and it was a source of great comfort to me in those austere and friendless times.

Had life gone on like this, then there would have been nothing for me to write in my letters home, should I ever have written one, and perhaps the world might never have heard of Sir Thomas Malory, for good or ill, but — perhaps thanks to the departure of Jiggins and Bundsay and the arrival of William and Robert Boyce — my stock was on the rise, and had I but known it, that arrow of mine was not falling, as I feared, but still on its ascent, and soon it would be Thomas Verney and William Peyto watching me ride out, and further afield than they could even begin to imagine, for in February of that year I was told I was to ready myself to join Sir Richard on a journey — a very delicate mission, very close to His Majesty's heart — that would take me halfway across Christendom—

Suddenly the boy utters a stifled cry and springs to his feet, sending the napping cat flying.

Brunt is back early! The badgers must have killed all the dogs, or the dogs all the badgers, for beyond Sir Thomas's door there is a stumble on the steps, and the sound of clumsy, drunken fingers fumbling at the unlocked locking bar. Sir Thomas watches the boy once more making all those calculations, but there is no getting away from it this time.

He is trapped.

But before Brunt can solve the mystery of the misplaced locking bar, the boy turns and springs to the window. He grasps the bars, and is out through them like the quarrel from a crossbow, ripping the linen as he goes and leaving behind a hole through which the filthy soles of his feet vanish.

The door begins to swing open on those creaking hinges, and it is only then that Sir Thomas spots the boy's pie-like cap, russet wool, left on the rushes. He struggles to his feet faster than he's managed in a long time, but when he bends to pick it up, he feels a stinging lash of pain in his back and is left gasping, half one way, half the other, neither up nor down, but at least his foot covers most of the boy's cap.

The shape of Brunt fills the doorway like a slovenly bear caught out in the rain. His face is slack and his mouth sloppy, but his eyes are livid red knots and those fists of his swing at his sides like sacks of sand he wishes to bring down on something or someone.

'Where is he?' he slurs.

'Who?' Sir Thomas manages, imperiously enough, though by Jesu it is not easy with a double-bent back.

'Don't you piss about with me. Where's my boy?'

'I was wondering the same,' Sir Thomas tells him, 'for I need a flame for my candle.'

'He's been up here, hasn't he? Listening to your nonsense. Your clatter.'

'You dare talk to me like that?'

'Talk to you any damned way I please.'

Brunt burps. He has those fists, and a cudgel in his belt, and a knife too, of course, and as Sir Thomas's keeper he has licence to use all four on him at once, in any way he likes. But he is also wary,

Sir Thomas sees, and Sir Thomas remembers his arrest in the garden, and how Smethwick cautioned his men to do him no harm, especially not to his hands, and Sir Thomas is suddenly struck with the certainty that Brunt must be under the same mysterious obligation, and so he is less afeared of those fists, that cudgel, even the hidden blade, than perhaps he ought to be.

'Get out,' he tells him. 'Get out, you churl.'

At which Brunt swings around, pulls back an arm as if to strike, and for a moment Sir Thomas thinks he has misjudged it, but no. Brunt clenches his fist and growls, but makes no move to close.

'When I lay my hands on him,' he growls, 'I will lay the little bastard out flat! Missing a badger fight so that he might hear your tripe! Makes me wonder if he is any son o'mine.'

And with that he stumbles back and must clumsily catch the door frame to steady himself. Then he leaves, crashing the door behind him and hammering down the locking bar before he goes staggering and bumping down the narrow flight of steps.

Sir Thomas lets out his breath, lifts his foot off the hat, and staggers, limping, to the window, through which wafts the sound, and smell, of falling rain.

'Boy?'

There is no answer save the hiss of persistent rain.

'Boy!' he calls again, louder this time.

But still there is still no answer, save a moment later there rises up from the street below a cry of alarm.

Jesu defend me, Sir Thomas thinks, what have I done?

CHAPTER 4

Of Sir Thomas's seventh day of confinement in Castle Newgate, and how noyousness turns to joyousness, in so far as that is ever possible for a poor prisoner-knight

The next morning Sir Thomas wakes from rage-wracked sleep with his usual panicked cry, save this time it is not for his own self that he fears, but for the boy.

Is he alive? Is he dead? How can he have survived such a fall?

He had heard nothing further after that scream: no running feet, no shouts of alarm, no sound of anyone weeping over the corpse of a child. Or perhaps he had? Perhaps he had heard all these things, and much more besides, but that would have meant nothing, not in these parts.

He rises gingerly, for his back is very sore, and he inches his way to the window, there to await daylight enough to see — to see what? Ten little fingers clinging on the roof's rim? Or nothing? He is not sure. After a while he steps up onto the noisome night soil bucket to take hold of the window's bars and he pulls himself up on the tips of his toes and peers down towards the street. He can see nothing from here, save pigeons and the roof-leads, mossy, rain-matted and sombre, and he gives up with a great sigh, and steps back, almost overturning the bucket, before then settling to scuttle about his cell in that familiar old circle, around and around, a spasm of pain with each step, waiting, waiting, waiting for someone to come.

They are late. What can that mean? Only that the boy is dead, he is certain. After some time he stops, for the pain in his back has become too much, and he lowers himself to his knees and prays with the intensity of a guilty man. At last he hears the locking bar lifted and the door swing hesitantly open, and his heart yammers in his chest almost as if whoever comes brings news not just of the fate of a prison servant, but of his own self.

Pray God it will be the boy! Pray God! But it is the girl! It is Susan.

'Jesu preserve me!' Thomas cannot stop himself crying, and Susan leaps back, terrified by this kneeling madman who is begging her for something she cannot give him.

'How is he?' he nearly roars. 'How is your brother?'

He points to the window and mouths the words as if it is he who cannot speak and she who cannot hear, but she shows no understanding of, or recognition of, his miming of a dive — complete with a whistle to signify the fall and two smacked palms to suggest the impact upon the cobbles — or even of Sir Thomas's impression of the boy lying dead, with his tongue sticking out, his neck at a broken angle, and after a moment she thrusts the loaf at him and the ale, which slops from its mazer, and she turns and runs, slamming the door behind her, and he hears the bar being rammed into place.

Which is a good sign, surely? For if her brother had been found dead the night before she would be distraught, and she would know what Sir Thomas meant by all his gesturing. He puts the bread and the ale on his coffer, but still cannot eat it, cannot do anything except pace as furiously as the pain in his back will allow, and he thinks nothing new, for there are no new thoughts to be thought on this matter, until, at last, the pain of his pulled back overcomes him and he lowers himself into awkward stupefaction upon the palliasse, and watches the cat cleaning herself.

Jesu.

Next he stares at his coffer, topped by bread and ale, sitting at the foot of his palliasse, just where it always used to sit, and for the first time he wonders why it is there. Not at the foot of his palliasse rather than over there, say, in that corner, but why is it in his cell at all? Did he ask Elizabeth to bring it when he was first taken up? Or did he mention it to Hartshorne perhaps? Time alone in a cell addles the wits, this he well knows, and so perhaps he did mention it to one or other? Or both perhaps? But why? Doing so suggests that he accepts he will be herein constrained for some time, and he is yet to do that.

Hmph. But, oh Jesu! What of the boy? Can he really have survived that fall?

Sir Thomas forces his trembling fingers to take the coffer key from his purse and unlock the box, and remove from it the top two trays and the bundle of clothes, and set these aside, and then from the coffer's base, he forces himself to take out his manuscripts, every last page, and pile them next to him on the palliasse.

It forms a low mound of rough-edged, irregularly sized paper — some pieces of fine vellum; others of hog-rough paper — covered in ink that is sometimes of deepest, purest lampblack (when he was in favour with the keeper) and sometimes faded to the palest lavender (when he was out of favour; it might have been his own blood). It is the result of nearly ten years' work undertaken in divers establishments — Ludgate, the Marshalsea, Colchester Castle, even the Tower itself, but mostly right here, in this room in Newgate — and completed in divers states of mind, too, ranging from bleakest despair to wildest joy. Sometimes the lines veer alarmingly, as if written while he was agued, or weeping, or — who knows? — drunk. He must have worn his way through a hundred reeds, two hundred feathers, including those of the pigeons of the type who are even now cooing beyond his window, much to the cat's poised interest.

Over those years he had slowly grasped the magnitude of the task he had undertaken — the drawing-out from the French books (and the telling in good plain English) of the complete story of King Arthur and his Knights of the Round Table, as well as the history of their achievement of the Sangreal, from the birth of King Arthur to his death – as well as why no one had tried it before: the unfinished book is already fatter than any Bible Sir Thomas is yet to come across, and more unwieldy too, for being unbound save in rough folds, sometimes stitched and sometimes not, so that it makes no neat stack, but slithers apart in a heap, as if each book wishes to thrust itself to the fore and not be hidden by the previous.

He takes up one of the folds of paper at random and finds it is the history of how the eleven kings agreed to gather an army to march against King Arthur, and he begins to read:

'The first that began the oath was the Duke of Cambenet, who said he would bring with him five thousand men-at-arms, which were ready on horseback. Then swore King Brandegoris of Stranggore that he would bring five thousand men-at-arms on horseback. Then swore King Clariance of Northumberland that he would bring three thousand men-at-arms. Then swore the King of the Hundred Knights, who was a passing good man and young, that he would bring four thousand men-at-arms on horseback. Then there swore King Lot, too, another passing good knight, and Sir Gawain's father, that he would bring five thousand men-at-arms on horseback . . .'

He is beginning to wonder how much would be lost if he were to trim this chapter – perhaps make it just five kings? – when without warning the door opens, and suddenly the boy is there, grinning.

'Came to collect my hat!' he says.

'Jesu preserve me!' Sir Thomas cries. 'I believed you dead!'

And he struggles to his feet as if to embrace the boy, but stops short, and instead passes him his hat that he has hidden behind his coffer.

'However did you get down?'

'Went along the leads, didn't I?' the boy laughs. 'Climbed in through old Lewd-Act's cell.'

He nods to the wall separating Sir Thomas from his neighbour,

Master Bewscel, he who is charged with committing some lewd act on Popkirtle Lane.

'Ha!' Sir Thomas laughs. 'A rare example of someone breaking *into* Newgate. But then — however did you get out of there? Surely his door was likewise locked?'

'Slept on the floor all night, and then, when Susan brung him breakfast just now, there I was.'

He is rightly proud of himself.

'And what about your father? Did he not miss you?'

'He'd had his ale by then, and cared not where I was, so long as I was not listening to your — your deeds.'

Sir Thomas ignores the slight.

'And did Master Bewscel not mind having you on his floor?'

'Done him a favour, in the end,' the boy supposes with a shrug. 'He's up in court this afternoon, so he's all astir, and he had some-one to talk to.'

Despite himself Sir Thomas feels a minor twinge of jealousy, but then remembers how he used to be on the nights before his own trials were supposed to start, back in the days when he knew with what he was charged, and he wonders aloud if Master Bewscel's trial is like to end well or not.

'For him, I mean?'

The boy pulls a six-of-one, half-a-dozen-of-the-other face that he will have learned off his father.

'Still,' he says. 'It means my old man'll be taking him down the Guildhall, so . . . ?'

So Sir Thomas is surprised how pleased he is.

'You mean . . . ?'

'If you've a mind?'

'Of course. Of course. Yes. And we come to a good bit today.'

'Agincourt?'

'Almost,' Sir Thomas havers.

At which the boy raises a sceptical eyebrow, but his attention is caught by the great spread of papers on Sir Thomas's palliasse.

'What you got there then?' he asks, very doubtfully.

Sir Thomas tells him. The boy looks almost disgusted, as if he has caught Sir Thomas in a perversion, a lewd act of his own.

'You wrote all that?'

'I did,' Sir Thomas admits, feeling half-foolish and half-proud.

'That's a lot of letters,' the boy says, stooping to peer. It strikes Sir Thomas that the boy might never have seen a book this close. A Bible in the distance perhaps; a psalter maybe, or some pronouncement nailed to the east door of St Paul's, but who'd bother looking at that if they could not read what was written?

'Yes,' he agrees. 'Each letter has its sound, and each sound adds together to make a word.'

The boy studies the page for a long moment.

'No,' he decides, standing back. 'It's not for me.'

Sir Thomas smiles.

'Look again,' he tells him. 'That letter. It's an A, you see? It is the first of Arthur's name. There. Another. And there again. And there too. Not each word that begins with an A spells Arthur, of course. This one is longer and is Agwisance, who was King of Ireland. This one is shorter and is "and". Do you see? There. And there. A. N. D.'

The boy allows that it might be the case.

'Find me two more,' Sir Thomas instructs, once more unsoundly confident.

The boy's grubby finger hesitates before finding two more.

'Ha!' Sir Thomas says. 'You are reading.'

'Simple as that,' the boy laughs.

Sir Thomas is just opening his mouth to ask him to find more incidences of the word Arthur but the boy must attend to his business.

'Be back after the bell for Terce,' he tells him, and Sir Thomas is left alone to leaf through the pledges of the eleven kings with a nagging sense that although it sounds brave and noble and true, perhaps there is something a bit flat about it.

After a moment he becomes aware that someone is at the harp again, and places his ear to the wall between his cell and Master Bewscel's and listens, charmed, and envious, wondering why he did not tell Elizabeth to bring him a harp so that he might once more play too. Or perhaps he might find something else? A rebec? A fiddle? Might he have a try at either?

He plans to speak to Hartshorne, listens a little longer, and decides that Master Bewscel is a gifted harpist. But what can his lewd act have been? He wishes the boy would just tell him, without him having to ask and so reveal his disworshipfully prurient curiosity. After a moment Master Bewscel stops playing, and so Sir Thomas returns to his coffer, where his flitting, distracted gaze is rebuffed by the further adventures of the eleven kings and settles on the new-ripped linen window covering. He remembers then how oftentimes in the past he paid for the privilege of taking to the leads, and so – his back notwithstanding – might he not do so again now? Might he not knock on Master Bewscel's window and wish him luck for today and might he not offer advice – only if it be welcomed, of course – as to how to endure the day, for is he not an old hand in such things? And might he not, in this way, also divine, from Master Bewscel's appearance if nothing else, just what manner of lewd act he is accused of committing?

He might, you know. Though it is easier said than done, of course, especially with a back that when he extends his leg feels as if he has been kicked by a horse. But still. He surveys the obstacles: principally the height and narrowness of the window above, which when he was here last, nigh on ten years ago, were no problem, but that was then. How many years is it, he wonders, since he broke out of the dungeon of Colchester Castle, scaled the castle's curtain wall and then swam the moat, all while still in iron fetters? Fifteen? Sixteen? Though his efforts proved pointless in the end, for he had not made it to Westminster in time for his summons before the Court of the King's Bench, the memory makes him smile, and he thinks how much the boy will like that story, if they ever get to it.

He gets up and gingerly turns the bucket aside, and then, in minute shuffles, manoeuvres the coffer into its place under the window. He steps up, bats aside the linen and heaves himself up to get his knee on the sill, on which he then pivots to force his head and shoulders through the frame, but now he cannot quite tuck his elbows in, and must wriggle himself through, out into space, with his arms trapped at his side, like a fish in a trap, and for a moment he is caught half in, half out, and must either retreat or press on, and he — being Sir Thomas Malory, veteran of Verneuil, and so on and so on — presses on and pushes himself forward, only to find himself sliding all too quickly out of the frame and careering towards the all-too-close and none-too-high parapet of the moss-and-dropping-crusted leads, beyond which, fifty feet below, await the unforgiving cobbles of Newgate Street.

He stops himself, just, and the pigeons erupt in noisy alarm and wheel overhead while he scrabbles back and sits against the wall, there to regain his breath and survey his perch, which is a strip of mottled lead two paces wide by twenty long, with a carved stone ball marking each outside corner. Master Bewscel's window, identical to his, is about ten paces along, and when he is recovered, he gets unsteadily to his feet and with one hand on the wall he shuffles along and is about to knock when he hears Master Bewscel has taken up his harp again. He is playing a melody that Sir Thomas half-remembers his mother playing, from his childhood, and now indeed is even singing, in a soft, pleasing voice that you would never imagine belonged to a man accused — but not yet, of course, found guilty — of a lewd act on Popkirtle Lane. Sir Thomas listens for a moment. Merry it is while summer lasts, and skies are filled with birdsong, but soon winter will come, and there will be long nights of sorrow, and mourning and fasting. The old song is beautiful: plangent, telling and so melancholic that Sir Thomas forgets his purpose of knocking, and finds himself leaning against the wall with tears misting his vision.

When the song is sung, he does not wish to break its spell, for Master Bewscel's sake as much as his own, and he steps quietly away from the window and returns to his own, through which he writhes back with no little difficulty, spraining his wrists in the slide from the frame to his coffer on the way down, and afterwards, sitting awkwardly on his palliasse, nursing his divers injuries, brushing the moss and bird smut from his cloth, he offers up a prayer to St Ivo – a Breton and a lawyer, which make his elevation to sainthood doubly remarkable – for his neighbour's success in trial.

When he is done he sits and awaits the sound of Brunt conducting Master Bewscel to his trial, and despite knowing he will learn nothing, he cannot break the habit of pressing his ear to his door to hear them pass – Brunt still limping, Master Bewscel's footsteps very light, as if he were frail, or God forbid, as if he were somehow already absenting himself from this earth.

He considers what to tell the boy. Brunt will have left him a list of tasks as long as your arm, he must suppose, so time will be tight, in which case, he wonders about skipping details such as:

➺ How at Christmastide Lady Elizabeth Beauchamp came to join her husband from Warwick, in a litter deep with soft furs, bringing with her letters from Thomas's father, with news that all was well in Fenny Newbold, though Spare-the-Rod was still awaiting trial. Trial? Thomas had thought him dead, and so was relieved at this reprieve, though now considerably puzzled and fretful. His father instructed him to buy William and Robert Boyce some cheese for Twelfth Night, for that would please them passingly well, and his mother sent a pair of woollen socks and a long roll of paper, very nicely made, which puzzled him, until it struck him they merely wished him to write letters back. He bought William and Robert their cheese — only a fool would not wish to please them — but put the paper away, and never, as far as he knew, wrote back.

**→ How Christmas in Calais passed just as it had at Warwick Castle, with much relieved and irresponsible eating and drinking now that Advent was over, and after-dinner jousts fought on piggyback that left one boy — not Peyto, sad to say — with a broken arm, and another with teeth in only one side of his jaw.

**→ How, if Sir Thomas were honest — and he is nothing but, upon his sword — he would admit to falling in with Peyto during this time, and drinking a great deal too much spiced wine, with a kind of desperation, and that he also joined in those after-dinner jousts (and, indeed, it was he who knocked the boy over so that he broke his teeth) and that he did so only because of the presence of Lady Elizabeth Beauchamp, whose attention he sought to attract in ever more foolish ways.

**→ How it was that for three nights in a row Folo had to carry him home over his shoulder, and how Goodwife Bundsay was hard pressed to attend to his linens. William Peyto gambled with dice and cried when he lost, though, so at least Thomas was not the worst disgraced among Sir Richard's new lances, but even so, most mornings Thomas woke wracked with shame, conscious that he was not leaving the bad and following the good, as he knew he ought.

He knows he has told the boy there is to be a long journey described, but he wonders if he needs tell him exactly *why* it was undertaken? Does the boy need, for example, to know the following:

→ How it came to be that Sir Richard Beauchamp was appointed as the king's representative to a General Council of the Church, which was to be held in the city of Konstanz, on the shores of a lake in far-off Tirol, requiring a journey of many weeks in winter, and possibly a stay of an equal length, before the long journey home.

→ How the reason this General Council was called was because at that time — the fourteenth year of the fifteenth century after the birth of Christ — there were crowned in Christendom not one, not two, but three popes, or, rather, one pope and two antipopes, though no man was able to state definitively which was which.

→ How, even though it was obviously very shaming that the One Catholic Church Indivisible should be so divided — with each of the three popes excommunicating the other two, and urging crusades against them — the real issue was that it weakened Christendom's resolve in the face of the Ottoman Turks, who were even then expanding like a storm cloud in the east, threatening the destruction of Christendom as a whole, and of Hungary in particular, and so this Church Council had been called by **Sigismund, the Emperor of the Romans** and the King of Hungary, to fix this schism and unite all of Christendom against the Turks and so save his country.

→ How there were only two things that Thomas knew about this Emperor Sigismund: the first that he had already once been beaten in battle by the Turks (because of the French, it was understood, who had, as was then still their wont, charged headlong into a shiny trap, this one set by the Turks rather than the English), and the second that Sigismund and his brother had once been poisoned by some enemy or other, but while his brother had died, he — Sigismund — had survived, because he had spent twenty-four hours hanging upside down.

⇥ How every cardinal and bishop of the Church was summoned to Konstanz along with the representatives of every king and queen in Christendom — including King Henry of England — in the hope they would pick a pope on whom they could all agree, and whom Sigismund could press into calling for a crusade to set the Turks back on their heels and, of course, eventually, to re-edify the walls of Jerusalem, which was a cause close to King Henry's heart.

Perhaps the boy would relish the detail of the upside-down emperor, it is true, and the absurdity of there being three popes, but Sir Thomas knows all too well that court sessions at the Guildhall can be over before they start, for reasons good or ill. When the boy comes darting in, not unlike the cat, with news that his father has ordered him to get the ale up to those inmates on the second floor before he gets back or he'll feel his fist, Sir Thomas wastes no time:

So the day after the Epiphany, Sir John Shirley summoned me to his office and told me that since the boy who was supposed to go with Sir Richard had lost half his teeth, and William Peyto had so disgraced himself that Christmastide, I was to help provide escort on Sir Richard's long journey to Konstanz.

'You will be provided with everything you need, Malory, and you need only bring your page and two men. And if you've a cook, bring her, too, so long as she is not also your personal harlot.'

It was felt strongly then that having a personal harlot was bad for general morale, and so if a man were caught with one, at the first offence she had all her money confiscated; at the second she had her left arm broken; and if he persisted, she would be hanged.

I thanked Shirley and walked away, my spirits buoyed at this somewhat undeserved turn of fortune, and set about gathering my little retinue. Folo I knew would be happy to come, but I was less sure about Goodwife Bundsay, who might wish to stay with Watkyn Bundsay. But when I put it to her she threw aside her ladle, tore off her apron and said: 'When do we go?'

'Soon,' I said, though I could not bring myself to tell her not to throw her apron too far, for of course she would be expected to cook on the road. I was most nervous about asking William and Robert Boyce.

'Why?' one of them asked when I did so.

'Because I tell you so.'

'You. Tell. Us. So?'

Both looked down at me for what felt like a long time, their dark eyes set very deep in their skulls, and I am not ashamed to say I began shaking slightly, and if they'd said no, then I do not know what I would have done, but in fact, I had misunderstood William's question. He was not in fact questioning my borrowed authority, he merely wanted to know why Sir Richard – and so we – were going to the Council.

'We are going to see the pope,' I told them. 'In Tirol.'

Of which none of us had ever heard, of course, and if I were pushed, I was not even sure if it was Tirol that I meant, but the idea of going so far into the unknown did not seem to bother them, and I supposed they had come from some bleak little valley in Wales, and here they were, looking after the son of an Englishman against whom they might or might not once have fought, while serving the English king across the Narrow Sea in Calais, so perhaps they had long since ceased to seek the whys and wherefores and had just learned to accept life as it came? As God's will?

And so they were not unduly fussed, or even interested, to find that in the week after Epiphany, despite the winter gales, Calais began filling with various lords and dignitaries sent over from England whom we would be escorting to Konstanz, including **Sir Walter Hungerford**, who at one dinner told me he knew my father from fighting in Wales, and from the House of Commons.

'A passing good man, Malory,' he said.

Sir Walter was a stern old knight, who described everything as being 'passing' this and 'passing' that, and who had once been an expert jouster. I vowed that 'passing' would become my amplifier of choice. Later, one of the two bishops Sir Walter had come over with – of Salisbury – told me that Sir Walter had once defeated the French King Charles in a tourney held right here in the Calais Pale.

'But that was about the time when Charles began to believe himself made of glass.'

Which made it less of a feat, it had to be said.

The Bishop of St David's, in Wales, had also come over with Sir Walter, and he was likewise there that evening, and, stuck for something to say, but never forgetting my lessons in such things, I looked him in the eye and asked him if he knew of William or Robert Boyce, they then being the only Welshmen I knew. He did not, though, and it turned out he was English anyway, and that he'd never even been to Wales, and in fact knew not a single Welshman at all, so that was two fewer than me.

In any case, soon after that we set off for Konstanz, wherever it was, on a dismal morning, and we wound our way through the Pale towards the Calais marches, led by Sir Richard and his captain Sir Baldwin Strange again – at the head of perhaps two hundred horses and mules and seven carts, each loaded high with all the stuff we'd need – including Sir Richard's finest tilting harness packed in straw-stuffed barrels – but mainly a great many gifts for Sigismund, including a small pack of fierce-looking alaunts, and no fewer than eight hawks of various kinds, none of which, sad to say, made it to Konstanz, being either killed or dying or stolen en route.

Thomas West – who seemed to know most things – explained that we were not doing all this solely to add England's voice as to who should or should not be pope, but so that Sir Richard could swap it for King Sigismund's support for King Henry's claim to the French throne.

'But King Henry has a right to the French throne!' Verney countered. 'He has God's support and he needs no support from some German!'

West agreed, patiently, as you would with a stupid child, but supposed it might help. Verney was not happy and accused West of denigrating the king, England and St George. West sighed and returned to what he called his *zibaldone*, the little book he kept in which to copy down the poems he read and the thoughts he had. He even drew in it: faces, horses, faces of horses, a boat under sail, a sword pommel he liked the look of, and intricate examples of stonemasonry, including a series of gargoyles. I had noticed Sir John Shirley had just such a book too, and I vowed I should buy one as soon as I could.

We made up to about fifteen miles a day, moving slowly on good roads in bad weather, through Flanders and Brabant, stopping for two nights in Aachen, where we heard Mass in the cathedral, and saw the Cross of Lothair with all its jewels, and Charlemagne's golden bust, where once again I was pleased Peyto was not there to call me 'flycatcher'. From there we went south through a hundred different realms the names of which need not detain us here, but through which I wondered – aloud, one night, to Sir Baldwin Strange at dinner, believing he'd find my observation marvellously clever – if King Arthur might have come on his way south to defeat the dictator of Rome.

'No, Malory,' Sir Baldwin corrected me, his cheeks florid and his nose like a little beak above his narrow, lipless mouth. 'He'd never have come so far east. He would have brought his knights down through France and then over the mountains into Lombardy.'

'I see.'

Sir Baldwin was a serious-minded man (I suppose you must become so, growing up with a name like that) and, having actually been with Sir Richard on his pilgrimage to Jerusalem five years previously, he probably knew whereof he spoke.

We finally reached Konstanz in the week after Candlemas, after more than a month on the road, and we rode in through the handsome little town's northern gate wearing all the finery we'd kept clean and dry against this very event, led by trumpeters and fifers and the like, and all the townsmen and women – my God, how many women were there? – came to see us pass. The town was on the shore of a lake so large it might have been a freshwater sea, dominated by its minster and filled to overflowing not only with clerics of every rank from pope to parishioner, each with his retinue; and not only with servants and soldiers but, I'm sorry to report, thousands of common harlots.

'Oh, here we go,' Goodwife Bundsay said when we arrived, already weary of such women, who here stood in groups of four or five at every corner, beautiful pale ladies, tall and oftentimes strapping, in their striped hoods, shamelessly offering their wares by exposing themselves with quick flashes of puckered flesh or by pulling the cloth tight across their breasts to give an idea of what was on offer. Most shocking of all was when a friar or a priest, or even, God admit it, a bishop, succumbed to their blandishments and went off with one or even two of them, feigning reluctance as he went, his heels against the cobbles, blushing but laughing, and the prostitutes' sisters and more or less everyone else in the street whistled and cheered to see him go. There was no shame.

The English delegation was allocated the Painted House, made mostly of wood, rather than of the grey stone in which the rest of the town was built, and not far from the minster where the sessions of the General Council were to be held. These sessions lasted more or less all day, and in all that time I never attended one, although those who did so came back so wracked with the effort of arguing with the French and Spanish and Italian delegations that we often ate our plain suppers in simple, drained silence.

The Bishop of Salisbury threatened to have any man who shrugged, or gesticulated with his hands, expelled from the room.

'Say what you've got to say, Malory,' he ordered, 'and say it quietly. Or else put it in writing.'

It snowed often, and was always cold, and every man shuffled back and forth with his head wrapped in a scarf and his cloak or gown invariably sodden six inches about the hem, but while the clerics and lawyers were sequestered in their endless conferences, those of us not involved passed the time agreeably – though expensively – enough, for the hunting in the woods was very fine, with every kind of quarry imaginable, including wolves and bears, which the locals ate as you might a cow, and I had the chance – missed – to shoot a wild boar, which I had long wanted to do.

I was also persuaded to buy another small merlin, which I set at the various sparrows and so forth that twittered in the trees to the south of the town, but she soon vanished in the mist that rose from the lake and I only saw her again a week or so later, being offered for sale by the very man from whom I'd bought her, but who on our second meeting claimed to speak no Latin or French or English, though he had been fluent in all three at our first.

I was interested to see Emperor Sigismund. I hoped I'd be able to tell that he'd once spent a whole day hung upside down, vomiting poison, but except for a typically (for that part of the world) sad and elongated face, there was nothing much to tell him apart from anyone else. Sir Richard and Sir Walter courted him and his wife very carefully, for West was right in saying our purpose was to seek his approval for King Henry's claim to the throne of France. But that was but one of the things they – we – sought, which I only came to understand later.

When Emperor Sigismund promised Sir Richard the pickled heart of St George (as a gift to King Henry), we knew we had achieved the greater part of our mission. That night we – the English delegation – held a dinner to which easily a hundred bishops of all nationalities except the French came to eat a monstrously fat fish caught fresh from the lake and cooked in cinnamon.

The pope on the other hand – **Pope John XXIII** – was not at all as I'd imagined he'd be. He was small, strikingly dark, like a Saracen, and had perhaps the least saintly expression I ever saw on any man, let alone a pope. He so obviously carried a knife in his sock, and I was not at all surprised to learn from Sir Walter Hungerford that he came from a family of pirates, a trade he'd only given up when he realised the Church paid better.

'And after two of his brothers were hanged for it.'

How such a man had come to be pope nobody would tell me without much rolling of the eyes and sighing, and there were hints at some very dark deeds, not only by those who backed him, but by him too. Nevertheless, he was pope, if only for now, and when he passed us on the street – in his camauro and robes on a very fine grey palfrey caparisoned with the papal coat of arms – we all bowed, even Emperor Sigismund, for whatever else he was, he was also the direct descendant of St Peter. Or one of them, at any rate. Given his reputation, it sounded to me that either of the other two might be better suited to the office, though I subsequently learned that they too were none too chaste, and one of them even charged money to kiss his copy of the Ring of the Fisherman.

I personally spoke to Pope John while I was there, which was regarded as a great honour, but I was not so sure. I had been with Thomas West, picking our way through the berms of swept snow that lined the street between the bishop's palace and the minster. It was on this street that the brothel Haus Zur Wilde stood, run by a man named **Leopold Nesselwang** who kept a wild brown bear on a chain with which to threaten any customer quibbling over his bill, and though this was where the most beautiful women in all of Christendom were supposed to ply their trade, it was the bear that West and I wished to see.

The truth is . . . the truth is that while the others among our party capitulated to the temptation of the women in such places, as I swear upon the cross of my sword, I did not, though I could not say why, not until I spoke that day to Thomas West, whom I noticed had also resisted their charms.

'It is mere lechery,' he told me, 'and no true knight would give his heart to such a woman.'

Thomas West was very straight-backed, very straight-nosed, with a fringe of fair hair that fell across his noble brow to almost cover the far-off look in his blue eyes, and at that moment, standing in the shadow of a church, a light snow beginning to fall, with his hand on his sword hilt, he embodied, to my mind at least, the very soul of what it meant to be a true knight. He looked as I imagined King Arthur must have done when struck by the idea of gathering the knights around the Round Table, and I found myself looking up to West with something like awe.

'Besides,' he went on, 'what need has a knight for such women when he has a lady of his own?'

It took a moment for me to understand what he was saying.

'And do you?' I asked. 'Have a lady of your own, I mean?'

He sighed, and we walked on.

123

'Oh, Malory,' he said. 'My heart is pledged, but alas! Our love can never be.'

After a moment I said, 'I see.'

The thought that Thomas West might have a lady, and for their love for one another to be doomed – it was too much for my nearly fifteen-year-old self to bear. I opened my mouth to say something.

'I too have a love,' I found myself saying. My mind scrambled to reinforce my tongue. What? Why? Who? All I could think of was Lady Elizabeth Beauchamp, Sir Richard's wife.

'And nor may we wed,' I added. Which was of course true, since she was married to my good-lord.

West stopped and looked at me with newfound brotherly respect.

'Ah, Malory,' he sighed again, and beat his breast with a clenched fist to show his fellow feeling.

We might have gone on to console ourselves over our loves that could never be, and we might have gradually wormed our way to the conclusion that given our status as frustrated lovers – his lady, it turned out, was only betrothed to another man, already knighted – we might be expected to be the natural customer base for the beautiful harlots who clustered at the street corners like goldfinches after holly berries, but – thank God, perhaps – it was at exactly that moment that we saw the pope ahead, coming from his palace.

He and his attendants – who held a canopy of cloth of gold over him so that neither he nor his beautiful grey palfrey would get wet in the feathery snow – were held up by a cart unloading wine barrels and we hurried to come alongside, and for some reason he turned then, and I caught his glance. It was a confusing look he gave me, I have to say, especially in the light of what West and I had been talking about, for there was something speculative in his eye that hinted less at concerns of the spirit than the flesh, and catching it, I instantly felt my cheeks burn, for though I was young at the time, I knew. I *knew*.

I hid my confusion in a deep bow, but when I looked up again, there he was, still in his saddle, still staring, an eyebrow arched. He beckoned to us. To me, I mean. Thomas West instantly started across to him, but the pope waved West away and gestured to me. His guards — Neapolitans with blue chins, dark, self-interested eyes and great long spears — looked at me in a weary way that made it clear I was not the first to be summoned in such a way.

'Who are you?' the pope asked in Neapolitan-accented Latin.

I told him.

'Thomas Malory, esquire, of Fenny Newbold, County of Warwickshire, England.'

He was briefly unsettled, but after a moment's pause he carried on.

'Ah. English.'

He stretched the word for a long moment. I nodded.

'Would you — eh — like to kiss the Ring of the Fisherman?' he asked. His voice was surprisingly delicate, with each word deployed as a piece on a chessboard, and after each sentence he seemed to step back as if to inspect its configuration.

'But you are wearing gloves, sir,' I said, truthfully enough, for he was, and he held up a hand gloved in beautiful, blood-red leather as if he had not noticed it before. It matched not only the other glove, but also the saddle and the bridle of his horse, the stirrup straps and his boots.

'It is no matter,' he smiled with yellow teeth.

He put forward his hand and I took it in mine, and bent right over it, with my lips nearly pressed against the smooth leather of his fingers. The fragrance that rose up outweighed that of the horse, and was the most beautiful thing I'd ever smelled; it smelled of things I'd never known, never have been able to describe, and if he himself was — reputedly — of the gutter, he smelled of the heavens, and I felt myself keeling, reeling with it, a strange, heady rush.

When I looked up, he was smiling at me, his lips very red and eyes deep and brown and glistening.

'Come and see me, English boy,' he said. 'My chambers.'

Just then there was a noise up ahead, a shout, a curse, the whipping of an animal, and with the barrels of wine now successfully delivered, the carter set off and the blockage in the street was gone. Without waiting for permission, the pope's guard likewise set off, taking the awning with them, and he had no choice but to touch the palfrey's flanks with his red-leather heels and follow, but he watched me as he went, staring back over his shoulder until one of his men bundled me aside with something spat out in his own tongue.

Thomas West gave me an equally curious look when I returned to the roadside. Although we had to some extent bound ourselves to one another with our confessions of love for our far-off damosels (even if mine did not strictly exist), our meeting with the pope had driven the matter from our minds, and by now the snow was falling fast, and the minster bells began to boom above, and we were late for wherever it was we were meant to be. We set off in haste, though I never forgot my audience with the pope, nor did I mention it to anyone else, not even to Sir Baldwin, for example, or the Bishop of Salisbury.

Many years later, at the Council's end, long after we had gone, they deposed that pope, accusing him of piracy, murder, rape, sodomy and incest, but it was said they suppressed the more scandalous charges, so he was free to carry on life within the Church, where he remained a cardinal—

Suddenly the boy cackles, and Sir Thomas realises that in his reverie of long-gone times, he has once again forgotten his audience.

'Sounds like he should be down below in fetters with the commons,' he laughs, 'not swanning about on some fancy horse. Having boys up to his chambers, I don't know.'

For some reason, after all these years, Sir Thomas feels protective of Pope John, and does not like to hear him judged wanton by a mere prison boy. He wonders if he should have told the boy any of this – if indeed it is of any account – but before he can say anything, add any cavils, or anything like that – some sense alerts the boy, and he rolls quickly to his feet and goes to check the window. He peels back the torn linen and thrusts his head out, standing straddled on toe-tips on the bucket's rim, and he tuts at what he sees.

'There he is, the old man, back already,' he says. 'Funny, I guessed he was on his way. Must've felt it in me bones.'

It will be some extra sense, Sir Thomas supposes, that develops when a child's father batters them.

'Is he early?' Sir Thomas supposes. 'Perhaps no jurymen appeared?'

'Jury always appears when it's a lewd act,' the boy says over his shoulder, and Sir Thomas smiles to hear this bit of prison lore in the mouth of a child so young and does not disabuse him of it.

'How do they look?'

'Not exactly skipping,' the boy admits.

Sir Thomas rises awkwardly, his back still sore, and crosses to peer out over the boy's head – which smells sweetly fetid – but by the time he gets there, they are gone.

'I'd best be off,' the boy says. 'Them on the second floor'll be spitting feathers.'

'Will you find out how it went with Master Bewscel?'

'Course.'

'And let me know?'

'Only if you promise we'll get to Agincourt?'

'Ahh. Well. Yes. Agincourt. Well, we'll see, eh?'

The boy groans and rolls his eyes, but he means it in jest, for Sir Thomas sees he is taking some pleasure in the story's distractions, just as he is too, although later, when the boy is gone about his business, Sir Thomas wonders if he really ought to have told him about the harlots, or about the pope? He decides that it was fine to do so, for surely he must hear worse every day from his father? And anyway, it is too late now. Sir Thomas sits back carefully and stretches his legs out, and he is somewhat astonished to find himself content, though, Jesu defend him, he cannot say why.

CHAPTER 5

**How upon the ninth day of Sir Thomas's incarceration
in Newgate, Master Hartshorne brings doleful tidings,
and how Sir Thomas and the son of a churl find
themselves ever more in accord**

It cannot last, of course. Though the night is peaceful enough, the
next morning Master Hartshorne is brought to Sir Thomas's cell
door wearing a very pained expression.

'What is it?' Sir Thomas asks.

'Do you know any shoema-akers, by any cha-ance, Sir Thomas?'

Sir Thomas is taken aback.

'*Shoemakers?*' he echoes. 'You can't surely want the name of mine?'

Hartshorne's shoes are very fine, the colour of Burgundy wine,
each pointed like a chisel, and symmetrical, while Sir Thomas's —
made by a man in Coventry called William the Shoe, to whom he
now remembers he owes four shillings — are round-toed boots, and
not at all symmetrical.

'No,' Hartshorne agrees. 'A shoema-aker named **Corne-elius**.'

Sir Thomas does not.

'Or a tailor?' Hartshorne wonders. 'Named **Hawkins**?'

Again, Sir Thomas does not.

'Why do you ask?'

'It turns out you are not the only one taken up,' Hartshorne con-
fides.

'Yes,' Sir Thomas says. 'My wife told me as much. Days ago.'

'Did she?' Hartshorne asks, disappointed to be the second person
to bring the news. 'But did she tell you who?'

'She said there had been a plot discovered, presumably against
King Edward, but she knew no names.'

129

Hartshorne is pleased to be able to provide these, at least, and he has a list, he says, but he can't find it now because he has brought no bag with him, perhaps because it would spoil the cut of his silk doublet, and his servant is God knows where, but anyway, he says that in all fifteen men are arrested, and he remembers some of them, because how could he not? **Humphrey Heyford** – the London sheriff, for the love of God, **Thomas Portaleyn**, **Sir Gervaise Clifton**, **Hugh Pakenham** and even **Sir Thomas Cook**. These are all men of substantial means and substantial influence. Cook was once Mayor of London.

Hearing these names, Sir Thomas feels himself stiffening and his chest filling with something like feathers, and he finds he can hardly breathe. It is as if it has all become serious now. Real life, with its sharp edges, has intruded upon his recent reverie to remind him of his peril. What has he been doing all this time, telling the boy his story as if that were all that mattered, when he could be – could be what?

'But what have they to do with – to do with your shoemaker?' he wonders.

'He is not *my* shoema-aker, thanks be to God,' Hartshorne says, and he crosses himself. 'He was taken up at Queenborough, accused of carrying messages from the queen in exile to Heyford and one or two of the others. It is said he revealed their na-ames under torture.'

Torture. Just the word is enough to sluice ice water down any prisoner's spine, and Sir Thomas does not trust himself to stand, so sits. He has allowed himself to cling to the belief that all this – all this *incarcerating* – might be a strange misunderstanding, an unfortunate oversight, perhaps brought on by the recent hot weather, but now, by Jesu, he thinks, this is no joke: the king is in deadly earnest.

'Do you know if – if my name was mentioned?' he asks.

There is the briefest lull between the two men.

'Not so far as I can find out,' Hartshorne admits, and then very carefully asks, 'Would it surprise you if it was?'

Despite his doublet and shoes, Hartshorne is no fool and that is a good question, which Sir Thomas chooses to ignore.

'Where are they kept?' he counters. 'Here in Newgate?'

'In the Tow-ower.'

Oh Jesu. The Tower. Well, at least he is here, not there, with the brake, the mere proximity of which can make a man piss vinegar and turn his hair grey over night.

'All together?'

'Yes.'

'So if I am taken up for the same reason, then why am I not with them? Why am I here?'

'I ho-oped *you* would tell *me!*'

They stare at one another.

'It changes nothing,' Sir Thomas tells him, 'for I have still done nothing!'

Hartshorne sighs, and folds himself up with many joint-clicks to perch a skinny buttock on the corner of Sir Thomas's coffer, and he sighs again.

'If you are not caught up in this,' he starts, 'and I believe you, Sir Thomas, when you say you are not, I do, but then — why? Why are you here? I have asked everyone I know, and am told it is at the king's pleasure, and that is all. I ask after charges, and all I am told is that they are being prepared. This is worse than the old days, for at least then we knew *why* you were here, or with *what* you were charged. At least we *knew* that your trial was scheduled.'

'For all that it mattered.'

'Yes, yes,' Hartshorne agrees, as if so many years in gaol awaiting trial was mere detail. 'But now it is just — there is nothing. I have written to everyone you can think of — yes! Even your good-lord of Warwick — but hear nothing back. I have been to see everyone you can think of, and am told whoever it is I wish to see is elsewhere, or too busy. Even when I see them in person, they feign ignorance, or tell me that now is not the time or that they are not the right person to speak to.'

Sir Thomas can see this must be frustrating for Hartshorne, and he almost feels sorry for him, but after he has removed his backside from Sir Thomas's coffer and taken his leave, sighing, Sir Thomas is left alone, still unsprung from Newgate's iron grip.

He paces around his cell again, and he tries to think clearly, but all he can really see and — dear Jesu — even smell, is the hot, savoury wisp that the shoemaker's flesh will have given up under the ruby-red grip of the tongs. He thinks then of poor old Spare-the-Rod, forced into his barrel by the riverside in Gloucester, and of the Armagnac witch Jeanne, made to stand barefoot upon her pyre, and through his window it seems as if the light of the day is made matt by clouds of billowing, greasy human smoke.

The boy comes with dinner. He is late but does not apologise. He is also pale and distant, as if something has happened.

'What's wrong?'

Sir Thomas fears he brings bad news about Master Bewscel's trial, but it is not that.

'Been a fight among the commons down below, hasn't there? Two women fell out over a cabbage, and went and killed each other. One with a blade, the other with her fetters.'

Sir Thomas knows this sort of thing can happen.

'Saves on the hangman's fee,' the boy supposes, aping his father, 'because they were for the drop anyway, but it means the Irish are here, doesn't it? Them from Southwark.'

Sir Thomas understands that by 'the Irish' the boy means the men who cart away the worst of the city's spoil — from the bear pits and the gaols and so on — who will bribe the nightwatch to let them out after curfew to dump their loads in Moorfields or, if it's nearer, the Fleet, or somewhere further out, but that does not explain his frozen, watchful look, which Sir Thomas recognises.

'Did you see the women kill one another?' he asks.

The boy nods tightly.

'It's always a shock,' Sir Thomas tells him, for dear Jesu, so it is.

'They're in the yard right now,' the boy says, 'with the bodies chucked in the back of the cart while my old man treats the Irish to ale.'

The boy looks at Sir Thomas, expecting something, but Sir Thomas has nothing to give.

'What about Master Bewscel?' he asks. 'I have not heard him or his harp all day.'

The boy shrugs.

'Jury didn't show up, did they? Or not enough of 'em, so he is back here a week or two. Reckon he thought he'd be found innocent, so he is glum.'

'Well,' Sir Thomas says, 'at least they did not find him guilty.'

The boy agrees, reluctantly, but lingers still. He does not want to go down to the bodies, or the Irish.

'You were going to tell me about Agincourt,' he says.

'Ah.' Sir Thomas understands. 'You have some time?'

The boy nods, more a tense little rocking motion, and abruptly he sits and buries his face in his hands, and he might burst into tears, and Sir Thomas is reminded once more that his story has become a means of escape for the boy, too, just as much as his: a refuge from the day-to-day struggle of the life he's been born into, though then again, when he thinks of what comes next, it is hardly cheerful, is it? Nor is it Agincourt. But perhaps, he thinks, it would do the boy good to hear something more soothing? And although at any other time he might not risk over-encumbering him with the softer details of his return from the Church Council in Konstanz, and how he came home to his family, and what he found there, today he feels it is meet, for it is diverting enough, surely, and then perhaps they will come to the matter of Agincourt.

So we left Konstanz that next week, in five barges, travelling north down the River Rhine under broad, rust-coloured sails, well-pleased with ourselves for having achieved what we'd set out to do: shown Christendom's other nations what we Englishmen were made of, secured Emperor Sigismund's support for King Henry's claim to the throne of France, and – the third part of our mission, though one unbeknownst to me at the time, and seemingly of little interest anyway – we had succeeded in having **John Wycliffe**'s teachings condemned in such a way that the king might now treat his followers – the Lollards – not merely as heretics, but as traitors, with all that that entailed (hanging, drawing, quartering, burning and so on), which seemed to me, then, to be fair enough, though I have since passed many a dolorous hour regretting that matter.

The great river carved through steep valleys between soaring mountain ranges and then took us out onto broad plains, and we spent a happy week or so floating downstream, passing our time telling stories, singing songs and playing tables. Sir Baldwin Strange recounted endlessly detailed histories of the movements of King Arthur and his armies against the Emperor of Rome, and oftentimes I was asked to share my stories of Sir Lancelot and his crossing into the land of Gore in pursuit of She-Upon-Whom-He-Would-Most-Wish-to-Lay-Eyes (Queen Guinevere), at the mention of whom I noticed West would sigh, or clench his jaw in a show of romantic agony. I once shared guard duty with him, and caught him sitting alone at the bow of the boat, wrapped in his cloak, sighing while studying the stars above. It was then he told me her name: Elaine.

I laughed. I admit it.

'*Elaine?*'

No one is called Elaine.

'Why not? What is your lady called?'

It was funny how we had settled on our ladies as possessions, when in fact it was we who were possessed. We were like dogs with owners. Well, he was. My lady did not exist, of course, except, perhaps, very vaguely, in the form of Lady Elizabeth Beauchamp. All I had to say was some other name than Elizabeth.

'Elizabeth,' I said.

He sighed gustily on my behalf.

'To think she might be looking up this very moment, Malory, and seeing these self-same stars!'

It was my turn to sigh.

We changed from barge to ship in a muddy port owned by the Duke of Burgundy and returned at length to Calais, coming in from the sea to discover Watkyn Bundsay hanging in a basket from the city walls.

Folo covered his face in shame.

'What you doing up there?' Goodwife Bundsay called.

'A misunderstanding,' Bundsay replied, but a guard told us that he had tried to kidnap a priest for ransom and that he'd been there a couple of days.

'Oh, just leave him be,' Goodwife Bundsay said.

She had enjoyed our journey to Konstanz, I think, and had been reluctant to leave, for she had fallen in love with a butcher – who had sold her a bear's head from which she made a curiously pleasant meaty bear paste, but who spoke no English.

'He was kind to me,' she told me later.

But it would be a while before we discovered Watkyn Bundsay's fate, for Sir Richard was determined to press on and bring the king word of our achievements in Konstanz in person, and so that afternoon, on an ebbing tide and before a fair wind, we set sail for England, making landfall in Sandwich a little after dawn the next day. Or we would have done so, had not the port been so crammed with boats of every shape and size – gathered there, we learned, in readiness for the king's imminent invasion of France – that it took us until late morning to set foot on dry land.

'The king runs swift about his business,' Sir Richard murmured, perhaps unsettled at all the preparations that seemed to have gone ahead without the need for our precious accord from Emperor Sigismund.

It was rumoured to be like this at every port along the coast of England, from Lynn to Lyme, and inland too; all throughout Kent and Sussex we discovered the roads were choked with columns of men on foot, columns of mounted men-at-arms, columns of carts and sumpter animals, and great flocks and herds of livestock, all pressing together between the hedgerows. They were all coming against us, so that our passage was passing slow, as Sir Walter Hungerford would have said, for constantly negotiating your way past groups of bored, belligerent and heavily armed Englishmen takes tact and patience, even if you are the Earl of Warwick.

Eventually we made it to Windsor, where the king received Sir Richard, but I rode on home to dear old Fenny Newbold. I was bearing divers gifts from Konstanz – nothing which I now remember save a small stuffed bear with very sharp teeth and a hideous expression, and a copy of the *History of Merlin*, which I had bought from a stationer near the Haus Zur Wilde, as it happened – and as I rode through the new-built gatehouse I considered myself a changed man, though when I pulled up my horse and got down, self-consciously aping the way my father used to dismount when he returned from his wars in Wales, I think I found them more changed than they me.

It was not that my brother and sisters were each a foot taller, though they were that, it was that my father and mother were each a foot smaller. My father's beard was snow-white now, while I found that my mother would hardly venture from her room.

'It is this business with Master Orme,' my father told me.

Spare-the-Rod! I had almost forgotten all about him.

'You told me he was taken?' I said, thereby admitting I had received a letter I would later deny receiving. 'I thought he was dead?'

'Not yet,' my father muttered, while trying to keep me from talking about him in front of my brother and sisters, who had, as had I, come to love Spare-the-Rod. Later, when we were alone, I learned that Spare-the-Rod had not died, but been accused – by that churl the Abbot of Coombe – of being a follower of none other than John Wycliffe: of being a Lollard.

They did not yet know about the king's new policy against Lollards.

What should I do? This was terrible. What should I say? It had never occurred to me that Spare-the-Rod might have been a Lollard, but later, when I thought about it, or knew a tiny bit more about it, it seemed obvious. Had he not always dispised *The Golden Legend*? Had he not always been dismissive of priests and bishops and even churches, with their 'figurines' and so on? 'They are like to come between a man and his God,' he'd told me when he'd confiscated my three-horned sheep's skull.

By going to the conference at Konstanz I found I had, even if only in some small way, contributed to the fate of my old master, although, of course, I did not tell either my mother or my father that. Perhaps if I had stayed with them we might have been able to do something for him, but that is not what happened, because that was when my mother and father realised I was about to go away to war, and their fears for me consumed their fears for him. My mother expressed hers in much weeping and twisting of snot-soddened cloth, while my father's were expressed in snippets of advice – basically: stand behind Robert and William Boyce, whom he credited with angelic powers of survival – and gifts of a warlike nature, including the most perfectly shaped misericorde dagger, a slender rod of steel as long as a man's hand, tapered to the cruellest point and created with the specific intention of penetrating any gap in even the finest armour, to find the flesh below. It was housed in a fine red sheath.

'Put it on your belt,' he told me, 'there, next to your sword, but never take it out, or play with it, or show it to anyone, or do anything with it, unless you absolutely have the need.'

'Why not?' I asked, taking it out.

'Because,' he sighed, 'if ever you do take it out, or play with it, or show it to anyone, when you do not absolutely need to, then when you absolutely need it, you will find you have left it elsewhere, and so it will not be there, and you will be dead.'

I slid the knife back into its sheath, promising to heed his words (which I did).

I left them later that week with many tears on both sides: theirs for me, mine for old Spare-the-Rod, for whose fate I held myself responsible, and the occasion was very wretched indeed, and I snivelled all the way to Warwick, partly thankful but also partly miserable to be alone.

From there we left for Southampton the week before Lammas Day, with Folo Bundsay acting as my squire, bringing two new horses (John and Likewise John having gone the way of all flesh in Calais, and these two unnamed, to my knowledge). William and Robert Boyce came too, though they rode with the rest of Sir Richard's bowmen, and only appeared now and again, looming out of the gloom, to bring me pieces of cheese they'd roasted, or odd pieces of meat they had brought down against all laws of the land. I wondered what instructions my father had given them in relation to me.

The roads south were thicker than ever with troops and horses and it seemed that every man in the country must be gathering in and around Southampton, where someone told me the king had caused all the priests and friars that would be left behind in England to be trained in fighting, in case his great enemy the Scots chose our absence to attack. We pitched our tents outside Southampton, on common ground, by a stream under a hugely fat weeping willow that soon became the precise place most men chose to relieve themselves, and we settled in to wait for no one knew how long. It was better than being at sea, everyone said, as some men already were, but as the warm weather continued, and the smell under the tree rose, I was not so sure.

At length we were summoned to Southampton itself to wait for embarkation.

'Have you written your will, Flycatcher?' Peyto asked.

I had not seen him for a few days, and he smelled very strongly of drink, and of something else: hedgerows and manure, and something that smacked of fertility, if that makes any sense. He had on his bits and pieces of patched plate – field armour, we called it – but he had grown taller over the summer, like a weed, and not even this fitted him. His huge hands hung at the end of long wrists almost down by the saggy knees of his rough brown hose.

I told him I had not written a will.

'You should. West has. He has left his property to his "lady love".'

Peyto sucked in his cheeks and fluttered his eyelids and then laughed lasciviously. I felt vigorously offended on West's behalf, and had a good mind to punch Peyto.

'Shut up,' I said. 'Shut up. You are a disgusting animal, Peyto, a knave, no better than a common churl, whoring and sullying yourself, whereas at least West is keeping himself pure for Lady Elaine!'

Peyto laughed and went off to find West to torment him for his chastity, as I supposed, only for Verney, of all people, to tell me that of course West's lady love was not called Elaine.

'No one is called Elaine!'

It had not occurred to me that he might have given her another name.

'He has borrowed the name from the tale of Lancelot, you dolt, for he does not wish to disgrace the real lady in question.'

I was left cursing my naïvety as we trooped up a gangplank into the deck of the merchantman's ship that was to take us across the Narrow Sea, only to find it already very crowded with troops, so that a man needs must stand, or sit on his saddle, and began what I came to think of as The Great Wait. It was, I have since come to think, not unlike when you are waiting on a woman to give birth to your first child: you think surely the baby will be out in an hour or so, as why would it not be? It does not have far to come. Then two days later, you are still there, and it is only on the evening of that second day that the baby comes.

It is, I should acknowledge, a somewhat greater ordeal for the woman.

Nevertheless, we sat there waiting at sea for five days. We ate all our food in those few days, and the water around the ships became thick with a slick of bobbing ordure that not even the tide could shift. At length though, the king came aboard his great ship the *Trinity Royal*, sent his last messengers ashore, caused that giant sail to be unfurled, and, among trumpet blare and drumroll, the rest of the fleet followed likewise, though for some reason three of the king's ships immediately caught fire and were burned to the waterline before they managed to leave Southampton Water.

How? Why? No one knew.

Despite the bad omen, it was a good crossing, this time not to Calais, as was expected, but further south, to Harfleur, in Normandy, and our little ship slid into the estuary of the River Seine that next night, and tied up to a bigger ship, which was in its turn tied to another, bigger ship, and so on, and we waited until dawn to see where we were to come ashore. When we disembarked – none of us before the king, who had forbidden it on pain of death (he would go on to threaten this fairly often) – most of us staggered on the lifeless surface of the beach for having lost our land legs, and I fell over in the gritty, grey mud.

'Same thing happened to King Edward the third,' Robert – or

William — told me as he helped me to my feet.

'And the first King William,' the other one added. 'Who is called the Conqueror. He also fell.'

It seemed I was in good company.

The sluice gates had already been lowered and the land behind the town was much flooded and treacherously marshy, so we set up camp on higher ground to the west of the town, which from there appeared a handsome little place, built across a river that ran into the mighty Seine. She had a moat, a tall curtain wall much punctuated by turrets and another even higher wall surrounding the docks within. On our arrival this outer wall was lined with all the townsmen and women of Harfleur, some with their babes in their arms and their children beside them, watching us, and I waved at them, just as if this were a game, until Robert — or William — stood by me.

'God. Save. Them,' he muttered.

'God. Save. Us. All,' the other added.

I stopped waving and looked at them anew, as at Christian souls, and a chill seized my heart. For the first time I wondered what they must be thinking. This is something I've often since pondered about the inhabitants of the various towns I've laid siege to: they'd been living their lives happily enough, going about their business, to market, say, or to Mass, when from down the river come enough men to turn the landscape black, not just with their — our — presence, but with their — our — malicious intent, which must surely pollute the earth, the sky and the water just as literally as does all their — our — ordure and woodsmoke.

We stood there awhile, looking at our newfound enemies, studying their unexpected and redoubtable defences, and the mood among us waxed grim. But then the king appeared before us. I had not seen him since his coronation, and I, like the others, turned towards him as morning flowers do the sun, and we watched him survey the scene, and then cross himself and say:

141

'Be all things in accordance to the will of God.'

He told us then that when we had taken the town, he had wonderful plans for a *chevauchée* – a great plundering ride – either into Normandy, to Rouen, and then to Paris herself, or south, through Gascony to Bordeaux. On hearing this, many men imagined they would make their fortune, but I was still swept up in a different kind of fervour, one that was at once harder and yet more ethereal: glorious feats of arms, and the winning of worship, so that my name would resound throughout England, and I imagined, I think, Lady Elizabeth Beauchamp hearing it, and saying, with a particular smile, 'Oh yes, Sir Thomas Malory, I used to know him.'

When the king had returned to his tent, followed by his brother, the **Duke of Clarence**, and Sir Richard Beauchamp, who had come over on the king's ship along with **Bishop Courtenay**, the rest of us set about pitching our own tents on the lower slopes. My aim was to be as close to the king's tent as possible, or failing that, as close as possible to the path he must take to get to the lines, so that when he passed by each morning he would be able to pick me out and remember me as the boy he had stood by while I played the harp so badly at Warwick Castle that day.

Such proximity had its price, though: in this case, quite a sharp slope.

'So long as we lie with our heads at that way, we shall be all right,' Folo said. He was never keen to have too much blood to the brain.

After that, the army spent the first few days pulling apart the houses that lay outside the town's walls, clearing sightlines for the king's great guns and his great siege machines, which the carpenters had brought over from England, all packed up and ready to be assembled where they were needed. Men argued about whether it was sensible to burn the houses, or better to keep the wood for fuel should the siege last any length of time, and anyone opposed to burning was told they had no faith in the king and therefore in

God, and they therefore must be a Lollard, and so it was that much wood was lost to the flames, which was something we would later come to rue, but at that moment it was a fine, warlike sight, and we cheered as each house collapsed with great woofs and towering columns of sparks.

I can only think of those early, innocent days of the siege with an incredulous shake of the head. What were we thinking? So certain of our purpose, so assured of it and of ourselves? There were setbacks, it is true: even after we thought we had surrounded the town, a great troop of Armagnac knights managed to get in through the East Gate to reinforce their defences, and there were sorties from the town itself almost daily, which cost us a fair few men.

I say that now — 'a fair few men' — but I was walking down from my camp when the first wagon carrying the English dead came jolting up the track, and the sight of all those bloodied bodies, each turned in a trice from man to meat, all jumbled up in the bed of the cart, I confess, struck me dumb. I began shaking and Folo had to guide me back to our little tent where William and Robert sat turning something petite and four-legged on a spit over the fire.

'Don't. Think. About. Them,' Robert or William told me.

'It. Will. Never. Happen. To. You,' the other one added.

Which I knew to be true — that it would never happen to me — but that was not the point. This was the first time I'd seen death as the aim of some specific activity. Jousting and fighting in a tourney were all about winning worship and avoiding death, and if someone was killed, then that was a misfortune, a sign that something had gone wrong. But now those men were being swung into a pit while a priest intoned their names — 'John, son of John of Bristol; Fulk, son of Basil, a priest; Seamus, an Irishman' — and their death had been the desired product of some Armagnac's morning's work.

And this extinction was to continue to be the desired product of all our activity for the next month, and how busy we all were going about it! The king's great cannons set about reducing the town to just enough rubble that it became impossible to live in, but not so much rubble that it would be impossible to rebuild after we took it, and they fired all the time, day and night, and each time they did, great flocks of birds took flight from the marshes around us, and the gunstones throbbed or howled towards the town, and we would watch and cheer if they hit something – those inner walls, or another house, or one of the barbicans – with a great crack, followed by a slithering crash of masonry and a roiling plume of dust that hung in the damp air until it was finally dispersed by the wind. The moon was very full and bright in those early days, and sometimes it was possible even at night to see the king prowling his newly constructed ramparts, urging his gunners to ever-greater efforts, before returning to his tent to play his harp.

Despite a few early days of fretting about those innocents within the town – the women and children – who might have given up their souls with the impact of each gunstone, after that first week I found I did not care for them at all, and the longer it went on, the less I did so. After a month, as the brash summer faded to subtle autumn, I even came to hate them.

I came to hate their resistance, their bravery and their resourcefulness: what we knocked down during the day, they somehow rebuilt at night, and if we ever came close to them, they shot at us, or hurled jars of quicklime in our faces, blinding many a man. The carpenters built a tower and rolled it towards the walls, but this they burned to the ground with pig fat and black powder. Then we tried to fill in the moat with bundles of faggots, so that we could get closer, but they set light to those too. Then we started digging under the walls, but they dug back, and they were better at it than we, and they killed all our miners and collapsed our tunnels. I began to think of them not as people but as rats, ruthless in their tenacity of life.

'Why won't the bastards just surrender?' we asked ourselves, and them, and God, for no one knew how they could stand it, day after day, week after week, but somehow they did.

And meanwhile the miasma from the marsh which we'd much enriched with so many rotting corpses began to rise and creep up the hill to our camp. It inveigled its way past the clouds of smoke from our fires, past the screens we set up, and through the canvas of our tents. While we slept at night it went down our throats, up our nostrils and into our ears. It even soaked through the little holes in our skin. Men began falling sick with a foul pestilence that caused their life to scorch its way out of their backsides in a scalding, blood-tinged torrent.

The bloody flux.

In those first weeks, a lucky few were evacuated back to England by boat; the unlucky many were dropped in a pit and scattered over with quicklime, and in this way, along with such men as the Armagnacs managed to kill in their constant sorties, and those who slipped away in the night — surprisingly many, whatever men may tell you now — our army was soon whittled away. When we came ashore, we numbered ten thousand fighting men, but soon it was very obviously fewer. Tents were emptying, graves were filling, but still the food and wood supplies were running out — how we regretted those early fires — and we had to roam further afield to find anything to eat, in the countryside where bands of Frenchmen now lay in wait to winnow our numbers further still. Our raiding parties became no longer a source of fun, as they had been in those first few weeks, but grim, heavily armed, usually unsuccessful, oftentimes fatal, excursions into hostile territory.

Yet still I clung to my belief this was an opportunity to win worship and renown. Folo and I moved our tent from its slope into a newly vacated spot — the previous occupants had died, one of drowning, the other of being murdered by his own servant, who was subsequently hanged – nearer the pathway down which the king and his retinue passed every morning to inspect the guns that were blasting away at the Porte de L'Eure, the big gate with the barbican on the west side of the town, and at dawn each day I put on my polished leg plates and my surcoat (which Folo managed to keep spotless) and waited in the hope that either the king or Sir Richard would see me and wave me over (just as they had after the swimming in Warwick that time, and just as they now sometimes did to others, such as Thomas West) to join them on a tour of the lines. How I would impress them with my martial vigour! And the king would give me something specific to do, some vital, daring task that would prove my worth, after which – by Jesu! – he would knight me in the field.

He never did, of course. He would stalk past, thin as a falchion, staring into the distance, eaten up with certainty. His men – including Sir Richard and Bishop Courtenay and those other lords in their armour and surcoats – would follow along in a concerned train, hands behind backs, nodding wisely, and all would ignore me.

I don't recall the exact moment when it was generally known that we were losing this battle, but in the space of a day, it was suddenly understood that time and tide had turned against us, and that if we did not take the town soon, or strike camp, then we would all be making our graves in the stinking, blood-rich mud hereabouts.

Worse, in a way, than that was the shame, for this would mean that it would be widely known throughout Christendom that God had found us wanting, and our king's cause unjust.

It was then that Bishop Courtenay fell sick, and he was dead within the week. He had been an old friend of the king's and it was the king himself who washed his feet and closed his eyes, and then ordered the bishop's heart cut out, and his body dismembered and boiled in a cauldron. No one was allowed to watch as the king's surgeon, with the help of the king's butcher, cut the king's bishop into pieces, but we could all smell him boiling, even above the stench of the camp and the marsh, and when his meat was softened enough to be slipped from the bones, the king's scullions tipped the cauldron over and separated out the contents, burying the cooked flesh but keeping the bones, which were wrapped in linen, ready to be sent home along with his heart for burial in Westminster Abbey.

And it was precisely then, while the greasy scent of the boiled bishop still hung heavy in the air, that I too felt the disease's burning fingers upon my shoulder. A choleric heat in my joints, a churn in my bowels as if something hot and heavy were alive in there, and the hardening of the ache in my head, and soon I could no longer deny the truth and I experienced an almost crushing despair.

'What I would give for some good English ale right now,' I told Folo.

He shot me a quick glance. Thirst was a symptom.

'Master Thomas?'

'Just thirsty,' I told him.

And we looked at one another and tears appeared in his eyes and tears appeared in mine too, and I realised we had become friends.

'Oh, Master Thomas,' he said.

'Oh Jesu defend me, Folo,' I said.

For we both knew this was a death sentence, as sure as any read out by the headsman.

'It may be – the smell?' he suggested. 'The bishop is——?'

He covered his nose and mouth and raised his eyebrows.

But no. My head beat like a bell being rung, and even as I spoke, my stomach was gripped as if in two fists. Ah Jesu. A fiery snake was writhing within, trying to force itself out. I ran – trotted in a way that was all too familiar to see – to a ditch. I was evidently not the first to do likewise, for the ditch was already much befouled with the vilest mixture of discarded oyster shells and the despoilments of other desperate men, but my need was uncontrollable. I will not describe what came out of me, for I was still at the stage in the disease when my stool was explosive, and copious, and, at that moment, seemingly purging, for I was yet to reach the stage when all I would produce was a spoonful of scorching, blood- and shit-tinged egg white, flecked with raw flesh.

It was exactly then that the thing I had been praying to happen for so long happened: the king and Sir Richard Beauchamp came past, down from seeing the bones of their friend the bishop being boxed up and readied for travel back to England. At long last they saw me. I could not hear their words from where I was squatting in the ditch, but I imagine the king saw me first, and recognised my surcoat, and he indicated to Sir Richard that one of his men was in trouble.

A moment later Sir Richard stood over me, or a little way off, his hand masking his face.

'God give you good day, Master Malory,' he said.

I could say little or nothing, for another great spasm was travelling through my guts, but I was pleased he had not forgotten me.

'How long has it been?' I heard him ask Folo.

Folo tugged his ear.

'Just now, sir,' he said.

Sir Richard nodded. He watched me squatting in my noisome ditch with great understanding, and some pity, and came to a decision.

'Malory,' he said. 'You are to go from this place and find passage across the sea with His Grace's bones and, if God grants you His mercy, you are to travel from there to my castle of Warwick.'

'I am quite well, Sir Richard,' I called from my ditch. 'It is the smell of the boiling bishop, and of this — this ditch.'

I could sense glory slipping from my grasp. My disappointment was visceral. My vision swam. I felt as if I might throw myself down in the mire and scream.

'Please sir!' I bleated. 'Please. Let me stay! I wish to be here when the town falls, sir! I wish to be the first to—'

But just then I needed to loose my stool again, and I had to gasp. Sir Richard hardly took a step back.

'Enough, Malory,' he said. 'I have seen you hanging around, trying to make yourself useful, and I am sorry nothing has come of it, but you are sick now, and once dead you will be of no use to your king or country, man or beast, and nor will my Lady Elizabeth ever forgive me.'

After which I vaguely remember Folo finding me space on the cart taking the box of Bishop Courtenay's remains down to the makeshift dock set up on the beach to the west of the town, and I remember stopping the cart so that I might pass stool again, and I remember looking across the marsh and thinking it looked as if we were waging war against horses, for their corpses lay everywhere unburied, and I remember stopping the cart again so that I might once more void my bowels, until the carter would no longer linger to watch me straining on the trackside, and Folo forced me back onto the cart, for my painful attempts were already fruitless in any event, and any further delaying meant we would miss the tide.

I remember the night was drawing in as we were taken aboard a fishing boat that had just delivered his catch to the king's army, and I recall them setting the sail – green, ragged, square – and as we set out across the Narrow Sea, I remember staring back at the dimmed lights of Harfleur, and at the prickle of fires and lights that signified the English army camped at her walls, and I remember my eye falling on the position of the king, but I did not see him, of course, and I experienced such a pain of melancholy and loss that it was like a lance to my bosom.

'A farewell,' I think I might have murmured. 'A farewell to worship.'

And I knew for certain then that my ambitious arrow had reached its peak, and I should have been inconsolable, save that I was also thinking of Sir Richard's words: 'And nor will my Lady Elizabeth ever forgive me—'

It is late now, nearly curfew, and sombre shadows have descended. Brunt's boy stands at the window, looking thoughtful.

'Never so much as met a bishop before,' he says, 'let alone smelled one on the boil.'

'I daresay they smell like anyone else,' Sir Thomas supposes.

The boy allows for this possibility.

'But of course,' he goes on, 'the likes of you'd always be alright, wouldn't you? Someone like me: no chance. No one to see me safely home. No one to see me boiled, even, and have me bones sent back here.'

'But would you want them sent back here? To Newgate?'

The boy laughs.

'Maybe not. My old man'd only add 'em to the soup anyway, or give 'em to the dogs.'

They both sigh a bit and then the boy supposes the Irishmen will be gone by now, and he is just about to make himself scarce when he realises something.

'Wait,' he says, 'if you were all sick and that – how did you get to Agincourt?'

Sir Thomas has to smile.

'Ah,' he says. 'You will have to wait and see.'

And the boy gives him another of those sceptical looks, and when he is gone, Sir Thomas rises slowly to his feet and stands in his vacated place by the window, and through it he imagines he can see the Irishmen's cart loaded with corpses, being wheeled out along Fleet Street, perhaps, to be unceremoniously emptied in the river, or at some convenient bend in the road, out of sight of all the bishops' palaces. A moment later, the Christ's Church bell starts a slow and funereal tolling, and he wonders if it is for the two dead women, but who would have paid for that? And then he remembers Hartshorne's news from this morning, and he wonder if any bells will ring out to say goodbye to Cornelius the Shoemaker? And then he wonders if any will ring out to say goodbye to Master Bewscel or, Jesu preserve him, to Sir Thomas Malory?

And so does the long night draw in.

CHAPTER 6

How Sir Thomas lives to see Trinity Sunday, but how he is dretched in the night, and how then he thinks back on certain times past

That night Sir Thomas goes back in time, to when he was first constrained here. He wakes before dawn on Trinity Sunday to the sound of his own shouts, and finds he is sitting up clutching his sweat-sodden linens in a breathless stew of his own confusion. He stares about, flinching from – what? A horned devil? An armed man? The shades of two murdered women? Or is it that soft-whispering priest at his door? But there is nothing and no one. His cell is empty save for the cat, who stares unblinking in the solid bar of moonlight that falls from the ripped window cloth.

Afterwards he cannot sleep, and he lies listening to the agonies of Newgate at night: the groans, the screams, the distant rattle of chains, the endless mocking laughter from far below, and through the wall, Master Bewscel is at his harp again. How he longs for home. Why is he here? Why need he suffer so? If the king truly believes him guilty of some crime, then why is Sir Thomas not in the Tower with those other men this shoemaker Cornelius has implicated? Why, as his wife Elizabeth wondered, is he back here in Newgate – and not just here but back in the very same cell, one in which he has already passed so many years of his life?

Is the king a cruel man, is that it? Does he think this punishment worse than having Sir Thomas's feet burned, or his body stretched, or his head struck off? Or is he somehow not certain enough that Sir Thomas has committed the crimes of which he does not even accuse him?

He tries to think about him, about King Edward, for he is become certain that it is something within the man's character that will decide Sir Thomas's fate. He has met him, of course, a few months after his coronation, back in the autumn of 1461. He struck Sir Thomas just as he struck everybody else at the time as a very fine youth: tall, strapping and handsome. Every man and woman looked his way in admiration of one sort or another.

Sir Thomas had been curious to see this youth who had won the field that day at Towton, a battle fought in thick snow on Palm Sunday, when so many Englishmen were killed that by evening fall their bodies dammed the river thereabouts, and a man could walk dry-shod from one bank to the other. Twenty thousand Englishmen died that day alone. Twenty thousand! And many more afterwards, of course, of their wounds, and it was said the Northern Parts reeked for weeks thereafter with the bodies of men who'd tried to escape lying undisclosed in every copse and ditch across the land.

What would you expect to find in the eyes of the man who ordered such a thing? Remorse? Contrition? Guilt? Shame? Surprise? Pride, even? Pride that he was the sort of man who might be able to move other men to fight in such ways – and kill in such numbers – on his behalf? Sir Thomas had expected to find a mixture of all of the above, only when he looked into those handsome brown eyes, he found instead what he could only describe as lively interest.

'You are Sir Thomas Malory?' the king had asked. '*The* Sir Thomas Malory?'

'One of them, sir,' Sir Thomas had laughed, for it was possible there were others.

They had been at the palace at Whitehall, with the king in purple hose, sitting on a throne in his receiving room, surrounded by his court, and Sir Thomas had by then, he had to suppose, garnered some mild fame for having spent so long under lock and key, so unfairly, and in all that time never once succumbing to the maladies that can be relied upon to carry away most men so confined for so long a stretch, such as madness, or gaol fever, or self-murder.

'But you have spent the better part of these last ten years in prison, have you not?'

'On and off, sir, and may God bless you for dismissing the charges.'

'I never like to see an honest man wronged,' the king said, leaning forward as if to invite a confidence, and then he said in that low, aside voice: 'But tell me, Sir Thomas—'

And then his words had seemed to dry up and he had licked his lips and looked about the room – whether for inspiration or to check they were not overheard, Sir Thomas could not have said – but he could see the king framing the next question, and he had known with a plunging heart what that question would be, and he understood then with inescapable certainty that even though the king had indeed dismissed the charges against him, he – Sir Thomas – would never be free of the slander that had put him in gaol in the first place, and that his tormentors were even now able to laugh at him from beyond the vale, for if the King of England – who might be expected to learn the truth of anything if he so wished – doubted him, then so must all men doubt him.

It was at that moment that Sir Thomas had understood what had been done to him, and that for the rest of his life – and beyond, too, if he were ever to be remembered for anything at all – whenever his name was mentioned, men would always lean in and look about the place, wherever they were, and they would always lick their lips, just as the king had, and wonder how to frame the question, and having hit on some acceptable formula, then they would then, regardless of answer, always, always, always presume him guilty.

And in that great chamber, then, with its jewel-coloured glass and smoky fire, with its hearth piled high with enormous hunting dogs, all asleep, and with all those gentlemen gathered around in their velvets and their silks, he stood while all looked at him as if they might be able to judge his guilt by the look in his eyes, by the way he wore his boots, by the way he removed his cap in the king's presence, all speculating like horse-traders, dog-dealers, hawk-merchants, each hoping to form an opinion that they might later relate to their wives when they returned home that evening, on matters about which they could hardly have known one single true thing.

But it was the king's youngest brother, Richard, with scarce ten winters to his name, though already raised to the dukedom of Gloucester, who had saved a potentially shaming day: he had been standing at the king's shoulder, and he had at that moment coughed and asked Sir Thomas — with charming politeness — if it were true, as he had heard, that Sir Thomas had kept his mind busy during so many long years in prison by drawing out the whole book of the adventures of King Arthur and his noble Knights of the Round Table into English?

Sir Thomas had been taken aback.

How could he know?

It was not that he had kept his scribblings a secret, but nor did he cast the information about like peas in a field.

Nevertheless, the duke had pinned him with a very sober sort of gaze that spoke of some quality or other that Sir Thomas could not then quite name. He had essayed a diverting banality or two and each had been met in silence, and so after a long moment, he had found himself admitting before the distinguished crowd — but really, before that strange little boy — that yes, indeed, he had set himself the task of drawing out, in English, the true adventures of King Arthur and his noble Knights of the Round Table.

'Only it is by no means the whole book,' he had found himself gabbling. 'For a book that I needed was stolen from my cell, so I have had to leave off until I find it anew.'

The duke had leaned forward.

'Nevertheless,' he had said. 'I should like to read what you have done so far.'

And Sir Thomas had told him that it was as yet a rough old thing – which it was – unfit for the eyes of man, let alone a duke, nor his nostrils, come to that, for it was written on odd scraps of paper and a few worn pieces of parchment, some of which had been imperfectly cured, or cured a long time ago, and so the thing smelled terrible and left your hands greasy.

'And as I say, Your Grace, it is not finished.'

'When will it be finished?' the duke had asked.

When? *When?* What business is it of yours, you little wart? Sir Thomas had wanted to say, but under those dark little eyes he had wilted and found himself answering: 'Why, this very next month, your Grace.'

'This very next month,' the duke had echoed, neutrally.

'Well,' the king said, slapping his palms on his knees. 'Good. That is good, isn't it, Dickon?' the king had said, the ghost of a smile at his younger brother's precocity gracing those handsome lips. 'We are most relieved, aren't we, Dickon?'

But the boy had remained staring at Sir Thomas, unconvinced, until at length he had nodded very slightly, and stepped back into the shadows, and Sir Thomas had felt as if he had somehow been relinquished, let go, like a cat's mouse; and he had been grateful to be ushered on, his place taken up by some mercer, or a fruiterer or some such, someone from whom King Edward wished to 'borrow' money.

That was then, of course. When was it? Six years ago? Seven? And had he since even thought about finishing his book of King Arthur's deeds?

No. Or never seriously. There were times on wet Sunday afternoons perhaps that he thought he might take it up again, but something always prevented him, and so it was never done.

And now Sir Thomas sighs, and would rise, but he is at last comfortable on his miserable palliasse, and he realises with a strange sort of satisfaction that his back no longer pains him as it did, and then, scarcely a moment before cock-crow, he glides into the sweet release of sleep, only to be woken a moment later by the clamour of the city's bells and the flurry of a million pigeon wings, and he lies befuddled on his palliasse, arranging such thoughts as he has, before rising to pray for the usual mercy and the usual deliverance. This having been done, he resumes his pacing, impatient for the boy's arrival, for it seems his bad night has stirred up some bitter lees, and he is suddenly pinched with complete certainty that his time runs short.

Of course, it is Susan who brings him breakfast this morning. She still believes him to be out of his wits, so puts his ale and bread on the floor and then steps back, as if Sir Thomas were a dangerous dog. When he has eaten, he finds himself pacing the rushes once more, and turning over the same infernal questions, until he can stand it no longer and he turns almost suddenly to his coffer, as if pouncing on it, flinging it open and thrusting aside the top trays and the clothes, and from its depths he once more digs out those pages of his manuscript that concern King Arthur's war with the eleven kings, and he begins reading in his reading-aloud voice:

'Also there swore King Urience that was Sir Uwain's father, of the land of Gore, that he would bring six thousand men-at-arms on horseback. Also there swore King Idres of Cornwall, that he would bring five thousand men-at-arms on horseback. And also there swore King Cradelmas to bring five thousand men on horseback. And also there swore King Agwisance of Ireland to bring five thousand men-at-arms on horseback. Also there swore King Nentres to bring five thousand men-at-arms on horseback. Also there swore King Carados to bring five thousand men-at-arms on horseback.'

Sir Thomas stops.

Eleven kings really is too much, isn't it? He wonders how the boy would react to hearing all that, but before he has the chance to guess, just then the door opens silently, as only the boy can manage, and in he slides in person, and Sir Thomas cannot help but smile, though he is carrying someone else's slopping night soil bucket.

'I heard you reading?' the boy says, putting the bucket down.

'Still pondering the alliance of the eleven kings against King Arthur.'

'Eleven against one? Don't sound fair.'

'But the eleven do not have Merlin,' Sir Thomas says, gesturing at the page where for some now long-forgotten reason he has written the word Merlin in red ink. The boy peers.

'Merlin,' he says, as if he has read it.

Sir Thomas laughs.

'That is an M,' he points.

'M for Merlin. Yes.'

'Spare-the-Rod would be impressed,' he tells the boy. 'Though he would have preferred you do it in order. A, B, C and so on. Look. There is that A again, for Arthur, as you know.'

He points one out. Then a B.

'They follow an order, the letters. That is how they are learned. All of them together in a stream so that you can repeat them. That is how I learned them.'

The boy is mildly interested. Sir Thomas is struck by a thrilling idea.

'I can teach you, if you like?' he offers. 'Your letters.'

The boy is this time genuinely sceptical.

'We've hardly time enough as it is,' he says.

This produces a lurch in Sir Thomas's spirits.

'Where is he today?' he wonders. 'Your father?'

'Taken a forestaller from the other stairs down to Southwark, hasn't he?'

The boy nods towards the other side of the prison, where another flight of steps leads up to more cells, and where the cell of this well-enough-to-do forestaller must be. Sir Thomas cannot really imagine a wealthy forestaller — oftentimes they are somewhat desperate ogres who meet you outside the town gates to try to sell you goods cheaper than the rate of the market being held in the town's market square — but he must suppose they exist. Sir Thomas thinks to ask if the boy has heard anything of Cornelius the Shoemaker, or any of those other men taken up and who are now in the Tower, supposing the boy privy to some sort of network of gaol gossip, but the boy has heard nothing, and besides:

'Can you hurry your tale along?' he asks. 'I've got to clear the slops from the top two floors before my old man gets back, and if we keep on like this we'll never get there, will we?'

He means Agincourt, of course.

'But a life isn't made up of its good bits,' Sir Thomas tells him sternly, never before having given this idea a moment's thought. 'What defines a man's life is the time that passes between the good bits. The gaps. They are what make him. Make you. Just as a marriage is not made by the wedding, but all that comes after.'

The boy remains unconvinced.

'So what makes you you,' he says, 'is nearly shitting your life out in a ditch outside some poxy French town?'

Sir Thomas thinks about this for a moment.

'Exactly. Well, sort of, for it defined me in one way, and it meant that I was not defined in another.'

The boy's face wrinkles. He senses Sir Thomas is up to something, some storytelling trick, some narrative sleight of hand, and it is true that Sir Thomas does have a surprise for him, which may be unwelcome, but the blame for that cannot be laid at Sir Thomas's door, can it? Because, after all, who chooses to fall sick?

Not me, certainly, and yet I was made to endure the full lease of the bloody flux; a terrible, deep and dark descent, very nearly to death's door. The pain was mighty — in my head, my teeth, joints, bowels, eyeballs even — and when my body was not gripped in ice, it was roasted by fire, as if in Hell itself. Oftentimes I was out of my wits, delirious, and ever-prey to dreams in which I was tormented by unearthly apparitions, or made to believe my arms and legs were separate entities, like to fly off at any moment, and every other sort of horror beside.

Folo told me that my screams echoed around the castle walls, and could be heard throughout the town, where men crossed themselves at night, and shuttered their windows extra tight, as if the Devil himself were abroad, and I believed him.

In my lucid moments, I prayed for an end to my torment. I prayed for death.

But Master Knowles, Sir Richard's personal physician, took charge of my care at Warwick, and made me drink many pints of ale reinforced with bitter herbs and curious, meaty pellets that caught in my throat, and so, by and by, very gradually, I recovered, owing my life to Sir Richard Beauchamp, who had sent me home from Harfleur, and to Folo Bundsay who brought me home, and to this Master Knowles, who coaxed me back to health, with neither of the latter two giving much thought for their own safety. Lady Elizabeth, I was told, came to see me more than once, but both Folo and Master Knowles agreed it was best she not linger too long at my bedside.

'We never knowed what you'd be like to say,' Folo told me later, when I was somewhat recovered, though still abed.

Both he and Knowles smiled.

'The mind—' Knowles said, gesturing to suggest it was filled with things both known and unknown. He never finished his sentences, Master Knowles, but you always knew what he would have said.

By Advent tide, I was able to get up and totter about my chamber on legs that were now no thicker than a child's. I managed a circuit on that first morning before collapsing back onto the palliasse, sheened with sweat, the cage of my ribs heaving.

'You are like a new-born foal,' Folo laughed.

'Drink this,' Knowles told me. 'It will—'

'Give me strength?'

By the Epiphany I could manage the walk down the steps to the chapel and by Ash Wednesday — early that year — I was able, with Folo as a crutch, to emerge into the feeble sunshine of the bailey and there sit a while, shivering like a greyhound, clothes hanging from my frame like fresh-washed linen drying upon hawthorn branches. I watched Sir Richard's new pages as they wrestled and fought under the eyes of Masters Grimes and Yarrow, just as I had when I was young, and even though I was still shy of sixteen winters, I felt incomparably ancient, as if my youth were fled.

And if my body was diminished, so too was my spirit. Sometimes while I sat out — in a broad-brimmed hat of rushes to keep the sun from turning me red — men and women approached me and wished me good day and asked if I had been 'there' and we always knew what we meant by 'there'.

Agincourt. Bloody Agincourt—

'Wait!' the boy interrupts, back on his feet, fists balled at his hips. 'Are you telling me you *weren't* there? You weren't at Agincourt?'

Sir Thomas nods painfully.

The boy is furious.

'But you said!'

'I said we would come to it,' Sir Thomas reminds him. 'And we will.'

He is used to this sort of reaction, of course, and even expected it, but the boy feels so cheated that Sir Thomas continues without telling him the following things:

161

≫→ How, in the months that followed the battle, whenever people saw him hobbling along the pathway and they asked, were you there, he would admit that he had not been there because he'd had the bloody flux, which he'd caught at Harfleur, also fighting the Armagnacs, and how, on hearing this, they would step back, disappointed, disgusted even, as if he were a coward.

≫→ How, on seeing this, Sir Thomas vowed to lie in future.

≫→ How he then began to lie, and to embroider his own figure into the tapestry: yes, he had been there with the Duke of York — or: yes, he was with the king when he stood over Duke Humphrey — or: yes, it was him who slew the Duc d'Alençon—

≫→ How consolation of a sort came in the form of Lady Elizabeth Beauchamp, who one day brought him a very fine psalter, and told him that it was hers, and that she had found much pleasure therein, and that she hoped he would too.

≫→ How he had been unable to hold her gaze for fear he would never be able to tear his eyes from her.

≫→ How the pleasures he found within the psalter were those of putting his fingertips where she had once put hers, and how oftentimes he sniffed the pages, which smelled of parchment, of course, but also of leather and of far, far distant meadowsweet.

≫→ How often he sighed.

≫→ How at length he set aside the psalter and began to yearn for something else, something to remind him of who he was, or had been, or even had once hoped to be; something like that *Tale of Tristram de Lyonesse* that his father had sent him in Calais, and which was now long since lost. He sent word to Lady Elizabeth, asking if he might visit the library at Bordesley once more, where she had taken him as a boy, and where he had seen the *History of Merlin*, and an account of *The Deeds of Sir Lancelot* when he was not disguised as the Chevalier du Chariot, and of Sir Tristram himself, too, before he fell prey to that love potion and became enamoured of La Beale Isoud.

↬ How he then learned that she – Lady Elizabeth – had left for London, for it now transpired that Emperor Sigismund had come across the sea to England, bearing with him as promised the heart of St George, and that King Henry had given him the use of the Palace of Westminster, and had made him a knight of the Order of the Garter, and there was to be a tourney held in his honour, to which Thomas was not invited.

↬ How Thomas did his very best to try not to imagine the glories and the opportunities that such an event afforded.

↬ How he then heard tidings from London that Thomas West had been knighted, and that he was now Sir Thomas West. Sir Thomas West. Of course he deserved it, and of course it could not have happened to a more worshipful man, but Thomas's envy burned like quicklime, and it could only have been more painful if he had learnt that William Peyto had somehow distinguished himself.

↬ How such unworthy thoughts were driven from his mind when he learned that Spare-the-Rod had been tried and found guilty of heresy – and therefore of treason – and that he had been packed naked into a barrel, along with a

quantity of tar-smeared straw, and been burned to death
by the riverside in Gloucester, sometime in the week before
Easter. There had been nothing anyone could do for him,
Thomas's father wrote, and he went to his death bravely,
it was said, even singing until the pain bit. Afterwards the
soldiers rescued the iron hoops from the barrel, and smashed
his bones and let the tide wash away the greasy sludge of his
remains, and that was that.

How it was because of this, in among the national celebration
of Agincourt, that Thomas's family were among the few left
mourning their losses – startlingly few Englishmen died at
Agincourt – but unlike those families who had lost men in
battle, they mourned alone, and in secret.

How for reasons Thomas could not then have explained,
when he heard of Spare-the-Rod's death, he often found
his hand shaping itself to take hold of a quill and write
something. He wanted to see a mark made in memory of
his old tutor, and he rummaged through the bags that Folo
had brought back from Harfleur, his mouth clenched against
the ever-lingering stench of rot and mud that took him
straight back to the marshes outside Harfleur, and he found
his ink pot (dry), his quill-pen container (half-full) and that
long length of blank paper (still blank) that his mother had
sent him in Calais so that he might write letters back. He
resuscitated the ink with spit and wrote: 'Master Nicholas
Orme was a good man, and he did not deserve to die in such
pain, for he taught me my letters, and to swim, and he never
intended any harm to the king.' It felt good to write it out,
for on paper, it so seemed, his thoughts became truths.

⇥ How that was as far as Thomas ever got. For just then someone came back from wherever they'd been and called to him, and he put everything away again, and after that forgot his letters. His hand straightened, or reached for something else — a sword hilt perhaps — and so the summer wore on, and he began to regain his strength, which was just as well, of course, for though the battle was won, the war was not.

And with hardly a breath he continues:

But Agincourt was not the end of it. For already by St John's Day that next year — the sixteenth of the century and the fourth of King Henry's reign — French ships were harrying England's southern shore, and one of their armies had set about re-besieging King Henry's city of Harfleur, with her navy blockading any resupply.

I can scarcely describe how much this cheered me.

After all the tales of the slaughter at Agincourt, one would have believed there was scarcely a French knight left alive, and my chance to find worship in defeating one lay likewise buried, so to find that the Armagnacs were still fighting — and so fiercely — gave me hope. I summoned Folo from his mother's house and, along with two new horses — Joan and Likewise Joan, both bays — we set out along the road to Sandwich, and thence to Calais, arriving there a week later to find the city busier than ever, and, most astonishingly, that Folo's father, old Watkyn Bundsay, had survived his ordeal of hanging from the town's walls and was still very much alive, and working in the same tavern as before.

'Jumped when the tide was in, didn't I?' he told us. 'Before they cut the rope. But I can still smell the water, sometimes, on my skin, like.'

He sniffed the tips of his fingers.

The inn was down a few steps, off one of the alleyways that abutted the town walls, with a floor of grit and ash, where men sat hunched on benches, spitting on the ground between their feet, and the atmosphere was violently inhospitable.

Watkyn Bundsay was now its proud owner.

'Thought you always wanted a cat farm?' his son asked.

'Got out of the cat-farming game when old John Jiggins died,' he told us proudly. 'And got into the ransom business, but properly this time. Bought a couple of French gentles off some of the Duke of York's men when they came here after the battle. Sold them on, and bought a few more, sold them on. Your basic law of trading, that is, son: buy low, sell high. Remember that. And Frenchmen are easier to deal with than cats. Cleaner, too, despite what everyone says.'

It turned out that after Agincourt the townsmen of Calais would not let the king's men in through the city gates unless they paid a scandalous portage from all the plunder they'd amassed after the battle, and the prisoners they'd hoped to ransom when they got back to England. So a market was established: the king's men – sick, tired, starving, wounded and desperate soldiers – sold their hard-won treasure and captives and so on to the townsmen of Calais – traders, for the most part – just to be allowed through the gates.

'Like stealing from babies, it was,' Watkyn laughed. 'We bought them for a tenth of what they was worth, and ransomed 'em ourselves, just as if it was us what'd captured 'em! Easy!'

As he spoke, explaining his wretched scheme, I felt I was being dragged down into choking gritty slime that was foul with spoil and corruption. Its stench stoppered my mouth and nose and filled my lungs and heart. This – this was not what we fought for, not what we lived for. This had nothing to do with worship, honour, glory of arms! This was mere grubby commerce.

'I cannot believe the king stood by while this continued!' I told him.

Watkyn Bundsay snorted.

'Saints, Master Malory,' he laughed. 'The king indulged in it most of all!'

Something within me stiffened. Apart from my father's hints at the coronation, I had never heard anyone even so much as whisper ill of the king.

'You are — mistaken,' I told him, and he laughed again, as if I were a simpleton.

'Am I?' he chortled.

I could sense Folo tensing beside me. Around us men had stopped talking to listen in.

'And he did worse!' he jeered. 'You ask any of them Frenchmen in chains. They paid their ransom in good faith, but the king — our king! — still has 'em locked up, hasn't he? Hardly what you call chivalrous, eh, is it now, Master M?'

It was the first — and last — time anyone was to call me Master M.

The red rage boiled up. I snatched for the dagger my father had given me.

'Love God. Honour the King!' I shouted. But just as I was unsheathing the blade, a pair of arms locked around me from behind, pinning me like barrel hoops. It was not that I was weak — though perhaps I still was — it was that they were strong. I felt the man's breath in my ear.

'No. Need. To. Be. Hasty. Young. Thomas.'

It was William Boyce. Or Robert Boyce. And we left in good order.

But I still could not believe what Watkyn Bundsay had told me was true.

'Tell me! Tell me it is not true!'

No one would, for no one could. For it was true: the king had reneged on his promises. And not just once. Many times. To many men.

167

The boy stands, downcast, and even now, after so many years, Sir Thomas finds himself sickened by the thought of the dishonour of those days after Agincourt. He gets up and pours the boy some ale from the jug.

'So you see?' he says.

'Can't believe it,' the boy says.

'There were worse things to emerge too,' Sir Thomas tells him. 'Things that few of the men who had fought that day had mentioned before, or were willing to talk about now: how the king had ordered the slaughter of many unarmed French knights in cold blood; how some of them had been chained in a barn and burned alive.'

'No.'

'Yes. And back in Calais, plump with the profits, no one was interested in the rights and wrongs of the thing. It was unbelievable. I had lived my life one way – in the pursuit of worship – only to find – what? That I was a fool. And to be told I was so by such a man as Watkyn Bundsay! I could not stand it—'

But William, or Robert, held me fast and walked me home, and he would not let me go until my rage had cooled to sorrow. I shrugged him off then and walked the darkened lanes of Calais on my own. A thin rain was falling and from behind half-closed doors I could hear drunken shouts from men and women, and the occasional crash of benches falling and earthenware breaking. I kept clear of the night-watchmen as they set about their business, and I followed my feet wherever they took me. I thought about the king, and how he had shamed himself and everyone who had believed in him and, in all honesty, I cannot remember a lower night in all my life.

But it was strange. Although everything had changed, nothing had changed: I was still in Calais, and we were still Englishmen, weren't we? Our identities as fighting men were burned into our bodies and souls, and so even if the braver thing would have been to renounce it all and go home to join one of the Holy Orders perhaps, I stayed. I stayed and over the next week or so, the coruscating shame and rage of the king's betrayal faded. I was subsumed once again into the ranks of Englishmen wanting nothing more than to go out and fight the French, only in my case the desire was doubly strong, for not only did I want to redeem my not having been at Agincourt, I also wanted to prove to the world at large that not all Englishmen were base-born traitor churls.

I learned from Robert or William that they had both been at Agincourt, but they did not wish to talk about it, and they had also been among those who relieved Harfleur from the besieging Armagnac fleet just this past summer, and neither did they wish to speak of that. But they had fought a skirmish at sea, one told me, which every man dreaded for fear of drowning should he lose his footing.

'Never. Fight. At. Sea,' he said.

'I should relish the chance to fight anywhere,' I told them.

'Never. Fight. At. Sea,' the other one echoed, more firmly this time.

But it was already September, the very end of the campaigning season, and there was little or no chance of fighting now until spring. Instead, I was back on guard duty, overseeing a couple of companies of Sir Richard's men, merely passing time on the city walkways, certain that I had missed every chance to prove myself, to get myself knighted, to become the man I had believed I was destined to be. I confess I thought about that arrow then, the one my father shot into the sky at my birth, and how it had deviated from its true path, and if I am honest, and I am ever that, I blamed my father for my predicament.

And it was almost exactly then that one of those great fat overladen Genoese carracks was sighted from the lighthouse, lumbering its way northwards through the Narrow Sea, perhaps hoping to find shelter up north from the stormy weather everyone was predicting in the south. It was one of the ships that men such as Robert and William Boyce had fought off Harfleur, and seeing it struggling in heavy seas off Sangatte, bells were sounded in Fort Risban, and from all over Calais men came running, including me. This was my chance! My chance to prove myself as good as if not better than any man who'd ever fought at Agincourt. I ran to the dockside only to find hundreds of men gathering in a great crush, and I pushed and pulled and forced myself forward towards one of the smaller boats. And whom should I find at the head of the gangplank?

Sir Thomas West.

I had not seen him since I had left Harfleur, when he was cold with me over letting William Peyto know that his lady was called Elaine. He was now much bigger than me, or so it seemed, and he stood there, perhaps as old as eighteen, so sure of himself in his brigandine and boots, his hand on his sword hilt, staring out from under the low brim of his steel helmet.

And he had a scar! On his cheek. It tugged his eye down and gave him an unnaturally sceptical look. I wanted so much to be him.

'Malory,' he said without much of a smile. 'God give you good day.'

I threw myself shamelessly on his good graces.

'Sir Thomas,' I said. 'Please let me aboard. I will do anything.'

He looked very scornful.

'We have a full contingent of men-at-arms,' he said.

He stepped back to let a troop of bowmen pass down the gangplank. I could not shoot a bow half as well as any one of them, of course, but just then a hugely burly man shouldered me out of the way. He had naked arms, muscles like gunstones, and he was carrying a barrel of what turned out to be black powder.

'If he can pick up that barrel,' the man said, nodding at me and then at a barrel that still stood a little further along the wharf, 'then he can be my mate.'

I hurried to the barrel. I strained every fibre picking it up, but I managed, and I toppled myself towards the plank. Every moment's delay was another during which the carrack would get further away, and so West stepped aside.

'Go on then.'

'Thank you, Sir Thomas!' I told him. 'Thank you. You shall have no cause to regret it.'

Down I staggered, carried by the weight of the barrel, down onto the deck of the little boat that the men called a balinger.

'Up here,' the master gunner called.

I had to put the barrel down before I dropped it, and I rolled it across the deck to the tower at the fore of the ship, in which he stood, doing something to a short, black-barrelled gun while his mate — now my immediate superior — was fiddling with the complex and cleverly constructed trebuchet that loomed overhead: a long pole balanced on a pivot, with a huge, lead-wrapped stone as counterweight.

Meanwhile many more men were coming aboard. I was pleased to see Sir Baldwin Strange among them. I assumed he — rather than Sir Thomas West — would be in command and would be the one to report back on the day's events to Sir Richard, or even the king, so now was my chance to show what I could do by way of deeds of arms. It was a chance I would not lose.

It turned out that I was lucky being the gunmaster's second mate, for it meant that I was temporarily excused my turn at the oars. This job was given first to strong-backed bowmen, who turned their muscles to bending the oars and guiding us, under the bellowed instructions of the ship's master's mate, past Fort Risban and out into the dingy, whipped-up waters of the Narrow Sea. Men in the fort's battlements waved to us and bellowed things we could not hear over the creak of the oars and the constant resentful swearing of the bowmen.

When we reached the sea proper, where the water turned green and became very choppy, the sailors hauled up the sail and the ship took lumbering flight. We still could not see the carrack, though we believed we were heading in its direction. Five other English boats came with us and I saw Sir Richard himself in one of them, and Sir Thomas West pointed out **Lord Talbot** in another, and we all knew we were in a race to find the Genoese carrack first, and in all the buffeting and salt-spray no man could resist grinning.

I gave the gunmaster's mate my name, but he did not wish to know it.

'Put a stone in the sling,' he told me.

Below the deck, on which the rowers were heaving their oars, was a pile of ten stones, each as big as a man's trunk. My task was to bring one up and lay it in the canvas cradle of the trebuchet, and then hook the rope on the end of the cradle so that when the lead stone was dropped, the beam would rise, hurling the stone a hundred paces or more. If it hit a ship in the right place, it would punch a hole through the deck and the ship would sink.

It took all my strength to lift the stone, but an idle man-at-arms helped me, and together we got it all tied up.

'Will the carrack have one of these?' I asked the gunmaster. He was head-bent over a smaller gunstone, tapping it with a hammer to shape it for his cannon.

'Five or six,' he said, not really looking up. 'And guns aplenty.'

I nodded and smiled and looked away. Just one of those stones could sink us.

'I can swim, you know,' I blurted.

He looked up at me.

'Can you now?' he said.

It was as if I had told him I read poetry.

We sailed all day, letting the wind take us, the oarsmen doing the best they could as the sea began to run high, and yet still we could not find the carrack. By evening I began to doubt its existence and feel it was all useless. I took off my helmet and sat on it. I wished I had brought some food. And then, just as the sun was dipping in the west, there was a shout.

The carrack's light.

We gave a ragged cheer.

We kept on after her all night – what else was there to do? – as the seas roughened and the wind picked up, and not a man among us was not sick, even the captain, so that at dawn we surveyed the carrack from a deck slicked with vomit and worse.

By Jesu! She was huge! Many times bigger than any of our little ships.

'Has she grown in the night?' I asked West, hoping to rekindle our friendship.

He shook his head and said nothing, but stared out to sea with his jaw clenched, and I was left feeling like a child. I would show him.

Meanwhile our men-at-arms had taken up the oars as a fire was lit on the cooking stone so the bowmen could light their fire-arrows and we – able to move faster than the carrack thanks to our oars – edged up on her, and now I could see her gunwale and castle were crowded with men with crossbows and shields and above them hung the trebuchets that the gunmaster had promised, and guns too, their black snouts wreathed in smoke.

We were not the first to engage. That honour was taken by Sir Richard in his boat, who came alongside the carrack from one side, while the boat commanded by **Sir Gilbert de Umfraville** came along the other side. When they were within bowshot, the archers sent their burning arrows soaring. I watched them rise, each a flaming comet trailing black smoke, so beautiful, so fragile, and then drop into the men on the carrack's deck. Even before they'd landed, more were on the way.

The slingstones were also launched from each boat, with a tremendous twang and swoosh as the beams hurled the great stones through the air, so heavy and ponderous that you might have caught one with an arrow had you a mind, but when they came down, each stone could be devastating. One of Sir Richard's stones crashed into the carrack's timbers, but the other splashed harmlessly into the sea.

Then the carrack launched its own slingstones, and though these both missed Sir Richard's boat, the splash each made towered over the deck.

Then there was a rippling thunder of gunfire from the carrack's two towers, and the sea around Sir Richard's boat erupted in a frenzy of splashes, as if the water itself were furious, and when the wind dragged the smoke aside, you could see damage had been done: the dead and wounded lay scattered among the shattered staves and ragged sailcloth, and after a moment's confusion the little boat yawed away.

Now it was our turn to bait the bear. My blood felt as if it were molten, and I was tingling all over my body. I could hardly breathe. I was going to fight. Here was worship. Here was the chance to prove myself. Although there was little I could do, my whole life seemed to have led up to this moment. The archers around me dropped to their knees and made a cross on the deck and then bent to kiss it. Then they nocked their arrows and waited, poised while their captain passed among them with a flaming torch, letting them set the fatted tow in their cages alight.

'Wait for it,' he said. 'Wait for it.'

I too waited on the master gunner's instructions. He was on the forecastle, his eyes narrowed, trying to judge the distance so that he could yank out the holding pin of the sling. We swayed with the motion of the rising sea. He kept glancing backwards as the waves surged in, and then forwards to the carrack's side.

'Draw!' their captain shouted at the archers. They bent and drew, and as they did so he called: 'Loose!' And there was a range of twangs and grunts and woofs of expelled air and the arrows sprang away. A strange, hellish smell filled the air as they lit more of their arrowheads and each man loosed three more arrows as we closed. The men-at-arms on the oars cheered them on. West was standing in the middle of the deck. He had a poleaxe ready and looked as if he could conquer anyone and anything.

'Ready?' the gunmaster called down to me.

I had no idea what he meant.

He gestured for me to step back, away from the stone, which lay at my feet, cradled in its sling of canvas. I stepped back. The gunmaster nodded, and then, judging the moment a wave tipped us on a favourable angle, he pulled the pin. The lead-wrapped stone dropped, the beam jumped and then strained and flexed with the weight of the stone. It seemed to bend as if it were of sinew rather than ash wood, and then as the deck of the boat came up, so the stone lifted off the deck in the start of a perfect arc. It began slowly then picked up speed, and I am certain it would have hurtled across the sea and cracked into the side of the carrack, had not something gone wrong. The cradle twisted. Or snapped. Or slipped off its hook too soon. The stone hit the beam and then slipped from the cradle.

And underneath it stood Sir Thomas West, waiting for his moment of glory, looking elsewhere.

The stone drove him down into the deck. It crushed his head to a paste, and hit the deck with a sullen boom, its impact muffled by poor Sir Thomas West's flesh. He lay there under it, and it lay there over him, a huge, grey, gritty and malevolent boulder, as if cemented to the deck in the matter from his brainpan. Every man not loosing a bow stopped and stared. Sir Baldwin Strange clenched his eyes and made the sign of the cross. All aboard did likewise, except me. I could not move.

But our little balinger ploughed on and now suddenly we were under fire from the carrack. Gunstones thumped down at us from above with terrible, shattering effect. One of the archers was hit in the leg and lost it below the knee. Another wheeled away with a wound in his belly as big as a clenched fist. The gunwale vaporised in a shower of splinters. A man was bellowing in pain. All I could do was stand, gripping a rope, and just stare down at Sir Thomas West, watching his blood spread across the deck, become dilute with seawater, other men's blood and the slicks of vomit, and I was struck by just how strange a sight it was, for he lay on his front, with his head buried under the rock, and it seemed the rock *was* his head.

Nothing else mattered. I could hear and see nothing else. Only Sir Thomas West's poor dead body. I cannot say then if I thought much of his good Lady Elaine, and his chastity, or anything, though I did later. I just stared at him.

Oh God. Oh God.

'Malory! Malory there!'

Sir Baldwin Strange was shouting at me.

'Take command!'

The rest of the day, after that single defining moment, became a blur. I suppose I now must thank all those hours I'd spent with Vegetius learning the command of men, for in the day that followed I did not seem to need to think greatly about what I was doing. Perhaps there was little that needed to be done? I cannot say.

All I know is that we heeled away from the carrack after our first attempt, and then after our second. We baited the brute all day, taking turns, one boat after the other, nipping away at her heels until night fell early because of the thick cloud, and the wind was shrieking in our ears, and the waves were tossing us as if we were nutshells in a mill-race.

In all that time, I never once caught the eye of the gunmaster. Not once. We both knew I was to blame for the slingstone's twisted cradle. We both knew I was to blame for the killing of Sir Thomas West. They made me pick him up, dragging his body out from under the rock – by his heels, after a slight, separating tug – and they stood back and watched while, hot with guilt and shame, I levered my friend's bloody, headless body over the gunwale and into the deep green sea. Scalding tears filled my eyes as I did so.

But his was not the only body we had to put over the side that day, for by its end five or six more had followed behind, including – though I was too numb to mourn him at the time – that of Sir Baldwin Strange, who had been killed by a crossbow bolt shot from the Genoese carrack. He was a wise old head who had been kind to me, in his way, and at any other time I would have wept to see him go. But we soon had other things to worry about, for the tempest that had been forecast was about to hit us, and it came as with the wrath of God. We spent the night on our knees, alternately praying and baling, clinging on to whatever we might, while driving winds and mountainous waves took us away from the carrack, away from one another and away from the shore.

'You caused this!' a bowman shouted at me. 'You!'

How far and fast we went I cannot say, but by the evening of the second day the storm relinquished its grip upon our tiny ship, and we came to believe we might live. At dawn there was nothing to be seen but the sky the colour of a duck's egg, and the guilty sea herself, sliding marble green and serene beneath our bows.

The ship's master took the tiller and pointed us eastward, and for two or three days we lived off fish and blood-tinged rainwater, until with God's grace we found a strip of land the captain took to be Holland, and we made our way south along the Flanders shore, across the mouth of the Rhine, from which I'd sailed on our way back from Konstanz in happier times, until finally we saw Calais. We limped in, in a sad and sorry state, a week after we had left, much diminished in numbers, health and spirits.

In all that time, not a man had spoken to me save to blame me for everything. My final duty – given me by the gunmaster – was to lift the stone from what remained of the wreckage of poor Thomas West's head. The sailors and the remaining men-at-arms and bowmen watched in silence while I prised the stone up. Any gore had long since been washed from the deck, but there were the twisted remnants of West's helmet and even, dear God, his rosary beads to which was attached a scrap of gauze that I knew to be a favour from his Lady Elaine. I confess to snivelling not merely in grief for West and his death, but in molten self-pity.

And there on the dock stood William Peyto, swaggering, grinning Peyto, veteran of Agincourt, who had already heard the word.

'What've you done with old West, Flycatcher?' he jeered. 'You'll never win your spurs that way! Not by killing the king's favourite knights! Pshaw!'

And just as they were that first time, Sir Thomas and the boy have been so intent on the story that neither hears footsteps in the passage without until it is too late, and the door is flung open with a crash, and into their sombre scene erupts Brunt the father in all his fist-flailing, pig-eyed, no-longer-drunken fury. The boy scrabbles back, but his father swipes at him and catches him such a buffet that he is sent spinning like a corn doll across the room to thump against Master Bewscel's wall. He slides to the floor, blood in his nostrils, and a little shower of dust from the daub above, and lies there, dazed out of his wits. Brunt strides across, aiming to kick his ribs, but Sir Thomas rouses himself from the past and from his bed, and he stands to intervene.

178

'No!'

But Brunt shoves Sir Thomas back and he trips and is sent sprawling, and his back spasms again. For a moment he is utterly stilled and can only watch as Brunt picks the boy up by his ear and drags him scuffling back across the cell and out through the door. There are fat tears in the boy's eyes, and he whimpers 'sorry' and 'please', but still his father sends him tumbling down the stairs.

Then he turns back to Sir Thomas, all quivering menace, but before he can spit out an insult, Sir Thomas is back up on his feet and faces him, close enough to smell the reek that comes off him, and even though Brunt dwarfs him, he holds Brunt's gaze and lifts his chin, and dares him: dares him to use that bog-oak club, dares him to use his much-scarred fists, dares him, even, to use that much-scarred forehead to butt him.

'You do not dare,' he tells him.

And Brunt clenches and seethes and by Jesu he does dare! He pulls back the fist, and if he unleashes it, it will pass through Sir Thomas's head, but — no. Some roving calculation is made, somewhere deep behind those piggy little eyes, somewhere within that massive head wherein lurks a brain the size of a walnut, and there is an infinitesimal waver, a hesitation as emotions war with one another, and caution wins, and so his focus slips and his gaze slides from Sir Thomas's, and Sir Thomas knows he has won.

'Get out of here,' he snarls. 'Get out. You churl. You bully.'

Brunt lowers his fist, feigning as if he never meant it anyway, with a sneering smile on his horrible wet lips.

'And if you so much as touch that boy again,' Sir Thomas presses on, 'then I swear upon my sword that I shall see you in the stocks.'

Brunt doesn't say anything, but instead hawks up a great quantity of phlegm from deep within and he holds it in his mouth as you would an oyster, and he looks down at Sir Thomas, his face a study of disdain. Sir Thomas braces himself to receive a face-full of the man's spittle, but at the last moment, Brunt does not even dare that, and instead he turns and shoots his gobbet of snot onto Sir Thomas's coffer, and then he turns and lumbers off after his son, pulling the door to and ramming the locking bar home.

Sir Thomas stands and closes his eyes, and he can feel his whole body shaking, and rarely has he ever felt so torn between joy — at his victory — and sorrow — for the boy — but also confusion: why did Brunt not dare punch him? Why did he hold back? What is the nature of his power over these men who hold him captive?

CHAPTER 7

How Sir Thomas is given cause for hope, and how he must console the son of a certain churl

It is four days later, the fourteenth of Sir Thomas's incarceration, and summer's first punishingly hot day, with at least ten flies cutting squares through the sullen air of Sir Thomas's cell, and Master Hartshorne sends word, along with a cone of Kentish strawberries, that he hopes will make up for his recent apparent want of care, caused – he writes with pride – by his being among those summoned this coming Saturday to join the king in offering prayers at St Paul's for the king's sister's safe passage across the Narrow Sea to Flanders.

His attendance, he writes, has necessitated some fiddly tasks, however; not the least of which has been to oversee the raising of enough money to buy two fine bowls of silver, each to be filled with fifty pounds in gold, on behalf of the guild of the Master Stainers – with whom Sir Thomas recalls Hartshorne has some obscure connection – to be presented to the princess as a wedding present upon her departure.

It is only then – on the letter's other side – that Hartshorne reaches the point of his writing, which is to say that also attending Mass, and then leading the procession down Cheapside and all the way out to Essex afterwards, will be not only the king, his sister – obviously – and their brothers of Clarence and of Gloucester, but also, most importantly in this instance, the Earl of Warwick.

The Earl of Warwick!

Sir Thomas looks up. He tries to imagine Hartshorne sidling up to the earl, stirrup to stirrup, and reminding him of his duty in regard to his long-suffering liegeman Sir Thomas Malory.

He cannot. Or, he can, but not successfully.

The earl will have him horsewhipped.

Still, though, that is some cause for hope, isn't it? That is some-thing to get him through this day.

He shares the strawberries with the boy, who brought him the letter, and who now stands at the window and peers out towards St Paul's, whose bells even now peal in celebration for the queen's sister. When the boy turns back to face Sir Thomas, Sir Thomas cannot help but wince afresh, for his eye is a gluey slit in a fat, purple bruise and his lips are lumpy as cheap sausages. The swelling has lent him a truculent mien which today suits him well, for it turns out he *has* a truculent mien.

'I will run away,' he mumbles. 'I will run away. Tonight. Like you done, across the Narrow Sea. I'll go to Calais and become a soldier. He'll never find me there, and if he does, my men'll kill him. Put him in that basket with a knife and a cabbage.'

Sir Thomas smiles one of his father's downward-pointing smiles – that's not quite how it happened, is it? – that the boy interprets as doubting.

'I will,' he repeats. 'Just you watch. I will.'

'Then to whom shall I tell the rest of my story?'

The boy tuts and gestures to the window.

'The pigeons wouldn't care that you weren't at Agincourt when you said you was.'

Sir Thomas sighs.

'Where is he today, your father?' he asks, knowing the boy would not risk being here if his father were anywhere within the building. It has taken him four days to muster the courage to come at all.

'Taken old Lewd-Act down the Guildhall again, hasn't he? They switched his hearing to this morning.'

It is strange, Sir Thomas thinks, that though he has heard Master

Bewscel singing, playing his harp, coughing occasionally and being shuffled to and fro for various reasons, he is yet to clap eyes on the man himself.

'He's been a nice old stick, you know?' the boy goes on. 'Always kind and that. Still, though.'

He ends with a shrug that makes him wince. It must also be strange, Sir Thomas supposes, to have such a quick turnover of – of what? Friends? Associates? Masters? Then he wonders again – or cannot stop himself wondering – what exactly Master Bewscel's lewd act involved? He still cannot bring himself to ask.

'They might find him innocent?' he offers.

'They might,' the boy concedes.

'Or perhaps the jurymen will not turn up again?'

Again that half shrug of those bony shoulders. Yes. It is always possible.

Then there is a silence, which Sir Thomas puts out of its misery by asking the boy if he'd care to hear of a real battle.

'An honest-to-God one?'

'An honest-to-God one, involving those five hundred magically attired knights of Lombardy.'

The boy had almost forgotten them.

'You said it was a thousand. And anyway, he's left me to muck out the stable, and says if it ain't done by the time he gets back, he'll black this eye and all.'

He points a dirty finger.

'You should do what needs to be done first,' Sir Thomas tells him, just as he used to tell his own son, 'and then you are free to do as you wish.'

The boy pulls an on-one-hand-and-then-on-the-other face. He looks exhausted, and when he sits on Sir Thomas's coffer he puts his elbows on his knees and his face in his palms, and Sir Thomas waits in pitying silence.

'So after you killed that bloke?' the boy asks eventually, looking up from behind his hands. 'The one whose head you dropped the stone on? They didn't hang you or nothing? That's not why you was in here for so long?'

'Oh. No. Sir Richard knew it was not intentional, and that I was not to blame. Or not entirely, anyway. Worse things happen at sea, he said. He told me about a group of knights sailing for France once who were kept ashore by unfavourable winds, and so they took up with the sisters of a local convent. Three weeks later the winds changed, so they set sail, but by then they were attached to the sisters, and the sisters likewise to them, so they took the women with them. Only it is bad luck to have women aboard, and so when a storm blew up and threatened to sink the ship, the men threw the women into the sea. The storm abated, the ship sailed on, and the men fought bravely for their king and nothing was ever said about it again.'

The boy looks unsettled.

'By our Lady,' he murmurs.

'So no, there was no official punishment—'

But my shame was complete.

As rumours of how I had killed Sir Thomas West circulated among the earl's retinue, partly – mostly – because William Peyto spread them like dandelion seeds on a summer's breeze, my father wrote and suggested I swap my red surcoat for one of blue. With a heavy heart I left Sir Richard Beauchamp's retinue, and Folo Bundsay, and his mother, and William and Robert Boyce, and Joan and Likewise Joan, and for the following few years I served in Normandy under **Lord Grey of Codnor**. Had times then been less scrambled I might have undertaken a pilgrimage to Rome, perhaps, or joined my uncle in the Knights Hospitaller and journeyed to Rhodes to crusade against the Turks, for what was required of me was a stretch of penance, a period of selfless expiation to atone for my sins, but times were turbulent, and no Englishman with skill in arms could be spared to wander off in search of personal salvation when there was work to be done in Normandy.

Instead, I shunned worship and honour, and accepted the meanest, least noble, least rewarding tasks. Nothing was too base for me: while King Henry led his triumphant knights through the streets of Paris to hear the Te Deum sung in the cathedral at Notre Dame, I was guarding a bridge outside Carentan; while the king was being married to his French princess, I was escorting a barge of imperfectly salted herring along the River Orne; and while the king took his new bride on honeymoon, I was captain of a party of eight Normans, not one of whom had all his limbs, overseeing the hanging of an Englishman who had stolen a silver cup from a church outside Carentan.

Sir Thomas can see this is hardly stirring stuff. So though he believes what then followed was and is important, or telling, he decides he will not overload the boy with such details as:

➻ How it was just about then, when Thomas was at his sickest with shame, that he came once more upon that blank spool of paper his mother had sent him all those months ago, which he had carried around untouched since the day he had written his small paean to Spare-the-Rod, and on which he now began, hesitantly, and far from prolifically, to write down such thoughts as came to him. How he so wanted to ape poor dead Sir Thomas West and the way in which he had filled in his *zibaldone*, with sketches and poems and appeals of amorous ardour addressed to, or about, Lady Elaine, but since he was consumed with far darker thoughts than those in which Sir Thomas West had indulged, he wrote no love poems,

185

made no observations about the changing seasons and drew no gargoyles or cleverly wrought sword crosses. He wrote occasional observations about hunting, about food, about a hole in his boot and about a horse that kicked a child.

↬ How he could not yet bring himself to call this scrap of paper a — let alone *his* — *zibaldone*, and how for shame he hid it very carefully at the bottom of his bag.

↬ How he was not completely cut off in his obscurity, for his father's letters found him, though rarely did they bring joyous news. One — written in the second week after the Epiphany in 1421 — brought the sad tiding that Lady Elizabeth Beauchamp had died, of causes unknown, which occasioned much grief. She was the perfect lady, Thomas had always believed, unmatched in beauty and in learning by any he was yet to lay eyes upon, and so kind and gentle in spirit that after her passing even her bear cub — the one Folo Bundsay had nursed as a child, but which had grown into something altogether more daunting — pined to death, as if it meant to join its mistress in Heaven.

↬ How later that year a second letter arrived, equally unwelcome, to tell Thomas that his brother John had drowned in the stock pond. He was yet to see his eleventh winter, and they believed he had been trying to fish out an arrow he had loosed at the heron.

↬ How towards the end of that year another letter came, this one bearing good tidings: the queen — the French princess, Katherine — had given birth to a healthy son and heir to King Harry, and to celebrate there were some efforts at feasting in the garrison (a half-pipe of brackish cider and a porpoise coddled in pig fat and bay leaves), for it was said that this boy, to be the third consecutive Henry on England's throne, and the sixth to date, would be the one to unite the two crowns, England and France, and so bring lasting peace to both kingdoms.

And indeed I may have lived out the rest of my life in this self-sought obscurity, had not sometime in the tenth year of the king's reign, by which time I had endured perhaps twenty-two winters of my own, another letter came, this time brought by a messenger accompanied by a muffled drum, bringing shocking, unbelievable tidings: barely six months after the birth of his son, King Henry — the fifth of that name, and may God assoil his soul — died.

It was said that he paid for twenty thousand masses to be said for the speeding of his soul to Heaven, and there was much lamenting his passing, for he was a noble king, and there was talk of raising him to become one of the Nine Worthies along with Arthur, and Charlemagne, and Godfrey of Bouillon. But it was not to be — though one of the carriages that transported the late king's body back to England bore the arms of that noble king: an azure shield with three golden crowns — and when we Englishmen had dried our tears, we looked around fearfully, for the Armagnacs, under their new 'king', Charles, had taken heart from the fact that we now had an unweaned babe for king, and they soon forged treaties with the Scotch and the Castilians for more troops and, receiving them, became emboldened to try to fight their way to Rheims, so they could crown this new king of theirs in the same cathedral in which they had crowned every monarch since Charlemagne.

Why do I tell you this? Because this turned out to be another one of those odd, distantly borne breezes that buffeted my wayward arrow back upon its true course: foreseeing an Armagnac onslaught, the new king's uncle — the old king's brother, the doughty **Duke of Bedford** — summoned every available Englishman in France to join him at Rouen. So in my twenty-third summer I was winkled out of my internal exile – my hermit's life – and for the first time since before the siege of Harfleur I set off to join an English army in the field.

I cannot say what would have become of me had I not: I suppose I should have been murdered in some depressing wayside scuffle, or married a Norman girl against her will and drunk myself to death on that apple spirit they have over there, as did so many other Englishmen. But what happened next marked another great change in my life and made me the man I am today.

I brought with me to Rouen ten archers and John Ap-Moffat, a man-at-arms to whom I was supposed to pay ten pounds a year, but who somehow ended up costing me far more. He was of Welsh extraction, with a long scarf-swagged neck he claimed was forever cold, even in summer, and who was so wearyingly self-deprecating that if you took what he said at face value you would be surprised he could put one foot before the other, let alone take himself to war and make a very handsome profit from it without ever seeming to stir his stumps.

I was also reunited with Folo Bundsay, thanks be to Jesu, who came from Warwick at my summons, bringing with him two horses – whose names escape me – a donkey and his mother's blessings.

From Rouen we set out for the town of Ivry, fifty miles west of the city of Paris, on a bend in a river, to which an army under the **Duke of Suffolk** was waiting – as had then become the custom – for the garrison to capitulate, as agreed, on Assumption Day, should they not be relieved by Armagnac troops before then.

But at Ivry that year it was different. This time the Armagnacs of the town garrison really seemed to believe they would be relieved, and so they called out to us from the walls – morning, noon and night – taunting us with the shame of losing to them at Baugé, two or three years ago, back in 1421.

'We will kill another of your English princes!' was the sort of thing they'd shout.

Which was absurd, of course, for though, yes, they had managed to kill the Duke of Clarence, we'd killed or captured almost every prince or duke they'd ever had.

'And we are twice your number!' was also something they'd shout.

'And we have the Army of Scotland!'

This made us laugh. The Scots!

And also: 'We have the Lombards, who have magical armour that no English arrow can pierce!'

Which gave us pause.

Really?

For we had heard rumours that such armour existed, and that it was owned by these horsemen from Lombardy, and though no man could credit such a thing — our bodkin heads could pass through a hand's breadth of seasoned oak, for the love of Jesu — it was clear the Armagnacs believed it, and they held high hopes not only of their town being relieved by these same Lombards, but also of them then beating us in the field.

When Assumption Day dawned, then, we waited, tense and anxious all day, but there was no sign of any Lombard or Scottish armies, and so at sunset we watched those same Armagnacs who'd taunted us come trudging from the town gates just as the church bells rang for Sept.

'Where are your Scotch friends now?' we all laughed. 'Where are your magic knights of Lombardy?'

The Armagnacs cursed us and said we were damned by God.

And still we laughed.

But it turned out the Lombards *were* nearby! There were more than five hundred of them, as was promised, as well as ten thousand Scots, and the same again of Castilian and French troops, which amounted to near twice our number, and they were to be led by

Sir Poton de Xaintrailles, which was a name to marvel at, as well as another Armagnac known simply as **La Hire**. This translated as The Fury.

'Who calls himself that?' I wondered aloud, and that night it was generally agreed that these Armagnacs and Lombards and Scots and so on thought too highly of themselves, and those of us who knew no better about false courage laughed, and that night we slept more easily, but in the morning it was discovered that this Sir Poton de Xaintrailles and The Fury and their men had come around behind us and cut us off, and were waiting for us, ready to do battle outside a little town calling itself Verneuil.

This news was too much for some of our Norman allies who, after we had broken bread and heard prayers, deserted our lines. Most went west, back home, but others broke their oaths and went east, transferring their allegiance to the Armagnacs and so unbalancing our numbers even further, which was compounded when the Duke of Bedford sent away his Burgundian troops because he did not trust their leader, **Sir L'Isle-Adam**, who had once been caught treating with the Dauphin, and whom he was certain would turn his troops on us in the heat of the battle that was to come.

He may have been right. Who knows? But we were now the rump of the Duke of Bedford's army, and as we collected our horses from the lines, I confess I offered up a prayer that we too would return to Rouen, to gather a greater force. But it was not to be – the challenge was too great, and so despite being vastly outnumbered, we marched on Verneuil.

Guns make every wagon train slow these days, but even then, when we were relatively unencumbered, and the land thereabouts flat as a dish of gruel, it took us two days to cover the thirty miles to Verneuil. We threw up such a quantity of yellow dust that we were lucky not to have choked to death before we got there. On the second night, with the prospect of battle before us, we set our guard in a forest from which our bowmen cut their stakes, denuding it save for the oldest trunks, and at dawn those of us who had slept rose early and set our consciences in order and then we stood to hear afresh the Ordinances of War read by one of the Earl of Salisbury's captains, and then we – Ap-Moffat and I – mounted up and set off to find our enemy.

I noticed Ap-Moffat had found himself a poleaxe, the like of which I'd first glimpsed in Konstanz, and occasionally since, but now had time to examine at leisure. It was a beautiful if chilling thing, the result of a clever man sitting down to work out how to make the nastiest, most efficient killing tool possible and then a hundred other men seeing it and saying to themselves that that was exactly the kind of thing they'd most like too. It was a shaft of oak, around four foot long, topped and tailed with various spikes of steel. At one end was a hammer punch, balanced out by a long spike like a huge crow's beak. Next to it, my own weaponry – the dagger my father had given me, still in its sheath on my belt, and my sword, which was quite sharp and quite well balanced, though the leather on the handle was unravelling – looked shabby and ineffectual.

'Wherever did you get that?' I asked.

He told me he had found it on a market stall selling cast-offs and bits and pieces of scrappy field plate, overseen by an ex-nun.

'You found it in a *fripperer's*?'

You only ever find noisome rags and unmatched and rusted stirrups at fripperers' stalls. Or at least I only ever have, but not Ap-Moffat, apparently.

'Whenever I go somewhere new I always have a look at the fripperers' stalls first. I never ever find anything, except very occasionally, though I am always robbed when I do. I think they see me coming!'

He laughed and rolled his eyes as if to wonder at himself.

On we trudged, along a narrow road through a forest of scrubby pines, and then, sometime in the mid-morning, out into vast fields given over to strips of onions and garlic, and whatever else it is that French peasants grow, where at last we found our enemy waiting: a broad front, almost horizon to horizon, standing many thousands shoulder to shoulder, under a great host of banners, and at each wing, left and right, a huge number of horsemen, already mounted: the magically attired riders of Lombardy.

'It is like the army of the eleven kings,' Ap-Moffat said beside me. 'I only wish we had Merlin.' I only wished I had never told him the story.

Our trumpets sounded and new orders were bellowed, and for half a Mass there was much distracted hurrying around and moving in and out of one another's paths as we had our horses led to the rear, where they were to be tied end on end to stop anyone fleeing, and the archers were sent to their places on the wings, and then we settled ourselves down into the formation in which we would wait to hear what the heralds had to say to one another, and then we'd . . . we'd fight.

By Jesu.

I found myself with Ap-Moffat to my right, and on my left a man whom I had never met before, who would turn out to be **Hugh Smith**.

'Oh dear,' he whined, in a homely accent I recognised as being from near Coventry. 'They are easily twice our number!'

He claimed to have been a veteran of the battle of Cravant, and offered advice such as 'you want to watch out for them riders with horsemen's picks, Master Malory', and complained about the price he paid for his greaves, which he said were – oh, I can't remember. But Jesu defend me! Had I known then what I would come to learn of him later, then I should have killed him there and then. I should have struck him down and thrust my dagger in the gap between gorget and visor. I should have snatched Ap-Moffat's wondrous hammer and dished his brainpan not once, twice or even three or four times, but a hundred. I should have taken my sword point and thrust it into his stinking guts until he lay in that onion field like butcher's spoil. But I did not.

I was merely irritated by his endless witterings, most especially those as to how he came to be at Cravant and now here, too – not how fate had brought him there that day, mind, but actually how he had travelled there from Coventry: 'I took the London Road, of course, travelling with some grey friars who were on their way to Banbury, and they were fine fellows, we stayed in that little inn, I don't know if you know it?', and on and on. I just wanted him to be silent, for I did not wish to be a brother in arms with such a man, but whenever he was not talking like this, he was crossing himself and mumbling and then standing on tiptoe so he could see the Lombard horsemen, before ducking down again and kissing his beads once more. He was short and very unsoldierly, and I was not at all surprised when he told us his family were wool merchants.

'And today I wish I were one, too,' Ap-Moffat laughed.

Oh, just shut up, I thought, both of you.

I will admit that I was likewise struck with the overpowering certainty that I had made a mistake; that I was here by error, and if I could just make my way to the rear and explain my case to someone, then it would be understood, and I would be conducted from the field, and led to wherever it was I was supposed to be: somewhere far from here. I was not alone in feeling this, of that I am sure, for when we were confronted by our enemy, a stutter rippled through our ranks like wind stirring a field of barley, and had but one man turned and fled, then I dare say we might all have followed him.

But, my God, there were some lion-hearted men among us that day, mostly provincial knights and gentlemen, gathered from divers Normandy garrisons, each with the cross of St George across his chest, and they pressed forward – across the planted cabbages and onions – and seeing them do so, I hesitated to flee, as we must all have done, for no man wants to be the first to go, and after a moment the chance vanished, and everywhere men gathered themselves with something like relief at a test passed, and we pressed forward and the world – which had until then been broad and flat and open and green – closed in on us in a series of buff-coloured surcoats, mail-clad shoulders, helmeted heads and thousands of bills and axes and pole arms and so on.

Smith was still gurgling his prayers.

'Ooooh God! Preserve Your hoooomble servant in his hour of need', and so on.

I was grateful that I could hardly hear him for my helmet and arming cap, and the din of the moving soldiery: all the clicks and scrapes of plate and mail, the shuffle of feet in the dirt, and then the drums and the fifes and bugles and so on, but I could imagine the sorts of things he was saying.

We trudged forward, each careful not to catch the heel of the man in front, until we must have been within three hundred paces of the Armagnacs, and there came a shouted command to stop. We did so and then we were ordered to spread ourselves wider, shuffling left or right to give ourselves space to move, to swing our weapons. Then we shuffled out further still so that each man stood in the space of perhaps ten paces, five on either side. It seemed absurd, but in fact, this was to be our saving.

Meanwhile, the bowmen on our left and right flanks were knocking in their stakes, though the ground was so hard. Then there followed a long pause until the heralds agreed – just as they always do – that the shedding of Christian blood cannot be averted, and then the Scots dishonestly insulted the Duke of Bedford, and we all knew what would come next, and it felt like the great flat sheet of the earth itself was holding its breath. The air grew heavy and dense and I felt it weighing down on me, filling my ears as if with tallow, stoppering up my mouth and nose so that I could hardly breathe.

My chest ached with it, and my limbs were heavy and numb.

Then came the shout. Then came the arrows. *Our* arrows.

A rippling drumroll from left and right as the bowmen drew their strings and loosed their arrows, and the air was suddenly full of their delicate lines, two smudges of them darkening the sky on the left and the right, a great feathered pulse in the corner of each eye, dense as any murmuration, rising with breathtaking vigour, hanging for a long moment, only to hurtle down with gaining weight and speed.

A moment later an answering salvo came back, the arrows sliding in among themselves, further darkening the sky as they crossed. The Scottish archers – the archers of Scotland – were much prized by the Armagnacs, who, having no archers of their own – or none to mention in song, shall we say – must have hoped the Scotch would do to us what we had done to them at every meeting since Crécy, nearly eighty years ago now, and their commander – The Fury! – must have stood watching, beetle-browed, expecting to see us wither under the storm. But we rightly thought little of the prowess of the Scotch bowmen, and we knew our bowmen were more than a match.

I cannot say how long the archery duel continued because a moment later I was distracted by something else: a great, swelling thunder that transmitted itself up through the soles of my boots to my shins and my knees. The ground seemed to hum and soften, even to liquefy, and rise up like smoke of its own accord, and the rumble only got stronger, travelling up through my thighs like a creeping thrill. I know for a fact that I was not the only man there that day whose bowels it shook loose.

Here they came! The magically attired horsemen of Lombardy!

But on our right our bowmen bent their backs and then released their arrows with a timpani of fluted thuds, and perhaps as many as two thousand yard-long, feather-fletched lengths of ash, each tipped in a finger's length of hardened iron bodkin head, slashed the air. At a hundred paces such an arrow might pass clean through a man. At fifty it might pin him to his saddle. At twenty it might pass through him, his saddle *and* his horse.

Experienced archers know to keep their arrows for the enemies' last fifty yards, and shoot then at their fastest and lowest, and now our bowmen were a blur of action, for the horsemen were a hundred paces out, and the noise changed character as the arrows found their marks: a rippling stipple, sharper than the thunderous roll of hooves, like a thousand hammers on a thousand anvils.

Such an arrow strike would kill any man, surely! No armour devised could deflect it. Yet not one fell. Not a man. Not a horse. The arrows hit them, but bounced off their helmets and breastplates and even the horses' barding. Or they stuck in them, but none fell. At fifty paces the horsemen still came on, impervious. At thirty paces, too, they remained upright.

I did not know if I was screaming or not but everywhere I looked men were turning to one another, mouths agape, eyes round in terror. None stood foursquare, and every man's body was canted aslant and every muscle in every body screamed, fly! Fly! Fly!

At twenty paces, their armour weathered the blows. They remained up and alive, their speed and purpose unchecked even by the stakes, for if they could withstand an arrow strike from that distance, what is a slim stick dug into hard ground? Not a thing. Even when they entered the final ten paces, and down came their lances, not a horse was felled.

And now accepting what they were seeing, a great cry went up among our bowmen, who threw down their bows and turned to run. But they were too late, of course, far too late.

The noise of the horses hitting our ranks ahead was deafening: a staggered, percussive wallop, loud as any bell in any belfry, and the violence was very terrible. Men were hurled into the air as those monstrous, steel-faced horses broke open our ranks. The horsemen broke their lances upon whoever they could, and then they brought down their hammers and picks on anyone left alive, and only the weight of the bodies of the men who could not avoid them – both the quick and the dead – slowed their pace.

They crashed through our ranks as if we were made of grass. Some of us turned and ran. But I did not. I fell to my knees, and held out my sword and closed my eyes, and I prayed to God to grant me grace. I know I screamed. Stamping hooves thundered past, and something crashed against my helmet, glanced off it, and caught my shoulder with the force of a horse's kick. A flash of green, a flash of black, and I was lying on my back, winded and afire with every kind of agony.

But now we thanked our God and the Duke of Bedford for spreading us so thinly. We had space in which to move. To throw ourselves back, aside, down. Yawning gaps opened in our ranks as men hurled themselves aside, and the horses naturally veered down these cleared ways and after those long and terrible moments when we were caught up in the raging storm, they were through. They passed us by, and were gone, and it was as if a great weight had been dragged through us, harrowing us more surely than any plough.

I pulled myself up, righted my helmet and found my sword in the dust. I was very weak, and trembling as if once more in the grip of the ague, and I stood and looked about. The warm air was strong and striking with the smell of ruptured guts, spilled blood, shit, piss, chipped metal, earth and onion and the recent passage of sweating horses, and all around me were dead and dying men, wailing and whimpering, and trying to drag themselves to safety, though Jesu knows where they thought they'd find that. Others lay twisted and broken, with blood easing through the joints of their compacted plate, and their limbs crumpled in those same awkward, misshapen tangles I had glimpsed all those years ago, that morning at Gosford Green.

197

Jesu preserve me, I thought, he was right, my father: this is what war is like.

Smith had gone – good – or was dead somewhere, but next to me Ap-Moffat was on his feet, bareheaded now, and studying a great dent in his helmet as if he were at a loss to know how it might have got there. When he saw me he asked after my health as if we had not seen one another for a month or two, and were met by chance upon the highway, and asked if I had seen his poleaxe.

'I'm always losing things,' he said.

'Will they come again?' I asked.

'I wouldn't if I were them.'

But they would, of course. They would surely now be wheeling back to ride through us a second time, to finish what they'd started and now more thoroughly and at their leisure. But for some reason the prospect did not so much frighten as dismay me, for I found myself utterly stunned that we had lost the day, stunned that we, an English army, had been beaten in the field without taking the chance to prove our valour and our prowess. I thought of Folo Bundsay, in the rear somewhere with the horses and the baggage train, and what he had said after John Jiggins had fallen to his death from the walls of Calais: not what you imagine when you think of God's purpose for your life, is it?

I cannot tell you the blackness of the despair that then descended upon me. I saw now there was no hope I would ever be redeemed. I had finally fought in a battle, only to be beaten. It was an unjust horror. I would now never match men even such as William Peyto. I would never come back from France having triumphed in battle, the very thing on which I'd staked my life, my name, my reputation, the only thing on which men would judge me. Not only had I killed Sir Thomas West, I had been at Verneuil when the English army had been driven from the field by the Lombards, by the Armagnacs and, most shaming of all, by the Scots.

Then I saw Hugh Smith, likewise having lost his helmet and arming cap, pinned beneath another man, covered in blood, but blinking as if he were being brought up from a cellar into sunlight.

'Oh, *please* help me,' he whined, and he extended his one free hand, for he could not move the weight of the dead man and his harness.

I dragged the dead man off him and helped him to his feet. He was very unsteady, but apart from the blood on his face – belonging to the dead man, whose helmet had been dished – he was untouched and pristine, though he stood in such a way as you knew he had soiled himself.

'Where are they?' he quailed. 'Where've they gone?'

I gestured, for you could still hear their horses, still feel them, still smell them, and everywhere you looked those who could still stand were sore perplexed and disconsolate, waiting for their end. No one knew what to do with their weapons. One man threw his down and ran. Ap-Moffat picked it up.

'Even better,' he said.

This is what it is like to lose a battle, I thought. Did it feel like a shame worse than death? The pain of it was lancing, and at that moment I swear death would have been preferable. I felt a seething dizziness, coupled with a gripping desire to lash out, to push back, to fight against this most shameful fate, to strike back, to smite someone. Hugh Smith, even. And how I wish to God I had.

But then I thought: for the love of Jesu! We are not dead yet!

'We can't,' I said. 'We can't just—'

In truth I did not know what we couldn't just do, but I knew we must do something, and nor was I alone in this. Ahead I could see the banner of the Duke of Bedford still held aloft, a symbol of life and hope amid all this death and despair, and then next to it divers smaller flags were being raised again, and those men who had run, had run, and now those of us who stayed, stayed. We looked one another in the eye and we gathered together, stepping over the dead and the dying, finding one another out, closing to stand shoulder to shoulder with one another, as brothers, in some way resolved.

And ahead, but a hundred paces across the field, came the broad-steeled, blade-stippled front of the Armagnac men-at-arms, five thousand Frenchmen rolling towards us like a tidal bore under full many a noble flag and banner, every yard freighted with blunt force, prickling with sharp-edged weaponry.

Seeing them come, the Duke of Bedford turned back to us. His broad face was florid, and he took off his helmet and unstrapped his bevor to let his beard spring free, and he took a great breath before bellowing:

'Sirs! Those whom God loves most, He first tests in the fire, and this day He has sent us a great test. We have been tested, and bested, and laid low. We have lost this battle, and we are all dead men. You, my lord, are a dead man. You too, sir: a dead man. And I, yes, I too am dead. For listen! Even now those Lombards are looting our baggage. We have nothing left. Our lives are forfeit and our property stolen, and all that remains to us now is our honour! Our honour which now these God-damned Frenchmen—' he gestured with his axe '—mean to take from us. But I shall not sell it cheap. I shall not give easy satisfaction to any man, be he French, or Lombard, or any God-damned Scotch. I, John of Bedford, brother of the king that was, uncle to the king that is, will prove myself worthy of those Englishmen who have gone before, worthy of St George and worthy of the Lord my God, for I will not move from this place until the day is done!

'So let fly any man who wishes to fly, for he is not my brother, but let tarry any man who wishes to tarry here with me, for to stand with him on such a field and on such a day, that shall I call an honour!'

It was quite a speech, delivered with ragged, enraged passion, and Jesu, how we cheered!

The duke's squire fastened his bevor and put his helmet back on, but then the duke paused before dropping his visor, and with no regard for the Armagnacs, who were now within fifty paces and closing very fast, he shouted: 'Sirs! Prepare you all this day to acquit yourselves as gentlemen. For God! For St George! And for England!' And with this, and a tumultuous bellow of defiant rage, we moved to meet France.

I will not describe what happened for the next four hours or so. There is no need. Or perhaps there is, but it is not a simple tale with clear lines of sight. It is mired in struggle and confusion, be-sweat with sudden alarms and moments of blinding terror. In such a melee you do not see your opponent as a man, you see only his arm, his fist, his sword blade or axe head. It is with these things you engage. You hack. You hew. You smite. You stab. You find the crease, the seam, the weakest point, and you plunge your blade in with not a thought for the man within.

In such circumstance, there is no sense of victory, only the presence of threat, and then by your own feats of arms, its absence.

The work is hard, harder than you can ever imagine. Your breath is short, your limbs ring, you sweat out your own bodyweight, and afterwards the pain in every part of you is very great, startlingly so, for you remember nothing of any buffets endured at the time.

But so it was that, grudgingly, moment by moment, inch by inch, man by man and struggle by struggle, the day was ours. At its end we had driven all five armies from the field before us, and those who did not run, we slaughtered. The fight with Scotland's army was un-matched in ferocity by anything I ever experienced again. No mercy was asked, offered or accepted. They did not run, for they had no-where to run to, just as we had nowhere, but they stayed and they fought and we slaughtered every last one of them. (Such a thing was unchristian, you will say, and I will say yes, but they would have done the same to us.)

And where were the Lombards, you ask yourself? Ha.

They came back, but only eventually, and only much hampered with the spoils they had plundered from our baggage train, and seeing their paymasters dead, or dying, or being driven from the field, they – like all good mercenaries – opted for self-preservation, and they turned their horses and rode away, and such surviving bowmen as we had nocked their bows and loosed arrow shafts to chase them off, and by God how we cheered to see that the armour at their backs was not so very magical after all.

I once heard it said that no man can be happy after a battle, for surveying the sorrowful mounds of despoiled corpses and hearing the fearful screams of wounded horses, how can he be sure of what he has lost and what he has won? But let me tell you something about the man who said that: he never lost a battle at noon, only to win it back by day's end—

The boy sits straight-backed, brimful of martial ardour. He reminds Sir Thomas of little Harry Beauchamp, Sir Richard's son, who once became King of the Isle of Wight – had he ever had his eye blackened by his father, which Sir Thomas doubts.

'That is it then,' he announces. 'A soldier I shall be!'

They both laugh until the boy re-splits his lip, but when he has dabbed away the blood he wonders why no one ever speaks of this battle as they do of others, by which he means Agincourt, or Crécy, perhaps, or even Poitiers.

'In songs and whatnot.'

'It is true,' Sir Thomas sighs. 'Verneuil is all but forgotten now, but as God is my witness, it was a feat of arms just as marvellous as any yet seen, and had we been led by a king, or by a king's son, rather than a mere duke, then the minstrels would sing of it to this day.'

Just then all through the city the bells begin to ring and the boy looks suddenly aware of his surroundings, and of the time.

'By our Lady!' he says. 'The stable!'

And he hauls himself to his feet, his slight little body wracked with almost infinite weariness, and suddenly he is a sweet child again, and Sir Thomas offers him a coin, which he takes with slender fingers, and somehow it vanishes up his dirty-wristed sleeve, and he is gone, and once more Sir Thomas is left alone, Hartshorne's letter still loose between his fingers, wondering where else Brunt hit the boy, and vowing that he will somehow save him, and exact some sort of vengeance on Brunt, if only Hartshorne is able to bring him anything more than deferred hope from his day with the Earl of Warwick.

BOOK II
Worship

CHAPTER 8

How Sir Thomas receives joyous tidings, and of what then befell him

It is two days later, the feast of St Mark and St Marcellian – martyrs, Sir Thomas recalls from his reading of *The Golden Legend*, and twins, too, who had their feet nailed to pillars on the Via Ardeatina and were left to hang upside down for a couple of days until Emperor Diocletian's men lost patience and stabbed them to death – and the city bells ring all morning to mark the departure of **Margaret**, the king's sister, for Flanders and her marriage into Burgundy.

But Sir Thomas is in no mood to celebrate.

Perhaps it is because of the desperate, hollow hope that Hartshorne's letter has stirred up in him – again – but he has passed these last few nights in a fearful state: sleepless and sweating malodorously in the unwanted heat, with his eyes fixed wide and starting at the imagined sound of St Sepulchre's bell and of that priest come snuffling at his door. So when that morning he surfaces from his nightmare-ravaged dreams, he sends for the priest – from Greyfriar's within the city, rather than St Sepulchre's without – to come and say Mass in the little chapel on the gaol's first floor, reserved for those who can pay.

The priest they send over today has a fine, almost musical voice, but nothing will soothe Sir Thomas's jangling nerves; nothing this day will distract him from the same old thoughts that are once more awhirl so pointlessly within his head; and when the Mass is done and the blessing is chanted, he thanks the priest, pays him his fee, and returns – as he has given his oath he will, which is the condition for his licence to attend in the first instance – to his cell, his body limp and powerless, there to wait for – what?

But it is as he is trudging his way back up those steps and along the narrowing passage towards his cell that he hears behind him the thumping of feet that he recognises with a stab of some wild emotion as belonging to William Hartshorne.

'Sir Thomas!' he hears his voice rising up the stairs. 'Sir Thomas!'

And Sir Thomas must stay himself, must repress the desire to turn and run down and grab Hartshorne by his no-doubt precious lapels and shout into his face 'what? what? what?' Instead, he forces himself to turn slowly and wait for Hartshorne to loom out of the depths, his usually dusty forehead glazed with sweat, and his coat – another new one, in silk dyed the colour of a ruby at the fireside on a winter's eve – already wrinkled and dark at the pits.

'By Jesu, Master Hartshorne,' he mutters, feigning that his heart thunders not, and that he is like to faint with excitement, 'can it be that you have run all the way from your chambers?'

'Aye, sir,' Hartshorne roars, 'and with good tidings, by our Lady!'

Sir Thomas has lived for this moment, and conjures up in an instant all the usual things: 'Gather your possessions, my Lord Malory of Newbold Revel', or 'The king wishes to see you raised to a dukedom!' or 'You are to be crowned King of the Isle of Wight!'

'What is it?' he asks, as if he does not know.

'A pardon!' Hartshorne exclaims. 'The king is to announce a general pardon!'

Sir Thomas turns his back on Hartshorne and leads him up the rest of the steps and into his cell. A general pardon? No, it is not what he hoped; it is not the release with an apology and some handsome recompense by way of title and gold, is it? But that doesn't matter. The only thing that matters is that he is to be free, free to leave Newgate and to return home to dear old Newbold Revel! It takes a moment to understand, though.

'Haha!' he laughs, when he does, and he turns to grip Hartshorne by the elbows and the two old men manage an awkward shuffling jig around the rushes. When they are too embarrassed to continue, Hartshorne throws his hat down upon Sir Thomas's coffer, and looks about in vain for something to drink.

'We've heard nothing about it,' the boy tells them.

They'd both missed his always silent arrival, but Sir Thomas supposes it must have been he who let Hartshorne in, and there he now is, leaning against the door frame, almost like his father: doubtful, sour-faced and with his bruised eye now a vile mixture of purple and green, despite which Hartshorne is surprisingly polite, and tells him that His Majesty only decided it yesterday, and that the announcement is to be read from St Paul's Cross later today, 'to mark the marriage of his sister into Burgundy'. The boy remains unsmiling.

Sir Thomas ignores him.

Ha! he thinks. A pardon! A general pardon! What better way to mark his sister's wedding than for the king to issue a pardon for any crime – disclosed or undisclosed, historic or future – in return for a sum determined by his own chancellor! Of course, it is a trick copied from the Church, who've been selling indulgences for years now, and it is of course to pay for his sister's wedding and dowry. Every petitioner will be made to dig deep, and the king will no longer have to kiss grocers' wives for gifts of their husbands' money, though come to think of it, he'll probably keep doing that anyway.

Sir Thomas is not vastly wealthy, it is true, but he has lived carefully these last thirty years, and thanks to all the divers enfeoffments and so forth, and all the other precautions taken at the time of his first incarceration, his lands have been protected from such hawks who've eyed them jealously, and Elizabeth his wife is careful by nature. It is true that he does not know yet of what crime he is accused and so is unable to gauge the price he is like to be asked to pay, and

because the king is ever needful of money, he is unlikely to sell anything cheap. But still. A hundred marks? That sounds about right.
Sir Thomas will buy it anyway, regardless of the injustice, regardless
of anything, really, and return at last to Newbold Revel. He will return to sleep in his own bed, to walk his own fields, to pat the heads
of his own dogs! He will see his wife and son again! And his little
grandson! And he will be permitted to pray at the church at least
once more before it is his time to be buried there.

And he will evict Appleby and his wife, that is for sure. His spirits
soar as does the unfettered lark: upward.

'Ha!' he shouts, capering feebly. 'Ha!'

He embraces Hartshorne once more, and then even moves towards the boy, who still stands at the door, his expression still that
of a shelled walnut, and Thomas feels his joy somewhat occluded.

'What is it?' he asks. 'Aren't you pleased? I shall be free!'

And it strikes him then, in all honesty, that the boy does not wish
to see him gone for he wishes to hear the rest of his story; he wishes
to learn how such an honourable man as Sir Thomas, who is so
obviously incapable of such crimes as those of which he is accused,
was held so unfairly and for so long under lock and key in Castle
Newgate, and Sir Thomas can scarcely recall ever feeling so strongly
for his fellow man.

'I will tell you the rest of my tale, my boy,' he says. 'Never you fear.
Upon the cross of my sword I swear you shall hear it all.'

But the boy just shakes his head.

'It ain't that,' he says, intending to be rude. 'It means the gaol will
empty.'

And Sir Thomas steps back, suddenly sobered, his vanity pricked.

Of course. A general pardon is bad news for the boy, or, really, for the boy's father, whose purse will hang so much the lighter,
since any prisoner with the wherewithal to pay for all those added
little extras – Mass in the chapel (tuppence), a walk on the leads (a

shilling a week), a walk in the city (tuppence), not to mention his shilling and sixpence every week for delivery of sharp red wine and greasy candles – will also have the wherewithal to buy their pardon, and so be gone, leaving the prison's cells empty save for the rump of chained and impoverished felons below, from whom Brunt can expect nothing but contagion.

'I am sorry,' Sir Thomas mumbles. 'I am sorry', and for a moment he genuinely is, but then that moment passes, and he cannot resist returning to his own news, and soon he is once more caught up in joy. Having been afforded a glimpse of what might have been, having suffered the threat of endless imprisonment or excruciating death, only for it now to be lifted, he is born anew, and despite the boy's glowering presence, his world transforms into a sparkling jewel.

He laughs his wheezy old man's laugh for half a Paternoster's time, and can feel tears of joy greasing the creases of his cheeks, and then, when he has recovered at last, he asks Hartshorne how soon he can expect to be free?

'Appeals must be submitted by this coming St John's,' Hartshorne tells him, as proudly as if he had arranged this himself, and purely for Sir Thomas's benefit. 'And we should hear back early in the week thereafter.'

Sir Thomas consults the number of lines scored under his window and calculates that St John's is but a week from now, so he has at the most two weeks more of this, perhaps. Two weeks to endure, but also: two weeks to finish his story.

He asks Hartshorne how much he thinks the king will charge. Hartshorne admits he cannot guess, but imagines something in the region of a hundred marks.

'Though we do not know what offence you are charged with,' he reminds Sir Thomas, further staring at Sir Thomas, as if Sir Thomas is like to tell him. But Sir Thomas is not. For Sir Thomas does not know.

'And your shoemaker, Cornelius,' Sir Thomas asks, slowly, deliberately changing the subject. 'Will he apply for a pardon? Do you think?'

Hartshorne pulls a face.

'Alas not.'

With which he confirms what Sir Thomas had suspected: that Cornelius the Shoemaker will no more stoop over his last, tacks pressed between his lips, waxed string and curved needle gripped 'twixt thumb and horny forefinger, for he has already met the headsman, and by now his quartered body parts will have been dipped in tar and despatched about the country as a feast for provincial crows. The London crows will have his head.

Sir Thomas crosses himself, chilled suddenly, as if in a damp shirt on a cold day, for, Jesu defend him, there but for the grace of God goes he.

When Hartshorne has taken his leave, off to his inn to write his petition for Sir Thomas's pardon, the boy hesitates to follow and stands at the door, still giving off that restive, sour energy.

'Looks like you're going to get away with it again then, Sir Thomas,' he says, and he gives the word 'Sir' a scathing slant, and Sir Thomas looks at him, not knowing how outraged he ought to be, but before he can say anything, or not say anything, the boy leaves, slamming the door behind him and ramming home the locking bar.

Sir Thomas is left alone with his previously high spirits somewhat dashed, and, unexpectedly, he feels very bruised, as if on the Tuesday after falling from his horse on a Sunday, and he and the cat stare at one another, very solemnly, and he thinks of some of the things that he would have told the boy today, had he had the chance, which would have included:

→ How, after he had washed the stench of that blood-glutted onion field from his skin and his nostrils, and after he had burned his armour-stained linen, and recovered his strength

212

— it was almost comical to see men hobbling along the road home in the week after the battle, not wounded, but merely stiff from sudden over-exertion — he returned home across the Narrow Sea in an autumn gale, at last no longer the man who had killed that good knight Sir Thomas West, but now Thomas Malory, veteran of Verneuil.

➻ How he and Folo rode up through London and along the old Roman road to reach Fenny Newbold just after St Martin's Day, with the smell of mushrooms and scorched pig-bristle thick in the air, and he was a happy, wealthy young man at last, buoyed up by renown (though as yet unknown), and intending if at all possible to take up the red surcoat once more, and to return to the service of Sir Richard Beauchamp, Earl of Warwick.

➻ How he brought his father back one of those Lombard breastplates, which he had bought from a battlefield looter for just twenty sous, which was reasonable enough, he'd thought, though as he'd bought in haste so he repented at leisure, for it soon turned out to be far too small for him, or even his father, who was on the wane, and who, though he was impressed with it, when they had set it up on a post by the ponds and shot arrows at it, could hardly draw his bow to shoot at it from five paces, let alone dent it.

➻ How his mother and sisters were more pleased with the other things he brought them: for his mother a large silver ewer, ingeniously worked by (and taken from) a silversmith of Lisieux, and for his sisters each a bolt of sanguine and yellow kersey, which in all honesty he would admit to having bought from a Flemish draper off Cheapside, asking him to assort the colours and paying his price without demur.

❧→ How he found his parents happy to see him but still much
saddened by the loss of his young brother, and every evening
before prayers they would walk out to that stock pond – now
caparisoned in late autumn colour, and watched over by the
self-same heron (perhaps) that his brother had tried to kill
– and they would stand for a while, his father's arm around
his mother's waist, her head canted on his shoulder, and then
they would come in, and order the fire covered, prayers said
and the household to bed.

These things he might have told the boy, and the boy might or
might not have been interested to hear them, but there are other
things that ought to be said, which Sir Thomas knows the boy will
not necessarily care to hear – he being a beardless boy with scarcely
twelve winters under his belt – such as:

❧→ How Thomas's father had been working to find Thomas's
three sisters suitable husbands, and would have sought him
a wife, if he had let him, but now that Thomas was a man
who had stood on the field of Verneuil, he seemed to feel it
was not his place, and instead he would only offer examples
of other men who had married, and how happy it made
them, including Thomas's old lord, Sir Richard Beauchamp,
who after Lady Elizabeth's death had married Lady Isobel
Despenser, the widow of the Earl of Worcester, who owned
divers lands in divers counties in the west of the country and
in Wales.
    'You will see how happy she makes him,' he had said.
    'Love must arise of the heart,' Thomas had replied, 'and
not by constraint.'
    'Hmmm?' his father had queried.
    It was something Thomas had read somewhere.

'I do not wish to be bound to a lady I do not love,' he had clarified.

'Right,' his father had said, or words to that effect.

→ How it was that, by one of those odd coincidences that are in fact all too common, Lady Isobel Despenser's father had been executed for his part in the very same plot which had seen Thomas's father sent to the Tower before he was born, and which had so weakened him that he shot Thomas's arrow askew, and how by another odd coincidence – though perhaps less common – Lady Isobel Despenser's first husband (killed by a crossbow bolt, outside Meaux, 1421) was named Sir Richard Beauchamp, as was her second.

→ How it was that Thomas was not uninterested in women, or in marriage, and nor did he have what might be called a dolorous relationship with either, but he had witnessed full many a man who had married in haste, or for dynastic reasons, or for reason of a seat with a hundred acres of the finest hunting – or, in Folo Bundsay's case, of which more later, a stew of apples baked under a rough pastry crust – and he had seen the constraints such men must then endure, the sacrifices they must then make, and then, inevitably, the divers shabbinesses to which they then fall prey. He also saw to what ends they subjected their wives, too, and he wanted none of those things, neither for himself, nor for his lady.

→ How earlier, when he had been in Normandy, not long after King Henry's death, an acquaintance – whose name matters not here – once told him that he was altogether too romantic a soul, and that he spent too much time with his nose in a book when he should be taking advantage of what was 'there to be taken'.

'You are like to end up alone, Malory,' he'd chided. 'As cold and pale as Onan on Candlemas Eve!'

→ How the man had laughed, but Thomas was at the time still paying for masses for Sir Thomas West's soul, and sometimes he believed himself to have come under a sort of enchantment that West had cast during those days afloat the swirling Rhine, when he sighed for the lost love of Lady Elaine, and whenever, or if ever, the temptation to 'take advantage' of what was 'there to be taken' occurred to Thomas while he was in Normandy, he could not help but imagine what West would have said and done in such a situation.

'It is mere lechery, Malory.'

Nor could he help contrasting it with what he supposed a man such as William Peyto might have done – might actually be doing – in the same position, and thinking these thoughts, any ardour he might be expected to experience thus wilted as does April's frost-cankered rosebud.

Nor, now, will the boy ever learn the following:

→ How Thomas did once – but once! – succumb to the temptation of what was 'there to be taken' and that this event occurred in the benumbed and heady aftermath of that tremendous day outside Verneuil, when having shaken Death by the hand, something made him wish to embrace Life, to plunge himself into its simple, earthly pleasures, and so once – but once! – did he allow himself to wander into disworship.

It was in an inn, thatched, upon a hillside that smelled of apples just then coming into fruit, in which served a chubby

216

blonde girl – and this was a time when chubbiness of that sort was in short and much-prized supply, especially among Normans – who, Thomas was told, as the evening wore on, had taken a shine to him. Thomas can remember the rising roars of laughter from a group of comrades, including bloody Ap-Moffat, with whom he was drinking, as she poured him more cider, and despite his life in Calais, and despite his trip to Konstanz, and despite almost everything he knew all too well, everybody but him seemed to know what was expected.

He remembers very little of it after that – a convenience, he will admit – other than that at evening's end he followed her up a ladder to a room under sloping beams and mossy thatch, and there they lay beside one another, and the shock of her body – naked as a needle – against his was as pleasant a thing as he'd ever encountered, and when he attempted to put his hand against her cunny, as Peyto had once boasted he had done – 'many a time and oft, pshaw!' – she had had to move it to where it should have been (lower down). Divining him then to be a virgin – if she had not already guessed beforehand – she guided him in the necessary, and in the morning he woke in the bed, mouth like a glove, head ringing as if cupped in a bell, to discover he was sharing it not only with her, still wonderly naked, but now also (unless he had not noticed them the night before) her two sons, likewise – though less wonderly – naked, all three sleeping like angels, and he too was naked, and everything smelled very strange.

↦ How he lay then there for a while, examining the rafters above and letting the cool air waft over his skin, and he had to admit it was not how he had imagined it might be. He had imagined himself first marrying a fair lady before lying beside her in a pavilion, or in a flower-strewn summer bower, perhaps, or even in a hermitage, and he had dreamed of divers other blisses he could neither picture nor name. But instead here he was in a Normandy inn listening to the rain, and the barmaid snore ever so gently, wondering if she had now become his wife. At that moment, he would confess to hoping she had, for the close proximity of her naked flesh was having the effect on his young body that might be supposed.

Sadly, or perhaps mercifully, it was not to be, for when he tried to rekindle the pleasures of the night before she pushed him away with many a rude grunt, and thus was he ejected from the bed, bent double, to lace himself into his discarded hose while both the angelic boys raised themselves onto their elbows and watched on in farmyard glee. The girl's father, or perhaps her real husband, met Thomas in the hall down the ladder and placed a strong hand on his arm and demanded – in likewise rough grunts – a price Thomas was only too happy to pay, if only to get away from her, from him and from that place, and to be on his own.

Afterwards he had been gripped by shame, and wondered if he had not been poisoned, perhaps, or given some potion or other, such as Sir Tristram and Isolde had accidentally drunk on their fateful voyage from Ireland.

When he shared his fears with Ap-Moffat, Ap-Moffat looked merely pained.

'Oh, I was much worse for wear than you, Malory, for I have no head for cider.'

Which was not true, of course. Thomas recalled him drinking cup after cup of it, and remaining steely as a heron all evening long, singing ballads in a wonderfully true voice, while the rest of them were rolling about like ruddy-faced bear cubs.

➻ How then, having sampled all the pleasures that love has to offer — a single night with a barmaid whose name he never learned and whose face he could not recall — Thomas believed he need not pursue them further, for their own sake at least, and that he was now free to dedicate himself solely to the pursuit of worship, and to feats of arms, as befits a man. He would forsake any yearnings of the flesh until he loved a lady, and she loved him, and he would prove himself worthy of such love, just as poor dead Sir Thomas West had proved his love for the Lady Elaine.

Much of which, if he is honest — and that he is, by Jesu — he would admit that he had not been looking forward to telling the boy, for the shame of it, but now the boy will never learn of such things, which is a blessing, but nor indeed will he learn of the following things, which is a pity, for they would have helped him understand more clearly such events as will soon come to pass, such as:

➻ How, soon after his return to England, Thomas rode unto Warwick Castle, just as his father had done all those years ago, to offer his services once more to the aforesaid earl. So much time had passed since Sir Thomas West's death, and so many others had likewise passed out of this world, including Sir Richard's own Lady Elizabeth, of course, that any memories Sir Richard might once have had of Thomas's part in West's death were faded, and when the earl looked Thomas over, as he did that morning, he did not see the man who had contributed to a good knight's end, he saw instead a man who was once his page of honour, of whom his dead wife had been very fond and whom he'd once seen shitting in a ditch, now come fresh from winning worship on the field at Verneuil.

'Still not knighted, Malory?' the earl had asked, embarrassed for Thomas's sake, and Thomas had shaken his head, and tried a laugh, but his cheeks flushed because, of course, he should have been knighted many months ago, but with an infant on the throne and so many men in search of just that honour, he waited still.

'Well,' Sir Richard had placated, 'I dare say there will be further chance aplenty.'

Sir Richard must by then have been about forty or fifty, but he had aged well, solid and muscular, rooted to the ground like an oak, and with the sort of frame you would hate to run into in the dark. He was likewise elsewhere valiant too, as was attested by the fact that his new wife Lady Isobel – hardly a handsome woman – was already stout with child, and every day a mass was said so that she should be blessed with a boy, for Lady Elizabeth – may God assoil her soul – had provided only girls.

How Thomas became, once more, Sir Richard Beauchamp's indentured man, and how they ripped in two halves their agreement guaranteeing that Thomas should ride with the earl when the earl had need of him, and how he – Thomas – would bring with him three men-at-arms, suitably accoutred for war, and ten archers, each mounted, should they be required, and in return Thomas should have the earl's protection in all matters, and forty marks per annum. They folded away their halves of the agreement, and shook hands and the earl embraced him.

'Malory,' he rumbled.

It was a homecoming.

➻ How Thomas was to be permitted lodging and stabling in the castle itself, and was encouraged to ride after the game in the earl's park.

➻ How to celebrate Thomas bought himself a very fine falcon, but as with his earlier birds, she likewise flew away, jesses and all, and was never, by him, seen again.

➻ How autumn that year gave way to icy winter, during which Smite Brook froze over, and for the year's turn Thomas took his mother and sisters necklaces of coral beads and his father the falconing glove, of which he now had no need.

➻ How in March that year Lady Isobel birthed a son — named Henry after the king — and how all the bells in Warwick were set to peal in joy for days on end, but there was but little time to celebrate further, for very soon afterwards Sir Richard was summoned once more to Normandy, where the Bretons had seized some towns to which they had no right, and so it was that Thomas celebrated his twenty-fifth birthday at sea, where Sir Richard kissed him and gave him a gift of an inkhorn capped in gold that had obviously been to hand, come into his possession in Normandy somewhere, and they sailed to the mouth of the Seine and past Harfleur, which brought Thomas to the gunwale, and he watched the town and the low rise of land where he had so nearly died until it slid out of sight, and then the ship followed the river to Rouen, whence they disembarked and went by road to Paris, to which he had never yet been, and within the walls of which Sir Richard had been allocated a very fine house near the river.

The more Sir Thomas thinks about all this, though, the more he wonders just how much the boy would appreciate its importance?

Would he not wax impatient at such quiet detail that involves no tourneying? No battles? No great deeds of arms? Especially as there is more of this sort of stuff to come, including two things that might at first — and especially to a mere boy — seem somewhat underwhelming, but which would, with more mature consideration, loom large, such as:

➤ How it was that during this time in Paris, the earl — perhaps remembering Thomas's interest in the books kept by the Abbot of Bordesley — suggested he look over the library of one of the old French kings, that had come into his possession.

'See if there is not something in there that Lady Isobel might care to look at. And take that bloody monk with you too, will you? He talks a lot of bookish twaddle.'

That bloody monk was John Lydgate, whom Thomas had never met, but who was much celebrated for having written divers poems for poor, dead King Henry, and whom Thomas expected to be a cadaverous pedant, for the poems were lengthy and serious-minded, but in fact Lydgate turned out to be a jolly little Benedictine, plump and mischievous, and while they walked together to the Louvre castle, he told Thomas he was hoping to find fresh inspiration among the French king's books.

'I need something juicy to get my teeth into, Malory, if I am to be mentioned in the same breath as Chaucer.'

The old king's library was kept in a falconry tower, which they entered by ducking through a low door, expecting to find the usual stinking mess the birds leave wherever they go, only to find an architectural joke, for once through the humble doorway the room was panelled in oak, and within were lecterns and tables upon which sat many a goodly treasure: manuscripts and bound books of exquisite beauty, including bibles, psalters, books of hours, the lives of the saints and so forth, each cover of wondrously worked leather, or sandalwood, or silver, or even bejewelled, and each page positively weighty with pools of burnished gold. Just opening some of the books felt like a sacred act, and the reader's face glowed in light reflected from the burnished initials. Lydgate, though, was careless of such things, and went through them like a squirrel in beech mast. Despite being a monk, he was not at all interested when Thomas showed him a Bible that had been translated into the French tongue.

'Boring,' he intoned, reminding Thomas of William Peyto yawning his way through Master Symmington's lessons back in Warwick Castle, and then he began up the steps to investigate the next floor.

Thomas had with him his *zibaldone* – about which, now that he was a hero of Verneuil, he was much more open and proud, and indeed he was onto his second or third of the little books – and in it he noted some of the titles he supposed Sir Richard might like to acquire for his own library – which are of no import here – and then he followed Lydgate up the stairs, where were kept the less gilded texts: the poems and romances of the sort that might be supposed to be of more interest to Lydgate and his chase to become the next Chaucer.

In fact, Lydgate was dismissive of these too, but here on this floor were things that caught Thomas's eye, and his breath: some true gems, including a version of *The Deeds of Sir Lancelot*, no, two versions; another two *Histories of Sir Tristram*, side by side; as well as a *History of Merlin*, alongside what looked to be something he had never before seen – a compilation of *all* the knights' deeds in one single book!

Tristram et Lancelot et de ses Faites de la Table Ronde! Thomas's heart thumped when he saw this. What an idea! He showed it to Lydgate, thinking this might be the sort of thing worthy of his attention, and felt a tremor of excitement that he might be present at the inception of some great enterprise, and that Lydgate would perhaps be forever grateful to Thomas for pointing out the opportunity, but Lydgate was scathing.

'A fairy story,' he sneered, making for the steps that led up to the third floor of the tower.

'A *fairy story*?' Thomas questioned. 'King Arthur? He was one of the Nine Worthies!'

Lydgate stopped on the steps and stared at him, laughing from under a cocked eyebrow. 'You don't believe he was taken away by fairies, do you, Malory?' he chortled. 'That he lies under a fairy hill, like some piece of mouldering cloth or rusting harness, ready to be dug up and brushed off, whensoever he's needed?'

Which was more or less precisely what Thomas had believed, though he had never thought of it in those terms, and never quite so literally, so baldly.

'Well——,' he began, but Lydgate had gone chuckling on up the steps to the third floor above. Thomas stayed below, leafing through another compilation: *Du St Graal et du Tristram*, which he found too wordy, and typically French in its use of eight words where one would do, and he found himself returning to that *Tristram et Lancelot et de ses Faites de la Table Ronde*, in which, however long-winded it might also be, could be read how the lives of Sir Lancelot and Sir Tristram intertwined with the rest of the Knights of the Round Table. He read the list of the chapters: how Sir Lancelot did this, or how Sir Lancelot did that, and how Sir Tristram and La Beale Isoud came out of Ireland, and so on, and so on, and he was so delighted that his fingers tingled.

After not very many moments more Lydgate came bouncing back down the steps, and finding Thomas bent-necked over the book, he laughed.

'Come on Sir Thomas du Lac,' he called and he led them winding their ways back down the steps and out of the tower and Louvre Castle itself, and it was only on their way back to the Hôtel Jean de la Haye, where they were quartered, that Lydgate slid that volume of poetry from his voluminous sleeve.

'What do you think King Arthur would think of that, eh Malory?' he laughed, his chins quivering. 'Is a bit of looting below a man who'd send a boatload of newborns to their death?'

Thomas said nothing.

And that was that.

'What have you got there?' Ap-Moffat asked when Thomas reached the Hôtel. His scarf was pulled very high around his neck as usual, and he was perched on a low stool by the fire, playing chess for money with Folo, whom Thomas was certain did not know the rules of the game.

'Just something I bought from a stationer down by the river,' Thomas told him, and Ap-Moffat launched into a tale about how he once found a medical pamphlet at a stationer's that had been written by the surgeon John Arderne that – oh God. It just went on, and basically even though he thought he had been rooked, and everybody laughed at silly old Ap-Moffat, it was very useful and he gave it to another surgeon who used the information to save the Earl of This or That's marriage or life, Thomas was hardly listening which, and he – the earl – was so grateful that he gave Ap-Moffat his daughter in marriage or something, but by then Thomas was deep into the second page of *Tristram et Lancelot et de ses Faites de la Table Ronde*.

→ How it was that Thomas was soon on the move again, after only a few months in Paris, because there then occurred another of those distant events, such as that which took his father to Warwick, or him to Konstanz, the breeze from which would alter the course of his life again, and this time the blame for it — or the credit for it, perhaps — lay with, of all things, a person. Or rather, a woman. In particular King Henry the fifth's widow, the French princess Katherine, who, after the late King Henry's death back in 1421, had remained in England to mother her son, the present King Henry, the sixth of that name.

Now it had so befallen that this task had not kept the dowager queen completely occupied, for it was learned at court that she — governed more by whim than worship — had taken up with a gentleman of her wardrobe whose name no one could then pronounce, for it was — and he was — of all things, Welsh.

And this being known, and it being believed that the late king could be heard spinning in his grave, the Council felt it wise to remove the boy — her son, the king, with perhaps seven winters to his name — from such a noyous influence, and since Sir Richard Beauchamp already had a young son of his own — Harry was just past his third winter by then — as well as a household filled with other wards of high blood — none of whom matter here — early that next year, Sir Richard was summoned back home to England to become the king's governor.

This was a great honour, apparently, and entailed enfolding the young king into his own household and teaching him letters, languages, nurture and courtesy, and, knowing of Thomas's interest in letters — not one over-widely shared among many of his affinity — Sir Richard summoned him to return with him to England.

'Show the king examples of times past, Malory,' he told him. 'Show him how virtuous kings come to good ends, how evil kings suffer accordingly. You know the sort of thing.'

⁂→ How it so befell that Thomas once more gathered his possessions, and Folo Bundsay, and Folo's newfound wife — whom he had taken on the strength of her buttery pastry and solid good sense, and of whom he was justifiably proud — and together they rode for home: Folo on a bay mare he had bought and named Jean, his wife on a mule he had named (a good joke this, Thomas thought likewise) Jean. She — Laure — was a sturdy little thing, with strong opinions, whom Thomas could see feuding with Goodwife Bundsay in the future, and the thought made him smile.

Helping to educate a boy of so few winters was a strange change in occupation, Thomas would have admitted, but he soon located his old copy of Vegetius, much abashed by poor old Spare-the-Rod's interrogating thumbs, and later that month he presented himself to the king, who was then at Warwick Castle with his tutor, affable **Sir John Somerset**, and various other household men, who, again, do not matter here overmuch right now.

At first glance the king stirred within Thomas the certainty that a mistake had been made, or that a trick was being played, for there was no trace of the father within the son — nor, really, of the mother, who was a famous beauty — and he found himself peering beyond the boy, over his shoulder, in search of the real king, who was surely coming, but no, this was he: the King of all England, and Lord of France, for now at least; he was one of those tall, pale and boneless boys with eyes forever glossed with about-to-be-shed tears; the least warlike child imaginable.

Nevertheless, they persisted in hoping something would change, and for his seventh birthday, Sir Richard had made for him a very fine suit of armour, perfect in every diminished detail, just as the child's own father had been given on his seventh birthday, and in which any ordinary boy would have wished to bathe and sleep, but the king set it aside as if he simply did not know what it was. He was also given any number of very fine — if blunted — little swords of the sort Thomas would have loved at his age, with which he was encouraged to lay about anything and anyone who stood nearby. These he likewise left untouched, and they were snatched up by the earl's boisterous son, little Harry Beauchamp — whom they called Child Warwick — who was also often there in attendance, of a sort, to the king.

And while the king was usually mildly pleased to see Thomas whenever he appeared carrying his *zibaldone* (which he now did with no embarrassment, and into which he had started to copy stories taken from that wonderful *Tristram et Lancelot et de ses Faites de la Table Ronde* that he had stolen in Paris in order to read them to the king), whenever he tried a new story, Child Warwick would insist instead on hearing again, and again, and again — while enacting it, too, of course, with one of those blunted blades — only that of how King Arthur pulled the sword from the stone.

At the start of Sir Richard's efforts to temper the king, they led him to the tiltyard, where they had set up a post similar to the tree trunk Thomas's father had once had upended for him when he was a boy, in the hope of instilling

228

within him some of that same martial vigour. They showed him how he might take his blade to the thing – whack! whack! whack! as little Harry Beauchamp managed – but the king could hardly lift the sword, and though members of Sir Richard's household stood clapping like fools every time – five of them – the king managed to land a blow, in the end he stopped and everybody waited a while longer, about thirty of them in a ring around him, while he leaned on his sword and looked very dolorous and then it began to rain, and so they went in, and that was that.

These were agreeable, easy months for Thomas and he grew fonder of the king once he had come to accept that he was not likely to become the man everyone had hoped he might, and that he would never come around to Vegetius, or ever lead English knights to re-edify the walls of Jerusalem as his father had once hoped to do himself. In the end, Thomas was grateful that he did at least once lose his temper with Child Warwick for affixing so mightily on the story of the pulling of the sword from the stone, and insist that Sir Thomas move on to reading to them some of the more peaceable deeds of the Knights of the Table Round, though he was so pious a boy, he would clap his hands to his ears rather than hear anything with even a hint of earthy, earthly pleasure.

'Leave we the story of Lancelot and Guinevere!' he would shout. 'Turn we now to the story of King Bagdemagus!'

Or whoever, which Thomas was happy enough to do, though likewise the king had little relish for tales of grievous buffets and dolorous strokes, and the terrible injuries that followed thereafter, so Thomas had taken to passing long hours going through those French books and drawing from them and noting down as many of these gentler, softer sorts of detail as he could, such as the quest for the Sangreal, and in this way the months passed and Thomas might have become fat and lazy and have developed a taste for Gascony wine and dried fruits brought back from the Holy Land, and he might have changed, very slowly, over time, into someone such as Spare-the-Rod, save without the Lollardy, or the rod, and that might well have been a better, happier end for him, especially given what was to come, but just as a chance wind – in the shape of the Dowager Queen Katherine – had buffeted that arrow of his, and blown him back to Warwick, so another woman was once more about to enter his life, and cause its path to make a sudden and dramatic turn, and not just any woman, but a certain specific woman.

Sir Thomas is conscious that any boy wishing to hear of Agincourt will most likely be put off by the arrival into his story of another woman, and were the boy here listening, Sir Thomas might glide over some of the details of what is to happen next, most especially:

➻→ How in the spring of that next year, while Thomas was with the king at Wallingford and, it being the first warm day of the year, they were outside, in the shade of one of the park's great, spreading oaks. It was hoped their proximity to the shadowy glades might tempt the young king to pick up one of the slender hunting bows the huntsman had brought against just such an occasion, and to venture out after woodland game. Sadly, the young king remained unmoved by the proffered cone of fresh hind turds, and was entertaining himself upon a spread arras with two corn dolls: one playing a priest hearing the other confess sins that were so feeble none there knew where to look.

As had become his habit, Thomas had brought with him his latest half-filled *zibaldone*, ready for the moment when the king's second doll had performed its tiresome penance, and someone — Sir John Somerset, probably — suggested he might like to hear tell of a stirring deed of arms as performed by a noble knight of his forebear's Round Table. And the king reluctantly agreed that perhaps he would, although not one that concerned buffets if possible, and Thomas opened his *zibaldone* and was about to tell the king how Sir Tristram met La Beale Isoud, and how he did ingeniously disguise himself as Sir Tramtrist, when through the park came a party of horsemen and, as it turned out, horsewomen.

The king's guards gathered themselves to watch them come across the sheep-cropped grass and all fell tense and silent, and Thomas later thought that they had all felt something strange was afoot, as if they had all known then that these riders brought with them tidings to change the world.

'Why, I believe it is my aunt,' affable John Somerset said, recognising the colours of the Earl of Westmorland on the first of the outriders' surcoat, and so with mixed relief it was decided that it must be **Lady Joan Beaufort**, another of the king's many cousins of some distillation, and that she should therefore be allowed to approach the king. The countess by this stage was very elderly and, having already borne more than fifteen children, long past the point of patient courtesy with any child, even the king. For his part, Henry accepted her brusque courtesies without complaint, for she had become notorious for her piety and was in fact, even then, she told them, on pilgrimage to nearby St Alban's Cathedral.

⇥ How for once Thomas found himself uninterested in the travelling arrangements of a pious old woman, for in among the party was another woman perched aslant a small grey palfrey, who slipped from her saddle without assistance of any servant, to land lightly on the grass. She was younger than Thomas, in a simple dress the colour of roses and a veil-wrapped and effectively pinned henin, and she carried her narrow self with lively spirit and bent her knee to the king with a mildly ironical flourish.

'My daughter,' Lady Joan was saying, 'Lady Anne.'

And that was the moment when Lady Anne, perhaps feeling Thomas's enraptured gaze, looked up, and, as if by some predetermined celestial logic, they caught one another's eye, and it was just as if there were nowhere else either might look.

Though now Sir Thomas recalls such things to mind, he warms to the details, as must all old men when recalling to mind all those youthful burgeonings of the heart, and he would now admit that he would have liked to tell the boy that his entire life halved upon that moment, and that from then on there would only be the time *before* **Lady Anne Neville** — she was of the Westmorland Nevilles — and *after* Lady Anne Neville, and he might even have risked incurring the boy's repugnance by expanding on this, and telling him more, such as:

⇢ How that from that moment and forever thereafter all others — men, women, the circling dogs, the whickering horses, the humming insects — ceased to exist; and that everything in the world from then on forever thereafter became brighter, fuller, more vivid because he knew that she — Lady Anne — lived.

⇢ How while they looked at one another, all time seemed to dawdle, and the air grow syrupy, and that though he could but only sense it as a rough, unshaped thing, he knew he had seen the purpose of his life, just as, perhaps, Sir Tristram had when first he saw La Beale Isoud – or, rather, after they had drunk the love potion – or, dare he say it, when Sir Lancelot du Lac first clapped eyes on Lady Guinevere.

➻→ How his feelings for Lady Anne were of a nature that even now, so many years later, he can only describe as spiritual. There was no wanton lust, no desire to lie with her, for, as he would swear on the cross of his sword, his chief delight that day was in the dawning relief that she existed, that she had been revealed to him, not as a woman, but as an idea, as intangible as worship, as honour, as the love of God.

➻→ How while their eyes were fixed upon one another's, everyday life did proceed around them as if nothing had changed.

'You are not drawn to the chase, sir?' Lady Joan Beaufort was asking the king, indicating the clutch of bows, and the arrows that lay still within their linen bags propped against the tree. He told her he was not. Not that day, anyway. Not any day, some of the men gathered there might have muttered.

'Then you are reading?'

'Yes, lady,' he said. 'Sometimes Sir John reads to me verses from the Bible.'

At this affable John Somerset bowed, allowing his fur-lined gown to touch the ground.

'And sometimes Master Malory reads to me of noble acts of King Arthur and his gallant knights.'

At the mention of his name Thomas was recalled to the present and stepped forward to bow like a proper soldier, stiff from the neck down. He was facing Lady Joan, but his bow was intended for Lady Anne, and it was intended to signal a lifetime's dedication to her service, and as he stood staring at the tips of her rose-coloured shoes, she spoke:

'The noble acts of King Arthur!' she started. 'Oh, how I should love to—'

But as Thomas looked up she cut herself off, as her mother's gaze turned on her, and rolled her eyes just enough to convey her affectionate exasperation with the old bat. She was quiet after that, though a smile was never far from her lips, even when the king asked after the health of her father, by whom he meant her husband, of course (for her father was long dead).

⤐ How the fact that Lady Anne was married came as a blow to Thomas, but then again, of course she would be married, as why would she not be? All women were, or were about to be, or had just been, and in those days, while men were away fighting, there was always a high chance of widowhood, and with this in mind, he was cheered to hear Lady Anne now telling the king, without correcting him, that her husband the earl was in France about the king's business, to which the king didn't have much to say, for although he was pleased to have an earl about his business, he had no idea — he having so few winters — what that business might be.

⤐ How Thomas deduced that Lady Anne must be married to Sir Humphrey Stafford, Earl of Stafford, whom Thomas then knew only as a worthy knight, having been at the old king's bedside when he went out of this world, and of whom there was, at that time, in that place, little more to say.

But by God and all his saints, Sir Thomas will soon have very much more to say about him, as the boy shall hear whether he likes it or not, but until then there are yet a few things more that might be safely got through without risking the boy's patience, including:

→ How the king then asked Lady Joan if she had come far, if she were enjoying her pilgrimage and if she liked her horse, and it went on like this for a while, but Thomas was conscious that he was waiting with his breath held, and when it looked as if the visit was ending, he felt something vital was slipping from his grasp. He grew hot and panicky, as with ague, as the countesses prepared to continue on the road to St Albans, and so, without conscious will, and by unsubtle increments, he placed himself by Lady Anne's side, and she smiled at him from the tail of her eye, but she did not look up at him, for she had no need: she expected him to be there, and had he not been there then there would have been a Thomas Malory-shaped hole by her side, and as they returned to her horse, where a groom waited to help her up, Thomas asked her if he understood correctly that she enjoyed the stories of King Arthur and his Table Round.

That is how he said it: 'his Table Round'. He could not say why then, nor now, but Lady Anne smiled, for she must have known what he was talking about, but Thomas gabbled on, and told her about *Tristram et Lancelot et de ses Faites de la Table Ronde.*

'A compendium!' Lady Anne breathed. 'All the stories woven together into one book? It must be long?'

She cocked her head and held her delicate hands apart, like so.

'Oh the writing was very small,' Thomas allowed. 'And there are no illuminations. It is a rough old thing.'

'Rough old things are always the best,' she said. 'Think of Sir Lancelot.'

He had not, until then, thought of Lancelot as a rough old thing, he had to admit.

'And anyway,' she went on, 'it is the words that matter, the ideas.'

Thomas agreed, totally. And to prove it, he could not help showing her his *zibaldone*, into which he had copied so many of the stories, the ideas.

Lady Anne was intrigued.

'You have taken the trouble to copy them out?'

She made it sound slightly suspect, and he had to explain that he had had to alter them slightly to make them suitable for the ears of the king and of young Harry Beauchamp. He did not tell her that he did not want anyone to see that he had such a valuable thing, and wonder whence it came.

'He acts them out, my lady,' Thomas went on, 'while I read them, and on very wet days it is the only way to wear the boy out, so always my knights are very quick to arms!'

She laughed at his story, a delicate little chime.

'How I should love to read them!' she said.

Without a moment's thought he placed his *zibaldone* into her hands with a bow.

'You must,' he told her. 'Here, please. Take it. It would be an honour.'

She held it for a moment in both her hands. She was flushed with pleasure. So was Thomas.

Over the years that separate that single act from now, Sir Thomas has oftentimes had cause to regret it, and had he known then what it would lead to, he knows a sensible man might have torn that *zibaldone* from Lady Anne's grasp and run for those shady glades and tried to live out his life as a hermit. But who among us is granted such foresight? None. And especially when in thrall to such feelings as then gripped him fast. And there is a part of him still, even now, even after all these years, and all the suffering he has endured because of his connection with Lady Anne, that thinks perhaps the price he paid for that strange, indefinable love was worth it.

And now, while he is in this recollective mood, and without the boy to impel him forwards to matters of a more martial tenor, Sir Thomas permits himself the luxury of lingering further upon the smaller, subtler details of what then happened, such as:

*→ How Lady Anne admitted that she had nothing to give him in return, and how he did waft away the thought.

'Perhaps you will write something in there yourself?' he suggested.

'A story?'

He smiled. That was not quite what he'd meant, but it was something.

'Why not? And if it pleases you, you might return it?'

'I might!'

She beamed, delighted with the idea.

And thus was their correspondence born.

*→ How it began fitfully at first, hesitantly even, though he believed it would become more regular once it settled into its true form, though what that form would take he had no inkling, for, in all honesty, he could not say how he imagined such a friendship might proceed, but he believed he had fixed upon a model, drawn not from the French books, but from real life: from that of Sir Thomas West and his Lady Elaine, and he saw himself very plainly as he had once seen West, on that barge on the River Rhine, sighing over the impossibility of his love for another, just as he – Thomas Malory – would soon sigh over Lady Anne, for their love, nascent yet, was likewise an impossible thing.

➻ How the countess's party then mounted up and rode away across the park, and Thomas was left gazing after them in reverential, transfixed silence, until, strange as it may seem, at that exact moment, a fly flew into his mouth.

➻ How in the days and weeks that followed, with Lady Anne gone with her mother to the town of St Albans, Sir Thomas took to sighing, and pacing the grounds of the castle, and in particular around an ornamental well in the garden, and to putting up a hundred hopeless what-ifs: what if he had met her before she'd met Sir Humphrey? What if her family were not the Nevilles of Westmorland? What if she had not been betrothed to Sir Humphrey since she was ten years old? What if Sir Humphrey died? Or was killed? What if he – Thomas – died? Or was killed? How would she feel then? Would she then shed a tear for valiant Thomas Malory? That sort of thing.

➻ How it was that Thomas started a hundred letters, only to scrape the page clean again, and his heart grew weary from all the plunging and soaring – so often! And so quickly! – and nor could his spirit stand the endless buffeting spells of high excitement chased by deepest melancholy that seized him as might the claws of a dragon, five, six, seven times a day, lifting him up and then letting him go, so that after a week he was worn out, his body sore through and through, and his spirit bruised all over.

➻ How it was that at last, fully seven days later, in connection with her mother's need to return to the Northern Parts where her family kept the Marches against the Scots, Lady Anne came back through Wallingford again, and once more Thomas was there to meet her again, in broadly similar circumstances to that first time, and how his heart waxed sore at the sight of her, for in her absence his strange, misplaced love was now so great and so true, notwithstanding the fact that she was another man's lady, that it was the centre of his life.

After speaking some time with the king, she sought him out in the park and passed him back his *zibaldone*, wherein she confessed she had had no time to write anything of her own, for she was so very much taken up with his stories, which she praised for being briefer than any of the French books she'd yet met.

'Why waxeth the French so prolix, Sir Thomas?' she wondered with a dreamy sigh, and for a moment he could not answer because his thoughts were occupied by the labour of dismissing the idea that she had mistaken his name – *Sir Thomas?* – because she had not made the effort to discover more about him. When he had succeeded – she had not made a mistake: she knew a noble soul when she saw one – he repeated something that perhaps Sir Baldwin Strange had told him about the French being ever more busy than bold.

'I should rather hear fewer words,' Lady Anne went on, 'and for those to touch upon worshipful deeds, and prowess at arms, rather than of knights sighing in gardens.'

Thomas did not tell her that she sounded like boisterous little Child Warwick, but told her instead that he was in the process of drawing out from one of the French books – he did not tell her, the one he'd stolen – the history of Sir Marhaus, Sir Gawaine and Sir Uwaine meeting three damosels in a wood, and each taking one for a year's adventure. In his mind he imagined taking Lady Anne for a year's adventure, and he imagined she was imagining such a thing too, but she told him then that she knew the story, and that she did not care for it overly, for it smacked of purposeless wandering, and further, she could not be sure if it was true.

'And what would three women be doing waiting by a fountain in the woods? And with so much time on their hands?'

Thomas could not exactly answer that, for he had not considered it, and so they walked on to find themselves in the garden wherein he had so often wandered and wondered all this last week, planted with roses and small hedges, and as they walked, with Thomas putting one newly polished riding boot carefully before the other, she told him how much she had enjoyed the story of King Pellinore and his fight with King Arthur, and how Pellinore broke Arthur's sword in two.

'Can you imagine it?' she asked, breathlessly.

To be honest, he could, quite easily. He had read that story many a time to Child Warwick, who liked it because it was all smiting of men and no kissing of damosels. Was it strange that perhaps Lady Anne and a five- or six-year-old boy were of a mind?

He told her that he had seen his share of such things in France.

'You were in France?'

She sounded surprised.

Again, Thomas fought to dismiss the idea that Lady Anne had not thought to ask anyone about him – less successfully this time, but eventually – and so distracted was he that he allowed himself some modest boasting of his own deeds of arms at the battle of Verneuil, the details of which she was likewise unsettlingly hazy about.

'Do you not mean Agincourt?'

➳ How when she left him, she called him Sir Thomas again, her noble Sir Thomas, and he felt unable to correct her, and she told him she would write of things that were close to her heart, and it was only later, while he was alone in the garden again, already yielding to autumnal sorrow at their parting and thinking on what she had said, that he was suddenly struck with doubts that reading stories of adventures to a group of small boys – however noble the adventures, and however noble the boys – was a worthy occupation for a man such as might be fit for a lady such as Lady Anne.

Was that any way to become a knight?

➳ How if that were so, then unbeknownst to him, the cure was at hand, for it was exactly then that a third woman was to enter his life, as she did the lives of all Englishmen, though in far less elegant or ladylike a style than had the Dowager Queen Katherine or Lady Anne Stafford made their appearance, which was, when you come to think about it, the very thing that did for her, in the end.

None of that will the boy learn.
Which some may hold to be a pity.
While others may not.

CHAPTER 9

How Sir Thomas attends the St John's Day procession, and how he is left bruised, both in body and in spirit

St John's at last: the twenty-second day of Sir Thomas's span in Newgate, and not only comes there no word of the general pardon, but for the sixth day in a row there is neither sight nor sound of the boy. Of course, the former vexes him far more than the latter, but Sir Thomas is surprised by how much he wishes to see the boy, and how much he wishes to continue with his tale.

'Ho there!' he now calls. 'Ho there! Boy!'

But there is no answer, of course, and it is a tired-looking Susan who brings him his bread and ale in her soot-smutted hands. She'll have been up late the night before, Sir Thomas supposes, keeping the vigil of the bonfires, probably with the boy. He wonders where he'll be now. The boy, that is. Off up to Smithfield perhaps, where there's usually a fair to mark the day, or perhaps he'll be down among the crowds along Cheapside, waiting for the Lord Mayor's procession? Or there is the bridge, too, of course, to watch the boatmen's flotilla set off for Westminster. It is too much to hope that he'll have been so inspired by Sir Thomas's descriptions of jousting and so on that he'll have set off for Windsor, or Eltham, where in years gone by Sir Thomas has spent many a St John's.

He exhales a noisy gust of warm air.

It is not *his* fault that the king is issuing a general pardon, is it? Not *his* fault that the wealthy inmates of all His Majesty's gaols will pay their ways out, denying Brunt and his like the chance to charge for all those extra candles and wine and trips to the Southwark geese. It is true he did not consider the boy's feelings, but for the love of Jesu! Who would? On hearing that he is to be free?

No man.

By the time Sir Thomas has finished his bread and ale, the day is already waxing overly warm, and he feels a thunderstorm in the offing. Even the slightest movement causes him to sweat, but so does sitting still, so he stands, dressed as yet only in his shirt and braies, and he swings his arms to and fro, to and fro, idly wondering where that cat has got to.

He lets his gaze drift around the all-too-familiar room, ignoring his coffer, and he sighs again. Now that the bells have ceased their clamour, and the pigeons are yet to start their cooing, he can hear distant music – pipes, cymbals and drums – coming from the street below, and the sounds of the crowd, too, and despite his divers vexations, he feels a lilt of excitement, and it strikes him that he might take to the leads today, as was his wont in days past – and is still his right, having already paid the one-penny fee for the week – to watch the procession pass by below, and so, in a manner, join with the world in celebrating St John's Day.

And he is suddenly very pleased at the idea of showing himself in his finest. He will wave to them, he thinks, and when they spot him, they will all wave back, and so he pulls from his coffer those plum and ochre hose that he has been saving, and the lightest pourpoint, in finest linen, which he ties together at the back and then steps into, finding the hose are loose on his withered legs, and the pourpoint flapping about his diminished shoulders. Once the points are tied at the front and at the hip, he is ready.

The pigeons erupt in noisy flight as Sir Thomas crawls out through the window's frame, and again he slips and only just manages to stop himself going over the edge, but this time he barks his shins and when he stops to brush the moss and pigeon shit from his hose, he sees with a sigh that he has ripped a hole the size of his

243

thumb in the plum wool above his left knee, which is now bleeding.

What a fool he is, he thinks, but he was right about the storm: that is definitely coming. Thick fists of ugly ominous clouds rise over Moorgate to the east, and elsewhere the sky is too dark and the air too dense. Shame, he thinks, thinking of the crowds below, and he crawls to the edge and peers down on them, where a band of strolling minstrels is playing a lively tune that Sir Thomas has never heard before. Behind them through the gate comes a man dressed as a woman with a wig of plaited straw, perched upon a pony that has been whitewashed, and he/she has on a collar from which extend long red and yellow streamers that are held by a ring of men on foot with rattling sea shells stitched to their sacking costumes – though why is anyone's guess – and after them through the gate come all sorts of other attractions, including a mule in a straw hat pulling a cart on which two mummers seem to be performing all the divers acts of the life of St John: baptisms in the main, of course, but also, now, just below Sir Thomas, the saint's final act of martyrdom. It involves the one wearing only dog-fur braies – the saint, presumably – kneeling to have his head chopped off by the other, who is now pretending to be a Saracen in a pointed hat and charcoaled face, waving about him an extravagantly curved sword.

It is strange and frustrating watching people from above like this, judging them only by the crowns of their hats, and since they cannot see him, his efforts to join them – and his parti-coloured hose in particular – are gone to waste, and are ridiculous, but he welcomes the visual stimulation, and the change from his confinement, and he lingers awhile staring down, smiling to himself to suppose that anyone looking up from below might mistake him for a gargoyle. It is while he is trying to see if that girl there – the one leading a sheep with blue ribbons in its wool – is comely under her straw hat, that he sees Brunt, standing on the other side of the street just as if he owns it, with a leather mug of something in his fist and a foolish, pickled grin on his foolish, pickled face, and Sir Thomas does not think he looks too distraught at the news of the general pardon, damn him! Or perhaps he has not yet heard of it? Perhaps the boy did not tell him? Were he the boy, he would not have rushed to break the bad news, not with those fists on the loose.

He sees Brunt is leering at the girl in the hat, from which it may be drawn that she – the girl – is most likely comely, and it is only after a long moment spent glaring at Brunt, trying to make him sense the full weight of the disdain thrown down from above upon his fat, churlish shoulders, that Sir Thomas notices the boy, standing a few steps away from his father, staring straight back up at him.

He starts and swallows hard, and once he has mastered his instinct to shrink back out of sight, he tries a smile, which he imagines will be seen as a grimace, and manages a stunted little wave.

Then the Saracen's sword flashes, and a red cloak is thrown over the head of the kneeling saint to signify the bloody wash from his beheading, and the crowd gasp in mock fright, and Sir Thomas would swear he can hear Brunt's mighty roar of laughter even from up here. A moment later, St John is on his feet again, resurrected to life, bowing and laughing with the crowd, flourishing his upturned cap and grateful in advance for any contributions. At which, of course, Brunt turns upon his heel and sets off down Cheapside just as if he had never been there, and Sir Thomas cannot believe how miserable it makes him to see the boy step out after his churlish father.

'Jesu,' he whispers to himself, never having felt so foolish as now, crouching on the prison leads in these silly parti-coloured hose, with his hand still held in that crimped half-wave, wishing for the company of a prison urchin.

At which point he is greeted by a voice from Master Bewscel's window.

'God give you good morrow, sir.'

It is, presumably, the man himself: old Lewd-Act, hatless this morning, and distinguishable only by a halo of silver-white hair. Sir Thomas makes his way over and ducks to peer through the frame to find a man almost as old as him peering back out. Under his unusually abundant silver hair Bewscel has a refined, scholarly face, with watery blue eyes and the sort of long, inquisitive nose on which you can expect to find eyeglasses. They exchange greetings and handclasps, and Sir Thomas finds himself staring at the old man, framed within his window, wondering if – if – *can it really be true?* Can such a man have done what this man is accused of?

And he sees a sorrowful look on Master Bewscel's face, who seems to be able to read his thoughts, and Sir Thomas recognises it as being the same that he wears when he is judged thus, and they both laugh ruefully in recognition, and thus is a fellowship born.

'Young John tells me you are telling him the story of your life?' Bewscel changes the unvoiced subject.

Immediately, the way it sounds (absurd and boastful) puts Sir Thomas ill at ease.

'I would not put it quite so,' he says. 'But he was interested in learning of the perplexed path that brought me to my present state.'

He does not really mean to boast that the path that brought him to Newgate is more perplexed and somehow superior to that which brought Master Bewscel here (though it is) but he has done so, and apologising will only further the offence, but Master Bewscel merely smiles to show he still has good, long teeth, and that he takes no umbrage.

'I dare say all paths leading to Newgate are perplexed in one way or another,' he supposes, which sounds very wise and generous. 'But John has been telling me some of the most memorable details, and I should like to shake the hand of a man who stood with the Duke of Bedford on that famous day outside Verneuil.'

Sir Thomas is wholly disarmed, for it is rare to meet a man who knows of Verneuil, and he takes the man's hand again, asks if he was ever in Normandy, though he doubts it, for Bewscel looks altogether too saintly, but Bewscel surprises him and tells him he served ten years, on and off, in the Duke of Gloucester's retinue – 'the late lamented Humphrey, that is – may God assoil his soul – not this new one'.

'No!' Sir Thomas exclaims. 'I nearly joined Duke Humphrey's household. He passed out of this world before anything came of it, though.'

'For shame!' Master Bewscel says. 'Our paths might have crossed earlier.'

'Where did you serve?' Sir Thomas asks.

'Only in Winchester,' Bewscel says, and he holds up a long finger, the waxy pad at the tip of which is dinted by the year-on-year pressure of gripping a quill. So, a scrivener then. That is no reason to judge ill of him, of course. Over the years Sir Thomas has met any number of them, and one of them, **Master Vernon**, with whom he once shared a cell in Ludgate, turned out to be a very fine fellow, in his way.

Sir Thomas thinks to tell him that he once saved Sir Humphrey's life at Agincourt, but he suspects Bewscel will know this is not true, since the boy would certainly have told him, and in fact, Bewscel's being the Duke of Gloucester's man explains why he recalls Verneuil, for the duke's brother of Bedford – with whom he later fell out – had been there.

He asks Bewscel where his people are from.

'Essex. Thaxted to be exact.'

Thaxted! Sir Thomas knows Thaxted well, having once spent a whole summer there in search of Hugh Smith and his accursed wife, just before he was confined to Colchester for – well, the less said of that the better. He tells Bewscel that from memory it is a fine little town, in good country, by which he means hunting country, and Master Bewscel doubts it not.

'Though I was never much one for that,' he admits, for it transpires that he does not eat meat. Sir Thomas can think of nothing to say in response to that and Master Bewscel turns, naturally enough, to the latest news.

'Have you tidings of the general pardon?' he asks.

'It is announced?' Sir Thomas asks with a painful jolt of hope. 'I did not wish to raise it in case it had not.'

'It has. Master Brunt told me yesterday. He was somewhat put out at the prospect of losing revenue, but I reminded him that in such times as these, gaols fill far faster than they empty, and that for every inmate he loses, he will gain two, by and by, and since each must pay his warden's fee, in the long run it is to his benefit also. He was somewhat mollified. He is a rough old boot, Master Brunt, but there is a soft side to him, and he is marked by tragedy. You know his wife died childing Susan?'

Sir Thomas admits he did, though he was not herein incarcerated at that time, but he does not wish to hear any good word about John Brunt the father.

'Has the chancellor suggested how much your pardon will cost?' he asks.

'Oh, I have not applied,' Master Bewscel surprises him. 'I am certain the jury will not convict me. And if they do, I will, I suppose.'

That seems sensible, though the prospect obviously worries him, and again, Sir Thomas thinks this must be about money. He could lend him the money, he thinks, even give it to him. Surely it would not amount to very much? A lewd act on Popkirtle Lane is not treason, is it? A matter of ten or twenty marks. A towering sum when you do not have it, yes, of course, but nothing much to Sir Thomas.

'But what is the punishment like to be?' Sir Thomas wonders aloud. 'If — God forbid it — they do find you guilty?'

'Oh. Let us not talk of that on this day of all days, Sir Thomas. Let us be happy and embrace the life we have left.'

Yes, yes, Sir Thomas thinks. Easy to say . . .

'But what of you?' Bewscel asks. 'Young John believes you will soon be free?'

Sir Thomas feigns doubt, though inside he celebrates at the very sound of this.

'My lawyer has petitioned,' he admits, 'though I cannot say how much it will cost for I am not yet told with what I am charged.'

Bewscel shakes his head in wonder and at that moment the cat — thought of as Sir Thomas's — passes his elbow to be greeted fulsomely by Bewscel just as if it belonged to him, and it leaps elegantly up onto his sill for a thorough stroke. After which Sir Thomas and Master Bewscel talk more of further divers imponderables and inconsequentialities until Sir Thomas feels they are in danger of becoming no better than two washerwomen at the wringing posts, and his knee is aching, and so after some time he feigns the need to move his bowels and bids Master Bewscel good day.

When he puts his head in through his own window, he cannot help but smile, for the boy is there, the blackened eye much faded and his lip healed enough for a shy smile.

'Oh!' Sir Thomas says. 'You've come back. Will your father not miss you?'

'Not him. He's gone up Smithfield, hasn't he? To meet his old pals to watch that witch burn.'

It will be some poor heretic, Sir Thomas supposes, some stubborn old wretch who will not bring herself to tell them what they need to hear.

'Well, it's one way to celebrate the day,' he supposes, his gaze drawn northwards towards Smithfield, above which he imagines will soon rise a plume of smoke if the storm does not arrive before the pyre gets going. 'Though I dare say not the one she'd choose.'

The boy grunts agreement.

'Should be able to smell her out there,' he says, 'if the wind's right.'

Sir Thomas does not wish to see the smoke of a burning woman again, still less smell it.

'Help me in, will you?' he asks.

And the boy does so, and when Sir Thomas is through, and upright, with no mishap, he waits while Sir Thomas brushes himself down without saying a thing about his parti-coloured hose, for which Sir Thomas is parti-grateful, parti-disappointed.

'So will your father be gone all day?' he asks.

'He likes to make a day of it,' the boy nods. 'Comes back all soused and gets us to smell his clothes.'

Sir Thomas thinks about Brunt for a moment. What a life: watching dogs tear a badger apart one day, paying Irishmen to dump dead bodies the next, jeering at a woman roasting in mortal agony the third. No wonder he takes his fists to the boy. Anyone would.

'Have you ever watched a woman burn?' the boy asks, and Sir Thomas almost denies it, but then admits he has, because, really, it is so neat.

'Tell me you have heard of Jeanne d'Arc.' he asks the boy.

'Jeanne – the French witch? Joan? You saw her burn? I bet she went up like a torch!'

'A torch? Why?'

'Well, stands to reason, doesn't it? Her bein' all evil and that.'

'Was she? Was she, I wonder.'

Like any Englishman, Sir Thomas finds it painful to think on Jeanne d'Arc's early victories—

But what I will say is that from the outset, and at all times thereafter, save for the fact that she was a woman, and that she dressed as a man, and that she was French, she was in all other respects a model of the perfect gentle knight, and that in other times she should full well have graced the Round Table – the Table Round – because for all her other faults, she was pious, worthy and noble. Further, she was more considerate of women, children, priests and those less fortunate than herself — prisoners, even! — than any man I did hear of, let alone meet, in all my days in Normandy.

She fought with great prowess, too, and though she could not wield a sword like a man, she did more to buffet our king's cause than any Frenchman had yet managed. She did not strive, like so many others, for mere bobaunce, for the empty glory of arms, which has been the undoing of all French knights since time out of mind, for she had in mind a greater vision than merely driving us English from France, which was to unify Burgundian and Armagnac, and to lead them on a crusade against the Hussites, which was a vision she shared — bar minor changes in personnel, and, in fact, destination — with our great King Henry, the fifth of that name, may God assoil his soul.

As a consequence of her arrival on the battlefields of France, we English lost not only much of the territory we had taken, but also our aura of invincibility, as from then on we were bested in every battle we fought — the names of which are not important here — and soon our hold on our lands in France became so uncertain that it was believed the only way to regain our ascendancy was to bring the boy King Henry — the sixth — to Rheims, and to have him crowned there as King of France in a magnificent coronation ceremony to show the glory of our court, and so impress upon the French the rightness of our cause.

But first the boy needed to be properly crowned King of England, a ceremony which had been felt likely to be too taxing on his scant physical resources, but now needs must, and so, in something of a rush, and with an intake of breath, as if for a plunge in a winter's pond, King Henry's coronation was planned for St Leonard's Day, in early November, later that year of 1429, when he yet had but eight winters to his name.

On the day itself — surprisingly fair — it was Sir Richard who took the honour of carrying the king into the abbey at Westminster, and once he had the crown placed on his head – at worrying peril to his reedy neck, I have to say – the boy walked out onto the abbey steps to wide acknowledgement, if not great acclaim, for this time the conduits were not stocked with wine as they had been at his father's coronation, and the only public spectacle was the burning of some poor sad heretic in Smithfield—

The boy adds something of his own: 'Wonder if my old man was there then? Bet he was.'

But at the feast that night – various roasted birds, subtleties that celebrated St Dennis as much as St George, and an unusually sharp Rhenish wine – I was given a better seat, on a better table than at my first coronation, and from this vantage point I had a clear view of the assembled guests, including, of course, Lady Anne, Countess of Stafford, who was seated on a very high table.

'Who is she then?' the boy chips in. 'This Lady Anne of wher-ever?'

Sir Thomas has forgotten he'd chosen not to tell the boy about his first meeting with Lady Anne, so he does so now, very briefly, by telling him that she was the woman whom he loved.

'What? As in . . . ?'

The boy leers and Sir Thomas sighs.

'This is why I did not mention her before,' he says. 'Because my love for Lady Anne was not unlike Lancelot's for Guinevere.'

'Eh? Didn't they—?'

'Or, no. It was alike unto Sir Thomas West's for his Lady Elaine.'

The boy suppresses a laugh.

'What is so funny?' Sir Thomas asks.

'It's just the name again: Elaine.'

'What about it?'

'It's just — funny. No one is called Elaine.'

'Well, she was.'

'No, she wasn't, remember?'

The boy is right, of course.

'But what about Elaine of Corbenic?' Sir Thomas comes back. 'Whom Sir Lancelot rescued from that enchanted bath? Or Elaine of Astolat, who died of love for him?'

The boy has nothing further to add on the subject of the name Elaine.

'Anyway,' he says. 'Go on. About the French witch.'

'I was telling you about Lady Anne,' Sir Thomas reminds him, and he is about to explain further how love was in those days — constant — as opposed to love today — unstable — but then recalls his audience, as well his vow never to wax prolix. Yet he must say something, to make sense of what is to follow, and so a little more of Lady Anne it is:

I had not seen her since she had left Wallingford, of course, though she had written in breathless urgency on more than one occasion — twice — addressing me as Sir Thomas de Lamory, after which I started signing my letters as such too, joining in on her joke, and in her last letter, sent before she came south for the coronation and written in haste, she wrote that she hoped to have the chance to meet me again so that we might have a few words, but we both understood — and indeed she phrased it very prettily — that the thing we most wished was the very thing denied us.

Such sentiments, they may seem laughable now, but in those days there was something noble about lovers' abjuration; an understanding of sacrifice of the self, and the knowledge that the love between two chaste and pure souls was a greater force in the world than either lover, for such love lasted forever, while the lovers' earthly bodies would grow weary and sicken and die. Lady Anne and I both understood that our love for one another was the better part of each of us both, and its unattainable nature lent it immortality.

Or so it seemed to me, at that time.

The boy merely blinks.

Anyway, perhaps because of this, King Henry the sixth's coronation feast was only the third time I had ever laid eyes upon She-Upon-Whom-I-Most-Devoutly-Wished-To-Lay-Eyes, as Chrétien de Troyes would have it, and that day she was by far the fairest lady in the hall, dressed in all her high finery, smocked about with swathes of luxurious samite and cloth of gold, and with a great golden brooch the weight of which was evident from thirty paces.

She surveyed the rest of those in the hall with that same ironical quizzing look as that with which she had greeted the boy king under that oak tree at Wallingford (I discovered later that her eyesight was extremely poor). I fancied she sought me out, though I, for the moment, preferred not to reveal myself, for seated at another table, even higher, was my rival: her husband, Sir Humphrey Stafford, Earl of Stafford, red-of-face, potted-of-belly and spindle-of-shank, who was by then already half-witted with wine and was staring about the hall like one of those grease-chopped simpletons you find outside inns towards the end of feast days. This was the first time I had ever seen him, and the last time I ever saw him looking so benign, and all I felt then was disappointment that Lady Anne should be forced to sully herself with such a man, whereas in fact I should have boiled with rage and hatred, and indeed had I got up, walked the thirty paces or so that separated us and thrust my dagger — still kept — into his gizzard, I should hardly have caused myself any greater trouble than that which he brought me in the end.

I did not actually do that, though oftentimes to this day I regret it. Nor in fact did I even speak to him until a few months later, when we — Ap-Moffat and Folo and I — once more found ourselves in Sandwich, awaiting a favourable wind for France. If I am honest, and I am that, when first I saw him I confess I was anxious, for I was not sure how much he knew about my friendship with his wife, or whether he knew that she and I wrote letters to one another, and so I was required to steel myself, which worried me, for it suggested, I believed, a less than saintly conscience. I had by then exchanged perhaps a half dozen (exactly five) letters with Lady Anne, and I had seen her once, though never alone, and in that time I had sent her a fair number of pages taken from my *zibaldone* just as I thought they might interest her, and a poem I very much liked that made a play on the words heart, as in the seat of love, and hart, as in the thing you hunt, and also — even — a play on the word dear, as in valued, and the word deer, as in the other thing you also hunt.

The point I am trying to make is that I had never once sought to keep what I was doing secret, or hidden, from Sir Humphrey, since there was nothing to hide or keep secret. It is true that I did love Lady Anne, but it was, as is aforesaid, a love quite as innocent as that between Sir Thomas West and his fair Lady Elaine, whoever she was. And if, as it may have befallen, I did not wish Sir Humphrey ever to see the letters I sent his wife — for he was like to misconstrue their real meaning — then that is no fault of mine, nor, Heaven forfend, of Lady Anne's, but rather of His Lordship's, and His Lordship's alone, for not thinking to ask what it was that the stout friar — a servant of Lady Anne's mother, it turned out, who had once like-wise carried her letters to and fro her own paramour — had hidden in his purse as he rode up and down the country on monastic busi-ness, while His Lordship was away in Normandy.

The boy gives Sir Thomas a sharp look.

Be that as it may, that day in Sandwich Sir Humphrey Stafford had just ridden down from Rochester, forty miles in one day, and now here he was, very road-smutted, sitting in the yard of Sir Richard's house, drinking ale while sat upon an old wine barrel with his saddle-stained legs spread wide and a hand cupping his cods.

'What are you looking at?' he barked, for I was staring.

He had a voice to cut through all other noises, and make every man and beast jump and turn his way. I took off my hat and bowed, and he growled, pacified, and returned to his ale. When he was done drinking, he threw the mazer aside and wiped his mouth on his sleeve and then adjusted his cods in such a way as no man – or woman – could not have known how matters lay.

'God-damned saddle,' he swore. 'God-damned bloody saddle. I won't piss straight for a sennight, now, and won't manage a shit for a week beyond that. Who are you anyway? And what are you doing standing around here like a woman?'

I told him. I supposed I was waiting for him to acknowledge me and our connection, our rivalry even, but no. He seemed never to have heard of me, and I felt the same pang of disappointment as when I had heard that Lady Anne had made no effort to discover more about me, though when I told him I was from Fenny Newbold, near Gosford Green, near Coventry, in the county of Warwick, he merely grunted.

'You know Caluden?'

Caluden? Of course I knew Caluden. It was the game park along Smite Brook, beyond Coombe Abbey, on the way to Coventry.

'Mine,' he said, pointing at his chest.

I had believed it belonged to the Duke of Norfolk, though I dare say things had changed since that duke's untimely death.

'It is a fine park,' I complimented him.

'Caluden's the worst park I've got. I've got better parks. Much better. I've got others I've not even been to, so I can't say more about them.'

I nodded, unsure what to say to this.

'But as long as they pay the God-damned rent,' he went on, 'and send my cooks enough dressed venison at Advent tide, then I'm content to leave them be. Though if ever they didn't—'

And now he gripped his fist around someone else's imaginary cods, and twisted. There was some further discussion of the pain he would inflict on more or less anyone who ever got in his way, and the pain he had already inflicted on more or less anyone who had ever done so in the past, and then he demanded more ale, and a servant went hurrying.

'Got a horse, have you?' he asked.

'Two,' I told him, truthfully.

'I've got many more than two,' he grunted again. 'I've got stables full of them. All the colours. Most of them are white. You got a white horse?'

Ap-Moffat arrived just then, and asked after the situation in France — as if Sir Humphrey might have privileged information — because by then Jeanne d'Arc was beginning to cause us extraordinary trouble.

'That fucking God-forsaken bitch!' Sir Humphrey bellowed. 'You know what I'd like to do to her?'

And he stood up suddenly, and gripped those cods again, in both hands this time, and he thrust his hips forward, and Ap-Moffat and I looked at one another in shocked disgust. Seeing our reaction, Sir Humphrey turned on us both.

'What are you?' he shouted, knocking aside his new-brought mazer to send ale splashing over our boots. 'To be blushing at me? A couple of God-damned maidens? Afeared of dirtying your dicks, are you? Think the French whore has teeth in her cunny? Get out of my sight, the pair of you!'

Which we did, gladly, sailing for Rouen that very next day, at dawn as if in a hurry, and without seeing Sir Humphrey again — he was bound only for Calais, thank God — until much later, as you will hear.

This time Sir Richard was to take command of the city as our headquarters in Normandy. We were to be garrisoned there for the next year or more, waiting for the king to make the crossing so that we might escort him to Paris to complete the second part of the plan to have him crowned king of both his kingdoms. With every passing day our situation in France grew worse, however, so that by the time he finally made it across the Narrow Sea, Rheims had fallen to the French, and Paris was only being held so that he might be crowned there instead. In the meantime, he had to be kept safe: first behind the walls of Calais for three months, and then, once it was deemed safe enough for him to scuttle south across country through which we could no longer guarantee his safety, he stayed hunkered down behind the even stouter walls of Rouen for up to a year or more.

But in May of that otherwise wretched year, the one after my twenty-ninth winter, the Burgundians managed to capture Jeanne d'Arc, outside a place called Compiègne, some leagues north of Paris. After some thorny negotiations, they ransomed her to the king's cardinal, **Cardinal Beaufort**, for ten thousand *livres Tournois*, which was a huge sum in those days, and so finally, at last, she fell into English hands.

I did not see her in the flesh until Christmas Eve, some eight months later, when she was brought into Rouen through the Bouvreuil Gate at dusk, under heavy guard, and I will never forget the moment: a thin snow filled the grey sky and I stood with Ap-Moffat and Folo and some other men who do not here matter one whit, having been charged with finding and bringing in a Yule log for the castle's great hall, and having done so, we stopped at the gate to let the guard party pass through the gate before us.

There was some sort of hold-up ahead, and the guard party came to a stop just yards from me, and there she stood, stick thin, pale as curd, with one of those bowl-on-your-head haircuts that William Peyto still favoured, and she closed her eyes and lifted her bony face to the sky, letting the drifting flakes settle on her skin, knowing, perhaps, that this was the last time she'd ever have a chance to do so. She was besplotched all over with blue, green, purple bruises and flea bites, yet still she had about her an aura that made us all – men, women, children, even dogs – stop and stare in total silence.

I can't say whether it was the possibility that she had heard messages from God, or from the Devil, or whether it was because she had achieved all she had achieved in so short a span of time and was still – I mean, look at her – a girl, a mere chit, nothing, but whatever it was, we all knew we were in the presence of something or someone extraordinary.

'Wonder which one'll be the first to go up in smoke?' Ap-Moffat asked, nodding to the ivy-clad log we'd cut down and were waiting to drag in.

'It won't come to that,' I was sure, for not even *we'd* burn a child, would we?

'Man is ever wolf unto man,' Ap-Moffat supposed, for he was better read than Folo, and had of late become similarly disillusioned with life.

'And when it comes to women,' Folo added, as if they had been talking about such things beforehand, behind my back, 'he makes wolves looks like donkeys.'

I looked at them both, slightly confused, but at that moment the hold-up was cleared and the guards set off again and the man behind Jeanne – obviously no longer overawed – banged a fist between her shoulder blades and she staggered forward, her wrists and ankles clanking in their manacles, and when she righted herself, she looked up and right into my eyes.

Jesu defend me! I felt the air sucked from my lungs. She had such beautiful, soulful and sorrowful grey eyes that I was unmanned, and knew not whether to bow, bend my knee or cross myself. A moment later, she was gone, jerked into the dark maw of the castle gate, where because of her previous attempts to escape, and because it was well known that the Armagnacs would do anything to have her back, she was to be kept in an iron cage, on the upper floor of the Treasury tower, within the castle donjon itself, shackled and guarded by a watch of never fewer than four of Sir Richard's men.

'Is that wise?' I wondered.

Most of Sir Richard's men were rough as hogs, of course, and in possession of great reason to hate Jeanne, believing her to be a witch, with hands much stained by English blood, so she'd be lucky to make it to the first day of her trial, I thought, without falling up and down those tower steps at least three or four times. I wondered if King Henry knew? It was not the sort of thing he would like: a woman, even one sworn to drive him out of his second kingdom, being badly treated and prevented from attending Mass.

If he did, though, he said nothing about it.

I did not see her again for some time, for life in the town went on as usual during the days in which she was locked in that cage while the priests interrogated her for evidence of witchcraft. The next time I saw her was a few weeks later, when she looked even worse: thinner, paler, bonier, dressed in rotting, grease-stained hose and a pourpoint, with a pair of very long, mouldy old riding boots she had tied about her waist, the points much knotted and intertwined in a great and complex tangle with those from her hose and her pourpoint.

By then we all knew that the Duchess of Bedford had examined the girl, and found her to be a virgin, which was something she wished — not unreasonably, you'd think, though, as we shall see, not everyone thought so — to protect. Hence the boots and the knotted points. Had the duchess found the girl not to be a virgin, then of course this would have been taken as proof she had lain with the Devil, and that all her powers must come from him below, rather than from Him above.

But would God really not speak to her if she were no longer a virgin? For some reason I cannot now explain, this was generally believed to be the case, though who first posited the connection I cannot say. A priest, of course. Yes. It might have sounded absurd when it was first ventured, but after a little while, once it had been repeated a few times, it became generally accepted as a fact, and so it was that much rode on the matter of her virginity.

It turned out Folo's Yule log made ashes first, which was something, I suppose. Its last tendrils of thick grey smoke vanished up the hall's stone chimney even before Jeanne's trial had started, which was in the week before Candlemas. Not long after this, perhaps a week or so later, on a day so filthy it was almost dark at noon, Sir Richard summoned me to oversee the watch on Jeanne's cell in the Treasury tower.

'Find some reasonably civilised men, will you, Malory? The last lot were altogether too excitable.'

It would only be for a few days, he said, and of course I was pleased with the responsibility, not to say the warmth. I took Ap-Moffat and Folo Bundsay with me, as well as two or three others who do not matter here. For some reason Ap-Moffat was unhappy, and on the first day of our tour of duty, while Jeanne was in the keep's robing room being questioned by all those priests and bishops, we took our places around the table in the guardroom outside her door — iron-barred, like a portcullis — and he asked how long our duties would last. I told him that Sir Richard had said just a few days.

'Then pray to God they do not find her guilty in that time,' he muttered, 'for I will not be the one to tie her to the stake.'

We all exchanged a look. In any event, we sat there all that day, unable to relish our idleness and the warmth of the brazier because of the thought that we might have to burn the girl, until towards evening, when she was finally escorted back from her day in the robing room by her old gaolers, her face ashen and her eyes sunken, but still holding a spark, and there was a tilt to her chin that suggested as yet unexhausted reserves of strength and spirit.

'Who are you?' she asked.

All save Folo Bundsay could speak French, so we introduced ourselves.

She said no more but shuffled past us and swung the door behind her. Through its bars there was only a tiny space in the room in which she could not be seen.

Meanwhile the old guards looked at us warily.

'You're not going to watch her?' one of them asked. He was, in fact, a youngish man, with a fat face that did not suit his cap.

'She is *pissing*,' one of his fellows added with a smirk.

'Go away, Goddons,' we heard her call.

Goddon was what they called us Englishmen because we cursed so often, and damned everything in God's name.

No one said anything for a moment. Ap-Moffat coughed to cover the sound of her pissing while the old gaolers looked confused and then left. We retook our seats. After a while we took her in some soup and bread. She was on her knees, praying. Folo took her bucket and emptied it down the garderobe. Then he returned it to her, and we locked her in her cell and hung the key on a hook banged into the wall by the loophole through which we were instructed to throw it into the river if ever the Armagnacs stormed the tower. We had one candle between us all, and, it getting dark early, we sat in its gloom for a moment, then banked the fire in the brazier, said our prayers, double-checked the lock on Jeanne's door, blew out the candle flame and lay on the rushes and hay in the corner, just as if we too were prisoners, and prepared for sleep.

'Good night, Goddons.'

'Good night, Jeanne.'

In a way it was comical, thinking back on it now.

The next day we received word that she was not to be taken to the robing room, but the priests and bishops would be coming to her cell to question her. Two women were sent in advance to gather up the rushes and hay and bring fresh stuff, fragrant with dried flowers, and three beeswax candles to sweeten the air further. Ten priests came, led by the fat, breathless bishop, and followed by an army of clerks with more stools and lecterns, and we were ejected while they questioned Jeanne.

At the end of that first day the clerics and clerks came trooping out of the tower weary with displeasure and we returned to take our places to find Jeanne asleep, exhausted by another day's defiance. It went on and on and her inquisitors made no ground. She rejected their authority, claiming God's above the Church militant's, or she demanded to see the pope, or she would tell them that she wasn't going to tell them anything else that day, or that they should just move on from whatever it was they were talking about. Yet every new day ten or more of them would come, each well-fed and well-rested, buttressed against the cold by layers of fat and wool and fur, and they would torment her – an ill, starving, exhausted, unlettered girl – with their sinuous suggestions and concealed lures to indict herself. And each time she bested them, for she was cleverer than them all by a time and a half.

'Do you believe yourself to be in God's grace?'

'If I am not, then I pray He puts me there, and if I am, then may He keep me in it.'

And for all that, for all the days they put into it, they could find her guilty of nothing more serious than the wearing of men's clothing – which one might have detected with a single glance – but which was against rules laid down in the Book of Deuteronomy.

Occasionally she talked to us, asking us about the weather and about the countryside beyond the city walls, and after any signs of spring, while I asked her about such things as her famous sword, and how she knew to find it in the churchyard. I was not trying any trick to lure her into telling me that she had placed it there herself, or that someone else had placed it there on her behalf, but she was wary and when I asked her such things, she would usually sigh and wish me a good night, or she would turn her face to the wall, but once or twice she got me to tell her stories from the history of King Arthur, some parts of which she found difficult.

'So wait, Goddon, are you really saying that King Arthur had all those children born on May Day put to death? Just like Herod, and just so that Mordred would die?'

Put like that it did sound bad, I had to admit.

'Not exactly,' I told her. 'He had them put in a boat.'

'Which he had pushed out to sea? And in the end, still Mordred survived?'

I was still then, I think, neutral in my belief as to who guided her, if you can believe that. Or I was in the gap between knowing and believing: God's truth and man's truth.

She was a great biter of her nails, I noticed, and I discouraged her in this, though as Folo said, it hardly mattered for she would not need them where she was going.

I'd noticed that to begin with everyone hated Jeanne for the harm she'd caused us English, but once you came to know her a little bit, then, I have to say, she became merely irritating. It was not that she was so pious — that was a good thing, of course. It was that she was so unbending, so certain in her endeavours and just *so* superior, with her mind appeared fixed on higher things, as if she always knew what you were going to say, and was always disappointed that you should say something so banal.

'Perhaps it's just that she's French?' Ap-Moffat wondered.

As the days passed, the bishops' and priests' and clerks' nerves became stretched tighter than cloth in a tenter frame. The whole might of Lancastrian England pressed down upon them, demanding results, and the thickening spring air seemed to thrum with their shame and frustration because, I feel sure of it, they also knew that what they were doing was wrong, and found themselves in a race between English impatience and their own self-disgust.

Either way, they needed to break Jeanne before they themselves were broken.

Into this already foul-enough brew, and back into my life, came an even fouler agent: Sir Humphrey Stafford, Earl of Stafford, who rode down from Calais on a cheerless afternoon in the week after Ash Wednesday, in a cap and travelling cloak lined with fox and marten fur.

I was sitting with Folo Bundsay on the outside steps of the tower, having just put away after rereading for the hundredth time, of all things, a letter from Lady Anne — sent in haste from a place called Hexham in the north, where she wrote that there was an abbey, and the weather was poor — when he came clattering into the bailey followed by a retinue of fifty men, each in the earl's black and red, with a badge of knotted rope rather than our cross of St George.

'Where is that whore bitch?' he bellowed.

He hadn't even got off his horse.

'Folo,' I said. 'Make sure Sir Richard is aware my lord of Stafford is come.'

Folo ducked under the horses and hurried off across the bailey to the keep, where Sir Richard Beauchamp was most like to be found. Sir Humphrey swung his leg over his saddle and came stalking towards the tower's door.

'Is the whore up there?' he bellowed.

'My lord of Stafford,' I began, standing up, forcing him to check

265

his stride. He was ruddy-cheeked and smelled like a horse who sweated wine.

'Who are you?'

I reminded him. Not a flicker of recognition.

'Well, get out of my God-damned way, then.'

He made to pass me but I remained resolute. I had been at Verneuil, remember. I knew how to withstand such things. But his men were a gathering weight behind him, and each was like to stab me if I so much as laid a finger on their lord.

'She is at prayer,' I told them.

'She prays to the God-damned Devil, so now out of the way.'

His breath was cold and meaty, and he tried to thrust past me but again I stood my ground, and he was forced to lever himself around me. There was nothing I could do to stop him, really, that would not have had me beaten to a bloody pulp. I followed him stamping up the winding steps, his horribly stained backside ahead of me, perhaps as many as ten of his men following behind.

'Where is she?' his voice echoed in the stone confines of the tower. 'Where is that God-damned French whore?'

I prayed that Sir Richard would come hurrying, for without him it was impossible to imagine this ending well. After three turns of the tower steps we reached the guardroom where Ap-Moffat was eating something and once more winning at dice with the other two guards. Jeanne's door was locked, thank the Lord, but through its bars you could see she was, as I'd suggested, on her knees, at prayer.

'Is that her?' Sir Humphrey shouted, as if she could be anyone else, and for the first time, Jeanne looked up and looked frightened, as if we'd let in a snarling boarhound or something, and now she was pleased that we had always been ordered to lock her in, for at least he was locked out.

'Call yourself a maiden do you, you French whore?' Sir Humphrey shouted. 'We'll God-damned well see about that!'

Sir Humphrey yanked the iron door fiercely. Then he turned on Ap-Moffat, who still sat there looking only partly alarmed, feigning not to know with whom he was dealing.

'Where is the God-damned key?' Sir Humphrey barked.

Now Ap-Moffat stood and pushed the bench back with his knees and made a vague patting notion, as if he might keep the key in his purse. He opened and closed his mouth and looked questioningly at the other two men as if either might have it. Both were round-eyed with fear, frozen still, for they well knew Sir Humphrey's badge and his reputation.

Footsteps scraped on the steps behind us. Sir Humphrey's men, hurrying to catch up.

'Sir Richard keeps the key,' I lied.

'Does he?' he growled. 'Does he now?'

Of course, just then all of us looked over at the key hanging on its nail by its loophole. It was impossible not to. Whatever else he was, Sir Humphrey was no fool. He followed our glances.

'Give it me, you bitch's whelp!'

Ap-Moffat looked surprised to find it there. I hurried around the room and plucked it off the wall and then feigned clumsiness, and tried to scoop it out of the window, but my fingers were cold, and instead I dropped it in the rushes.

'Don't let him in, Goddon!'

'Shut up, you French bitch!'

I stumbled and managed to kick the rushes over the key and then pretended to fumble for it more. Sir Humphrey shouted a name and a large man in a buff coat strode across the room and shouldered me aside. He found the key. I snatched it from him as he picked it up and I made for the window again. He banged my arm aside as I threw it. I missed the aperture and the key fell to the floor again. This time he gathered it with more care. He curled a scarred lip at me, and strode to hand it to Sir Humphrey. I hurried to stand between Sir Humphrey and the doorway to Jeanne's cell.

'No,' I said.

Sir Humphrey looked at me dangerously.

'Who are you again?'

'Thomas Malory,' I began, 'gentleman, of Fenny Newbold in the county of Warwickshire, I am my lord the Earl of Warwick's indentured man, and I am charged with the safe—'

He smacked me with the back of his hand, the sort of blow that might shake loose every tooth. Stunned, I could only let the big man in the buff coat haul me aside. Ap-Moffat almost caught me but I gathered myself and I charged at the big man, driving my shoulder into his belly. Ap-Moffat extended one of his perfectly polished riding boots to trip him and he stumbled back into the other men at the head of the stairwell. But Sir Humphrey had twisted the key in the lock and had swung the door open. The big man was back on his feet and more of Sir Humphrey's men were shouting and filling the room. Jeanne was backed into the far corner of her cell.

'You'll soon be no virgin, you bitch!'

I caught the duke by the shoulder and turned him. He was – as God is my witness – fumbling with the points of his codpiece.

'Get out of my way,' he spat in my face. 'You God-damned peasant!'

'Think of your wife, sir! Think of Lady Anne!'

It was all I could think of. He stopped then and looked at me properly for a long moment, and I believed I had shamed him enough, and that this would come to an end. But then he roared something spit-flecked and incomprehensible and he reached for his dagger. I knew he would kill me then or kill her, or kill us both, and for an instant, I wondered if I was doing the right thing. I pushed him back. My hands slipped on the broiling sweat that seemed to froth through his cloth, oily as goose fat. He drew back the dagger. I began to reach for mine, but then, over his shoulder, I saw or heard that I had done enough. Behind them, through the door of the cell, came storming the bulk of Sir Richard Beauchamp, big, solid Sir Richard Beauchamp, armed with muscle, title and inbred authority.

'Stafford!' he bellowed. 'Stafford!'

In the small cell the sound resonated. He caught Sir Humphrey properly and pulled him away from me, and from Jeanne. By now Sir Humphrey was befoamed like a horse, struck out of his wits with a form of madness, and he kept lunging at me to get past, to get at the girl, shouting that she was no virgin, and that she was a whore, and that all we had to do was look at her to know it. But Beauchamp was not giving in and he wrapped Sir Humphrey in his arms and dragged him backwards out of the cell.

'Lock it, Malory,' he said, 'and yield the key to no man save my-self.'

Sir Humphrey was struggling and trying to throw him off, but by now he was wrapped about in his own cloak and his arms were pinned, and the bigger, stronger man was in command. All he could do was continue to shout that we had only stopped him from having her because we wished to have her for ourselves, and that if we were real men we would have seen to this many months ago, and that she was servicing us all and we were fools if we thought he did not know what was going on.

His men backed slowly down the steps as men in Warwick's colours began to outnumber them, and by now Sir Humphrey was bent over our table, the dice scattered, still bound in Sir Richard's arms, his breath reedy and laboured, like a mare giving birth, and he was looking up at me through those bright, demented eyes of his.

'You!' he seethed. 'Thomas God-damned Malory! How dare you! You churl! You will pay for this! I. Will. Never. Forget. You. Or. What. You. Have. Done. This. Day. What you said. You used my wife's name in front of that God-damned French whore!'

He gave another great spasm, but Sir Richard held tight.

269

'You'd best go, Malory,' he soothed. 'Take the key. I will call for you later.'

'I'll remember you! Thomas God-damned Malory! By God, sir, as long as I have breath I shall remember you!'

A ferocious peal of thunder erupts above their heads, and both man and boy lurch startled to their feet, staring about in wild-eyed terror as the first raindrops hit the window hard as bodkin heads.

'What about the witch?!' the boy cries out.

It takes a moment before Sir Thomas knows him to mean the Smithfield witch.

'What about her?'

'She'll only go and smoulder now! Means my old man'll be back early and he'll be livid for not having seen her go up. God's bones, I'd best be off.'

For once Sir Thomas is not unhappy to see the boy go. Perhaps it was talking to Master Bewscel, or the shock of that thunderclap, or perhaps it comes from having riddled the embers of his memories of such dolorous times, or perhaps – even – it is something to do with the date of the announcement of the king's pardon passing unremarked upon, but Sir Thomas feels none of the joy he knows he ought. His spirit feels as bruised as his body, and after the boy leaves, he slumps back on his palliasse and watches the roof leaking, and he thinks of dear old Newbold Revel, and how the roofs will be faring at home under such rain.

After a while he gets up to move his night soil bucket under the fastest drip, but then fears it will soon overflow, so he moves it back, and then he stands at the window a while, conscious of new miasmas that the rain has stirred up, and he offers up a prayer – forlornly – that the Smithfield witch's flames will be quenched, and that she will be permitted to step off her pyre and, like him, go free.

CHAPTER 10

How a mystery arises to perplex Sir Thomas, and how he then offends the son of a churl, whereupon he is much abashed, and of one other thing

It is already a week after St John's, his twenty-ninth day in New-gate. After another very poor night's sleep, Sir Thomas wakes at dawn, gripped once more by dread, for there is still nothing from Hartshorne about the general pardon, and once again the threat of imminent execution looms large.

He lies on his palliasse and watches the flies dance, inferring from their strange and remorseless habits not a single useful thing, until Brunt himself comes to collect that which Sir Thomas owes for the week ahead. After their last encounter their relationship is necessarily strained, but instead of trying to bully him, today Brunt is almost cowed, and will not catch his gaze.

'Just a shilling,' is all he says, as if in pain, his hand outstretched.

A shilling? That is almost nothing for the wine and the candles and the good bread and ale that Sir Thomas has — he would not go so far as to say enjoyed, but certainly taken comfort in.

'Who is paying for all this, Brunt?' he asks, making a show of fumbling for a coin in his purse.

'Not for me to say, is it? Being as I am a churl and all.'

'Or does this only cover a day or two?'

Brunt says nothing, but gestures for Sir Thomas to pay up. Sir Thomas withholds the coin.

'Have you heard word of a general pardon?' he asks.

'Just give it me,' Brunt growls. He means the coin. Sir Thomas still won't pass it to him.

'Has it been announced?' he asked.

'How should I know? I've got no time to swan off down St Paul's, have I? No time to stand around listening to procla-fucking-mations.'

'I would have thought the gaol's keeper would say something re-assuring? After all, it is you who will lose out.'

'You'll all be back within the week, the lot of you, and if it ain't you, it'll be some other fucker just as bad, so don't you go worrying your woolly old head about Master John Brunt. He'll be all right. Always falls on his feet does Master John Brunt. Come on. A shil-ling. Now.'

Thomas presses the single coin into that fat, flat outstretched palm.

'And I will hear Mass this morning too, Brunt,' he tells him. 'Send your boy for the priest from Greyfriars.'

Brunt scoffs at this, though why, Sir Thomas cannot say.

The pardon is announced, he thinks, which is good news.

But no word from Hartshorne, which is bad.

He sits for a moment, waiting, and he hears Master Bewscel at his harp — a livelier tune this morning — and Sir Thomas is taken back to, well, the days when he used to listen to men who could play the harp, playing the harp. It occurs to him to write to Master Hartshorne and ask him to apply for a pardon on Master Bewscel's behalf. It will come late, Sir Thomas is aware of that, but **Bishop Stillington** — of Bath and Wells, and also the king's chancellor — is unlikely to refuse an extra sum, and it cannot require so very much money, can it, for a lewd act? And if Master Bewscel is found not guilty, then so be it. He will give it to him anyway, against future necessity.

He opens his coffer, and sets about the note, using up his last piece of paper. While he writes, he hears the harp, and is very con-scious of doing a noble deed, and when it is done he sets it to dry upon his coffer, just in time for Susan to come to tell him the priest is here for Mass.

Sir Thomas descends to the little chapel on the first floor, where the priest from Greyfriars awaits, and with the warmth derived from his noble act, Sir Thomas finds enough consolation in the Mass's soothing familiarity to be distracted from all his many other distractions, and he feels almost benign as he pays the priest his two pennies and then starts back up the steps to his own cell, as he is sworn to do, only when he gets there, he stops dead.

What is this?

His coffer has been ransacked. His clothes are strewn all over the rushes and the trays and their contents are spread across his palliasse.

His first thought is: Brunt.

He will have come back to steal that which he had felt unable to steal while Lady Elizabeth looked on, when the coffer was first brought in.

'Brunt!' he shouts down the stairway. 'Brunt!'

He returns to his cell to see what has been taken. All his pens and his inkhorn have been taken out of the trays and thrust back in the wrong order; the twists of paper in which he keeps his gum and copperas have been loosened, as if for inspection, and thrown back into their slots any old how; and though his hammer is where it should be, his galls have been spilled from their pouch. He sees his *zibaldone* has been left to slip behind his blanket.

Sir Thomas's clothes — those beautiful parti-coloured hose, his very fine linen pourpoint, his shirts and socks and braies and what have you — they are all just thrown aside as if the thief had no care or time for them, and yet . . . not even Ap-Moffat would have been able to find linens of such quality on any fripperer's stall. Even Sir Thomas's sponge is still there, and that block of Castilian soap.

The last time he was robbed in gaol — when that copy of *Le Chevalier du Chariot* was taken — the thief stole absolutely everything — including his night soil bucket — and left only his manuscripts.

And then a sudden, implausible fear seizes him.

His manuscripts!

He leaps to the coffer, throws back the lid, and – but no. There they all are, and apparently untouched.

Brunt arrives and surveys the mess.

'Having a tidy-up, are we?' he asks.

'What have you taken?'

'Taken? What would I want with any of this stuff?'

This is bluster, because he would want everything, if only to sell to buy ale.

'Do you swear upon our Lord Jesus Christ that you have taken nothing? That this was not you?'

'I'm not swearing on anything for the likes of you, you God-damned gaolbird. If you're accusing me of stealing anything, call the beadle. See where that gets you. Let out the old hue and cry, go on. I dare you.'

Brunt is a horrible man, and would have stolen everything he could, of course, given half the chance, but the fact that he does not even seem to be defending himself gives Sir Thomas pause for thought, and when he says nothing more, Brunt scoffs as if his point is taken and leaves him amid the wreckage of his coffer, banging the door shut behind him and ramming home the locking bar.

Sir Thomas sits and looks at it all.

It is as if the thief – if that is the right word, and it is not – had been looking for something in particular that was either here, and found, or not here, and so unfound.

Or were they looking for – and did they find – something Sir Thomas did not know he had?

And why the clumsy care of the pens, and the manuscript, and the ink, and none for the clothes?

He can think of nothing.

He looks back at his manuscript, and then looks again. Wait. He left it with the episode of the eleven kings on the top, didn't he? Now it is no longer on the top. Its place is taken by the story of how Sir Lancelot cured Sir Urry, the Hungarian knight, and it – the episode of the eleven kings – is buried an inch lower.

Someone has been through the manuscript. Why? Have they taken any of it? And if so, what? And if so, again, why?

Sir Thomas sits and hauls the whole thing onto his knees. He has to read through it all to see what is missing. He starts, and likes what he reads, but he is soon distracted from this distraction by those flies, still cutting to and fro above his head, and he finds he has lost concentration while trying to get through, of all things, the promises the eleven kings made to bring all those men-at-arms.

But if it is not Brunt, and Sir Thomas is prepared to think it might not be, then who?

It can only be the boy.

For some reason – probably because it is already two days after St John's, when the pardon was announced, and still Sir Thomas has heard nothing from Master Hartshorne – this betrayal enrages him far more than he feels it ought. After all that he has done for him! All his divers kindnesses and considerations – this is how he is rewarded. His private papers gone through? Anger flares, and for a hot moment he means the boy actual harm, and were he here, he might cuff him, just as his father did, but then, strangely, the anger burns out, to be replaced with a kind of bruised sorrow.

'Why did you do it?' he asks, when at length the boy answers his summons.

'Do what?'

'You know. Go through my coffer. You need only have asked me if there is anything you wish to see, or know about, or, by Jesu, *have*, even.'

The boy looks very wounded.

'But I ain't done nothing. I never went through your coffer.'

'Don't lie to me, by Jesu. I thought we were friends.'

Now the boy's eyes bulge glassily. He is very quickly on the verge of tears.

'But I never,' he says.

Sir Thomas sighs.

'I don't mind that you did,' he tells him. 'I only mind that you do not tell me the truth.'

'I am telling the truth. I never done it. I never done nothing.'

The boy gestures sharply, desperately, a flap of both hands. He is scared, and used to being hurt when accused of wrong-doing, and he looks ugly now, repellent even, and it is clear he has come from some foul-smelling task to do with night soil, but before Sir Thomas can say another word, before the tears spill, for the second time in less than a week, the boy turns and bolts through the door, slamming it behind, ramming home the locking bar as if to cage an evil spirit.

'Wait!' Sir Thomas calls after him. 'Boy! Come back! I didn't mean—'

But the boy is gone, before Sir Thomas can even get up, and he is left alone sitting in a new-brewed mire of mixed emotions: guilt, shame, regret and now, of course, doubt.

It really could have been anyone, couldn't it? Even Master Bewscel, of course.

He sighs and grips the hair at the side of his head and could happily tear it out.

Why, why, why? That is all he ever has: questions. Questions. Never a single answer.

And now there is no one to distract him from his infernal circling thoughts by listening to the next part of his tale, to which Sir Thomas has given a weight of thought, and though it is not necessarily the sort of thing the boy finds most interesting, it contains certain specific details that will show him just how the world stood then, and how it could come to pass that a worshipful man such as Sir Thomas might – through no fault of his own – come to be condemned to languish under lock and key for so many years, accused of a crime that in no ways could he have committed. Details such as:

➺ How the dishonest trial, the attempted rape and then the burning of Joan was only the first nail in the coffin of Thomas's belief in the God-given right of Englishmen to own Normandy.

➺ How a second nail followed swiftly thereafter when English armies captured not only Sir Poton de Xaintrailles – the Armagnac leader who had escaped the slaughter at Verneuil – but also William the Shepherd, who was the Armagnacs' desperate attempt to find for themselves a new Joan after the English had burned their last. He was a sad, simple little shepherd boy whom they'd cajoled into claiming that he too had heard the voices of divers saints and martyrs urging him to lead the Armagnac forces against the English. No one believed him, least of all those whom he was supposed to inspire, and he was easily trapped and taken alive outside the town of Beauvais.

Both he and Sir Poton de Xaintrailles were brought back to Rouen, and while Sir Poton was made most welcome in the castle's great hall, where he dined with the young king and Sir Richard and Sir Richard's wife, Lady Isobel, and was measured up for a ransom, William the Shepherd had his hamstrings cut, was stitched into an ox-hide sack and thrown alive into the Seine as it flowed to the south of the great castle.

Thomas watched all this from the quay, noting that nothing is so valueless that you should throw it away like that save a human life, and when the party of soldiers were done, they walked past him, wiping their palms on the woolstuff of their buttocks, on their way back up to the castle for the well-earned barrel of ale they had been promised in payment.

'Thirsty work,' one of them confided.

How the final nail was hammered home in Gisors, when one day he met a man from Birmingham walking free, fêted even, and bought drinks, because it was well known that he had once eaten a whole French nun.

How Thomas oftentimes thought of Lady Anne, of his father and his mother, of his poor brother who had drowned in the stockfish pond, and his bickering sisters, and of dear old Fenny Newbold, and he fell prey to gnawing melancholia, which Folo Bundsay diagnosed as homesickness, and Thomas agreed for the first time that he should like to be at home.

How it was that he then came home, with thirty-five-odd winters to his name now; wealthy enough, and not horribly maimed by war, and how he understood it was his Christian duty to find himself a wife and settle down somewhere to hunt, to game, to produce a family and to live out these next few years of his life in the unspoken anticipation of the death of his father, and of the coming into his estate.

How it was that he could not do this. Or not properly, for that same dogged melancholia to which he had been prey in Normandy followed him home, and so he spent his days doing nothing more than riding the drear tracks around his father's estate, along Smite Brook, past Coombe Abbey, where he would be reminded of Spare-the-Rod's burning, and where he would oftentimes clench his fist with rage at the abbot, and then past Caluden Park, which that malignant blot of grease the Duke of Stafford had once boasted of owning and where he hoped perhaps he would one day lay eyes upon Lady Anne come hunting, perhaps, with bright eyes and her slender frame all caparisoned in green – why not? – clutching a slender bow. Nothing would have pleased him more, and indeed without her by his side, nothing seemed to please him at all.

How at length Thomas even stopped hunting, and would not go with his father to the Pentecost tourney at Gosford Green, though they all knew it would most like be his last, and later, how he would even not eat fish or flesh for a while, and he began to waste away, and the world seemed a dim and ashy place, its lights blurry and every corner filled with a reminder of the dead. His father – who had just paid money to the Crown so that he might *not* be made a knight – seemed to understand, and he let Thomas be, though Thomas oftentimes caught him watching him through the shutters of his counting house.

How Thomas's mother wondered if it was a woman.

'Not one of those Frenchies? You always had a soft spot for Frenchies. Remember your first nurse? Always trying to look up her skirts, you were. Oh no! It's not that witch, is it? Joan? She's not put a curse on you, has she?'

His mother crossed herself.

She had become silly, Thomas thought.

His father rolled his eyes.

'Everybody needs a purpose in life, Tom,' he said later, when he was overseeing the hanging of an arras that his brother – Thomas's uncle – Robert had sent him from somewhere in Flanders. 'You need something else to do, other than wait for letters from whoever it is.'

As Thomas started to say something in denial, his

father was overtaken by one of his coughing fits and the conversation ended with Thomas helplessly and mutely patting his father's back, which was become like a bag of chicken bones from which could be heard and felt the grating of cracked and broken ends. The old man had shrunk so much that when he and Thomas's mother ventured out for their evening walk around that stock pond – now almost the only time his father ever left the house – his mother needed to rest her head against the top of his, rather than on his shoulder, as in times past.

➽ How the cough that wracked his father's frame was very sickening to hear, and how Thomas began to look away from his bloody linens, and abjure his company, which was dishworshipful and reflected badly upon him.

➽ How Thomas's father was right though: he did little else save wait for the letters from Lady Anne, the tone of which had changed over the years. From those early gushing enthusiasms for the adventures of King Arthur they had slipped by monthly increments into more formally expressed courtesies, so that where once Thomas might have told her he yearned to talk to her about King Pellinore, she now wrote that she had travelled to Brecon ('damp'), Maxstoke ('ruddy in a certain light') and even Calais (where 'the seagulls are ever impudent'). Sometimes she wrote regarding the weather – 'passing fair', or her health – 'passing well', or her movements about the country – 'to Lichfield for Shrovetide', and twice she mentioned Sir Humphrey had become Count of Perche.

➽ How early the next year, or the one after that, while there was snow on the ground, his father died. They had all been waiting for it, and one night the coughing just stopped and in the morning they woke to silence. It was all over. They called the priest from St Edith's, a successor to the successor to the man who had baptised Thomas, and they buried his father in the churchyard there, and so Thomas came into his own estate, though his mother retained her share.

⇥ How he wrote to tell Lady Anne. She wrote back to tell him that she had lost her own father – Sir Ralph Neville, the first Earl of Westmorland – many years earlier, and without quite meaning to, perhaps, she managed to suggest that his own sorrow was somehow childish.

⇥ How after that nothing much changed.

⇥ How May passed with little fuss, and then it was summer, then very soon after that it was autumn again, beyond which: winter again. And so on. And so on.

⇥ How a year passed.

⇥ How then another passed.

⇥ How a further year passed with little or no change in Thomas's estate.

⇥ How it was that just after Easter during the seventeenth year of King Henry's reign, when Thomas was past his thirty-ninth winter, Sir Richard Beauchamp, the thirteenth Earl of Warwick, died in France, and how Thomas rode with Sir Richard's son, Harry – who had once been Child Warwick, but was now raised to become the fourteenth earl, with scarce fifteen winters to his name – to Sandwich to receive the boiled bones of he who had done so much to shape Thomas life as a boy.

⇥ How he and Sir Harry stood bareheaded on the dock in Sandwich, with the watch called to silence as the box of bones was brought down the gangplank by two men in black velvet, raindrops clinging to the peaks of their caps like silvered seed pearls, and how the boy could not help but sob as a muffled drum beat like a slow heartbeat.

⇥ How this tragedy came not unaccoutred with consolation for Thomas, for the earl's passing seemed to bring to the king's mind all the earl's past kindnesses, and with them those of Master Malory too, for upon St Michael's Day, at Hertford Castle, at the hand of his gracious lord, King Henry, the sixth, Thomas was finally, at last, raised up to become Sir Thomas Malory, knight.

⇥ How this was the thing he had most earnestly sought all his life.

⇥ How his sponsor in this was the self-same Sir Harry Beauchamp, and in among the solemnity there was some mirth, when they recalled the stories Sir Thomas had read to both king and newly raised earl when they were younger.

'Why, there can be scarcely a man alive who knows more about what it means to be a knight than you, Master Malory!' Harry Beauchamp had said.

'I recall you reading us the old stories from your *zibaldoni*,' the king had said, giving the word an unattractively undercooked limpness. 'And believed for some little while that you had written the stories yourself!'

Sir Thomas had told the king and the earl that his services were theirs to command, should they ever desire he read to their own sons, 'come the happy day'.

There had then followed a brief pulse of awkwardness,

for neither man had yet produced an heir: Sir Harry because he had yet to see his seventeenth winter, and his wife — **Lady Cecily** — her sixteenth, and because the king — though with perhaps twenty winters by then — had not changed in essence since he had first offered those unfavourable impressions as a child, and lingered yet in what is oftentimes called 'that awkward stage', being very flushed of cheek and lank of hair, with greasy down upon his upper lip, and oftentimes a man wanted to wash his hand after shaking his.

↝ How, nevertheless, he was Sir Thomas's king. He was the man who gave him his spurs, and to whom he pledged lifelong fealty.

↝ How the order of the ceremonies of knighthood that followed over the next few days had been passed down from the days of King Arthur, and every act was symbolic of great honour and solemn oath.

↝ How at the heart of the ceremony was the moment when humble Thomas Malory knelt before his king, wearing a red gown to symbolise nobility, a white vesture for purity and black hose for death, and he — Thomas — though faint from his night prostrate before the altar, had sworn never to traffic with traitors; never to give evil counsel to women — wed or unwed; ever to observe fasts; and ever to go to Mass every day.

↝ How then he had his spurs attached to his feet, and his belt cinched about his waist, and then the king placed the flat of a sword blade upon his neck and said 'I dub thee Sir Knight' after which, when he stood, base Thomas had been transformed to golden Sir Thomas.

➤ How after that there was a dinner, held in Sir Thomas's (and two other new knights') honour, and the next day Sir Thomas rode against one of them for the first time in the lists.

➤ How he had been imagining this for many years, but nothing really prepares a man for charging headlong at another man, except doing it.

➤ How Folo Bundsay's wife was sickening, so he could not leave her, and so Sir Thomas had sat astride a stallion while his new, temporary squire, a man named **John Appleby** had lowered the great helm over his face, and then passed him up his lance and finally his shield, the design of which came revived from the arms of his grandsire, of Winwick, with its three lions passant, red chevrons and field of ermine tails.

➤ How Appleby had stood back, leaving Sir Thomas as the cynosure of half the eyes in the yard, and of how he kicked on, bringing the restive stallion surging into the tiltyard, and how there was so little to be seen through the helmet's mouth, and still less to be heard, that it took him a while to sight the cynosure of the other half of the eyes in the yard: his adversary, one of the other new new-made men, at the end of the field.

➤ How Sir Thomas tried to calm himself, to slow his quick-beating blood, and so communicate steadfastness to his stallion, but saints, it was hard, and the stallion was already over-boisterous. After what seemed like an age of nervous wrestling, he saw the signal given – by Lady Cecily, Sir Harry's wife – and heard the herald bellow his cry – '*Laissez les aller!*' – and he couched his lance and brought his spurs to bear, and he began his career down the yard.

➼ How he was brought home to Fenny Newbold upon a litter and how thereafter he remained many weeks abed, vowing never to return unto the tiltyard save as a spectator.

➼ How, when returned to life and able to walk his estate again, Sir Thomas found Fenny Newbold no longer grand enough for a knight, and that his mother had become near dangerously witless, and so, with all that remained of his unfulfillable love for Lady Anne – those letters – locked safe within his coffer, he resolved to eschew the perfect in favour of the good, and find himself a wife.

➼ How, in the week before his forty-second Pentecost, in May, with apple blossom petals in the rain-washed air, he did marry **Elizabeth Walsh**, of the Leicestershire Walshes: a pretty girl, narrow of waist, broad of shoulder and long and strong of leg. She was from a good family, unsurpassed at needlework, though with little interest in books, and his junior by an unspecified number of years. She did not weep on their wedding night, as Sir Thomas understood that many other men's wives did, and they got along very well from that moment on despite each moving within distinct zones of interest, and for the life of each, neither could quite divine how or why the other filled their days as they did.

➼ How from then on, and for a long while thereafter, life passed agreeably enough, and Sir Thomas rarely thought of Lady Anne. He hardly ever opened the coffer at the foot of his bed wherein he still kept all her letters, and so never once did he think for a moment that in keeping them he was running any kind of risk, for what was written was in no manner disworshipful.

➡ How Sir Thomas remained within the new-made Earl of
Warwick's household as the earl's indentured man, and how
throughout those years he was oftentimes in attendance upon
the earl, especially his castle at Hanley, south of Worcester,
where more than once he was summoned to read from his
zibaldone a story of King Arthur, or Merlin, or Sir Tristram to
the earl's wife, Lady Cecily, who was passing fair, but, if Sir
Thomas were unsparingly honest – as he would swear upon
the cross of his sword he is – also passing dim.

'Why would he *do* such a thing?' she was forever asking.
'That is very wicked.'

'I think that is the point, dearest,' Sir Harry would say. 'If
you do bad things, bad things come to you.'

'But surely it is a shame that the whole country must be
made to suffer for what its king has done for his own end?'

There had been a moment's pause when she said that and
Sir Thomas had thought, by Jesu, she is no more intelligent
than Folo Bundsay.

'Well. Yes,' one of them had agreed, sort of.

'And Lancelot,' she'd gone on, 'how many men does he kill?
In the tale of him rescuing Guinevere from the fire the first
time, or maybe the second – or is it the third? – he kills a
carter and then a porter without so much as a thought.'

'But they are churls, dearest. They do not count.'

Cecily had harrumphed and Sir Harry had laughed.

'You are like my sister,' he had told her. 'She too finds these
details difficult to grasp.'

➡ How Sir Thomas oftentimes also read to this sister – another
Lady Anne – who was most perplexed by the relationship
between Lancelot and Guinevere.

'But what are they doing when they are alone in her room

and so silent?' she had asked and Sir Thomas had thought of his own love for the other Lady Anne, who never had the joy of what she loved, and told this Lady Anne that love in those days was different from now.

'It was a virtuous love,' he told her, 'which is as real as any, but lacks for lechery.'

'But then why does he have to pull the bars from her window if he only wants to talk to her?' she had asked. 'Can he not say what he has to say through the bars? And then why does he say he will prove her virtue by fighting any man who doubts her virtue, when he must know her virtue to be incomplete because he himself has lain with her?'

'That is to do with God's justice,' Sir Thomas had told her.

Yet she had, he was certain, remained unswayed.

All this and more would Sir Thomas have told the boy, were he here to listen. Would he – the boy – have found it interesting? Sir Thomas cannot be sure, and perhaps none of it mattered overmuch in the great scheme of things, but what does matter, and what he wishes now he could explain to the boy, and what will transpire to be central to what then befell Sir Thomas, is:

⇥ How it was that about then England began her sorry slide into her late sad state, with her nobles riven broadly between two parties: those with estates in France who wished them protected (and so were in favour of continued war, whatever the cost to the weal) and those with no estates in France (who no longer wished to pay English armies to protect the estates of those who did).

⇥ How those of the first party – the war party – were led by Sir Humphrey, Duke of Gloucester (with whom Sir Harry stood, and so, as a consequence, must Sir Thomas), who believed all that was needed was one more Agincourt, one more Verneuil, after which everything would go back to how it was before, under the old king, may God assoil his soul.

↦ How those of the second party – the peace party – believed that since the Armagnacs had finally, at last, learned not to charge headlong at anything shiny, as was once their wont, but to sit back and blow it to pieces with their much-improved guns, England's venture in France was doomed, and that expenditure on further fighting was a pointless waste of money and lives.

↦ How this party was led by **Cardinal Beaufort** and the **Marquess of Suffolk** and, crucially, none other than Sir Humphrey Stafford, Earl of Stafford.

↦ How it was that just when England needed a strong king to balance these two competing factions, all she had on her throne was that sixth Henry, he who waxed ever more bishop than king, and more like to lead his nobles in prayer than battle.

And:

↦ How that is, in fact, what he did: every morning, reciting aloud the whole psalter from memory, which is a feat right-wise impressive on hearing for the first time, and the second and third times too perhaps, but the spectacle ages fast, and with each repetition, Sir Thomas noticed an ever-increasing restiveness among even the king's close gentlemen of the wardrobe, who were no stern knights themselves, and memories of the king's father were set aside in favour of memories of the king's French grandsire: he who had believed himself made of glass.

➻ How the king would grant any favour to any man, for he wished to please whoever knelt before him, and how because of this — and for no other reason — in the year 1444 he raised Sir Humphrey Stafford, Earl of Stafford, to the dukedom of Buckingham, which was an appointment entirely undeserved, and which made him the pre-eminent lord in all the land, save only the Duke of Norfolk.

But:

➻ How then, less than a sennight later, and for no other reason save fond memories of their shared childhood, he then elevated Sir Harry Beauchamp from the earldom of Warwick to the dukedom of Warwick, and crowned him King of the Isle of Wight, which raised Sir Harry to be the pre-eminent lord in all the land, save only the Duke of Norfolk, and so now Sir Harry — son of the new-made Duke of Buckingham's age-old and most-hated rival, and a scarce-bearded youth — had overleapt him!

➻ How this made the Duke of Buckingham wrathful out of all measure.

➻ How with these two nobles at daggers drawn, and the court divided between the two factions, and with the king an inconstant ninny, the outlook for England in general, and Sir Thomas in particular, was bleak, and only likely to become bleaker still when in the summer of what must have been the twenty-second year of his reign — and the forty-fourth summer of Sir Thomas's life — the king took a French wife.

➳ How this in itself was not so shocking – his father had done the same thing – but what was shocking was that not only was England to receive no dowry, she would – against all custom – cede the entirety of Maine to the girl's uncle, the French king!

➳ How the arrival of this wife – **Margaret**, daughter of King René of Anjou – reinforced the peace party's ascendancy at court, for she was a strong-laboured woman, a she-wolf in silk and linen, and moreover easily twice the man that King Henry ever was.

➳ How King Henry was very smitten with her, for she was a beauty, with abundant roan hair, and once married, it did not take long before she was ruling England in all but name.

➳ How her arrival saw the prospects of those in the war party – among them Sir Thomas Malory, knight, of Fenny Newbold – occluded, while the sun shone on those in the peace party, and most especially upon the Duke of Buckingham, who started to expand his interests in the county of Warwick in direct challenge to his newfound enemy, the young Duke of Warwick, and, of course, all his liegemen, among whom, of course, Sir Thomas numbered himself. But at that time, having become Sir Thomas Malory, and being a knight of the shire, he was much taken up with the Affairs of the County, and in January that year – in the year of his forty-fifth winter – he followed his father in becoming Member of Parliament for the County of Warwickshire.

➳ How his fellow member was **Sir William Mountfort**, who had been among those who stood with his father that day when Sir Thomas's arrow was shot in the sky to celebrate his birth.
'Glad to see you knighted, Sir Thomas,' Sir William had

said when they met again. 'Was worried about you when that arrow of yours fell on our heads. Thought it was an ill omen. Thought you might have gone to the bad.'

They had both laughed, and Sir Thomas had told Sir William there was still plenty of time for that, and Sir William had said that he was glad to hear it, and Sir Thomas realised, with no little pleasure, that he had at last become That Sort of Man.

⇥ How Sir Thomas started enlarging his own retinue, adding more men to join Folo Bundsay and John Appleby and divers other tenants – of whom more later – and he began stockpiling helmets and arrows and billhooks, and bought up barrels of salted herring to keep in the cellar, and saw to it that the shutters and gates of the house were reinforced and made secure.

'I don't know why you worry so,' Elizabeth his wife told him. 'Sir Harry loves you out of all measure, and is not like to let Sir Humphrey harm a hair of your head.'

⇥ How on St Barnabas' Day in the forty-sixth year of the century, after a mild summer during which Sir Thomas imported a Hollander to dredge that stockfish pond in which his brother had drowned and started laying the foundations for a substantial wing on each end of Fenny Newbold, it so befell that Sir Harry Beauchamp, the first Duke of Warwick, with scarce twenty winters to his name, died.

⇥ How such things happen according to the will of God, of course, as is well known, but Sir Harry's death came as a bolt of lightning from a summer sky. He was well one day, sick the next, dead the third. No one could explain it.

➳ How Sir Thomas recalled that earlier that summer he had read to Sir Harry and Lady Cecily from one of the French books the story of how Sir Pinel le Savage had tried to poison Sir Gawaine by doctoring the apples he loved so much, and how it was revealed to him in a dream a week or so after Sir Harry's death that the very self-same thing had happened to Sir Harry, save in this case the poisoner had been successful. But why would anybody do such a thing?

All men loved Sir Harry.

All men, that is, save, of course, the one man who benefited from his death: Sir Humphrey, Duke of Buckingham.

➳ How Elizabeth his wife reminded him that anybody might be called out of this world at any time.

'You must stop being fanciful about poison,' she said, 'and find yourself a new lord.'

➳ How Elizabeth his wife was right in this second part at least, for with Sir Harry's passing, Sir Thomas was vulnerable once more to anyone with greed or grudge, including, most especially, the Duke of Buckingham.

➳ How since Sir Harry's daughter Anne was not yet two years old, her wardship fell to the king, who, lamb-like, passed it on to the queen, who set about undoing all the ties that once bound the duke's household by handing all his offices and appointments to those in her own affinity, including, most especially, the Duke of Buckingham.

➳ How the queen cut Sir Thomas's retainer, and with it his annuity, so that not only did he now lack for a good-lord, he was twenty pounds a year the poorer.

How Sir Thomas joined the affinity of that other Sir Humphrey, the Duke of Gloucester, the king's uncle (and whose life he had oftentimes claimed to have saved at Agincourt), who was no well-wisher of the Duke of Buckingham, and a man who had always raised his cup to him in respect of his presence on the field at Verneuil.

'Any man who fought with my brother that day', and so on, even though he had fallen out with his brother of Bedford.

How they were in the process of drawing up Sir Thomas's indenture when, despite being in excellent health, the Duke of Gloucester too died of what was said to be 'heaviness', in Bury St Edmunds, deep in the Earl of Suffolk's lands. Suffolk was another of the peace party's leaders, and the Duke of Gloucester had been lured there to a meeting of Parliament, which had been switched from Winchester at the very last moment.

How very soon thereafter rumours were aswirl that the Duke of Gloucester had been done a great wrong, and so the Duke of Suffolk felt it necessary to put the old man's body on show in the abbey in the city to prove there was no mark of violence upon him.

How this suggested a guilty conscience.

How Sir Thomas asked his wife Elizabeth: 'So who now is being fanciful about poison?'

How from then on Elizabeth watched their cook very carefully, and she even found a new pepperer, though that did not prevent her waking Sir Thomas before dawn one morning a few months later by being violently sick. Her face was the colour of a storm at sea, both green and chalky at

293

once, and Sir Thomas believed that just as instead of killing Sir Gawaine, Sir Pinel had killed Sir Patrise, so instead of killing Sir Thomas with a poisoned apple, Sir Humphrey Stafford had managed to kill Elizabeth his wife in his stead, and so he threw up his hands and cried aloud 'alas!' and 'alack!' and so on.

'You fool!' his wife cried, wiping the string of vomit from her chin.

→ How seven months later, Sir Thomas found himself sat on a newly strung rush chair in the new chamber that he had had built in the newfangled house (the name of which he had changed from Fenny Newbold to Newbold Revel so as to disassociate it from its damp reputation) listening to his wife, whom he loved, birthing his firstborn son upstairs, while before him, on the table, lay an as-yet-to-be-nocked hunting bow and a single broad-head hunting arrow.

→ How later that afternoon, watched by Sir William Mountford and others, Sir Thomas nocked the bow, then the arrow and sent it skywards, signifying his son Robert's release from womb to world, and how despite his divers worries, he professed himself a happy man as he watched that arrow turn on the wind and drift to land harmlessly in one of the other two surviving stockfish ponds.

→ How it would have made him laugh if it had killed that heron.

→ How there is one last death that now must be mentioned in order to finally set the scene for what happens next: that of poor Lady Anne, Sir Harry's fat and fierce little daughter, the fourteenth Countess of Warwick, who died in Ewelme just past her fifth winter, where she had been taken under the wing of the Duchess of Suffolk, and all her estates and titles, vast and widespread, fell through her aunt — after whom she was named (who was Sir Harry's only sister of the whole blood) and who had once voiced all those doubts about the love shared between Sir Lancelot and Guinevere — to her husband, and thus did the next man to rule Sir Thomas's life — and all English lives — enter unexpectedly through an unremarked door: this **Richard Neville**, this new-made **Earl of Warwick**.

He imagines the boy might gasp at finding this last name entering the fray of Sir Thomas's tale, for it is on everyone's lips these days, for good or ill, but how would he have responded to hearing all those other background details? All those other background names? Possibly his eyes would have glazed over, or possibly he would have soon shouted that something must happen, and happen soon, as he did when Sir Thomas first started his tale, or perhaps he would give up on it, and resolve to live out his life in ignorance, but then again, perhaps Sir Thomas underestimates the boy? Perhaps the boy would want to know the background to what comes next, in order to fully understand Sir Thomas's plight? Yes. He would want to know everything.

If, that is, he ever returns to grant Sir Thomas a second chance.

CHAPTER II

How a welcome discovery is made, and how a seemingly unremarkable day ends otherwise, and of other things

Trackless days later, nearly a month after petitions for pardon were sought this St John's Day last, and finally, *finally*, word comes from Master Hartshorne. It is just a letter, brought with his breakfast by Susan, and Sir Thomas surges to his feet, buoyed up by joy, for it must at last contain news of his pardon. He takes a deep draught of ale – disgusting – and re-breaks the seal with trembling finger. Master Hartshorne commends himself unto Sir Thomas (yes, yes,) and must apologise for appearing so lax in sending tidings over these past few days (weeks!) but the reason he has not done so (or something) is because there are none to send.

Sir Thomas feels himself deflate back into a kind of blunted nothingness, and he returns to Hartshorne's note.

The king – he writes – and his court are much preoccupied with the trials of those men arrested this Pentecost last—

Sir Thomas stops reading.

What? Surely Hartshorne cannot mean the fifteen men that included Sir Thomas Cook and so on?

He does. Sir Thomas Cook and Thomas Portaleyn and Hugh Pakenham. They are already on trial! No! No! In fact, they are already on to their *second* trial! The first jury found them not guilty of treason, so a new jury was appointed the very next day and they too found them not guilty, and so the king has had to content himself with the lesser charge of hiding treason.

Sir Thomas is incandescent.

Two trials! *Two!* While he has been stuck here waiting to learn what it is he is even being charged with!

He strides across the cell – two strides – and hammers on the door, just as if this were his first day in Newgate.

'I demand to see the keeper!' he bellows. 'Where is he? Where is Master Arnold! I demand to speak to Master Arnold!'

There is no reply. He hears a distant scream. He lets the letter fall and thrusts his fists into his eye sockets and would scream too, if he did not know that it would do no good in this purgatory. He paces for a while and then presses his ear to Master Bewscel's wall, through which he hears nothing, and he's reminded of course that today is the day of the old man's rescheduled trial, and once more he flies into a fury.

Why is *everybody* on trial except him?

After a while, when he can think of no new thoughts on this matter, he manages to think that it is a shame that he and the boy are estranged – he has not seen him since the shameful business with the ransacked coffer, which seems like so many wasted weeks ago. Today Brunt has escorted Master Bewscel to the Guildhall, and they might have found some consolation or distraction in Sir Thomas's tale, from which the boy would learn much – for they are getting closer to the nub of why he is so unfairly herein constrained. But that is not to be. The boy is still absenting himself and Sir Thomas blames him not.

He takes the time to offer up a prayer to St Ivo for Master Bewscel's acquittal today, but failing that, for the man to see sense and petition for a pardon, and then he remembers that letter. Jesu! He had forgotten about that entirely! Perhaps that was what was stolen! He leaps to his feet and flings open the coffer and searches again.

My God, he thinks, if someone stole that, then – but why *would* they? And how could they have known he was writing it? But they *must* have done so because it is not now – oh. There it is. Lying tucked between coffer and palliasse, edges curled and insignificant. His spinning mind comes to a rest, and then stops. Yes. Now he kicks himself for not having sent it. For having forgotten all about it. He will still try to send it, though. It may be a day or two or even longer late, but his argument – that Stillington's office will not refuse a little extra money, even if it does come late – still holds, he is certain of that, for he knows how hard-up the king always is. He will give it to the boy to take to Hartshorne's inn, that is what he'll do, along with any reply he might make in regard to this latest letter.

Then he remembers he is still no longer speaking to the boy.

He picks up Hartshorne's letter again to read him signing off with the usual nonsense, in the usual way, and that is that. What does it mean?

Nothing. It means there is nothing to know.

He stares out of the window: grey skies with the vague threat of more rain. By Jesu.

Suddenly he is alarmed to hear fast-racing feet stamping on the steps beyond his door and he whips around, his heart thumping. The steps are surely too light to be Hartshorne bringing any kind of tidings? Nor can they be the king's men – Smethwick, say, dear Jesu, he has not thought about Smethwick in some time – and when the door swings open, there is the boy, breathless, beaming and clutching a package half-wrapped about in waxed linen.

'Look what I got!'

'Whatever is it?' Sir Thomas asks.

'Paper!' the boy says, thrusting it towards Sir Thomas, pink with pride, and Sir Thomas prises open the linen and within are many sheets of very fine paper, folded in quarters.

'Wherever did you get it?' Sir Thomas asks, very pleased to be able to forgive and forget.

'It was down in the yard, wasn't it? Just sitting on a barrel.'

'Someone must have left it in error. One of the attorneys, per-haps? Whoever is acting for Master Bewscel?'

'No, no. He's speaking for himself, and anyway there was a man stood by, and I thought it was his at first, but when I asked him about it, he just looked at me like I was made o' shit, and asked me who I was. When I told him he just walked away as if I smelled of it, too.'

'What sort of man?'

'A gentle, he was. Your sort. You know. Good boots. Hat with a feather and that.'

'Well,' Sir Thomas says, 'perhaps we should keep it until he comes for it? Or someone lays claim to it? It is worth something.'

The boy looks disappointed, though Sir Thomas cannot imagine to what earthly purpose he would put it instead – sell it?

'Maybe,' he says. 'Oh. And there is this.'

He has another letter. For a heart-stopping moment, Sir Thomas thinks this is also from Master Hartshorne, with real news, but it is from Elizabeth his wife.

She commends herself to him and writes that the shepherds have said there are up to seventy new lambs, and that the pea harvest is successfully taken in, and that the swallows and swifts are ever busy about the eaves of the hall. But the tidings are not all good: the cat has distemper, a windmill has burned down and **Alan the mustard-maker** has ruptured his fundament on a wheel spoke. She writes of their son, and their grandson, and of Appleby's wife, whom she has caught stealing butter again, and she tells Sir Thomas that she misses him and wishes he were safe at home once more.

When Sir Thomas has finished reading, he looks up and finds the boy staring at him with an expression he might describe as hungry.

'What is it?'

'Just never seen a man read. Not without speaking the words aloud.'

Sir Thomas puts the letter down. The boy's gaze follows it. Sir Thomas turns it around so that at least it is the right way up. He remembers the boy's interest in the manuscript of his book of King Arthur.

'Can you recall what the letter A looks like? As in Arthur?'

The boy nods and after a moment points one out in the jumble of Elizabeth's somewhat scrappy writing.

'A for Alan,' Sir Thomas confirms. 'Good.'

The boy smiles. He is missing a tooth.

'Phew,' he says. 'Thought you might have to get the old birch rod out.'

Sir Thomas laughs.

'Let us see if you can find the letter B, shall we?'

The boy fails, but Elizabeth's Bs are unconventional and inconsistent, and once he has worked this out, he fillets the short letter very quickly of its Bs.

'What about Cs?'

Again, the same thing. Sir Thomas feels a slight tug of excitement. The boy moves his finger along the line from left to right, so Sir Thomas supposes him to be a natural.

'Watched your eyes move,' he confesses.

'Clever,' Sir Thomas admits, and they try a few more letters, and then the making of a word, until Sir Thomas realises they have been at this for some time.

'What about your father?'

'Taken old Lewd-Act down the Guildhall, hasn't he?'

'Will the jury turn up?'

'He says he thinks so. He's given me a full day's worth of tasks anyhow.'

Sir Thomas sighs inwardly.

'But what happened with that duke? The one who was going to kill you? Him what you stopped having a go at that French witch?'

'Ah. The Duke of Buckingham. Yes. Well. I didn't see him for many a year after that, thank God, but what happened when next I did changed the course of my life completely.'

It was Advent, the year of my forty-ninth winter, and the Earl of Warwick — yes, him: Richard Neville, the sixteenth to be so called — invited perhaps a hundred guests and their households to celebrate the feast with him at his newly inherited castle. My wife said she would not come, for she was with child once more, and she said she could not face the company, which reflects well on her. But I told her that I must still go, for I intended to offer Sir Richard my services as his liegeman, if he would agree to become my good-lord (which was such an obvious connection that we both knew could have been achieved within a Mass's time, and on any old day), which perhaps does not reflect so well on me, but if I am honest — and as you know, I am nothing if not that — I confess I was restive, and wished for something more than sitting at home alone with a sick wife and a toddling child.

I admit that as I waved them goodbye — Elizabeth grey-green again and scarcely able to restrain that child — and wished them a happy Christmas (for when the day came), I felt a twinge of disquiet at my disworthyness, which lasted the length of our ride along Smite Brook, where once more and as always, I pointed out to Folo Bundsay all the usual sights that had not changed in thirty years except to become wilder and more overgrown. Folo was my some-what-in-two-minds companion on this visit to Warwick, for he had a burgeoning family of his own, with whom he had been looking forward to sharing Christmas, but needs must: he was my servant and squire, and he cheered up by the time we reached the familiar gates of Warwick Castle itself, where it became clear this new earl intended to entertain his many guests royally, as indeed he did.

There was a King-over-Christmas (a fat harper given his own

throne and canopy, as well as a jester and a gibbet on which to threaten to hang those men who would not do his bidding), various acrobats and jugglers and so on, and two companies of masked players who put on various plays that began on a pious note but all too often ended up in riotous disarray. On Christmas Day itself, to the noise of kettle drums and pipes and so forth, five swans were brought out, each roasted with other birds within, and a score of oxen, and those not invited to sit around the fire in the great hall were permitted to take away as much beef as they might carry on their daggers.

The real centrepiece of the occasion though was the three days of tournament with a gold cup offered as a prize, in which was set a single red ruby the size of a baby's fingernail. I forsook participation, of course, for tourneying, as I had discovered, was a young man's game, and even had I not learned this lesson the hard way, I would have had to withdraw from the lists anyway, in part because I had no horse or harness, and also because I was suffering an excess of sanguinity, or choler, or both perhaps, brought on by too much of the earl's excellent wine and game-bird pie, and so I was good for little more than being wrapped in furs — squirrel and cat for the most part, though trimmed at the collar and cuffs with marten — watching the action from a chair by the smoking brazier a little way along the dais from the earl and his countess, with my cap pulled low and a beaker of warmed wine never too far from my gloved hand.

That first day I watched with pleasure as various young knights in wonderful polished harness and shields of bright design broke lance after lance upon one another, and I thought back to my own tilt at Hertford, and of being sent flying from my saddle to land so heavily as to have every breath knocked from my frame, and every thought knocked from my head. I might very well have died. And for what?

Mere bobaunce.

Perhaps it was becoming a father? Or perhaps these were the first tremors of an old man's dread, but I realised then that my participation in this tournament had changed in character: no longer was I a man sitting this round out, I was, sad to say, a man who would never enter the tiltyard again.

Nevertheless, the tournament remained a gripping spectacle, and watching these young knights and their horses thunder across the frost-stiffened sand, each of them steaming vented wisps from the joints in their armour, and then colliding with a ringing crump of steel, muscle and spray of brittle wood shards as their lances shivered their shields and the crowds cooed with admiration and awe, gave me hope for England.

'Oooooh, isn't it foonny how it sounds different in the cold?' my neighbour of that first day volunteered to the woman next to him. I had noticed this myself and was about to agree with him, but he was a local man, I detected from his accent, and probably a merchant of some sort — why he was raised on the dais was anyone's guess — and answering him was almost certainly beneath my dignity, so instead I gave him a stern look.

Now, I do not pride myself on never forgetting a face, but I did not recognise this man at all, even when he gasped and stood up with an astonished look on his otherwise unremarkable and un-memorable face.

'Well, blow me!' he cried. 'Look, wife, as I live and breathe, it is my old friend and comrade-in-arms Thomas Malory!'

I still did not recognise him and was about to remind him, or inform him, that I was Sir Thomas Malory, when he stood and extended his arms as to enfold me in a hug and kiss me a hundred times.

'Don't tell me you have forgotten your old comrade-in-arms!' he cooed, not at all offended at my inertia. 'It is I,' he said, pointing a thumb at his chest, 'Hugh Smith.'

'Ah!' I murmured.

It took a long moment, but then I remembered him. Hugh Smith, whom I had last seen waddling helplessly in beshitted linens upon the field of Verneuil more than twenty-five years earlier. He had obviously prospered since that day – he no longer stank of his own shit, for one thing, though that is hardly a mark of great success, is it? – and he was pleasingly well-padded in soft flesh and good cloth. He gave me another unexpectedly enthusiastic hug and a kiss on both my cheeks and then held me at arm's length the better to inspect me, as if I were some triumph of his own creation.

Had I once saved his life? I cannot recall.

'I've heard all about what you've been up to since we last met!' he laughed, and I was so startled by his generous nature that it did not occur to ask why he had heard so much about me, or from whom, or in what spirit such news might have been imparted.

He embraced me – a third time? Like Peter and Jesus, I would later think – and then turned to introduce me to his wife, who was sitting a little behind, just then out of my sight behind a bulky manservant in ruby-red velvet and parti-coloured hose, black and green.

'Joan,' he called. 'Joan. This is Thomas Malory. Or Sir Thomas Malory, I should say, who was with me that day at Verneuil. He's since been in France and he's even been knighted by the king himself, and is become a member of the Commons, isn't that right, Sir Thomas?'

'Ooh, I've heard ever such a lot about you, Sir Thomas,' his wife said, in exactly Hugh Smith's accent and tone, and again I did not think to ask myself – or them – why she had heard so much, or from whom she had heard it, for now she rose from behind Smith, and stepped out of the shadow of the manservant, and when I laid my eyes on her completely, I will admit – for it is no secret that she was passing pleasing to the eye – that I was very struck by **Mistress Smith.**

She was not beautiful in the way that Lady Anne was beautiful. There was nothing delicate about her, she being blonde-browed, solid and even broadly abundant. But she was younger than Smith by perhaps two decades or so, and there was something about her that drew me back to that first time, the first girl, with whom I lay among the roof beams of that inn in Normandy.

'Mistress Smith,' I found myself saying, my mouth suddenly very gummy.

'Ooh,' she said, reaching out, against all rules, to touch my forearm. 'I know you, sir! We've met before, once, long ago, in Monks Kirby!'

A shadow passed over Smith's brow. He evidently had not known this.

'Monks Kirby?' I asked.

It is the village where I was baptised. Very small.

'Whyyy, yes. Monks Kirby.'

'I am sure – not,' I managed, for unquestionably I should remember such a woman. She had eyes of periwinkle blue and the most wonderfully broad smile, which exposed the twin hurdles of her oddly regular and very white teeth. The tip of her nose was pink in the cold.

'Oh, you won't remember me, Sir Thomas, no,' she laughed, coming to stand by me, and turning to her husband, making him the audience of our complicity. I could feel her breast against my elbow, and her proximity was unsettling out of all measure, even on such a cold day.

'But Sir Thomas even spoke to me once, husband, when he was ever such a young man, out riding with his father and a fat man, who might have been his tutor.'

Now she turned to me.

'You stopped and asked my father for some ale, and my father sent me to fetch it and when I gave it to you, you said "thank you".

305

I was only a very little girl at the time, but I will confess, though I shouldn't, that I was smitten. Smitten, I was.'

I could remember no such thing. Nevertheless, she laughed a full, earthy and somewhat delightfully unladylike laugh that, Jesu preserve me, even on that January morning brought to mind sunlit meadows and flower-flecked woods in the month of May.

'In Monks Kirby, you say?' I wondered. I knew every man who lived in Monks Kirby, and even, in a way, owned them, for I owned much of the village. But Mistress Smith's father turned out to be, of all things, the miller — which would explain her perfect teeth — and tenant of Hubbock's Mill, one of the few buildings in the village not held by us but by the Carthusians at the Priory, and so, since I never needed to collect rent from him, I would scarcely have had reason to speak to him.

'Extraordinarily fine flour,' I found myself saying. 'Yes.'

'And he would have been more than happy to hear you say so, sir,' she said, and her face — wondrously expressive in all things — took on a look of such devoted sorrow I nearly laughed.

'Would have been?' I repeated. 'He is no longer with us?'

'No,' she murmured. 'May God rest his soul.'

She closed her eyes and crossed herself and Smith now moved to put his arm out for her, and she detached herself from my side and went to him, and he spoke in a low voice, coddled with what was not even counterfeit sorrow: 'Five years ago now, but he's not forgotten.'

'Six,' she sniffed, at which Smith looked mildly chastened.

'I am sorry to hear that,' I said. 'But you no longer live in — in Monks Kirby?'

'Oh no, we live in Coventry now, but every year I come back to hear Mass said to mark his Year's Mind.'

'Easier to remember that one,' Smith intervened, hoping for re-demption, 'for this year it is the day of Pentecost itself.'

'The day prior,' Goodwife Smith corrected with a little shake of her head that loosed a glossy tear from her brimming eye. I almost reached across to wipe the tear from her cheek, and do you know what? I would have sucked my finger, I admit it.

'I will keep watch for you,' I ventured, which I knew to be true, but which I ought not to have said. Now she blushed prettily and thanked me, and I could think of little more to say, though Smith filled the gap with welcome prattle.

'I have made a small wager on the knight with the silver fern,' he began telling us. 'I know as I shouldn't, Sir Thomas, but if you cannot have a little flutter at Yuletide, when can you have a little flutter?'

Mistress Smith touched his sleeve and directed an admiring smile at him.

'And I've put sixpence on for you too, wife, so that you do not feel left out. How do you feel about that?'

'It is ever so kind of you, husband,' she said, and she sort of shucked her shoulders and rolled her eyes to signify that he was somehow slightly wicked, but she loved him all the more for it, and in turn I found myself bewildered, and then gripped with what I can now see was a strange over-confidence: if she could love him for that, I thought, wait until she learns of me, and what I can offer. All thoughts of Elizabeth my wife were banished in a bonfire of practicalities and when I retook my seat I was unable to prevent myself stealing glances at Mistress Smith, prettily perched on the bench next to her husband, in deep green velvets, trimmed with a gaudy pink fur I did not recognise as belonging to any animal of my knowledge.

You will say I was entering my dotage. You will say I was already become an old fool and was misconstruing a woman's slightest kindness as an offer of something altogether more serious. Perhaps you are right.

That first day under a low sky of beaten lead we watched the nameless knight whose symbol was the silver fern set aside all comers, and it seemed he was destined to win Hugh Smith and his wife their bets as well as the cup with the red jewel, for he be-shivered his lance with unmatchable prowess. I spoke all this aloud, and all through the day Mistress Smith hung on my every word, and it seemed Hugh Smith only encouraged her too:

'Wife,' he said, 'let us swap places, so that you are between us, as a rose sometimes grows between two thorns, and that you may hear what Sir Thomas has to say on these matters, for there are few in the county who know more of these things than he.'

She moved next to me then, and turning to me on more than one occasion, she leaned closer than she ought and breathed: 'It is ever such a treat to be shown what is what by a man with such experience!'

From that moment on, I believed Hugh Smith was rendered the proud-smiling, little-knowing, onlooking third point in a triangle of his own device, and whether he could tell this, from the fixity of my smile perhaps, or the syrupiness of my eye, I cannot say, but though she were fifteen – twenty! – years my junior, in that moment I was convinced Mistress Smith and I had struck an unspoken accord and that even though nothing might yet come of our pact today, or tomorrow, or perhaps ever, we both knew that in another life, at another time, in another place, something could, should and would have happened. I found I did not even need to look at her to know she knew this too, for it was obvious to any man with eyes in his head, save Hugh Smith.

When then the next day dawned even colder, the omens for the knight with the symbol of the silver fern were better yet, for each ice-glazed piece of plate of every knight in the tourney took upon its surface a pattern in the shape of new-sprung bracken frond, not unlike his own badge, and I was preparing to remark on this to Mistress Smith – something along the lines of Nature's homage perhaps, I had not quite decided – but the ice had melted before she appeared and soon it was apparent that neither she nor Smith would be attending that day. I knew not why. Some illness perhaps, but I was left crestfallen, not merely because my barber had been up before dawn to take great pains with my chin and cheeks, or that despite the cold, I wore my high-cut jacket, my very finest-spun blue-dyed hose and my new-made (by Coventry's finest shoemaker, William the Shoe) black-stained calfskin boots, with each toe extravagantly piked so as to make walking nigh on impossible.

I sat shivering, thinking again of the falseness of women and watching the tourney through jaundiced eyes, while sure enough the first ado fell to the knight with the silver fern, on account of his breaking two lances on his opponent's shield before knocking him clean out of his saddle, and I was looking forward to seeing him take the day, for he was a pleasure to watch, when a little before dinner, Folo Bundsay appeared at my shoulder, bearing a thick riding cloak and tidings.

'The Duke of Buckingham's on his way,' he said, looking at my clothes as if I were gone out of my wits. 'He'll be here within the Mass.'

'The Duke of Buckingham? Here? Within a Mass?'

'He sent a message ahead to tell the earl that he is passing through on his way to Caluden Park, where he is expected for a week's hunting.'

As he would do, naturally, to avoid any misunderstanding.

'And the earl has insisted he attend the tourney.'

Likewise, as he would do, naturally, wishing to show largesse.

'And the duke has accepted.'

Again, as he would do, for the duke, like any man, would wish to accept largesse, and to watch a tourney.

'So the duke is coming here within a Mass.'

Once I understood, the news set my blood racing. I had often-times glimpsed the duke since that day in Rouen's Treasury tower, but only ever at Westminster, and always among a swirling crowd, and if I am honest, I had always managed to stay hidden, or at least seen a path I might take or a door I might open. Here though, sitting on this dais, even in one of the minor positions of honour, I would be thoroughly exposed to his view. Would he dare do or say anything if he were the guest of Sir Richard Neville, whose badge I wore? But then I cursed my stupidity. I had not yet finalised the indenture with Sir Richard! I was not his indentured man, his liegeman, and so could only count on his protection insofar as I was his guest!

I recalled the words of this earl's predecessor, that other Sir Richard, after the business with Joan in the Treasury tower in Rouen, when he sent me back to England: 'My lord of Buckingham is wroth out of all measure, Malory, and if there were ever a man more like to seek pardon than permission, I am yet to meet him.'

Nor was Folo done.

'And with him is his duchess,' he added.

The duchess! Lady Anne!

Just then the Knight of the Silver Fern was knocked into a swoon by a blundering ox of a man in rust-fretted armour, and there was a great cry of disapproval, and we all leapt to our feet, even me, or especially me. But I was no longer interested in the tourney.

Instead, I gripped Folo's elbow.

'Lady Anne is coming here? With Sir Humphrey?'

Folo tried to get me to keep my voice down, but no one was listening to me, for everyone about us was watching the stunned Knight of the Silver Fern lying on his back, his arms and legs twitching like a louse in its last throes. His esquire was rushing across the sand, but he seemed more interested in the horse, which was struggling for breath with the saddle strap twisted tight around its girth.

By now Folo was studying the milky sky above with over-exaggerated care.

'It looks like the snow will come before shutting-in,' he pronounced loudly and pointlessly.

I did not want to think about the weather. I was thinking about Lady Anne, Duchess of Buckingham. If we should see one another, would I necessarily be placing her in a position in which she might find herself being false and untrue? I looked at Folo, he at me. The fear of being thought cowardly did battle with saving a lady's reputation, and the two came to an agreement.

'We have many leagues to ride before then, sir,' Folo went on in the same clarion voice.

I now understood.

'We must away, Folo,' I said.

'Yes, sir,' he agreed. 'Sadly, we must.'

I took the proffered cloak and with an elaborate bow to the earl and Lady Anne Neville along the dais, I stepped away, half pretending to be making my way to the use of the close-stool, and I noted the earl murmur something about old men and their bladders, and I did not disabuse him.

'Hurry, Folo,' I urged as we rushed towards the stables, all dignity to the wind.

But we were too late.

There in the rising mist were gathered a large crowd of steaming horsemen in red and black: the Duke of Buckingham's fore-riders, and now, clattering in behind, came the duke himself, astride a great grey stallion, and at his side, though just behind perhaps, was his wife, Lady Anne, wreathed in pale furs, perched upon a very fine grey mare.

I tried to hide, and turned from them both, to bury myself in the hurly-burly of the stable yard, but of all things it was she who called out to me.

'Why, Sir Thomas! Sir Thomas de Lamory!'

I stopped dead still, my back suddenly wet with iced sweat.

Behind me even the horses had come to a stop in anticipation of what must surely follow.

'My good and noble Sir Thomas de Lamory of Fenny Newbold!'

Her voice was musical and filled with very out-of-place laughter. I turned very slowly. One of the horses snorted as if laughing. I took off my hat and bowed gallantly.

'My lord,' I said, 'my lady.'

The words felt very dry, and I felt very naked and exposed, as if every man and woman were looking at me, waiting.

'Why, Sir Thomas,' Lady Anne called from within her nest of furs, 'you are not leaving the tourney already?'

'Alas, my lady, we have many miles to ride for home,' I said, gesturing to the sky above, from which snowflakes might be expected to spin at any moment, 'and—'

'I bloody know you!'

Buckingham.

'My lord,' I said again.

'Malory, isn't it? Thomas bloody Malory.'

I could hardly say 'my lord' again, or bow again to accept the insult. And I was conscious of a great pressure growing in my head. Why had she called out to me? Why had she drawn attention to me? And why was she now still smiling as her husband the duke forced his horse towards me as if he meant to trample me, or smite me to the brainpan?

'God give you good day, sir,' I said, mastering my nerves. 'Have you come for the tourney?'

'Have I come for the tourney?' he barked. '*Have I come for the God-damned tourney?* What the devil is he talking about?'

He turned to the man at his right, an unexpectedly lumpen figure who sat dumped in his saddle. It was, of all people, **Thomas Greswold**, a lawyer whom I knew from nearby Solihull, and whom I believe might by then already have been the county coroner. He was enveloped in an old-fashioned coat of padded grey wool and his nose — large, all the better to truffle up preferments — was red with cold. He looked like a mole, a great, fat, mounted mole, and what he was doing riding alongside the Duke of Buckingham I hardly thought to wonder — though by God I should have — before Lady Anne brought her horse between me and the duke, and faced him as if the two were in the tiltyard. I stepped to one side. I saw Lady Anne's cheeks were coloured, her chin up and her eyes suddenly very lively.

'I did not know you knew one another?' she asked the duke. 'You have never mentioned meeting Sir Thomas?'

Under the sugar of her tone was pure gall, and her husband, a boar at bay, turned his bulging eyes on her.

'Never mentioned him? Of course I've never mentioned him. I hardly even know who he is.'

'We met in Rouen,' I reminded him, informed her. 'In the company of Sir Richard Beauchamp. Before the business of Jeanne, the French woman.'

Was this a wise thing to say? No.

He lurched back to me, his eyes hotter and more furious yet, dark as the glazed currants on an Eastertide loaf, much greasier though.

'Don't talk of her!' he bellowed, smoke from his mouth. 'Don't mention that French bitch's name before me.'

'No, well,' I said, letting my point prove like said loaf.

But my gaze was as ever drawn to Lady Anne.

What was it about her? Even now I cannot say, but there was something about her that was a rebuke to mankind: an example of that which we ought to strive for, rather than squandering our hours in vainglorious bombast and easy, earthen pleasures, and I regretted again my silly high-cut jacket and my absurd piked shoes. All thoughts of Mistress Smith fled from my mind. Whatever had I

313

been thinking? At that moment there was nothing in the world more important than that Lady Anne should find me admirable.

And then the duke, blue-chinned and beetle-browed, roared at her.

'How do you know him?'

She laughed prettily and covered her mouth with her palm.

'Sir Thomas de Lamory and I are old friends, are we not, good Sir Thomas?'

I stammered a sound that was neither confirmation nor denial, and wondered how despite every appearance, and despite everything I wished to be true, she could be so silly. All this Thomas de Lamory stuff. Funny once, perhaps, but nothing such as that survives examination, or even time perhaps. Though that was hardly the start of it, and soon I could scarce believe what she was saying.

'He writes to me,' she was now telling the duke.

And I saw only then that I was caught in an old, old argument between these two and that the best place for me might well be anywhere but here.

'He bloody well writes to you?' the duke snarled. 'I should whip any man who wrote to my wife.'

'And I write back,' she trilled, tormenting him.

'You do – *what?*'

While he glared at her, and she laughed and repeated herself, I resolved to quietly make my withdrawal, my escape.

'I wish you a good day of it,' I murmured. 'My lord, my lady.'

I nodded slowly to each in turn, without them noting, and I stepped back, and, with Folo behind me, both our breaths still held, we walked quickly for the stables, my ears tensed for a whiplash summons to return, the rest of me tensed for worse – a boot, a fist, a dagger or sword, or even an actual whiplash, but the only thing that fell upon me was a single snowflake, spiralling to land upon my sleeve, and by the time Folo had reclaimed our horses from the stables, it was falling in silent ghostly curls, just as foretold.

I said little to Folo on our way back up Smite Brook, and he little to me, and it was only afterwards — after we'd reached dear old — dear new — Newbold Revel, after I had brushed the snow from my hat and cloak and taken off my absurd piked shoes and sat in my chair and warmed my toes before a fire of oak and beech wood, with a cup of warmed wine in each hand — that I thought of the appearance of the lawyer, Thomas Greswold, alongside the Duke of Buckingham.

Whatever was all that about?

I had had a few dealings with him, of course, over a few bits and pieces connected with my father's estate, and I had heard him mentioned even as far off as in Westminster as being a coming man, but he was still of that class I then most despised: the sort who seeks to haul himself up through unfair knowledge of the law, or of business, or mere enterprise of some sort, the sort whom I blamed — rightly — for having brought England to her current sorry state.

Had I known then what I know now, would I have done anything different in relation to his person? Of course. I would have run my father's dagger into his heart. But back then, knowing nothing, I was content to hold him in contempt. The Duke of Buckingham, however, I was not.

'Summon the men,' I told Folo, glad I had recruited a few more against just this sort of thing. 'Even the useless ones. We will wait for the duke here.'

But since her alterations to my hall, Elizabeth my wife would not have any men through the door.

'No, no,' she said. 'You take your men and you meet the duke elsewhere. I am not having any of them in here. We have only just finished the plastering.'

This was not quite true: that had been done in the autumn, while it was still warm enough, but I took her point, and anyway, perhaps she was right? Perhaps it would be better to forestall the duke, if he were to come, so as not to be trapped rat-like within? The more I thought of it, the more I liked the idea.

'Folo? Gather the men in the yard!'

Hearing we were not to pass the night by the fire in the hall, however, Folo seemed to have a change of heart. He looked out of the doorway to where the snow had settled, though it had stopped now, and the fields were pale under a thick sliver of yellow moon, and Folo suggested it would be much better to stay within. But now I took the contrary position.

'We are old campaigners, Folo, are we not? Remember Rouen? Remember how it snowed there?'

He did, of course, which was the reason why he was set against this venturing out, but I was re-energised. I might have been nearly fifty winters on this earth, but by God it does a man good to be back in the straps every now and then. And what would Lady Anne think if she could see me now? What about Mistress Smith? Such thoughts warmed my blood, and I was spurred to boldness.

'Very well, Folo,' I said. 'You stay here. Keep watch on the house, and Elizabeth my wife. And Robert my son.'

He was relieved with this, which disappointed me somewhat, but perhaps he had never been much of a one for this sort of thing? So I sent Appleby to collect my harness from its coffer in the strong room, and I set about having myself dressed for the field: thick hose, arming jacket, arming cap, but I would not wear full harness, and instead I opted for a lighter brigandine, which fit me still, though was tighter than I recalled, and my helmet, the stays of which I would have to have adjusted in the morning. I strapped on my sword belt.

'Will you need that?' Elizabeth asked.

I could hear her rolling her eyes. She was very doubtful of the whole enterprise.

'Perhaps not,' I agreed. 'But then again, what if I do?'

It sounded the sort of thing my father would say, and I confess I was pleased with myself. The rest of the men wore their heavy tow-stuffed jacks and helmets, some pimpled with rust, about which I would have to have words, and they had with them their longbows. There must have been about ten of us, and I fancy we did not look too shabby.

'Right,' I said. 'Let us be about it.'

No one asked what 'it' might be, but that is in the nature of the thing. Instead we trooped out of the gate under a thick sliver of yellow moon.

'But is it not too late for this?' Appleby asked.

'You do not know the duke as I do, Master Appleby,' I said, glad that Folo was not able to hear this. 'He is much vexed but will either come now, or not at all, for by tomorrow his choler will have cooled and he will have regained his wits.'

I was not sure this was entirely true, but did not wish to contemplate the implications of him not doing so. We rode on down to Smite Brook, and then along it, following that old familiar path on which I was certain the duke would come, if he came, and we rode half a league perhaps, with the mist rising up to the fat balls of mistletoe in the trees on our right, and it was all very unkempt, with briars and strands of travellers' joy tangled among the over-wintering trees, and out of habit I pointed out the spot that my father had always said was perfect for a bushment, and I had to smile.

I must say I missed him then, my father, and I thought of him as I swung my leg out of the saddle and led my horse along a small path through the brambles to the far side of the trees that had long since grown up from the fallen ash we'd seen on that first sunlit ride to Gosford Green, long ago. It was as if he were here now though, directing the affair, and I was grateful for it. We hobbled our horses in a clearing and gathered together under the thinned canopy. Everyone agreed my father had been right: this was a perfect place. Five of us on one side of the track, five on the other, staggered somewhat so that we should not end up shooting one another.

'Should it come to that.'

Appleby, taking command of the five or so on the other side of the track, looked anxious.

'Do we really shoot them?' he asked.

One of the outside men, **Geoffrey Gryffyn**, wondered.

'I will give a signal,' I told them. 'If they are few, then we will scare them off. If they are many then — well, we shall see.'

That seemed to satisfy them, though I knew I was postponing the decisive moment, and if Folo were here, he would have pressed me to be clearer, but he was not, and so we stole off into our positions to see what — or who — would come our way.

The crows were long since settled and the owl had given the first of his yips that always makes a man feel colder than he is, and my back and knees were stiffening by the time we heard the first clop of a horse's hoof.

I gripped the arm of the man next to me, **John Harper**.

'He comes!'

I admit I was caught by high excitement. We craned our necks and strained our eyes. Out of the gloom, along the path from Coombe Abbey, emerged a clotted knot of deeper darkness, about five or six horsemen. They were coming on as purposefully as they dared in the gloom along snow-filled, unfamiliar paths, and they were strung out, one rider further ahead than those few in the middle, and one rider lagging behind. The one at the front was the Duke of Buckingham, I was certain of it.

'What do we do?' whispered Harper.

I dithered and could not decide. This was a great step to be taking. If I killed the Duke of Buckingham, then nothing after would ever be the same again. I could not make up my mind, but by then my hesitation had proved decisive for the duke was almost through the trap, and if I let him continue a moment longer, we'd not be able to murder him, even if we wanted to, and Newbold Revel would lie before him.

I admit it now: I panicked.

'Cry God for England!' I shouted, and then: 'St George! And for Sir Thomas Malory!'

It was not something I'd planned. I just wanted to make some terrifying noise as I hacked my way through the briars and out onto the track to block their path. The words erupted from my mouth unbidden. But then the others came roaring out with similar cries as they charged from behind their positions, each man bellowing for as much as he was worth. The effect was wondrous.

The duke's horse reared and nearly threw him, but he clung on, and managed to turn, and he thundered back the way he had come, barrelling past those in the middle of column, who a moment later followed his lead and did likewise, careering back after their fleeing leader, but the laggard – he at the back – was less fortunate, for he was no horseman, and as his fellows galloped past him on the narrow track, his horse reared. He let go the reins, threw his hands up, cried out and fell, rolling back over the horse's tail as the horse bolted. He landed with a crack and a scream in a loose-limbed sprawl and was blessed not to be trampled to death by his horse turning as it cantered away into the dark after the others.

A triumph!

As the hooves faded, we stood with our hands on our knees, laughing breathlessly, delighted at our success, smacking one another on our backs, great plumes of pale smoke uncoiling from our mouths, while the man who'd fallen on the track rocked from side to side in the mud, mewling and crying out for someone's help.

'He wants his mama,' Geoffrey Gryffyn laughed.

We gathered around. Someone – Harper – had had the sense to bring a lamp, which we got going so that when we bowed over him, our faces were brilliantly orange in the night.

'Who are you?' Appleby asked.

But I'd already seen enough to know who it was: Greswold.

Despite his moaning, he seemed largely unhurt, and after a moment he stopped his caterwauling and took his hands from his face, only to see us all looming over him like fiendish gargoyles come up from Hell itself, and he started screaming in mortal terror, scrabbling in the mud of the track, digging in his heels and pushing back. Unfortunately — for him — he was surrounded.

'Get away!' he shouted. 'Help!'

'Oh shut your gob, you soppy turd,' Gryffyn barked.

Greswold resumed his mewling. He had lost his cap, and his thinning hair hung limp from his pointed head.

'We should kick his arse!'

'No! No! Get away!'

This was undignified and we stopped laughing, and then it became serious, and nasty too — which, as will become apparent, it always did with Geoffrey Gryffyn, who lowered his bill to Greswold's chest and his voice betrayed his desire to use its blade on something more solid than mere hedgerows, just for the sake of seeing it done.

'What you doing riding in the woods when all fine folk should be abed?' he asked of Greswold.

'I ride with the Duke of — the Duke of Buckingham,' Greswold cried. 'We are — we are about our lawful business. You have no right—'

'I reckon I got plenty of right,' Gryffyn interrupted. 'I reckon this here blade, and this here darkness, and me being where I am, and you being where you are, I reckon they give me the right to do more or less what I like. Unless you're telling me otherwise?'

He forced the bill into the cloth of Greswold's jacket, just below his throat. Greswold whimpered.

'Mercy!' he wailed. 'Have mercy!'

That was probably when Greswold pissed himself. I stepped forward and ushered Gryffyn away into the darkness. He had two teeth, brown and hooked like two dog claws, and he smelled of hot iron and devilry – like a hawk – though he had his uses.

I turned to Greswold and repeated Gryffyn's questions but without the threat of instant death.

'What were you doing? Where were you riding?'

And he in turn repeated his answers.

'I was riding in the service of the Duke of Buckingham. If you let me go, I will placate him. I will tell him none of it is true. I will tell him he has no reason to think – to think that you and the Lady Anne have – have – had a to-do with one another.'

Suddenly the night was very quiet. I saw the gleam of ten pairs of eyeballs rise to me in mute speculation.

'I don't know what you are talking about,' I said.

'You are Sir Thomas Malory,' Greswold blundered on. 'Sir Thomas Lamory whom Lady Anne holds in great favour above all other knights.'

His words held a mocking echo, as if he had read our letters perhaps, or had been privy to one of our meetings, and already I regretted having announced myself as I sprang the bushment. I could easily have remained an anonymous outlaw, looming out of the dark to attack the duke and steal his purse. Now it was known who I was. Damn.

I should have killed him there and then, of course. Of course I know that now. How much pain would I have spared myself had I done so? A lifetime's. But I did not. A death – even a wounding – would have spoiled the night, and besides, I was struck with contempt for the wretch: imagine being like that, I thought, imagine being so spineless as to sit all day in a chair, doing nothing but passing pieces of paper across a lectern. No wonder he'd leapt at this late chance for adventure. And no wonder he had fallen short.

So we got him to his feet, and I told Harper and Appleby to take his shoes and throw them in the river, and to cut the points of his hose, and with my own boot I kicked his soggy arse to set him on his way stumbling after his horse, and that was the last I saw of him that night, and, as it turned out, for a few months thereafter, but by God, I was to rue my mercy in the years to come.

That night, as we regained our saddles and rode back through the still-falling snow to Newbold Revel, we were fairly pleased with ourselves, for it was held that our little *chevauchée* had, with God's grace, gone as might be hoped: we had achieved perfect surprise, sent the enemy packing and no one had been unduly hurt on either side. The lawyer Greswold had suffered humiliation, yes, and would have some bruises to show for it in the morning, it was true, but no blood had been spilled and no bones would need resetting.

When we reached Newbold Revel there was much loud celebratory chatter and the dogs were roused, and the geese too, and Elizabeth my wife or one of the other women banged a shutter in protest — there was generally much bad-tempered to-ing and fro-ing from above, and the cries of a child — but it did not stop me calling for the fire to be rekindled, a barrel of ale broached and a ham taken down from its joist, and like old soldiers we sat in the hall and we relived our adventure for the benefit of Folo, who remained pale and sceptical. There was much laughter at who had said what to whom, and how Greswold would fare. It was only Harper who ruined it by asking what Greswold had meant about me and Lady Anne.

'A to-do?' he asked. 'You and the Duchess of Buckingham? No wonder the duke was after you, Sir Thomas!'

There was a ring of throaty laughter, and mugs were raised to shiny red faces and split-pea grins, and these men, these churls who knew nothing about anything, they stood there in my own hall, winking and nudging one another, laughing their great buttery laughs. I felt — what? Pried upon? Scrutinised? Discovered? Ashamed? Proud?

Angry? A mixture of all these things, but most of all I violently wanted them to be gone, to leave me be. Their knowledge about my friendship with Lady Anne was akin to them despoiling my hall with their muddy boots and their beshitting dogs. Their presence was now a pollution.

Folo saw my change of heart and quickly disbanded the evening with pushes and shoves. He confiscated their mugs at the door and sent the men reeling back out into the snow with swift and forceful thanks for their efforts that I knew I might have to back up with something more tangible come morning. Meanwhile I climbed the steps to my bedchamber, leaving the clearing-up to Folo and Appleby, and I found my way to Elizabeth's side, though as was become usual she would not let me touch her even when my hands and feet were thoroughly warmed-through.

Despite all this, I supposed I should sleep the sleep of the just — as the old saying goes — tickled, I hoped, by pleasant dreams of Lady Anne or, more likely, of Mistress Smith, perhaps — but instead I lay awake and listened to the colossal silence beyond my shutter and I thought about what had happened and what I had done.

Nothing, was the answer, really.

That fool Greswold might come away from the night complaining of chilblains, true, that was nothing compared to what might have happened had we not caught the duke so cold, and it was nothing compared to the sorts of things that were already then happening all over England, where there was much riotous disorder from men dispossessed of their lands and livelihoods in France, and who were now destitute and living only by begging with menaces, or open banditry, and so I pulled the blankets up to my chin, and my cap down over my ears and I turned, satisfied in all things, to sleep.

Yet it did not come. I was up well before dawn, like some black friar about Matins, and I supposed my wakefulness to be a remnant of the old soldier within me, fearful of some sort of early morning reprisal from the duke and his men. I sent Folo out to summon back into the hall those men I had sent out the night before, and we were gathered together – much sobered – with our bowstrings and our nerves nocked, and when Elizabeth came down, late, as had become her habit, she saw our tired faces now pinched with worry, and she cried out:

'Oh dear God, what have you *done?*—'

'And what *had* you done?' the boy cries with delight. 'By our Lady! You attacked a duke! You waited in some old woods and then jumped out on him! Jesus God above, Sir Thomas, I ain't surprised you passed so long inside! I am more surprised you ain't dead in a gallows' grave!'

Despite all the time that has passed since the event, and all the shame and disworship that followed, Sir Thomas still cannot help but laugh aloud at what he – they – did that night. Had it not had so many dolorous consequences, and had his love for Lady Anne not then been spoken of by rough-tongued churls, then it would have been a great adventure, and he cannot believe, even now, that if Lady Anne ever heard the truth of it, a smile would not have graced those beautiful lips. Sir Thomas de Lamory, indeed.

'But that isn't why you were locked up?' the boy continues.

'It is *why* I was locked up,' Sir Thomas says.

'But it ain't *what* you was locked up for, is it?'

Sir Thomas is tired now, and fleetingly wonders if it was ever a good idea to start telling his story to a churlish boy such as this? How can he be expected to understand its subtleties? It is true he had no choice, save Susan, who is deaf – and dumb too, of course – and not like to jeer or cross-question him on every little detail.

'I'm tired,' he tells the boy now, and indeed the day has worn by, and Brunt should surely soon be back from the Guildhall, bringing with him news of Master Bewscel's success or his failure, and so he gestures to the boy to be away about his business, and the boy takes this as a strange sort of triumph, as if he has somehow proved something, or beaten Sir Thomas in some point only he knows, and his departure into the world of chores is cheerful enough, so that Sir Thomas is permitted to drift peacefully into sleep, as if lulled by his own words.

He wakes later to hear a pair of voices beyond his door. Master Bewscel, he is sure, back from the Guildhall, with Brunt. He cannot hear what is being said, but Master Bewscel sounds cheerful enough. Brunt mumbles something in reply, his voice much deeper in tone, and then their footsteps shuffle past, and Master Bewscel's door is opened and there is another brief exchange of words, which sound as if Master Bewscel is thanking Brunt, and Brunt is telling him it was something like a pleasure, perhaps, and that he ought to get some rest, and then Bewscel's door is closed and the locking bar is dropped almost reassuringly, and then Brunt returns back along the passageway.

His footsteps slow, and Sir Thomas is almost certain he can hear Brunt breathing at the door, and he is suddenly sure there must be a crack or something in the wood to which Brunt is pressing his eye, in which case he would see him standing there, glaring at the door, but there is nothing like that in these upper cells, nor is there a shutter over a grille that the keeper or turnkey can lower to peer into the cell, as in Colchester or the dungeons below, and after a moment Sir Thomas hears a soft chuckle, as if Brunt is laughing at him, and then, at length and at last, the steps recede. Sir Thomas is left not knowing what to make of it.

He presses his ear to the wall when he hears Master Bewscel has once more taken up his harp and begun to play that same age-old tune that Sir Thomas enjoyed while he was on the leads, the one his mother used to sing, and the words come back to him now, and he finds himself singing: merry it is while summer it lasts, with skies are filled with birdsong, but now nears winter's blast and weather strong, oh oh! How this night is long, and I with so much wrong, will sorrow and mourn and fast.

When he finishes there are tears in his eyes, for the song is so hopeless – and it is then that Sir Thomas remembers he has forgotten to give the boy the letter to deliver to Hartshorne.

CHAPTER 12

How Sir Thomas learns certain specific things that bring him great shenship

It is the next day, the fourteenth of July, and Sir Thomas Malory has been in Newgate for exactly six weeks – longer by two than the number of days our Lord Jesus Christ spent in the wilderness – and in all that time the thing he has missed most, and the thing that he has never laid eyes upon, is, of all things, a tree. But today he cares not to dwell on that, for this morning the first pardons have been issued, and some prisoners have already been freed from their cells to set the gaol's upper passages ringing with bellows of unaccustomed joy.

'Haha!' he laughs. 'Hahaha!'

He smells of Castilian soap, and despite the day's growing heat he stands in his ochre and plum hose, and his cleanest shirt and pourpoint, waiting when the boy arrives late with the bread and ale.

'Where have you *been*?' Sir Thomas asks, with intimation enough to convey the fact that he has missed him.

'Had to help out on the women's tower,' the boy tells him, nodding towards the other side of the building. 'You know what they're like.'

Sir Thomas doesn't. He has never – knowingly – met a woman who has spent any time in Newgate, not even glimpsed them, for they do not share a staircase.

'How many of them are there?' he wonders.

The boy blows a greasy hank of hair out of his eyes.

'About twenty-five in the upper storeys,' he supposes. 'Mostly thieves, or accessories to thieves, or women what have helped thieves escape, but there is also half a dozen murderers, of husbands mostly; a couple of wounders; an arsonist; and one woman is accused of petty treason, what is murdering a gent, as I suppose you know, and likewise she denies it. The common bawds and harlots and what-have-yous are mostly down in the dungeon.'

Sir Thomas is surprised.

'That is quite a roster,' he says.

The boy nods.

'They are a lot of trouble, if I'm honest, which I am, of course.'

He smiles, pleased to be aping Sir Thomas.

'I like your hose,' he says.

'Why, thank you,' Sir Thomas replies. He does think they look good with his boots.

'Old Lewd-Act has a special pair too,' the boy goes on, 'with one leg dyed sky-blue and the other grass-green.'

'And what news of the man himself?' Sir Thomas asks.

It seems there is none, or none that is conclusive, and the boy is vague on the legal niceties:

'The jury turned up and all, but then the judge had to change halfway through the day to go to Westminster or something, where there's all sorts of stuff going on, so they had to start again, and then they ran out of time or something, and he had to come back here before it was decided. I don't know. He did tell me. But my old man thinks he'll probably go free, the old coot.'

There is admiration in his voice. And in Sir Thomas's, too, when he tells him that he only managed to gain his freedom after seven long years, and that with the help of Lord Fauconberg, rather than a judge and jury.

'But old Lewd-Act's only crime was getting caught in a lewd act with some common strumpet up Popkirtle Lane,' the boy says. 'He didn't tumble a duchess, did he—'

Sir Thomas almost hits the boy.

'Neither did I!'

'And nor then did he ambush the duke with a load of bowmen in the middle of the night, and send him packing! Nor did he knock his lawyer from his horse and kick his backside.'

Sir Thomas has to grant him that.

'But it was not quite like that,' Sir Thomas tells him.

'Well, how was it then?' the boy asks, sidling towards his usual spot on the floor. 'Did he come for you straight away? The duke, I mean, the very next day?'

Sir Thomas shakes his head in pained regret.

'Would that he had,' he begins—

For then at least whatever would come, would come, and it would have been over and done with, there and then, one way or the other, but the duke's revenge came not that day, nor the next, nor indeed the next, and by the end of the week I began to believe it never would. As each day melted into its successor, the great press of fear under which we had been living – packed into the shuttered hall and starting at every noise – began to lift, and then, the week after that, it was removed entirely, when we heard from a passing salt merchant that if the duke had ever been at Caluden Park, he was gone now.

'And not surprising,' he said, 'for he'll have been called away to London, for they've only gone and hanged the Bishop of Chichester.'

This was a surprise.

'They?'

'Some sailors. Down Portsmouth way. It's said they was tired as having been so long denied their salt.'

'Surely the Bishop of Chichester is not responsible for the pay of common sailors?' Elizabeth asked when I told her.

'**Lord Moleyns** – who was the bishop – was also Lord Privy Seal,' I told her, 'and a great supporter of the Duke of Suffolk.'

329

She made a snoring noise and rolled her eyes when I mentioned the Duke of Suffolk, about whom I had recently spent much time in complaint, for he was the man on whom we had apportioned the chief blame for letting slip our grip on Normandy. I was no longer surprised at how little Elizabeth cared for what was happening beyond the boundaries of Newbold Revel, for matters of state were just then convoluted, and hard to explain, even to a man, but it mattered gravely, I kept telling her, for the divers rivalries between the divers Dukes of This and Earls of That were passed down through their affinities to us ordinary men, catching us all up in their webs of obligation.

'It threatens great disruption at every level throughout England herself,' I told her.

'Oh, stuff and nonsense,' she said. 'This is not old England, with one half cleaving to King Arthur while the other takes Sir Lancelot's side, where the ordinary commons must fight and die just because the king and his friend fell out over a woman.'

I was taken aback.

'Have you been speaking to Folo?'

It was the sort of thing he was always saying – about King Arthur's contempt for the commons, and especially his use and misuse of them in his battles with Sir Lancelot, about the putting to sea in a boat of all the children born on that same May Day as Mordred. Elizabeth told me she need not talk to any man to know something wrong when she saw it, and she thanked the Good Lord above that she was not alone in this.

'You'll see,' I might have said, or should have said, because Moleyns's murder – coming so soon after Sir Harry Beauchamp's, and Duke Humphrey of Gloucester's – was just another straw in the wind.

'Murder breeds murder,' I further warned her.

'Well, what about you?' she retorted. 'Riding around the woods

330

at night, setting ambushes for dukes? How do you suppose that will end?'

'That is altogether different,' I told her.

She scoffed but even so, despite this, we were happy together, released from our fears and our confinement, and we sent all the men away from the hall and back to their wives, and I rode out to inspect my estate, and to revisit the site of our bushment, the memory of which, now that the deed was not likely to be avenged, made me gleeful. I promised I would pay the priest to say a few more masses for the safe passage of my father's soul through Purgatory, in late thanks for this last gift of his.

Snow still lingered among the briars within the wood, but saints! It was good to be about and I rode on along Smite Brook, scarfed with a mist of my own making, passing Coombe Abbey and noting that woodsmoke rose from just the one chimney — bound to be the abbot's private chambers — and I pitied those under his pastoral care. Then I crossed the old Roman road and came at length to the hedges of Caluden Park, where I came across a couple of barefoot children out collecting twigs and so on. They saw me and ran, dropping their meagre bundles, and I wanted to call them back, to tell them to take what they needed and more besides, and I'd even help them — I was in that sort of mood — but they fled through a hole in the hedge that ringed the park.

After a moment, and out of nothing more than curiosity, I dismounted, my legs weak from my confinement, and I pulled apart the interleaving wands of poorly laid hedge, and began following in the children's footsteps until they diverted into an altogether too unattractive dell, whereupon my own steps led me out into the park, where I saw the salt merchant had been right: if the duke had ever been here, he was no longer, for there was not a soul to be seen or heard. There were tracks of deer and pigs in the odd patches of snow that lay here and there in folds in the soft cloth of yellowed leaves underfoot, and even in the deadening cold, the ripe smell of vixen lingered like a ghost between the trees.

The lodge, when I came to it, was a small thing really, across a dipping, grassy clearing: not much more than a couple of halls with a steeply pitched roof, piebald with moss and garlanded with ivy. The beams were painted that deep blood-red you sometimes find in such places, as were the shutters. There was a run of stables and kennels beyond, and a mews for the birds, and another clutch of outbuildings for hanging the day's catch, and there was another, smaller house, from the eaves of which sifted a lingering tail of pale woodsmoke. This was presumably the keeper's, or the warden's, or whatever they chose to call him, happily about his own devices now that the duke had taken his household off to deal with whatever matters arose from Moleyns's murder.

I wondered about Lady Anne. Would she have relished coming here? It was less grand even than Fenny Newbold had been, and far less grand than Newbold Revel now was. The whole household would have had to sleep together in the hall, packed about the fire in the old way. I stood there, wondering whether I should write her another letter, or go to see her, for surely matters were unresolved? I was pondering my next steps when I heard a shout and a dog bark and I saw the keeper had emerged from his cottage, a fat, pale dog at his side, and they'd seen me and probably believed me to be a poacher.

Rather than staying and explaining myself to the churl, I turned and ran back the way I had come, my boots slipping, following my own tracks through the sopping leaf-fall. I could hear the dog barking as he came bounding after me and I thanked God he was no lurcher, who might have overhauled me in moments, but one of those Talbots, of little use or beauty, and one in this case who could not catch my backside of fifty winters as I crashed back through the hole I'd made in the hedge. I untethered my horse and was quick into the saddle, and I rode off with the strangely lonesome barks of the dog still stuck behind the hedge ringing in my ears.

My adventure unsettled me somewhat, leaving me feeling foolish rather than anything else, but Elizabeth my wife was disapproving.

'You are too long in the wild woods,' she said. 'You need to put yourself in the centre of things once more.'

Perhaps she was right. Was I not becoming the very thing I had scorned as a boy? A rascally knight of the hedgerow?

I resolved to act, to ride for Westminster that day, to have my say on the great affairs of the day, and to have it listened to.

I set off with a reluctant and still disapproving Folo, and one or two others, well-wrapped against the cold, and all the way down to Westminster I rehearsed what I would say should fate offer up another encounter with the Duke of Buckingham. I can recall none of these well-planned remarks now, for never once did our paths cross during that first session, which turned out to be among the most fraught ever witnessed.

Both Lords and Commons were already astir with the dire news from Normandy, where the Rouen garrison had yielded to the French after a well-aimed cannonball had blown a hole in the Duke of Somerset's children's nursery wall. In fear for their lives – and under pressure from his duchess – he panicked and gave away that which we had spent so much blood and cruelty acquiring. We hung on in places such as Caen and Cherbourg, but with dwindling hope and fewer expectations. Meanwhile pirates – French, Breton, Flemish, even Englishmen to whom the king had sold licence to do so – infested the Narrow Sea, raiding villages and towns along the south coast even as far north as Cromer (though I had no idea where Cromer was), and so the wool trade, on which we all, in our various ways, depended, suffered badly.

The king was at fault, but we his loyal subjects held steadfast to the tradition of blaming his counsellors, for he had sent many a

good man from his side – men such as the Duke of York, for example – and replaced him with bloodsuckers of the Peace party, of the
Duke of Suffolk's affinity, men most like to have been brought up
in the lore of the Church or the law court, men such as Greswold,
with scarcely a handful of them ever having served a single day in
the king's jeopardy.

Further to that though, as I heard from Sir William Mountfort,
my father's old friend, who had now left the Commons to become
sheriff of the county, that before Bishop Moleyns had died – not
hanged by sailors, as that salt merchant had had it, but beaten to a
thick pulp by the townsmen of Portsmouth – he had freely confessed
of his part in the yielding up of Anjou and Maine, but claimed the
greater blame lay with the Duke of Suffolk, who, it was also said,
was now planning to assist the French in invading England.

'He is said to have made Wallingford Castle comfortable for
them,' Mountfort confided. 'With sweetmeats, good wine and so
forth, and he plans to marry his boy to one of Somerset's girls, and
claim the throne in her name!'

'And he the son of a wool merchant,' I noted.

Mountfort looked at me down his long nose as if I were very
shrewd.

'And she the scion of a bastard,' he returned.

And I felt the flush of belonging to his select group.

Since no proof of these charges against Suffolk could be found,
others were made against which he could only defend himself by
declaring that if he were guilty, then he was guilty of nothing more
than of carrying out the king's agreed policy, and how then could
that be a crime?

But popular feeling now ran very high and the commons were
wroth out of all measure. Every church door was blanketed with
screeds of lewd ribaldries accusing the duke of insatiable covet-
ousness and of worse, and stones were being thrown and there

was much pushing and shoving in the streets around the palace at Westminster. The king had a wine-drawer hung and drawn and his quarters dipped in tar and sent around the realm – to Stamford and Winchester, and a couple of other places, too – to calm things down. And hearing of this man's fate, once more Folo mused – just as he had after poor dead John Jiggins was lost in the moat at Calais – on the purpose of such a man's life, but this time, feeling the man had deserved all he got, I had something of an answer.

'Every man has his story, Folo,' I told him, 'and each must have its ending.'

Folo looked at me very unblinkingly then.

So the Duke of Suffolk was at bay and must yield, but if he hoped the king would come to his defence, he was sore disappointed, for the example of the tar-dipped wine-drawer had not placated the crowd. The king became so afeared of them that he offered up the duke as scapegoat and banished him from this realm for a period of five years, after which he would be free to return, so long as he promised not to seek redress against those who might have caused his exile (which would be almost everybody, but most especially the king).

Parliament broke for Easter and was to be called again after Ascension in Leicester, a city known to be less rowdy than London, and, as luck would have it, more convenient for me. So of course I went, but any hopes that this session would be less tempestuous than the last were dashed even before Folo and I raised the city's spire, for we heard on the wayside that the ship taking the Duke of Suffolk to begin his exile in Ghent had been intercepted and boarded, and after a brief trial the boarders – common sailors, for the most part – had found the duke guilty of treason and had struck his head from his shoulders on the ship's gunwale. This – his head – they'd then skewered with a pole stuck in the sands below the great castle at Dover, and how men laughed, for the duke's name was De la Pole.

After hearing this, Folo of course repeated my earlier words back to me — 'each must have its ending' — and he made me sound very callous, but it was not Suffolk's end that came as the chief shock (though granted he would not have seen it like that), it was that common sailors might set themselves up to sit in judgement upon a duke, and worse, upon a king, for it emerged that certain words had been spoken during this so-called trial to make it clear that its verdict — guilty — was as much a damnation on the king as it was on his duke.

Is this important? Looking back on it now, and in light of what was to come, it seems perhaps not, or perhaps it was, or perhaps only as another link in the chain of events that began with the death of Sir Harry Beauchamp and ends with where we are today. Perhaps, in fact, it was merely the most alarming indication yet of the depth of our descent into the sort of wild vexations I had already begun to fear we Englishmen always bring about wheresoever we go.

I was mulling just this exact thing later that week, with Folo again — and of all people John Ap-Moffat, who was in Leicester conducting some business of his own, and had civilly invited us both to dine at the house of his wife's sister, or somesuch, in a pleasant quarter to the east of the cathedral. We were alone, and he had managed to get hold of a delivery of the new season's lampreys before even the king or the Earl of Warwick, who usually prided themselves on such things.

'It's extraordinary,' he had told us with his usual slow-spreading smile. 'I met this chap and—' I stopped listening immediately, because I knew it would be another story of something ending unexpectedly well for him, and I could not help noticing how gracefully he had aged, hardly seeming to sag or wilt in any direction, and with just a great number of very fine lines that spread all over his face, each one a filament of white hatched across a backdrop of taut, weather-beaten skin, and I thought to myself, my God: he smiles even into the rain.

'I fear the chief default of us Englishmen,' I was telling them, 'is that all too soon we wax dissatisfied with whatever we are given, and we must forever strive for some newfangled thing. So it is that now the commons believe themselves worthy to sit in judgement on a king!'

At this, Ap-Moffat mentioned that he had heard of a new uprising planned in Kent, under a man calling himself Jack Cade.

'It will come to nothing,' I told them, dismissing it only because I could not stand to think he might know more than me. Folo was there, greatly pleased to be included in the invitation, but his manners were bestial, and I hoped it'd not happen again.

'My wife,' he began, speaking around something he was chewing, 'says the chief default of us English is not that we wax dissatisfied, it is that we are boring.'

This took me aback a bit.

'Boring?'

'Yes,' he went on. 'But she also agrees with you. She says we are also greedy and covetous incompetents. She says that we are careless of what we already own, and that we think only of what we might next acquire, whether we need it or no, and furthermore, that we are careless of who or what we despoil in order to get it. She also says we dislike one another, and that we are right to do so, and that this is what has brought us to our current pass.'

There was scarcely a moment of silence before I rejected this analysis, and the evening might then have descended into the usual ritual examination of Norman and French shortcomings, but Ap-Moffat steered us in a more ruminative direction.

'Well, she has a point, hasn't she?' he ventured. 'Look at King Arthur and his fellowship: it started out well enough, with the commons acclaiming they would have no other king but Arthur, yet within only a few years they changed their minds and wanted Mordred in his stead.'

'Is it any surprise?' Folo now wondered. 'King Arthur brought the country nothing but strife and war – with Sir Lancelot over Queen Guinevere, remember, about which the commons can have cared little – while Mordred promised them great joy and bliss.'

This was shocking. Folo seemed to be siding with Mordred against King Arthur!

'No, no, no, Folo!' I said. 'You misunderstand. King Arthur was the most king and knight of the world!'

'Yes,' Folo appeared to agree. 'And yet.'

'And yet nothing! The French books authorise it! And, by Jesu Christi, he pulled the sword from the stone!'

'But that means nothing,' Folo countered.

I almost laughed.

'"Whoso pulleth out this sword of this stone and anvil is right-wise born King of all England" means nothing?'

'It was just a stone,' Folo said. 'Someone must have carved the words into it, surely? So whoever carved the words was the one who made it the condition to become king.'

I was not having this.

'No,' I cried, cutting across anything further he had to say.

And the evening wound to its unsatisfactory end.

Folo's words stayed with me though, bringing with them a sense of lingering threat, of everything being turned on its head, that persisted for many days. That Folo of all people, whom I had known for more than thirty years, might think King Arthur was not – well. I could hardly bring myself to think about it, let alone talk about it, and in fact I did not think about it or talk about it, or to him, in all the days that followed while we were in Leicester. Had he apologised, I might have, but he did not, though he knew he had offended me, and so we spent the rest of our time together in bruised silence

338

until a few days before Pentecost, when it was time to return home to dear old Newbold Revel.

May is the most marvellous month, of course, and beyond the ditches that bracketed the road home every tree was smocked in blossom, and as we passed the bee-jewelled heads of cow-parsley they seemed to nod in approval. Beyond the hedgerows the fields and folds were filled with bleating lambs and their answering dams, and above us the celestial sky was alive with trackless slips of swifts and swallows. The sun warmed our faces, and I found it impossible to suppose Folo had really meant what he had said, and so I began to talk to him of the land of Logris, which was the land of Arthur, and was this land too, and I spoke also of Gore, and of Listinoise, and of Surluse, and even of Lonazep, too, and when I saw that Folo was listening with drowsy intent, I found that in the course of that short journey along the old Roman road, I had forgiven him his outburst, and I found myself believing then that if I could do that, then surely so might anybody be reconciled to anybody? And knowing this I took great glad heart, for it meant that nothing worse might yet befall us, or this land of England, and I breathed in the rich-scented air with pleasure.

Which only increased upon my homecoming, with the sight of my wife, whom I found once more to be full meek and passing fair, once more with child, and my bounding dogs, too, and my sons, Robert and now young Thomas, who shook his fist in cheerful greeting.

'Home is where a man is happiest, Elizabeth,' I told her as I kissed her a hundred times, never once for one moment thinking what it might be like to be holding Lady Anne, as once I used to, or indeed a woman such as Mistress Smith, of whom I had not had a thought since a good many days, in her stead.

In my absence, Appleby had been assisting in the running of my estates and they thrived, he said, 'though there is one or two who are still in default on their rents'.

'We shall see to them later,' I told him, for I was struck most powerfully by echoes of my father's homecomings, which had been a time of gifts and forgiveness, and I did not want to think of such things as rent arrears and repossessions on a day such as this. I wanted to think of apple blossom, and of sweet ale, of pea shoots defying the predations of the crows, and of going a-Maying, and of other things.

'What else?' I asked. 'Not heard anything from our old friend the Duke of Buckingham, have we?'

I knew we had heard nothing, for, like me, Buckingham had been in Leicester this past sennight, but I wished to recall to Appleby's mind the occasion of the Coombe Wood Bushment, and, having done so, we laughed as old soldiers do over an old adventure, and Appleby's eyes became all bright in their whorls of little creases.

'I feared we might be seeing him again,' he laughed, 'but I suppose he must've got the message that Sir Thomas Malory ain't a one to mess with! Not like poor old what's-his-name, who had his house set upon by one of the duke's cousins, I believe, and only saved himself and his family from a most terrible death by barring themselves in the church!'

I had heard of no such thing, but Appleby had a connection to a boatman on the Thames who traded in such stories.

'He was lucky, it's said,' Appleby went on, 'for the duke's cousin came with near on two hundred men, only they could none of them get the church to burn, and so had to content themselves with pillaging his house and farm!'

Appleby sniggered at their incompetence, but this was worrying news.

'Whose farm was it?' I wondered.

'Oh,' Appleby said, as if it might not have mattered very much indeed. 'It was Sir Robert Harcourt's.'

I was drawn up short. Heat flooded my face, ice down my back.

340

My head felt light.

'*The* Sir Robert Harcourt? *Our* Sir Robert Harcourt?'

'What I've heard,' Appleby answered, as if this was still darkly amusing.

'And who was the cousin? Was it Sir Humphrey Stafford?'

Appleby was momentarily confused by there being two Humphrey Staffords, but I meant, of course, the Humphrey Stafford who was cousin to Humphrey Stafford who was the Duke of Buckingham. When he grasped this, he agreed it was so.

'Yes,' he said. 'Him.'

Now this required some thought, because it was well known that Sir Robert Harcourt – *our* Sir Robert Harcourt, since there were two or three others – had, once, in a scuffle during the Pentecost fair in Coventry, swung his sword at Sir Humphrey Stafford's son Richard, and in the ensuing melee, the son – Richard – had been killed. Sir Robert had not been found guilty, because of some shrewd lawyer's trick, and he had walked away, and so now, if Appleby was right, the father had tried to take vengeance, and would have done so, had his soldiers not been so hopeless.

'When was this?' I asked.

'A fortnight ago?' Appleby supposed.

'And has there been any comeuppance? Any consequence?'

Appleby shook his head.

'None so far.'

By Jesu! Sir Robert Harcourt had been one of Harry Beauchamp's men! He'd been a sheriff of the county. If a relation of Buckingham had attacked him, and there was to be no punishment or reprisal, then who would be next? By Jesu, in that moment I saw an image of the Duke of Buckingham as a goshawk, and I was gripped by that familiar flailing panic. I cursed my laxity. I cursed Appleby's laxity. I was the foolish bride who had not saved her oil, and now it was growing dark. But it was not yet quite, absolutely, too late. There was still time to – to – to gather up more oil. To arm myself against what might yet come.

'Appleby,' I said, 'summon the men for the morrow, especially that man with the two teeth' – I meant Geoffrey Gryffyn – 'if he is still alive, and we shall see to those rents.'

The next morning, and in that fraught atmosphere, we started out on those little pieces of what might be called housekeeping: the collecting of rents overdue since Lady Day, and which, with the threat of Buckingham brought to mind and hanging heavy above our heads, could not be allowed to linger over to St John's.

It was just as well we started when we did, for no sooner were we on the road – ten of us in all, including the two-toothed Geoffrey Gryffyn, there to be unleashed as a last resort, and each of us arrayed as if for a *chevauchée* in the wilder parts of Maine or Anjou – than word came that the commons of Kent were still unsated by their murder of the Duke of Suffolk, and – perhaps in response to the rumour of the plan to punish them for the murder by turning the whole of Kent into a deer park – they had risen up under a captain named Jack Cade, just as Ap-Moffat had predicted, and were camped, a friar told us, forty thousand strong, upon Blackheath, south of the city, and the king had fled to the safety of St John's Priory in Clerkenwell.

The friar told us that it was Bishop Waynflete, with whom I was on passing good terms, who was sent to deal with the rebels, and that they had a petition of fifteen complaints they wanted the king to address.

I have since entertained myself by wondering if that cursed lawyer Thomas Greswold was somehow behind the drawing-up of this petition, though that is unlikely, or if he merely read it and noted its content when copies finally reached us in Warwick? Whatever the truth, I find I can almost laugh at it now, from such a distance, and after such a time, for though I believe the rebels' grievances were genuine, it is impossible now not to see their petition not as a list of things they wanted stopped, but as a list of suggestions to any local tyrant short of ideas on repression beyond basic rapine.

One tactic they wished outlawed – and so suggested – was the bringing of false accusation of treason against a man so that his estate might then be easily snapped up. Another was the bringing of false charges in a distant court, which forces a man to travel, and where, as a stranger, he would inevitably be found guilty. Another was the bringing of false legal challenges to a man's right to his own property, which tie him up in lawyers' points so that he knows not whether he is coming or going. A further tactic (suggestion) was the taking of a man's possessions without payment while claiming to be a purveyor of the king, who has the right to live off the commons.

But these things, then, seemed distant in time and place, and were of less concern to me than getting in what was due by way of rents, and so we continued riding through the county, moving from tenant to tenant. Sometimes we might have had to lean harder than I should have liked on those who owed money, for this was a bad time of year to be collecting rent: the pea crop was not yet in, and the wool was not yet worth shearing, and so money was tight, with people coming to the end of last year's provisions. Now, I am not one to put a man off his land if he cannot pay his rent for a month or two, but I learned in France that if you are collecting rent – or taxes – you cannot leave empty-handed. You must take *something*, anything. A cow from a farmer in Brinklow, a dog from a shepherd in Stretton-Under-Fosse, a bee skep here, a latch gate there, and a bucket and a length of rope somewhere else. Though it was grim work, it needed to be done.

And then, on a day late in the week, under a sky the colour of the Blessed Virgin's cloak, I found myself back in Monks Kirby, where I decided we must take something – anything – from a brewster named Meg King, who hung her spray of wilted twigs above the doorway of a small cottage at the bottom of the village on which she was supposed to pay rent, and from whom, as a consequence, I had never bought ale. She was surprisingly stout for someone with no money other than a single much abraded sixpence, so we sent in Geoffrey Gryffyn to winkle out either the rest of the money owed, or something else of value.

He had come out with a leather mazer in the bottom of which was a good inch of pitch-black tar, which in other circumstances might have seen her ear clipped, or worse, for defrauding her customers, had she any, with a short measure.

It was while I was examining this item, marvelling at its brazen dishonesty, that I found myself in the shade of the great yew that had spread its boughs well beyond the churchyard wall, to the detriment of any stray cattle or horses, I thought, and it was just as I was thinking this that I heard two of them — horses — tethered to the churchyard gate, noisily cropping the lush grass. They were good horses: a quiet grey mare that might be ridden by a lady, and a smaller pony that might be ridden by her servant, both well-saddled, and with dusty fetlocks, as if they might have come some distance. The sun slanted down, bees filled the air with their drowsy hum, and there came the gentle murmur of voices from within the churchyard. A man and a woman.

I should have known who it would be. It was, after all, the day before Pentecost, and once past the horses and into the deeper cool of the shadow of the church tower, I saw her: Mistress Smith, standing exactly where she said she would be, dressed in wool the colour of dried sage leaves, with a servant girl, presumably, nearby, with two patches of dirt on her apron where she had been kneeling. Mistress Smith did not see me, for she had her back to me, and was talking to a cleric — it was **William Rowe**, he who oversaw the affairs of the priory to his own advantage, and had a face as smug as a rat in a cistern – and he too seemed mesmerised by Mistress Smith's appearance, for he did not take his eyes from her to look over to see me until I stood close behind her.

He was entertaining her with the fact that during the last century the name of St Edith's had been changed from St Dennis's because of that saint's sad connection with France, and she was listening absently, and under her headdress of simple linen, her neck was very fine, and, blame it on the weather, or the time of year, I was gripped with the urge to place my lips on it, and inhale the smell that I believed without question would make any man swoon.

'Mistress Smith,' I said, my voice deepening as I spoke.

She turned around.

'Oh 'ello!' she cried, flushing a wonderful shade of rose, and she greeted me with an impulsive kiss, as if she had no clue how to behave with such a man as myself, and I was once again struck by her all-enveloping corporality. Even though she was full meekly dressed, one could not help but know that she was covering up something that would be very wonderful to behold.

I murmured something about being in the vicinity, and of wishing to take the opportunity to offer my humblest sympathies at her father's eight-year mind. As I spoke I saw Rowe looking at me with flattened eyes – part-angry that I was come to chase him away from Mistress Smith, part-afeared I had come to collect moneys he might or might not owe – though to his credit he stood his ground and tried to maintain his dignity, but really, how could he? He wore an old gown, much repaired, that came to his baggy-hosed knees, and shoes of donkey leather, like meat pies, that fit neither foot. I just happened to be wearing my moss-green velvet brigandine that fitted me somewhat snugly, with two red leather belts wrapped about my waist, one holding a sword in an ornate scabbard, the other my father's dagger, likewise ornately sheathed, and a heavy-hanging purse. My only slightly dusty riding boots were well-made, and turned down at the knee to reveal my horseman's thighs clad in new-spun good quality wool the colour of mustard, and I carried a helmet under my arm. I could see Rowe looking at me with foul envy as Mistress Smith regretted to say that I had just missed the mass said for her father, and as I asked her to show me the old man's grave so that I too might say a prayer.

'For the love that you bore him.'

Now, I have never before knowingly stood over the grave of a miller, and see no reason to do so again, for it was a humble little thing, entirely in keeping with his station, and utterly unremarkable other than having been recently scraped free of leaves and lichen and the like, and I could think of little to say, so I kept my head bowed, and listened to some shouting coming from the brewster's house as Geoffrey Gryffyn went to work.

After some time — rent with a scream and a crash and what might have been a cloud of masonry dust — I lifted my head, touched the little gravestone, and sombre as Death himself I walked with Mistress Smith back towards the church, and I confess to not wishing to take my eyes from her or her form.

Clouds were gathering, and it looked like rain. I asked after her husband. She was, unexpectedly, hesitant.

'Oooh,' she started, a warbling falling tone of thwarted hope. 'He is called to his papers again.'

'His papers?'

'As happens all too often these days,' she said with an edge of complaint.

'These are uncertain times,' I sympathised. 'Wild and scrambled.'

'Oh yes,' she sighed, as if she'd heard all this before, and we were silent for a moment. I waited to see if she would go on, for it was clear she had much on her mind. She plucked listlessly at the tips of the bushes that we passed, and she tore the leaves neatly before dropping them beneath her feet. She sighed again.

346

'Do you spend so much time away from your wife, Sir Thomas?' she asked, not entirely unexpectedly.

'My wife? No. She is – she – hah! – she spends most of her time away from me.'

I meant it as a joke, obviously, but Mistress Smith was in no mood to laugh, or even to listen much.

'I know he is older than me,' she went on as if I had not spoken, 'and he is a busy man, what with all this new work with Master Greswold, but—'

Greswold! Ha! I nearly spoke up, to try to cheer her with my story of ambushing the Duke of Buckingham, and of capturing only Greswold, and of kicking his piss-sodden arse, which I was certain she would appreciate, but she was already moving on with her plaint.

'You too are nearly as old as he, Sir Thomas, I dare say, and you are not stuck all day behind a desk, lecturing me on how I should not spend money on a piece of silk at such and such a price, but should haggle a cheaper price, or make do with simple linen, if you please.'

I agreed, because that was true.

'He is much – ah – taken up with work with Master Greswold, is he?' I wondered.

'It is all he ever does. To begin with I was very pleased. I thought we were going up in the world and of course we are, but—'

She blew out through her lips.

Another scream from the brewster's cottage.

'Whatever can be going on?' she asked, finally noting the noise now that we were by the churchyard gates where her servant waited, casting a fading shadow as the clouds drew overhead, and peering south to see whatever it was that Geoffrey Gryffyn was about. Whatever it was, it would not show me in my best light if Mistress Smith saw ten of my men, well-armed and in steel helmets, pushing around an elderly, albeit fraudulent, brewster. I said something about stopping it, whatever it was, but in fact, when I showed Mistress Smith the mazer with its cheating disc of tar, she was outraged.

'Disgusting, I call it,' she said. 'She should be whipped.'

I could not decide if this reflected well on her or not, but to avoid further unpleasantries, I threw the cup away, untethered her horse, and began leading it westwards, away from the village, presuming her business here was done (it was).

'In the absence of your husband or any other escort present,' I asked, 'can I see you safe home, Mistress Smith? The roads are not safe for two women alone.'

Her servant girl looked somewhat browbeaten, and no good in any kind of a fight, should one arise.

'That's very chivalrous of you, Sir Thomas, and in the absence of my errant husband, I should welcome your protection.'

She was half joking, of course, playing the part of a lady, and she took my arm and I could not help but hear echoes of Lady Anne in her exaggerated, haughty tone, mimicking the ladies of Arthur's court. I held her stirrup and as she clambered up into her saddle, I confess myself warmed by her hand and weight upon my shoulder, and I then swung quickly up onto my own horse and settled myself carefully. The servant girl would have to look to herself, as she did, riding like a man, a few paces behind us, her bun-face collapsed into a frown, as we set off at a slow clop away from the church, and from William Rowe, with no farewell.

'That's the spirit,' I said.

But it turned out that she was not riding back to Coventry that day, but only to her father's old house by the millpond, which was her husband's property now, having passed to him through her. It was a ride that lasted as long as it might take to say the rosary.

I asked about Hugh Smith, for I realised that I knew virtually nothing about him other than those first distant and perhaps untypical impressions I'd gathered at Verneuil. I discovered that after the battle, he had given up soldiering and retrained – late in the day, I thought, but perhaps wisely – as an attorney, or perhaps he was one already? It was slightly unclear. I supposed that was how his collaboration with Greswold had come about, but it turned out the two were old friends, a fact which seemed to reveal Smith in a gloomy light.

'He has started spelling his name with the letter Y in all his correspondence,' she told me. 'In the belief that people will not think his father's father was a blacksmith from Wolverhampton. But I don't see what is wrong with that, do you, Sir Thomas? No one looks down upon him for that, do they? I do not, in any event. I take as I find, I always say.'

I didn't disagree, of course, although I did, violently, but neither did I agree. I said nothing as she prattled on a bit like this, perhaps enjoying talking to someone content to listen, as I did, vaguely ruminative, without offering overmuch by way of advice or instruction in return.

'He knows the best way to get anywhere,' she said, 'and he knows the names of all the roads. Fosse Way and Watling Street and whatever.'

I had not thought of roads having names, but why not?

We arrived at the mill just as it started to rain, a proper late spring deluge, and we hurriedly dismounted and led our horses into the gloom of the stables. Mistress Smith told the maid to run fetch the boy from wherever he was like to be hiding, and the girl hitched her skirts and ran splashing through the puddles across the yard. I tied up all three horses and we stood together at the door, shoulder to shoulder, close enough to touch, and in the din of the rain on the thatch above, we watched the drops pelt the quickly spreading puddles.

'It is like the sound of arrows falling at Agincourt!' I laughed.

She had not known I was there, of course.

I told her it was I who had stood over the wounded Duke of York, and I who had killed the Duc d'Alençon.

'Ooh, Sir Thomas!'

We stood for a while enclosed alone in a strange stillness. I was intensely aware of her, and I would wager she was intensely aware of me. My blood seemed to have turned to quicklime, for my extremities seemed to fizzle and I could feel the beat of my heart even in my teeth. I was certain I was on the cusp of something unlooked for in that merry month of May, and Jesu defend me! I knew that if I just turned to her—

But then the boy came running, a grubby stable lad with dirty bare feet and a felt cap like a Shrovetide cake, and the moment, if it had ever truly existed, was gone. I adjusted myself, and she scolded the boy with more than necessary vigour, as if she too had been discomfited by how close we had come to – to whatever it was that we had come close to, and then the rain let up, and I, still quick of heartbeat and short of breath, caught myself. I knew I should go, and go now, and we both knew I must – for now – decline her offer of ale, and I made my farewell to Mistress Smith and to her household, who stood staring mutely, and I mounted up – carefully again – and promised to come again, and I said I should bring my wife and so on, for I knew that was what was expected of me.

With my dignity preserved, I rode slowly back towards the sandstone church tower in Monks Kirby and the brewster's cottage to find Gryffyn and the others, but from then on, I was aware that a box was opened, a corner was turned, and a path to a new, unexpected destination was laid out before me. I had found something that was not there before, and I felt immeasurably enriched and enlivened.

'You all right, Sir Thomas? You's all flushed and that.'

It was Appleby, with the faintest smile twisting his lips.

We rode home in silence, and the smells that the newly wet earth gave up were heady and pungent, and under now bright sunlight again, clouds of insects rose up from the steaming puddles, and even though my brigandine, beginning to dry now, was shrinking to grip me uncomfortably tightly about my middle, I confess I could hardly prevent myself from breaking into one of those May Day songs that the commons sing, about the summer coming in and so on, and I felt a great lurch, and could not help but smile when I thought of Mistress Smith's slight nod when I had suggested I should call again.

But for one reason or another — one being my wife, the other being a message, finally, come from Lady Anne — I did not see Mistress Smith again for some time. In part it was because I wished to preserve the possibility that something might unfold, and in part because I feared that I had become a silly old fool and merely imagined the attentions of a bored young woman were anything more than — more than — I don't know. There was, too, the notion, the knowledge, that she thought me one thing, as Sir Thomas Malory, knight and soldier, and admired me for that, and the one thing that would prove I was not the thing she thought I was, was if I did what I wished to do. In a sense, not yielding to my base temptations, that only made me even more admirable in her eyes, and in a way, I possessed her even more fully, didn't I? By not possessing her? Or was that vanity? It was very noble, in any event, and it reminded me of love in the old days, when knights most loved that which they could not have.

It was hard to ignore, though. I knew by then the only way to escape this sort of self-laceration was through work, through activity, and so I threw myself into my daily tasks with uncompromising vigour, and in this way, summer was got through. With Gryffyn's assistance, I even managed to coax five pounds from William Hales, a notorious tight-fist.

But if our eyes were drawn to the business at hand, our ears were ever cocked for news of the rebel Jack Cade and his commons of Kent, who were known to be menacing London still. This duly came, a few days after St Barnabas, and it was very bad: the king had had enough of it, and had sent his supporters after Cade's men, only for them to be routed, which was the bad bit; but the good news was that in the rout two of Buckingham's kinsmen had been killed, including his namesake who had attacked and tried to burn alive Sir Robert Harcourt and his family.

'What do you make of that, Folo?' I asked, as if it proved some distant point I could not remember making. 'Just deserts, wouldn't you say?'

The next week, though, there came news from across the sea that distracted us from what was happening in Blackheath, and in my own heart: Caen had fallen. Folo and I looked at one another, all our differences set aside, and wordlessly we remembered what it had cost to take, and the unforgivable aftermath, and we shook our heads in sorrow at the pointlessness of it all. Then, just a week after that, we heard that Jack Cade and his men were back in London and they had managed to murder yet another bishop – of Salisbury this time – whom they felt deserved it, for he had officiated at the marriage of the king and his French wife.

The boy has crossed his ankles, rested his head against the wall and closed his eyes. He is snoring very softly, and Sir Thomas has not the heart to wake him. He's not surprised to find he has squandered the boy's attention with all these sorts of details, but in them lie the answer to his oft-repeated question 'why?' and – until the boy wakes and tells him that something must happen, soon, for the love of God – he continues this part of his tale in a quieter voice, vowing to wake the boy when it is time.

And so it went on, the world we knew fraying at its edges, all certainties abraded to nothing, and I expended much thought and anxiety on the state of the realm, worrying about the larger world, when indeed I should have had an eye on affairs of a closer nature, for little did I know then – for who could have known? – that my arrow, that fateful arrow shot to symbolise my passage from womb to world, was just then, unbeknownst to me, at its very zenith. All the buffets it had so far received, all those small changes of direction, were as nothing to that which was about to take it, and fling it hurtling across three, four, five counties, and to bring it down not in some mildly unexpected place – as might be suggested by its landing in the courtyard, rather than in that third stockfish pond – but in gross infamy, ignominy, disgrace and such disworship as no righteous man did ever deserve.

But while so many of the buffets I had received throughout my life had arisen from elsewhere, from beyond the horizon, or by freak chance, this final blow arose from an incident that occurred much closer to home: in Coventry, upon the day of the Feast of the Transfiguration, and it involved none other than Mistress Smith.

At which point the boy wakes with a start.
'What?'
'It involved none other than Mistress Smith, I said.'
He nods.
'The blonde lady, yes. Go on.'

The bell for None was ringing, and I was riding back home from having spent the morning with my attorney, William Hartshorne, at his offices on Earle Street, talking over something or other which I can now scarce recall but was probably to do with an enfeoffment, as was our usual business. I was completely alone, with neither Folo nor Appleby, which was, I concede, odd. I was thinking to myself that it was too hot to be in town, and that I should prefer to be at home in the shade of my rose bowers, perhaps, at liberty to do little or nothing, dressed only in my shirt and pourpoint, when there ahead of me I saw a party of well-accoutred horsemen gathered outside a house that I confess I knew – because I had taken steps to find out – to be Hugh Smith's hall on Pepper Lane. They were about five or six of them, and I judged them to be waiting anxiously for something, or someone, and since they looked far from carefree. I spurred my horse towards them and I recognised one of them: **William Weston**, whom I knew to be involved with the Knights Hospitaller.

'God give you good grace, William,' I called.

He started and did not look overly pleased to be so hailed. He looked caught out.

'Warm, is it not?' I asked, pulling at my collar to indicate the escape of bodily steam.

He was grudging.

'You look very fine, Sir Thomas?' he asked.

It was true I had made an effort, but not so very great a one as to be unusual.

'And what brings you along Pepper Lane?' he asked.

By now his companions were turning in their saddles to study me, and they too were unfriendly, as if it was my attention that was unwelcome, as if I had caught them out in something.

'I am on my way home,' I told him, and now them. I would have explained that I had just been to see Hartshorne in his offices, but had they then asked where his offices were I would have had to reveal that I had not taken the most direct route home, but had diverted my horse's steps just a few hundred yards out of my way, for the pleasure of riding past Hugh Smith's hall, about which, of course, I had heard so much.

'And what are you gentlemen about?' I asked, for their faces, and

their horses, were turned towards the hall's gateway — an archway
set in two other houses that was presently open — and I was become
curious about their intent.

Weston told me they were waiting for someone.

'Master Smith?'

He shook his head very minutely. And it was just then that I
saw Mistress Smith's bun-faced servant appear in the archway to the
yard of Smith's hall. She looked harried, and pale, and furtive. They
could not be waiting for her, surely?

'What is it?' I asked Weston. 'What's going on?'

The other men with him were leaning forward now, peering over
at me.

'Do you know Smith?' one of them asked. I sensed they would
judge me on my answer.

'He fought with me at Verneuil.'

If I thought that might carry weight, I was wrong.

'Did you know he beats his wife?'

I confess I was surprised at this question for two reasons: the
first was by the thought that Smith might do it, for he was elderly,
and though Mistress Smith was in no sense beefy, it was obvious
that should he try, she would beat him hands-down in any footrace,
hampered by her skirts or no; and the second reason I was surprised
was that this man — whom I did not then know — should feign such
outrage, for he was one of those uptight little men of about thirty
winters, with tight little lips, flared nostrils and narrow-set eyes,
who had also taken great care with his appearance — with rings and
gloves and a sword and so on — so that I might gauge him worth
easily forty pounds a year, and as such I knew him to be precisely of
the sort to regularly beat women.

'Is Mistress Smith harmed?' I asked.

'Not yet,' the third man said, who also had that giveaway tension
about the nostrils.

I turned to the bun-faced girl again, who was still in the archway, hands clasped, peering out, first away from us, then again at us.

'You seem very concerned for her?' I wondered.

They looked at me askance but said nothing. Now I saw the bun-faced girl signal to someone behind her and she stepped aside to let two oxen bring a well-laden cart out into the street. The sumpter man turned his cart away from us, as if meaning to leave the city by the Gosford Gate. Once it had turned, the bun-faced girl disappeared back through the archway, presumably into the yard, and a moment later she led out the fine horse that I had last seen in Monks Kirby, and on it sat a woman whom, though she was hooded and cloaked, and her head seemed to hang heavy, I knew at once to be Mistress Smith.

Weston and the others pulled on their reins and nudged their horses to join her as she followed the cart.

'Weston,' I said. 'Favour me. What is happening?'

Weston was not such a bad fellow, and though he obviously wished to put himself at Mistress Smith's side, he lingered a moment.

'A bad business,' he said. 'Mistress Smith wishes to leave her husband's household.'

This was a shock.

'With you?'

He shook his head sorrowfully as if to impart the thought that this was altogether too sorrowful an occasion to suggest he wished it were so, even though he obviously did.

'**Potter** there,' he pointed at the back of the first of the two with whom he'd come. 'He knows her brother. He and **Brown**. They are taking Mistress Smith to Barwell to be away from her husband, to be away from Smith.'

Potter? Brown? Smith? It suddenly sounded the sort of affair in which I did not wish to be involved.

'Does Smith know?'

A stupid question: had he known, he would have stopped her.

'He is in London,' Weston said.

I exhaled loudly. It seemed very shabby to me. Heartbreakingly so, in a way, and I thought of poor Mistress Smith, creeping away with a cartload of chattels, reduced to the company of men named Potter and Brown. That it was done in broad daylight – rather than in the dead of night – was merely a mitigating grace.

I decided I must intervene, if only to put Potter and Brown in their place, and to remind Mistress Smith of my existence, and so I turned my horse and spurred him down towards Gosford Street to catch the cart and its sorry retinue.

Mistress Smith sat upon her horse with her head drooping, her face half-veiled, and she herself half the woman she had been when last we met, this time in blue wool and rough-hewn clogs. She looked like a penitent on her way to some awful place of pilgrimage in the Northern Parts, and I rode alongside her, setting my horse between hers and that bun-faced servant girl's.

'Mistress Smith,' I announced myself. 'May God give you good morrow?'

She looked up at me from under her brows, anxious and tear-stained, and this time there was no cheery greeting for Sir Thomas Malory, only a sniff and then a fresh bout of tears.

'Come, come,' I said, finding and passing her a clean linen kerchief.

'Oh, Sir Thomas,' was all she could say before she noisily blew her already reddened nose. 'I am going to Barwell, to be away from my Hugh.'

Barwell was about ten English miles away, to the east of Coventry. If she really wanted to get away from him, I thought she'd have to do better than that.

'What will you do in Barwell?' I asked.

357

She shrugged her shoulders quickly, and blew her nose again. A rather fine mouse-coloured greyhound trotted along by her side.

'May I ride with you?' I asked.

Why? Why did I ask that?

I cannot say, really, other than I could not stand to see her so miserable, and I wanted to offer some succour.

But even now I still think about that moment, and I picture myself there on that road out of Coventry, and I look about, and I wonder if there was hidden from me anything by way of a sign — some small symbol perhaps? — as you might hope would come in a man's life, to warn him that his life is now at its zenith? That just like his arrow, he has reached his turn, and that hereinafter anything that remained to happen to him would be governed by what had already happened, and that from that moment on — in my case the moment I asked Mistress Smith if I might ride with her — he was on his return journey to the earth's cold clutch?

No.

Mistress Smith looked at me over my kerchief gripped to her nose and she began to weep again, as if my presence reminded her of the gravity of her plight, but she nodded to signal that my riding with her would be an honour, and I thought then that she was right, for if she must desert her husband and leave the city, then she must at least do it in style, and what could be greater in style than riding out with Sir Thomas Malory, knight of the shire, at your side, atop his finest horse, and dressed in his best green hose and a doublet of linen dyed the exact shade of a bullfinch's egg, and wearing a sword and a dagger at his hip, and on his freshly barbered head a velvet cap of midnight blue, from which swung a single pearl bigger than a pea?

Vanity you will say, vanity, and I can only agree with you, but there are greater sins than vanity, aren't there? And meanwhile William Weston rode alongside us, watching Mistress Smith from under one arched brow and out of the tail of his eye, while Potter

358

and Brown rode ahead, occasionally turning back to glare at me as if I had somehow snatched their prize, and the bun-faced girl was balanced on the cart, likewise looking back, but with more genuine concern for her mistress, and the few crowds stood aside to watch us pass, and in this way we processed in silence onto Gosford Street.

And it was there, just before the Gosford Gate, that we encountered, of all people, that accursed lawyer Thomas Greswold, coming from the east with an escort of ten or so men, a mixture of grey-backed lawyers and armed guards in indeterminate livery. When Mistress Smith saw him, I heard her gasp, and her hand nearly shot out to clutch my arm, but she restrained herself, and then she seemed to shrink in on herself, and pulled her wimple lower yet.

I laughed aloud, to calm her, and show good cheer, and thought that now she might appreciate my tale of our besting him in the Coombe Wood Bushment.

'Have no fear of Master Greswold, Mistress Smith,' I told her, 'for I can relate an amusing story about him.'

As we rode towards where he sat in his saddle like a sack of rags, I regaled her with divers details of the night we had turned back the Duke of Buckingham, and it was just as we approached, with Greswold looking on in calculating consternation to see the wife of his friend riding out, that I came to the punchline, spoken overloud:

'And so we brast his buttocks with our bootys, and sent him home, weeping for his mother and his laundress!'

No one laughed, it is true, least of all Mistress Smith, who sniffed and sobbed with each awful detail, but I put on a very fine show of nonchalance, and I greeted Greswold as if I had just that moment noticed him, and I gave him an extravagantly satirical bow, and in this way we passed him by, and rode under the Gosford Gate, and left the city, and never once did I look back to see Greswold's expression. By the time I gave it, or him, any further thought, it was too late.

I rode with Mistress Smith's strange unhappy party for a while, but took my stilted leave of them at the crossroads, where I turned my horse towards dear old Newbold Revel, and as I rode away, I experienced such a strange sense of calm elation as I have never forgotten since. I was conscious of a great surging relief that though I had come precious close to the brink, I had not after all made a fool of myself with Mistress Smith. I had not brought shame and disworship on myself. I had not betrayed my wife, whom I loved, nor my family, both past and present, and the joy I felt was a kind of escape from bondage, a freedom from servitude that I have since wished I could have bottled and drunk as an elixir.

I was full conscious that I was riding on a good horse, well-saddled, with England's summer sun shining on my face. I was likewise clothed well, in linens and silks and woolstuffs appropriate to my station as a knight of the shire, with that sword at my hip and a purse on my belt weighty enough against any eventuality, and I was riding home, along a familiar track, to a well-loved and handsomely appointed home, in good health. My name was wreathed about with worship and honour: I was a Member of Parliament, known to have served my king in Normandy and to have kissed the pope's ring, and – most crucially – I had the good-lordship of England's premier lord, the Earl of Warwick, and because of this, I had seen off, with force of arms, all attempts on my person and property, and while I enjoyed such blessings, and so long as I followed the worshipful path of loving my king, country and God, there was not a man – not even the mighty Duke of Buckingham – alive who could touch me.

Or so I thought.

If Sir Thomas had hoped to catch the boy's full attention for this climactic moment, he is disappointed, and the moment slips by almost unobserved, for the boy is beetle-browed and distracted, with a finger up as if to interrupt.

'What is it?' Sir Thomas asks, disrelishing the interruption.

'Someone coming,' he says, and he gets to his feet with that same nimble spring he used when he leapt out of the window and he goes to the door to listen. Had he more time, Sir Thomas would marvel at his ability to interpret the sounds in Newgate's corridors and feel tremors in its fabric that Sir Thomas cannot even guess at, but Sir Thomas will have to think about that later, for the boy has determined who it is.

'You lawyer fellow.'

And Sir Thomas feels awash with pure molten pleasure.

Hartshorne, here at last to spring him free and to take him back to dear old Newbold Revel, back to his wife and family and his dogs and his old familiar fields. He cannot quell the smile, nor stop tears escaping to splash his pourpoint. 'Gather your things, Sir Thomas,' he will say, 'you are free to go!' and so on, and so he stands, and does not know what to do with his waiting hands, and though he is almost witless with joy, he steels himself to behave with no undue celebration, for the sake of the boy, as much as his own personal dignity, though, by Jesu!

But then he hears the footsteps, coming up, and they – they drag, do they not? They are effortful. This is not how he thinks Hartshorne walks when he brings joyous news. Sir Thomas's irrepressible smile falters. Confusion clouds his vision.

'What—?'

He turns to the door just as it opens, and there stands Hartshorne. He is flushed from the heat, and the climb, and stands wordlessly at the cell's threshold, and they stare at one another for a long moment, lawyer and client. Sir Thomas is no fool. He knows someone who brings good news from someone who brings bad news, and he knows Hartshorne brings bad.

All his prepared levities are forgotten.

'Does the king ask two hundred marks?' he asks.

361

He is clinging to the wreckage of his hope.

Hartshorne just stares, his eyes very round. He cannot even shake his head.

'Three hundred?'

Now he can shake his head, minutely.

'*Four* hundred?'

Again, the shaken head.

Sir Thomas loses patience.

'What then?' he shouts. 'What, for the love of God! A thousand? A million?'

'It is not mo-oney,' Hartshorne finally bleats. The last word stretches comically long and at another time Sir Thomas might make a mockery of him.

Not money? Sir Thomas does not even know where to look.

'The ki-ing,' Hartshorne manages, 'the ki-ing – he has ex-e-empt-ed you from his pa-ardon.'

Exempted?

Sir Thomas is stilled. All thought and feeling flood from his mind and body, and then he falls, as if his legs are cut off from under him, a tumble of loose limbs like a de-strung puppet. No one says a word for a few long moments. The room, his cell, seems to slowly rotate before his eyes, as if the floor were going one way, the walls the other and he yet another. The two faces watching him elongate and then clench. He feels a ripple of pain down one side of his body.

At last it passes and he finds his voice.

'Exempted?'

Hartshorne nods as if he also is in too much pain to speak. An-other long moment passes in silence. Some force – be it life or anger – grows within Sir Thomas, like a flame catching and taking hold in a new-laid fire. He struggles to his feet again. Hartshorne steps back. The boy lingers, ready to bolt at any moment, in that state of frozen watchfulness.

Sir Thomas speaks.

'So of all the men in all the kingdom that are to be pardoned,' he starts, gathering his thoughts and words, 'of all the murderers, rapists, bigamists, pirates, whoremongers, sodomites, thieves, abortionists, embezzlers, the treasonous plotters and, and, and all of them — of all the men who have had their crimes discovered, and those whose crimes are yet to be discovered, which could be utterly monstrous, it is just me, Sir Thomas Malory, me, me, who is exempted? Just me?'

Hartshorne's mouth is very dry. They can all hear it creaking as he opens it.

'Not only you,' he says, and he holds out a list he has remembered to bring this time, and Sir Thomas snatches it.

Eleven names. His is not the first — that honour goes to **Sir Humphrey Neville**, a notorious traitor whom the king has been hunting high and low with the specific intention of having him hanged, drawn and quartered — but he is next: 'Sir Thomas Malorie, knight'. He reads the rest and — Jesu preserve me! he thinks. They are all, every last one of them, traitors! They are all adherents to the old king, to King Henry, and sworn enemies of the new king. And him.

'Where are they? All these others?' he asks.

Hartshorne pulls a terrible face.

'They are at large,' he says. 'Escaped or never captured.'

Just the word 'captured' shows how he is now the enemy of the king.

'It is just me?'

Hartshorne nods his horsey old head.

Sir Thomas is alone. The sole focus of the king's wrath.

'But *why*, Sir Thoma-as?' Hartshorne is bleating. 'What is it that you have do-one?'

He is almost as desperate as Sir Thomas. His hands are pulling his cap down over his ears just as Sir Thomas's are now gripping his hair as if it belongs to someone else and he means to pull it out by its roots.

'Jesu defend me!' he cries. 'I have done nothing!'

He subsides headlong onto his filthy old palliasse, pressing his face into filthy linen. He closes his eyes and weeps and he does not hear Hartshorne leave. Perhaps he falls into a swoon, as he has seen happen, for when he wakes, it is dark; the room is empty and his door is locked. Through the window the stars are extinguished and there is no moon. He cannot guess the hour. He cares not how long he has lain here, unmoving, as if in death.

After some time, he gathers himself.

It is just an exemption.

Just an exemption.

Such things may be appealed against.

There has been a mistake.

Yes, he thinks, that is what he believes they must do.

Appeal.

Gradually he becomes used to the faint light cast from wherever. The night is deepest blue, and in it, the cat's eyes.

He stands.

A rod of some inner power, a core of conviction, it gives him strength.

'It shall be well. Each thing, it shall be well.'

A part of him knows that is not so, but experience has taught him that if he can fool himself now, if he can get through this night, then tomorrow will begin another day. There is always hope.

And then he hears it.

The midnight bell.

Ding ding. Ding ding.

His heart is aflame. Panic blooms from his guts.

Ding ding. Ding ding.

And there – he can hardly believe it. A line of yellow candlelight appears at the base of his door. Footsteps shuffling. Whispers. Dear Jesu! The silver-bearded priest is come. He is come to whisper at Sir Thomas's door. He is come to hear his last confession.

Sir Thomas hears the keening of someone weeping, such deep sorrow, such deep terror.

And it is him.

His time is come.

At last.

Glossary

ague	fever
assoil	absolve of sin
bobaunce	boastfulness, pride
braies	long underpants, made of linen
demesne	land attached to a manor and retained by the owner for their own use
disworship	shame
dretched	troubled
falchion	type of sword
feutered	usually of a lance: to set it in its rest to point at the enemy
hose	trousers
noyous	hurtful, unhappy
pourpoint	waistcoat, to which trousers are attached by points
shenship; shenful	disgrace; infamous or disgraceful

TIME

Matins	'the night office', a prayer around midnight
Lauds	prayer around 3 a.m.
Prime	prayer at the first hour, around 6 a.m.
Terce	prayer at the third hour, around 9 a.m.
Sext	prayer at the sixth hour, around noon.
None	prayer at the ninth hour, around 3 p.m.
Vespers	prayer 'at the lighting of the lamps', around 6 p.m.
Compline	prayer before retiring, generally at 9 p.m.